C000108313

Us of Legendary Gods

THE WEST HAVEN UNDEAD BOOK 1

Us of LEGENDARY GODS

4 Horsemen
Publications, Inc.

NICK SAVAGE

Us of Legendary Gods
Copyright © 2023 Nick Savage. All rights reserved.

4 Horsemen
Publications, Inc.

4 Horsemen Publications, Inc.
1497 Main St. Suite 169
Dunedin, FL 34698
4horsemenpublications.com
info@4horsemenpublications.com

Cover by J. Kotick
Typesetting by Niki Tantillo
Editor: Arno Breedt

All rights to the work within are reserved to the author and publisher. No part of this publication may be reproduced, stored in a retrieval system, or transmitted in any form or by any means, electronic, mechanical, photocopying, recording, scanning, or otherwise, except as permitted under Section 107 or 108 of the 1976 International Copyright Act, without prior written permission except in brief quotations embodied in critical articles and reviews. Please contact either the Publisher or Author to gain permission.

This is a work of fiction. All characters, organizations, and events portrayed in this novel are either products of the author's imagination or are used fictitiously.

Library of Congress Control Number: 2022947613

Paperback ISBN-13: 979-8-8232-0093-6
Hardcover ISBN-13: 979-8-8232-0094-3
Audiobook ISBN-13: 979-8-8232-0091-2
Ebook ISBN-13: 979-8-8232-0092-9

DEDICATION

*To Nick Gerger and everyone who believed
this story was worth telling.*

TABLE OF CONTENTS

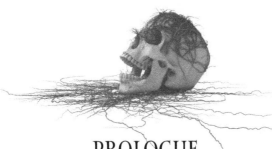

PROLOGUE

"There is no beginning,
And there is no end to a story.
There is only where you come in
and where you depart."
~B. DeSalvo~

There is a notion in each of us that there is something we can't see, just out of our reach, but we know it is there. Theories go back centuries of mysterious peoples living underground or secret societies in control of our government institutions. There are mythologies in every culture of undead creatures stalking the night, legends of wolfmen who howl at the moon, and walking corpses who feast on brains. Type the word "vampire" into a Google search engine, and there will be millions of results. None of the above are ever verified, but the beliefs in them and the nagging notion of their existence persists; otherwise, the rumors would have faded.

But even in rumors, conjecture, mythology, legends, and conspiracy theories, there is a kernel of truth. With these little kernels, we learn that they didn't fall too far from the cob. The dead that walk, the moon howlers, and the secret institutions do exist, just not entirely according to legend. They live in plain sight, yet no one sees them. It's how they survive. It's how they thrive. But to be in The Nation, you have to be a Legend. You have to be one of the creatures we were scared of growing up. You have to be in The Nation to know the Legends exist. To anyone not in The Nation, vampires and werewolves are nothing but campfire stories and scary movies. So you have to ask yourself … Are you in?

CHAPTER 1

"Forget those grand-scale goth-romantic full-moon fright-night satin-lined-coffin stories you've been told growing up about werewolves, vampires, zombies, fairies, and supernatural creepy crawlies of all kinds.
The Legends, the Immortals, the truth much stranger than the fiction."
~R. Chandler~

The hum of the fluorescent lights drones behind the tapping sound of tears falling from Tracy DeSalvo's brown eyes as they land on the double line that reads *Positive*. It obscures the result, but her mind has already engraved it in—two lines, not one. Right now, two little lines are changing her life and everything that will ever happen.

There's a hesitation creeping inside her mind to keep this quiet. She doesn't know why it's there or where it came from, but it's there. An innate knowledge that she knows the hesitation is correct, that she's feeling it for a reason. She doesn't know the reason, but she trusts her instinct that she shouldn't call up her husband and son to share the news.

After all, she doesn't understand how this happened. While a small part of her wants to smile and be happy, a much larger part is scared. An enormous part of her trembles at the fact that what she sees shouldn't be.

A bigger part of her pushes out those other parts. The part of her that sheds tears and screams inside to make sure this new baby is safe; the maternal instinct to make sure she protects her family has taken control.

She stares at the two blurred lines that try to shine out positive news to start her week, but she can't focus. Two ladies enter the office bathroom chattering about in a jovial manner, blissfully ignorant of the mixed emotions they unknowingly disrupted in the closed stall.

While Tracy—wife, mother, and mom-to-be-again—would like nothing more than to continue hiding in this bathroom stall contemplating the uncertainties of this impossible situation, Tracy the social worker has a patient coming in a few minutes that needs her help.

She knows she needs a clear mind to best support those who need her help, but the conversation on the other side of the stall disrupts her attempt at calm. All Tracy can think about is everything that is inconceivable right now; the number of things that could go wrong over the next nine months—if everything goes right. This isn't how she wanted to start her week. This shouldn't be. She already had one child. She is infertile.

A noisy ventilation fan jolts to life. The rattling sound distracts Tracy enough to realize both of her legs fell asleep from sitting on the toilet too long. She lets the pins and needles sting away because in her hand is a simple test with simple results that are anything *but* simple, and her racing mind can't comprehend them at this moment.

She stands, unsteady on her sleeping legs, struggling to pull up her pants. The pins and needles stabbing her waking legs and feet are a pointed reminder of everything that has changed in the last few minutes. The lighthearted ladies exit, leaving only the fan's rattle, the lights' hum, and the heaviness of her situation for company.

Alone again, no one to see her exit the stall a changed woman. She pulls the packaging from her pocket and slips the white plastic stick inside. Gripping it in one hand, she pushes against the wall to hold herself up with the other. She staggers on jelly-like feet to the sink while the waking pain in her lower appendages intensifies as, step by step, they wake up to their new reality. She turns the faucet knobs to wash her hands and splashes a little water on her face. Wiping off the excess, she looks into the mirror but seeing herself causes her to break down and cry. Her mind races with how this could have happened and what it could mean for The Nation.

Of all the questions and concerns tearing through her mind right now, the only answer she has is that now she knows why she is a week late. She runs like clockwork down to a four-hour window. This month was not clockwork, though, and now she knows why. But many, many more questions remain unanswered. She knows she needs to find these answers. The questions slice through her mind like knives.

How was she able to conceive? What impact will this have on The Nation? Will the child be healthy? How will Ken react? How does she tell Ken, her husband of twenty years, that they are having an impossible child? What does this mean for their son, Connor? What does this mean for her? How will this affect her condition?

She dries off her tears and calms herself down again. She needs to be composed once she walks out of the bathroom. She tugs at her blouse to straighten it up as she sniffles away the last few tears. She checks her eye makeup, which, much to its disclaimer, is water-proof. She pockets the test and exits the bathroom.

Tracy forces out a smile as she passes a few open doors while she tries to walk unnoticed down the hall to her office. She attempts to maintain a professional composure: straight back, shoulders up, head high, confident walk. She can't let on that anything might be wrong, even though she is sure so much is.

She opens the door to her office and invites the waiting patient in. She takes a seat in her chair and grabs her yellow legal pad so she can begin her session. She hides the used test in the bottom desk drawer.

She turns her attention toward her patient, but there is a lingering notion in her mind. A notion that she needs to talk about this, that sitting here isn't helping. But who can she turn to?

><><><><><><><><><><><><><><><><><><><><

Scarlett stands in front of her bathroom mirror, staring at her freckled face. A face she has seen daily since she was old enough to possess self-realization, yet this day something seems different. As if her face may not be good enough anymore. As if her face might not be representative of her junior class. Still, she stands staring at herself and the keynotes taped to the mirror.

The usual suspects of a sixteen-year-old girl decorate the counter surrounding her bathroom sink: half-empty face wash, an electric toothbrush set upright on a stand, a brush, a blow dryer, and a few other implements to help style her past-shoulder-length copper red hair. A small neutral-tone palette of eyeshadows and brushes sits next to a collection of varying red shaded lipsticks. All of which at this moment seem both overwhelming and inconsequential. She hopes her loose curls are disarming enough to win over her peers. Stark red lipsticks and lip stains will contrast her usual natural tones of eyeshadows and blush. A bold statement for sure. Her uncle Ken has helped guide her speech and prepare her up to this point. He has told her that making a statement will make her stand out—if only she knew what statement she was making.

Her eyes turn to the bullet points taped to the mirror. She rereads each one: Peer tutoring, Fine Arts Funding, and Open Campus. Her eyes squint at the thought of the decision she'll have to make, so she turns to her makeup that will finish off her look, the look that gives her the edgy professionalism she hopes will help her win.

"Thank you, class of 2019. I hope everyone…" She lets her words trail off. "Why am I thanking them?" she ponders, taking a deep breath. "Hello, class of 2019. For too long…" Again she trails off. "Good afternoon, class of 2019." A small smile breaks across her face. "Good afternoon, class of 2019. Thank you for the opportunity to fill the great shoes of our former class president." She stops. Scarlett stares into the mirror. "Why elect me?"

She picks up a couple of different hues of lipstick. One labeled Sunset Strip and the other called MisRed. She twists them up and down, over and over, unable to decide which color should adorn her lips. She knows it is going to be either of these two. Not any of the other eleven shades of red sitting there. She's too preoccupied thinking about the upcoming debate, why her class should elect her, and the possibilities she could offer them so that her class should vote Scarlett McAllister for the empty spot. There's a doubt that lingers in her mind. A suspicion tells her it will be someone more popular, someone with more friends, because isn't that the way it works? Elect someone not based on what they can offer but on how many friends they have. Perfectly logical.

"Because I can offer a new perspective. See things from a different point of view and give the students what they've been missing. They will recognize that and vote for me." She nods at her reflection.

Ken has told her to look "approachable but professional" to come across as "confident but not arrogant." All things are great tips to know, but past the surface of his words, all are rather vague. It is the vagueness of his words that frighten her, causing this momentary indecision. On more specific notes, she knows a longer skirt or dress is better than short but that pants put her on the same level as men. She knows all these things, but she can't seem to decide on something as mundane as a lip color.

She again reads over the bullet points taped to the mirror. The first calls for a better tutoring program—one which grants access to kids who can't typically afford it. The second point touches on how she will help allocate more money to the fine arts without taking money away from the athletics department. The third bullet reads of an open campus for seniors. She knows, in her head, she needs to eliminate one of these points, at least for the speech today. Her heart, however, can't decide which one.

She practices how she'll present each bullet point as she has a hundred times before. The tone of voice she'll use. The inflection on certain words to bring home her points. All pointers given to her by Uncle Ken, West Haven legislator. Not that Scarlett remembers precisely what he does.

She never could figure out politics, but here she is, about to dive head-first into high school politics. She'll either make a splash in the political pool or splatter herself on the deck surrounding it.

She looks back at the bullet points taped to her mirror, rehearsing the promises she'll make to better the student body's high school experience. Then she realizes that making promises comes with fulfilling promises, and fulfilling promises means deciding how to fulfill them. She then has to determine a course of action to make her promises a reality—deciding which from her list of potential

5

pledges to make. The slippery slope of campaign commitments yet to be sworn and eventually carried out.

She laughs out loud and looks again at the girl in the mirror. Her pale blue eyes stare back. She thinks that if she cannot decide on a shade of lipstick—a decision that, in the end, has no real consequences—or which bullet point to leave out today, then how is she ever going to make crucial decisions as a class president? Her thoughts turn to the notion that maybe her run for class president wasn't the best idea.

Self-doubt sets in as she thinks that forcing herself to do something extracurricular this year may not have been in her best interest. She would call out sick if she didn't have posters plastered all over the school hallways pleading for votes. She could stay home, play Ferris, and watch reruns of *West Wing* or *Criminal Minds* until she remembers each episodic plot outline by heart. But she knows she can't back out and needs to give it her best. If not for her, then for her closest friends and classmates who are excited to hear the speech she said she's been preparing.

She wants to make her parents proud. The fleeting thoughts of surrender vanish from her mind as she steels herself again. She focuses on her stance. Shoulders level, back straight, chin held high to project confidence.

She stares at herself, practicing her smile. Thinking, much like most teenagers, her smile isn't beautiful enough. It looks too fake if she keeps her lips closed; she seems like someone thinking superior thoughts about the people she'll be smiling at. So, she doesn't want to do a closed-lip smile. Then she tries a toothy grin, enough to see her pearly whites. But then she thinks she looks all-tooth. A red-haired, freckled, Julia Roberts' smile. A mile wide and all teeth. How she thinks it makes her look like a horse. But between the two choices, she'll take a tooth-exposing Cheshire grin. It made Ms. Roberts millions of dollars; it may get Scarlett elected class president. Then she thinks she might be overthinking the message a smile conveys.

A voice from just outside the door calls to her that they must leave for school. Sunset Strip it is. If she's going to sell herself for president, she might as well do it wearing lipstick named after a street famous for prostitution.

The morning light outside beams down on the parking lot as Scarlett walks away from a blue Camaro with black racing stripes. She waves goodbye to the two boys standing nearby.

In a black, graphic t-shirt for the metal group The Atlas Moth, poised in a pitcher's stance, stands the prized possession of the Maine West Haven High varsity baseball team and captain, Connor DeSalvo. His shoulder-length, sandy brown hair waves in the wind.

Connor stands a few feet from his car, ready to throw a slow pitch knuckleball to his counterpart and lifelong friend, Jack Taylor. Jack has always been second to Connor in baseball, but they have made their mark together, and that's how Connor feels it should be. After all, it was practicing side by side, on the field and in the streets, that Jack helped develop Connor's Gyro, Shuuto, and Knuckleball to the point of both being scouted for college scholarships.

These quiet morning moments are more than just regular pitch practices. They are relaxed moments between two lifelong friends where they can both breathe easier. No coach lurching over their shoulders. These are the moments Connor can wear his ripped jeans and Jack his Linkin Park shirts. No catcher's mask and pads. No batters to worry about. Just two friends hanging out.

Connor watches for the signal as they stand in a semi-crowded parking lot. They toss balls every morning here, never a care in the world. No other people around as Scarlett disappears into the school at the other end of the lot.

Connor's hand combs through his hair and unties the flannel from around his waist for better pitching momentum. He tosses it aside.

"What the heck is four down then one whirly finger?" Connor shrugs at Jack, losing his pitching stance.

"Well, uh," Jack starts in his usual stammer, "I thought we agreed that would, well, be a low right gyro."

Connor returns to his pitching stance. "Right. Forgot we changed the signal. My bad."

Connor winds up and throws one at Jack, who catches it without a problem.

To Connor and Jack, baseball has always been fun. A sport to play to kill time and procrastinate from studies. Neither thought their senior year would revolve around picking a college to play for. But that's how it turned out. So, they take these morning moments to remember where their love for the game came from; two-person games of catch in street clothes and no one around to tell them how they're doing it wrong.

"How many more days, uh, do you think we have?" Jack asks.

"What does that mean?" Connor returns the question.

Jack stands up and tosses the ball back. "I mean of this." He gestures around him. "Of, well, not really having any responsibility." His voice rises in pitch with each word of the last sentence.

Connor winds up and tosses the ball back to him. "As long as we want, bro. As long as we want."

Yet they both know moments like these have a shelf life, especially if they don't go to the same college, so the boys take them as often as they can.

Jack tosses the ball back to Connor, but the throw gets away from Jack. The two watch as the ball flies through the passenger side window of a red Ford Focus. No alarm sounds, and no one else is around to hear the glass shatter. The two gape at each other for a moment and run to the car.

"Connor, bro, like, well, what do we do?" Jack looks around in a not-at-all-inconspicuous manner.

Connor reaches into the car and grabs the ball. He, too, looks around, seeing that their misdemeanor went unnoticed. "Tell no one. It was an accident."

"I don't have the money to replace it." Worry and concern weigh heavy on his words.

"Replace what? Nothing happened," Connor assures Jack. "Head inside. I'm gonna make sure we're safe."

Jack nods in agreement, grabs his backpack, and starts walking in. "It just got away from me."

Connor nods in an understanding gesture that sends Jack jogging toward the school.

As Jack hurries off, Connor looks around the lot, seeing no one. He reaches for his wallet and pulls out five twenties; the majority of his two weeks' pay working part-time at a local pet store. Young

Mr. DeSalvo opens the glove box and puts the money inside. He just hopes it's enough to pay for the repair.

><><><><><><><><><><><><><><><><><><><><><

Scarlett takes a deep breath as she looks around the Maine West Haven High School fieldhouse. Her stomach rumbles in a mix of nerves and hunger. Ambivalent teachers and far fewer judging eyes from her peers than she expected fill the bleachers. All seem to be enjoying the break from class, not paying much attention to the happenings on stage. The teachers relish the break from the daily grind's monotony. To Scarlett, the lack of actual attention being paid to the reason classes have been postponed doesn't matter. No. All she can think about is the speech she has to give. The one she has been rehearsing in her head for a week before applying the Sunset Strip lipstick this morning. The address she should have had solidified more than a week ago but wanted to finish herself to make her parents proud. But also a speech that irks her insides as if it is just not good enough. An unnamed feeling inside her whispers she doesn't deserve to win. A sabotaging notion to sink her back into her comfort zone, her safe place where she isn't pushed or challenged. This moment, right now, in front of the student body, she wants to win. She wants to do more than be another faceless and forgotten student in the ever-changing sea of high school, but she is nervous even after all the preparation for this.

None of that matters because the current candidate just sat back down among the other three on her folding chair that was anxiously awaiting her royal derrière. Brianna Waldgrave, old friend and current frenemy. The popular, 5'7", size 3, blonde-haired, green-eyed leader of the pack. A few years back, Brianna was part of Scarlett's group, inseparable from them. But then high school began, and popularity called. The "In Crowd" only had room for one, and they chose Bri. Now, though, as the teacher finishes introducing Scarlett to the sea of students, all she can do is take a deep breath and pray she doesn't make a fool of herself.

Scarlett, stomach rumbling, stands from her seat, trying to keep her shoulders level and chin held high but not too high. She steps up to the microphone, smiling nervously, and clears her throat. The time for being scared has passed. She must say something—anything. All the preparation she did before today, and everything she rehearsed between finishing her makeup and being driven to school is all out the window. The words of her much-prepared speech escape her mind and slip off her tongue as the students wait for her to say something—anything. Now the judgment in the student's eyes is palpable.

She begins, "Open campus for seniors. We all will get to that stage in our high school careers, and we should have the privilege of eating at Wendy's instead of forcing down another mystery meat burger topped with old, fermenting ketchup. A responsibility for, and privilege of, the uppermost classmen."

She looks out, seeing that while most students still ignore her and the rally, a few have turned their attention toward the main stage.

"I know that's a big fight. But if elected 2018's class president, I'll fight for the small victories, too. Like better chicken sandwiches and stuff."

The reality of her entire speech so far being based around food has made her realize that, perhaps, she should have eaten something for breakfast before speaking at today's event. But too late now, she has spoken, and apparently, on the platform to lobby for better food.

Forgetting every other point she had rehearsed in the past few hours, she smiles her toothy, horse-faced smile. And perhaps out of nervousness or out of watching too many, or too few, political speeches, she raises her right hand, giving the queen's wave to the crowd. "Thank you." She steps away from the podium, trying to keep her head high, but the weight seems too much to hold at the moment, so she stares at the ground, a self-deprecating smile across her face, tight-lipped and broad with squinted eyes. She takes her seat among the other candidates as the teacher commandeers the podium once more.

Scarlett lifts her head, staring into the sea of bodies, not focusing on anyone in particular. She is looking past them to try and find a reason for doing what she so spectacularly failed at moments ago. The teacher on stage speaks of voting from today through Friday and the results coming out next Friday. Mid-sentence of some mention of a fundraiser, the teacher and Scarlett are saved by the bell.

Now all Scarlett can do is think about the remaining week, the long days ahead, and the fallout from her speech. She knows she isn't going to win and has already conceded to that fact. A sting in her mind lingers because she wanted this; she actually wants to do something more significant, something more than just a random extracurricular activity. Maybe an opportunity will present itself next year.

><>><>><>><>><>><>><>><>><>><>><>><>><>><

A few feet from her desk, behind an overhead projector, stands Linda Espinoza in a well-worn, tie-dyed Pink Floyd shirt and strategically torn jeans—biology teacher and high school boys' shower fantasy.

Her short stature diametrically opposes the boundless energy possibly stored in the remnants of her more rebellious years—her studded belt and leather boots. The perfect mix of high intellect and classic beauty in her brown eyes and long, flowing light brown hair bring alive the otherwise few sleepy male heads in the class. She is an athletically built woman who academically engages all her students in the classroom and runs a mean women's varsity soccer team outside the classroom. Looking out toward her twenty-four honors students with a smile plastered on her face, she twirls an infinity pendant around her neck.

Most Harvard and Yale dreamers in here dress in pressed jeans, polo shirts, button-downs, and slacks. Connor and Jack sit as standouts among the rest, united in their caring more about baseball than Bio. No matter how the students dress or where their priorities lie, they all have notebooks open and pens at the ready.

Connor stares at the UV pictures projected onto the whiteboard—a side-by-side comparison of a girl without makeup. On the left, she appears as humans would view her. On the right is her picture as seen within the UV spectrum: freckles, fine lines, and shallow arteries hidden beyond the abilities of normal human eyes; the details of the human body concealed within the spectrum of Ultraviolet. Data and a message fill the exposed whiteboard that borders the UV photograph, "50 questions 30 minutes." After reading the test info, Connor looks back at the pictures, and the two images look identical. The photo on the left also shows the freckles, fine lines, and shallow arteries as the one on the right. He continues staring at the matching pictures that not even seconds ago were different. He squints his eyes, giving them a good rub before widening and blinking them clear, but the images still look the same.

"Of the total light spectrum, humans can see 84%. This picture, for example…" Linda Espinoza points to the projected photo, "…is how bees see us. Of course, if it weren't for UV photography, we wouldn't be able to experience this. Similar statistics go for audio range as well. We are all familiar with dog whistles. The high-pitched range that a properly calibrated whistle outputs can only be heard by a canine. Twenty to twenty thousand hertz. That's what we hear. The range of canines is much higher. Who can tell us where the other 16% of the light spectrum starts?" She looks out at the crowd and sees Connor rubbing his eyes. "Connor."

Distracted by the tricks his eyes were playing, he missed her question. "Yes?"

"Yes? Not the answer. Do you know the start of the light spectrum?"

"Sorry, waking up still," he says, faking a yawn. "Infrared are the lowest waves of light that we know of. Ultraviolet are the highest."

Jack rolls his eyes at Connor's response. He leans over in his chair and whispers, "Dude, bro. Really? We only have thirty, uh, minutes for the test."

Connor tosses Jack a laugh, then looks back to the board and projected images. The two projected photos are back to being different. The left looks like a standard photograph, and the other with the special UV filter.

Linda raises an eyebrow as she grabs the test papers off her desk and begins passing them out face down. The first student flips it over but is quickly met with a playful whack upside the head with the other test papers. "Not until I say so. You know the rules." She turns her attention back to Connor. "What do you mean?"

"Just 'cause science hasn't found anything beyond the UV and Infrared spectrums doesn't mean those begin and end the spectrum." His feeling of self-satisfaction dissolves when he sees Jack, forehead in hand, giving a minute shake of his head in disbelief.

Jack eyes Connor. "Dude, we aren't getting out of the test by, well, your stalling. Come on."

Connor concedes fighting the good fight against the inevitable test, and sighs. "Just procrastinating, Mrs. E."

Linda smiles as she finishes passing out the test. "Maybe one day you can elaborate for us."

Jack interjects in an attempt to move things along. "Well … stupid theory, Mrs. E. Trust me, you don't wanna hear it," he finishes in his natural tonality of increasing pitch and volume as he drags out his sentences. A marking of his lack of self-confidence and social awkwardness.

She turns back to the class as she takes a seat at her desk. "Thank you, Professor Jack." Her eyes turn to the rest of the students, bringing the point around. "You'll have thirty minutes to complete your tests…" She eyes the second hand of the clock counting down the last ten seconds until it reaches a full minute. "Starting now."

Connor flips his test over and scribbles his name and today's date, Sept. 5, 2017, across the top. Connor glances up to see a few students scribbling out answer after answer as others fumble through. Jack seems to have started the test with ease.

Linda sidelines the stack of papers she needs to grade for the moment so she can watch her students. The razor-sharp intent in her stare is a little unnerving for those whose eyes stray from their test. No energetic smile across her face, only eyes piercing each teenager as they navigate the exam. The minutes tick by but not nearly fast enough for Connor. Of the thirty allotted, only fifteen have passed as he turns the page to question fifty. Before answering, he sees question fifty-one.

51) Given a 3-gallon bucket and a 5-gallon bucket, assuming no spillage, how do you get 4 gallons?

Without lifting his head from the test, he eyes the board to reread the words in dry erase '50 Questions.' He fills out the answer to number fifty and rises from his seat. Jack shoots him a worrisome look as if he is not going to pass this test. Connor sees Jack racing through. He smiles and nods his head as he hands his test to Linda. A radiant smile crosses her lips as she takes the test from his hands.

As Connor returns to his seat, Linda opens his test to the last page and sees he did not fill out question fifty-one. She looks at him for a moment to find him slouched back in his chair, counting the seconds until the bell rings. She continues working her way back to question one, skimming his answers as she goes.

With a few minutes left in both class and the exam, Jack turns to the final page. Some of the middle questions slowed the fast start he had to the test. Jack sees question fifty-one and does the same double take to the board that Connor did. Quick, quiet snaps possess his fingers in an unsuccessful attempt to catch Connor's attention. Unsure of what to do, he scribbles in a guess for the final question before handing in his test.

Again, Linda flips to the back of the test. She smiles as she sees Jack's response to fifty-one. Linda continues to make her way through the rest of the test, skimming each answer as she did for Connor's. Jack, making his way back to his desk, notices the janitor peering into the class through the open door. Jack stares at the vertical scar that runs above and below the janitor's right eye. He wonders if any rumors are true, that the janitor is an ex-navy seal and hiding here in witness protection, or if he got the scar while being attacked by a large animal, or if the truth is stranger than any of those. Jack watches as the janitor runs a plastic, black comb through short-cropped, black and slightly salted, unkempt hair.

Jack continues watching the janitor push his mop around outside the door. Jack taps Connor, pointing in a not-so-subtle manner to the janitor who seems to be leering into the classroom as he mops, eyeballing the pictures and info on the board more than the floor.

"What's up with Raymond?" whispers Connor.

"Who's Raymond?" asks Jack.

Connor swipes at Jack's pointed finger, pushing it down, "For all the finger pointing you're doing and rumors that circulate about him, take a second to read his name. It's sewn onto his jumper."

Jack shrugs as they watch Raymond the janitor dip down the hall, pulling his mop and bucket to the cafeteria as the bell rings. The deluge of students drowns Raymond and his work from sight.

>◇◇◇◇◇◇◇◇◇◇◇◇◇◇◇◇◇◇◇◇◇◇◇◇◇◇◇◇◇◇◇◇◇◇◇◇◇<

The rushing flow of students slows to a trickle as the bell rings, signaling the start of the next period. For the students in the lunch line, however, their wait has just begun. Scarlett watches Raymond give a silent nod to a security guard, large and unfit, bulging out of his two-sizes-too-small uniform. She smiles as Raymond mops spilled food up off the dining hall floor. Scarlett has never speculated on the scar that stands out so prominently above and below his eye. She figures if he doesn't talk about it, he probably doesn't want anyone to ask. But a voice in her head has mentioned on a few occasions, most decisively, that it was not an animal attack, nor is he in witness protection. The voice that has played in her head dictates it is from something more unbelievable yet equally real.

Scarlett steps up to the ever-silent but always friendly lunch lady. Her jubilant way of slopping the food onto the trays plays into her namesake of December. The school's very own proverbial Mrs. Claus helps keep the stomachs of the growing bodies filled. At this moment, the joyous nature of the lunch lady is lost on Scarlett. Brianna and her clique of half a dozen standing behind Scarlett steal her attention with their condescending, short, stuttered laughs. She watches as the group waves their hands about in a carefree yet somehow holier-than-thou way. Each laugh slings their heads back with such force that they might snap clean off. Scarlett turns around, thanking December as she finishes flinging slop onto her tray. All she can think about now is before they all entered high school when Brianna wasn't so artificial, when looks weren't her top priority.

To Scarlett, the hormones of teen years take more of a toll than just growth spurts and mood swings. They have abducted a good friend and turned her into something she despises. But Scarlett hasn't lost faith.

>∞∞∞∞∞∞∞∞∞∞∞∞∞∞∞∞∞∞∞∞∞∞<

Tracy sits alone in her kitchen having canceled the rest of her appointments for today. A move she knows isn't the most professional, but even professionals have problems of their own to deal with.

Ken has long since left for the office, and Connor and Scarlett are well into their school day. A rare moment when a mother can put aside her worries for everyone else and spend them on herself.

She looks around her kitchen, searching for something—though she isn't sure what. Perhaps searching for an answer to the questions she has asked herself. She knows she will not find it. She picks up today's paper that Ken left on the table. She flips through it, still searching for some unknown direction that isn't in there.

She puts down the paper and swipes her phone alive. She runs her finger up the screen, scrolling through her contacts but stops after only half the alphabet. Unsure of what to do or who to call, she turns to her refrigerator. Staring at the crowded inside, she spots a bottle of red wine peeking out from the back, behind yesterday's leftovers. A thought enters her mind that she should have scrolled further down her contact list. An idea brings a smile to her face and a momentary calm to this storm, someone she can turn to in this personal struggle. She grabs her keys and, slipping on her shoes, dials a contact in her phone.

Tracy drives through West Haven to the other end of town, tapping the steering wheel with every slow down and adding a double-timed foot accompaniment every time she stops. In this clear traffic, it's a short fifteen-minute drive yet seems never-ending in her current state of mind. The thoughts coursing through her head of how she will tell him and accompanying concerns dominate the drive.

She eventually pulls up to her destination and finds herself standing outside a well-maintained three-story brick house. Columns decorate the front porch and a stainless-steel door gives the overall classic look a modern touch. She raps on the door in rapid successions of repeating triplets. She holds her cell phone to her ear, waiting for the call to connect, but it goes straight to voicemail. She hangs up, stops knocking, and stands for a moment, "Come on, Vistrus. Where are you?" Her foot taps out the fast triplets now. She realizes that talking to herself doesn't help more than pushing an elevator call button over and over, but she does it anyway. She rings the bell hoping maybe he's upstairs. His Pontiac Solstice is in the driveway, but his Porsche is gone, perchance hidden behind the closed garage door a few feet away. Perhaps he's not home. She tries peeking through the front windows, but the drawn shades and blinds block her attempt. "Come on, Vistrus. Call me back."

She swipes to unlock her phone and types Vistrus a text.

[Tracy: *Call me.*]

She goes to hit send but wants the message to sound more urgent. She also doesn't want anyone to see the message and deduce the meaning. So she stands on his porch, thinking for a moment about what she could say that prying eyes couldn't interpret. She adds the words,

[*found something.*]

Send.

As she drives back home, she calls her doctor's office. She doesn't know if she can fully trust him on this matter. Having taken three over-the-counter tests and three positives, maybe she doesn't need licensed medical confirmation, but she can't get a hold of Vistrus and she doesn't know how this will affect her health.

She needs to do something though. So Tracy books the next available appointment with the doctor, which isn't for another two weeks. But it will have to do. He's the only doctor who knows about her condition, making him the only doctor who can treat her properly.

Senseless, fragmented buddings of would-be thoughts fly in and out of Tracy's mind. She can't concentrate on any one idea long enough to make sense of it or rationalize her current situation. Her ability to keep calm has long since gone. The fact that she still hasn't heard from Vistrus is making her more and more nervous. Instead of heading home, she takes the ramp onto the 294 expressway to see him at his work, the West Haven Museum of Natural History and Art.

In this time of need, of not knowing what to do or who else she can turn to, the museum is at least a destination. A half-hour later, she arrives at a large museum. Roman columns and intricately carved masonry support the outside vaulted entranceway. Two wings span hundreds of feet on either side. She exits her car and heads in.

More Romanesque stone columns and a marble tiled floor that echoes the sounds of everyone in the entrance hall greet Tracy upon her entrance inside. In the middle of the room is a circular help desk. The superb craftsmanship matches the rest of the museum.

She takes brisk steps to the desk, keeping her skirt straightened. The androgynous individual behind the counter looks up from the computer screen in front of them. "How may I assist you today?"

Tracy's mind reaches for words amid the worry. "Hi." Tracy's eyes break contact, and she scans the halls for Vistrus. "Do you know how I may get a hold of a Mr. Petrovsky?" Her eyes catch a man standing apart from the crowd, his eyes looking in her direction. She can't tell if he is looking at her or if she happens to be in his line of sight, so she forces her focus to connect again with the desk attendant.

"One moment." The attendant's eyes dart back to the screen, and fingers spring to life, typing at speeds only someone with advanced keyboard skills can. "I'm so sorry, Miss, but he seems to be out at the moment."

"Of course he is," Tracy interrupts. She realizes the rudeness of her action and apologizes. The attendant forces a polite smile before continuing.

"I can ring his office and leave a voicemail for him if you'd like."

"Do you know when he'll be back?" Tracy pleads, eyes still darting around.

"I'm sorry, I don't. Would you like to leave him a message?" the desk attendant responds.

"There's no way to get a hold of him?" Tracy urges.

The attendant senses Tracy's urgency, "I'm sorry. I'm just a front desk pawn. I have their office numbers, but they don't know me from the other employees."

Tracy smiles and nods, thinking for a moment, still scanning the area, hoping the attendant is wrong and Vistrus is around. Her mind isn't only thinking about getting a message to Vistrus. She is also thinking about if prying eyes see her leave a message or if unsuspecting ears hear something they shouldn't—like that guy who is still staring in her direction. Maybe she'll make it simple and tell him to call her. But then she'll have to say her name, and while people may have seen her, she worries about the random happenstance of things and how they get back to the ones she is trying to keep the information away from for the moment.

"Ma'am. Is everything okay?" the desk help inquires.

Tracy forces a sad smile as the clerk's question shakes her from her thoughts. "No. Yeah. Sorry. Everything's fine. Thank you."

The kindness of the desk attendant sticks in her mind. A kind act from a stranger when Tracy knows she is acting strange. The moment somehow helps her calm down a bit. She takes a deep breath and, for the first time since reading the results of her pregnancy test, can breathe just a little bit easier.

Trying to organize the countless thoughts in her head, Tracy walks away from the desk and exits the museum. A text alert goes off on her phone as she reaches the doors. She snatches her cellphone back out of her pocket, hoping Vistrus has received her texts. This text, however, is from her husband Ken.

[Ken: *I just stopped by your office for a surprise lunch date. Said you left for the day.*]

She stops in her tracks, knowing she needs to say something in response. She can't say she's somewhere eating because he might surprise her. She also can't say she went to see Vistrus because she's too afraid to tell her husband she's pregnant against all known accounts of her kind. But she has an idea.

[Tracy: *A patient was having a nervous breakdown. Had to make a house call. Heading home in a bit.*]

She continues walking to her car. She wonders again why she's afraid to tell Ken the fantastic news. Who would he tell, or to whom would he let slip that she's pregnant? And why is it a bad thing? It happens when a woman who's been told she can't conceive finally conceives. But never in the history of her people has anyone conceived a second child. The conception of a first child is hard enough. It must mean something. It's this something she wants to find out before sharing the news with her betrothed.

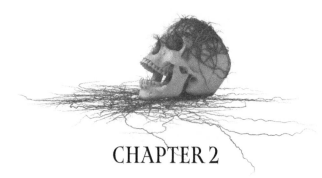

CHAPTER 2

"These things that haunt us...
That we personify in the demons and monsters under our beds...
they aren't real.
The things that haunt us, I mean.
The monsters, well...
they don't like being called such names."
~R. Chandler~

The bright sun in the partly cloudy Midwestern sky creates a beautiful afternoon for athletes to run drills on the practice fields that line the outskirts of the school property. The lacrosse players on the far field are running their game. The track runners circle the very outer boundaries. The innermost field that sits next to the parking lot of student cars, SUVs, and crossovers, is the baseball field. The outfielders are tossing balls back and forth. The basemen are fielding ground balls thrown by the coaches. On the pitcher's mound stands the pride and joy of the coach, Connor, who throws everything from heaters to sinkers with a particular concentration on his signature pitches. Jack is crouched down behind the batter's box, his hand getting battered even through his catcher's mitt. He sweats under the heat and full weight of his catcher's gear.

Jack stands and throws the ball back to Connor. "She's, um, got a better chance with the chicken sandwiches. They took away open campus back in, like, the 80's. The 1980's."

Connor stands, tossing the ball up and down in his right hand, listening to Jack while trying to read Jack's signal as to what to throw next. "Dude, that was two days ago. And I didn't think you meant the 1880s. Even so, you already voted, so what's it matter? Party at your place tonight?" He accents his question with a fastball right in Jack's mitt.

The ball hits Jack's mitt hard. He shakes off the sting of the catch. "Damn, Con. I think that's… that's enough fastballs for today." He takes off his mitt, tossing it and the ball to the ground. He rises, rubbing his hand. "And no way we're, well, throwing down on a Thursday. That's just weird. They were supposed to be home two days ago and … still no word! Not cool!" Jack tosses the ball back to Connor before picking his mitt back up. He puts it on and crouches down again.

"Don't you have their flight info? Watch this!" Connor winds up and throws a perfect knuckleball that slowly floats to Jack. After what seems like a stretched minute, the ball finally crosses the plate.

"Perfect pitch! Yeah, the flight info … it's in my phone." He throws it back without standing up.

Connor stands up to wait for Jack's signal. "Look it up and call the airline. See if they were on their flight. Then blow up their phones." Jack throws down a couple of fingers, signaling a curveball, low and inside. Connor squints to see the signal in the bright overhead sun, then steps back, raises his arm, and throws. This pitch is off the mark, causing Jack to jump low and outside. The ball misses the inside of his mitt and rolls behind him. Jack chases the ball a few yards.

"Thanks! That actually, well, slipped my mind," Jack says, picking up the ball. "Did you misread the signal?" He tosses the ball.

A black police car stops in front of the baseball team on the main drive next to the field. The officer inside stays concealed from the student-athletes by only rolling the tinted window down a quarter of the way.

"Nope," he responds, catching it. "Low and inside. Just got away from me."

After a moment of idling in one spot, an arm reaches out the squad car window and waves for the coach to approach the car. The head coach stops throwing grounders to the basemen and jogs over to the officer.

Connor stops throwing and palms the ball in his glove.

"You don't think?" Jack yells as he strides over to Connor. Connor shakes his head at Jack. The ominous feeling of a random police officer hiding in his car creates cause for whispers, especially after the other morning with Jack and Connor's broken window incident. The rest of the infielders come in around the pitcher's mound.

Jack leans into Connor, fearful that somehow the officer will hear him. "Is this about…"

Connor interrupts Jack, "No way. And what did I say?"

Jack tilts his head down, knowing he needs to remain silent.

A senior class teammate, growing out a beard beyond his years, chimes in, "Can't wait to hear all the rumors tomorrow. I'm sure someone will hear that one of us got arrested or some shit."

Connor turns to the outspoken teammate. A stern, serious look on his face tells the rest of the team this could become serious. "That's the thing. Whatever is going on, there will be far more speculation than fact. And the speculation is what's sensational. That's all that will matter."

The team stands around, the confused looks on all their faces a clear signal to Mr. DeSalvo that clarification is needed. "Vampires," Connor says plainly.

The looks on all of the faces read even more confused. Raised eyebrows, upturned lip corner with squinted eyes, all signs that the one word did not help eschew obfuscation. So Jack chimes in with the thought on everyone's minds. "Now I think, we're, uh, even more confused."

Connor searches for a moment as he tries to straighten out the words in his head. The players patiently wait for the words from the captain they hope will make sense. "There's no proof they exist. No evidence. Bedtime stories and campfire tales told to keep children from wandering out of their beds at night so parents can sleep. But it's a fascinating story with such wonderment that people would rather believe the rumors."

The team nods in a unified understanding, finally removing confusion from that single spoken word—at least somewhat removed.

"Everything has become contempt prior to investigation. People form an unwavering opinion that refuses to change, no matter the facts," adds Jack in an uncharacteristically precise manner.

"Or, more probably, they are just old friends or something," Connor says, finishing the conversation. As Connor says that, the head coach, as if overhearing him, points from next to the police car toward the team. Coach speaks to the police officer, words inaudible to the players, except for Connor. He spins around in place, looking for the source of the sound. The sound of the coach speaking close by, saying Jack's name. Connor, unsure of the events but aware he must look like a madman trying to keep eye contact with a buzzing fly as he spins side to side. He stops to find Jack staring at him, head cocked to the side.

The coach shifts his body to the team and shouts, "Did I say to stop practicing?!" He returns to leaning on the squad car and resumes whatever private conversation they were having.

With that command, the players disperse and return to fielding balls and running plays.

"You okay, Con? You looked like, well, crazy. Spinnin' 'round and all."

Connor knows what he looked like and knows what he heard. He can't say that he heard the cop because it defies all reason, but he heard it clear and crisp.

"Yeah. Yeah," Connor says as his thoughts wander. "Thought something was buzzing in my ear."

But his mind lingers on what he heard in a whisper from so many yards away.

><><><><><><><><><><><><><><><><><><><><><><><

Allison and Scarlett sit on a black, plush comforter of Allison's queen-sized bed. The pink sheets peeking out from underneath lend a bright contrast to the dark black lying on top. Government textbooks and spiral-bound notebooks sprawl across the bed top.

Allison's torn jeans, Nine Inch Nails t-shirt, and asymmetrical A-line haircut dyed red with black tips warn everyone that, despite her petite size and childlike features, she will lash out if she feels threatened. She is forever trying to overcompensate for the tiny, pint-sized frame she feels cursed to possess.

The Ramones, KMFDM, Skinny Puppy, Motorhead, and countless other band posters adorning the walls of Allison's room cover almost every square inch leaving any visitor hard pressed to find the pink-painted walls beneath.

An iPod dock playing Marilyn Manson's "The Golden Age of Grotesque" sits on top of a well-kept, antique dresser off to the side of the room.

Allison's frustration at this moment reads in every jerky, quick, overreacted motion she makes. The mounting stress of the upcoming government test is taking its toll on the young girl of 17 years. She reaches for one of the two glasses next to her and takes a sip of dark cola. "That one was yours," she says disappointedly. She sets it back down and picks the other one, a little lighter in color. She takes a satisfying drink, "That's what I'm talkin' about." After setting down the glass, she slides out a flask hidden between the comforter and the sheet. She dumps the amber-colored, spiced liquid into her beverage. Then sets the container next to the drink.

Scarlett shakes her head at Allison, not sure if she's impressed or let down by Allison's actions. "You'll never pass this test if you keep turning every study session into a drink fest. And if I can't tutor you enough to pass a test, how will they ever launch my program?"

"Sorry, Scarlett. I'll try harder," Allison says with sad, puppy eyes.

"Now, which amendment states your right to face your accuser in the court of law?" Scarlett starts again.

"I'll say … third." She sips her drink.

Scarlett takes a breath of frustration. "And I'll say you're wrong. Third states that the government is forbidden from forcing us to house soldiers during times of peace." She looks at the flask. "Isn't your dad home?"

Allison taps her tightened lips as if thinking hard enough to strain her brain, "Fifth amendment. And no. He's out on business for the week. Some new acquisition for the museum."

Scarlett's head falls back in defeat. "You're getting closer. Fifth is the right to remain silent and the whole self-incrimination."

"That's right. How could I forget?" Allison feigns as if she has known in the first place. "It's the sixth."

Scarlett laughs, the dry sarcasm in Allison's previous words amusing her. "Now you're just guessing. You're right, but you're guessing."

Scarlett admits defeat in her attempt to teach Allison about the Constitution. She pushes the books aside and lays down. Allison collapses next to her. They both stare at the poster of a shirtless Ville Valo on her ceiling.

"This is what I'm good at, Scar. This, right here," Allison says, looking upward, arms out wide.

Scarlett looks to Allison, whose mile-wide stare is facing upward. "What, Al? Lying in bed?"

"Yup. And thinking about music. The meaning of it. All of his songs. They're so … tragically beautiful. Like me." She turns and takes a swig from her flask.

Scarlett chuckles. "You're tragically beautiful? What the hell does that even mean?"

It's a phrase Allison has thought about before. The meaning always seemed obvious to her and, without the need of an explanation, now suddenly needs explaining. She continues staring into the dreamy eyes of H.I.M.'s lead singer plastered up on her ceiling, searching for words to do his music justice. For in her mind, they are all she has.

"Tragically beautiful. I'm seventeen. I look twelve … at best. I feel like I'm a maturing young woman trapped in a child's body."

Scarlett sits up. "Oh, come on, Al. You are a very attractive girl."

Allison pops up from her prone position. "There. That's the tragic part," she says, pointing at Scarlett. "You admit I'm beautiful but still said 'girl.' I just said 'young woman' like two seconds before."

"Not what I meant. I know you're a woman," Scarlett defends.

"But it's not what you said. It's not what anybody says. It's not what anybody sees." She takes a long drink to finish off her flask. She slips the flask back between her comforter and her sheet before she lays back down to stare at the ceiling again.

Scarlett scooches next to her and hugs her. "I'm sorry. I'll choose my words more carefully next time."

Allison turns to her and smiles. "It's all good, Scar."

Scarlett breathes in and pulls back a slight bit. "Whoa. I know he's out of town right now, but slow down. Your dad is going to kill you if he ever catches you. Even if he gets within hugging distance, you're toast."

"It's all good, little Lett. I got it covered. I'm sharp."

"Yeah, like a marble, Al. Sharp like a marble." Scarlett starts cleaning up the books. "I meant any time in the future, Al." Those last words fall on deaf ears as Allison already has a thought in her head.

"More like I'm sharp as a razor." She shoots upright in her bed. "Speaking of which. Did you hear?"

Scarlett momentarily stops. "What's-her-face from Connor's gym class?"

Allison swings her legs off the bed, letting them dangle down. "Yup." She proceeds to make slicing motions across her wrists with a pretend razor. "Right in her tub. Messed up, right?!"

Scarlett resumes her packing. "I didn't know her. Didn't know her situation. What she was running from or what led her to that."

Allison realizes that maybe doing a mock suicide on the side of her bed was not a way to bring up such an event. She also knows she is with her best friend, and sometimes decorum, or an appropriate way to bring up such a subject, is unnecessary. "Me neither. I'm just saying. It's whack. Imagine her parents not only finding her dead but dead and naked. In a bathtub they have to use every day. Not how I would do it."

Scarlett stops and turns to Allison. "You've thought about how you'd do it?" She finished up her packing.

Allison is a bit taken aback. "No. Not really," she backpedals. "I mean, I think we all have a passing thought about it here or there, but…"

Scarlett stands at the doorway of Allison's room. She holds her backpack and has her finger on the light switch. "You'd better not do it at all."

Allison crawls under her comforter and sheets, snuggling into a body pillow. "Just saying, if I was to do it, it wouldn't be that way. Too messy. Someone has to clean that up."

Scarlett stands in disbelief for a moment. "That's your reasoning? Too much blood?"

Allison is already half asleep. With one eye open and a half-efforted arm raise, she points to Scarlett. "Respect."

Scarlett flips the switch and shuts off the lights. "I'll see you tomorrow, Al. Better not be any mess for me to clean up."

Scarlett leaves Allison to fall asleep in the darkness of her room and under the protection of her posters. She hopes that the little bit of studying they accomplished sinks into Allison's brain. There's a more profound worry steeping inside Scarlett. A concern for Allison that Scarlett can't quite put her finger on.

As Allison tries to settle into a peaceful slumber, the images already invading her mind keep her restless. Twisting and turning side to side as countless minutes tick away on the digital bedside clock, trying to find a comfortable position that puts her mind at ease, she finally passes out. The strange and uncomfortable images still invade her mind. Her face twitches in uneasiness, accompanied by sudden arm movements. Her loud cries from within her dream barely escape her lips in muffled pouts.

A man's voice narrates the scene inside her head. A voice she has never been able to put to a face. The curious voice is both soothing in sound but disconcerting in that clarity of a voice she's never heard outside her sleep. Within her sleep, this is a voice that she has listened to time and time again, a voice that knows her, her name, and her friends and her family. For the most part, she knows that the voice is her subconscious creation. Maybe Allison's unique interpretation of a voice she heard once as a child or some long-forgotten actor. Then there's a sliver of a notion that pokes at her from time to time that this voice isn't imaginary, isn't her subconscious creation, that this voice is a separate entity within her head.

The words whispered in her head slip from her mind as the blurry dream world comes into focus. Allison finds herself peering through the window of her old friend, Brianna's house. Even within her subconscious, she feels anxious pangs from spying on this house. She has an unnerving notion that Brianna is not the one she is supposed to focus on.

Allison cannot see Brianna through any of the fuzzy borders or set within the clear image her dream shows. She sees Brianna's mother, Sylvia Waldgrave, as she sets about the house with a raccoon skin and a bottle of gin. Floating a few feet above the ground in a blue and white bohemian-chic dress, Sylvia douses keepsake-filled shelves with gin. With the raccoon skin, she violently smears the gin around, sending the keepsakes shattering to the ground. As suddenly as she started her smear campaign, she stops and calmly hovers to the window, staring Allison in the eyes.

Startled by the eye contact but unable to wake up from her strange dream, Allison finds herself inside the Waldgrave residence. The keepsakes again line the shelves as if Sylvia never shattered them. Her long curls flow in the silent wind of Allison's dream. Allison notices an old tube television in the background. A static image of an ornate, multi-level house surrounded by white noise displays on the screen. The house looks like hers, but Allison can't entirely be sure in her altered state. The rest of the Waldgrave residence is blurred out though she can make out a couch, some framed artwork on the walls, and the usual assortment of household wares.

Sylvia performs grand, dramatic arm gestures indicating for Allison to follow her into the kitchen, smiling and laughing as she walks. The kitchen becomes focused as the living room blurs, except for the television display. That remains in crystal clear focus.

The kitchen is stainless steel trim with an almost lime-green color to the cabinets. A circular, picnic-style table of blues and yellows has three chairs around it. A broken, jagged glass pitcher sits on the counter next to a similarly broken drinking glass. The razor-sharp points of glass lining the tops of the glass and pitcher glisten in the neon lights above. Allison looks around the kitchen and sees no broken glass anywhere else. She also notices that nothing appears to be dirty or out of place, not a dish in the sink nor a dirty dish rag. Only the broken pitcher and glass sit on a wiped counter surrounded by dusted ledges.

Sylvia pours an invisible liquid from the pitcher into the jagged drinking glass. She sets the pitcher down and pushes the glass to Allison. Sylvia smiles, and her lips form the word, 'drink,' but Allison can't hear her. Sylvia turns around to put the pitcher into the dishwasher, but a hand reaches out. From Allison's point of view, the hand should be Allison's, but it is not hers. This hand is far more muscular, far more lithe. The nails on this hand are off-color, tinted grey, and, compared to Allison's short-kept nails, long. Thicker than human nails, they are sturdy and appear as if meant for digging or shredding. The skin is pale. The veins bulge out, lending a blue tint that makes the extremity look sickly. It reaches out to shove Sylvia to the ground.

Sylvia smacks her head on the ground as she lands. She turns to Allison, looking confused. Sylvia cries, though no tears flow. The hand rends Sylvia's flesh. Each slice into her face sounds the bring-bring-bring of an old, ringing, rotary phone. The exposed muscle contracts with each cry against the attack. Blood gushes out from the wounds, filling the tiled floor under her. The assault rages on as flesh-rending blow after blow continues tearing Sylvia apart, though she sheds no tears. As blood fills the space of Allison's dream and Sylvia, about to disappear into the crimson pool surrounding her, her fleshless, muscle-torn face looks at Allison one more time. This word Allison hears in its deafening echo, "Why?"

Allison jolts awake in the moonlit bedroom protected by the musicians forever stationed in their posters. Her heart pounds with so much force she can hear it in the quiet night. She feels it beating through her chest. The power of which may cause it to explode. "Why?" She looks around to make sure she's alone. A double check to verify that all she witnessed was, in fact, a dream. Yes, it all was just a dream, except for the ringing phone. The feel of her vision is so vivid and lifelike that she has to check her hands to make sure they are still hers. She feels her face—the smooth, flawless skin of 17 years. No cuts. No slices or exposed muscle. However, a painful sensation runs through her face. Large gauge pins and needles stab through her head, front to back and side to side. A feeling that though she is familiar with, she is never ready to experience again and never welcomed by her.

The ringing stops, and a thought enters her mind. Did her father try calling her at the late hour? She never answers the landline. That's a business-only line. But if she missed his call, maybe he would try the landline. So she checks her cell phone for a missed call. Nothing but the time reading 3:40 a.m. She sets it back down. Did she imagine the ringing landline? Was she still caught in the twilight between the sleeping world and the waking world while she heard the phone?

She sits staring at the ceiling for a few moments, waiting for the pain to pass. She can now concentrate long enough to jot down the experience her subconscious mind just shared with her. She opens the drawer to a small, black wood nightstand beside her bed. She pulls out a leather-bound, parchment journal whose permanent bookmark shows it is more than half filled. She opens it to that page and begins writing everything she can remember. Starting with the current time of 3:50. Perhaps those few moments were a little longer than she thought. The meaning of her dreams ever eluding her and growing more strange as she gets later into her teen years. A subject she has yet to get a hold on. She dreads having this conversation again with her father and is too scared to approach Scarlett or Connor over some unfounded fear they will pass judgment. She fears that they, too, may exile her from the group the same way Brianna mysteriously ostracized all of them.

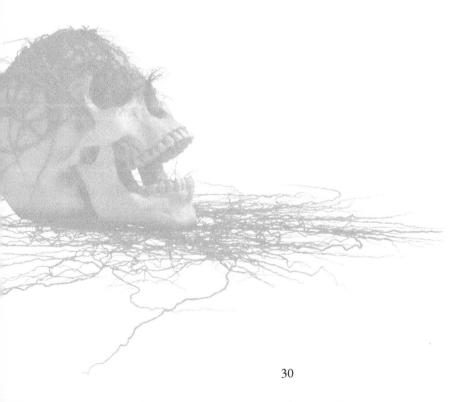

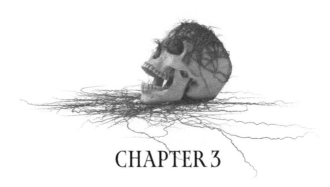

CHAPTER 3

*"I believe the world is
a far more understanding place
than you give it credit for being."*
~S. Waldgrave~

Scarlett's alarm sings its dissonant tune earlier than usual. Today she makes her monthly pilgrimage to have a few private moments with people she can't remember except through photographs. She finds solitude comes most effortlessly when everyone else she knows is still asleep. So after going about her daily routine of showering, eating breakfast, and applying whatever red suits her lips this morning, she heads out the door.

These people are not that far away. Only about one and a half miles. But even at this time of day, a fair amount of traffic buzzes by her as she walks down the road. She listens to the birds singing their morning praises to the light and sun. The occasional car blasting music at far too loud a volume for this hour disrupts her bird songs and introspection for a moment. But the breeze at her back seems to carry her a little faster.

She stops outside the main gates as they open up for the morning. The sign spans the gap between the two roadsides and reads: West Haven Cemetery. Stepping past the threshold, she heads toward the far end.

The chill breeze serpentines through the grey stone tombstones and old ash trees of the West Haven Cemetery. Mausoleums that dot the grounds stand in beauteous disrepair. The intuitive and unnamed feeling of the long-deceased caress the spirits of the living that visit this hallowed place.

Scarlett sits in silence, watching a family off in the distance. The black-veiled widow dabs her tears away with black-gloved hands and a white handkerchief. Scarlett sees the casket lower into the ground, the widow hiding her crying eyes into the shoulder of a nearby woman. Scarlett whispers to the family condolences of inner peace and the ability to cope while holding back a sympathetic tear. Their loss is something that young Scarlett knows too well.

Scarlett wears a black, long-sleeved, lace-trimmed, button-down top matching her black skirt. Even her makeup is dark today. From the eyeliner applied slightly thicker than she typically wears it, drawn out just passed her eyes, to the dark red lip stain she settled on, only her red Converse sneakers hint at happiness.

Scarlett turns to the marbled gravestones she leans against. She reads the epitaphs she has read countless times before. *Hillary McAllister, Devoted Wife and Loving Mother.* The engraving on the other read *James McAllister, A Family Man.* There are no dates on either stone. No dates to tell of their births or their deaths. Just that they are now together.

Scarlett stares at her parents' graves, having a silent conversation with them. A one-sided discussion she has repeated every month that she comes, sometimes more, whichever Friday or two a month she sets aside to come to see them. A conversation with them about the times they never had.

She tells them that their daughter is doing well; that she is not a bully. She walks a straight line. She talks to them about her best friend, Allison. The worry she has about her frequent drinking. Worry that it might turn into more. Scarlett always waits for a silent answer from beyond that never comes. She tells them about her cousin and confidant, Connor. His baseball games and coming college days. The times they have. She speaks to them through the six feet of dirt about her work to make tutoring more accessible to low-income children.

The wind blows her hair across her face as she talks to her parents. She doesn't move it. She doesn't let it distract her from a conversation she needs. A connection to her parents that she can only imagine. But the wind tries by whipping her ginger hair across her face. Her pale blue eyes blink in defense. The time with her parents is too valuable to be interrupted by trivial distractions.

The conversation ends as it always does. Scarlett shifts to a kneeling position placing her forehead on the gravestones and takes a deep breath. She stays there for a moment and whispers, "One day." She holds her head for just a moment longer before standing up. She turns away from her parents' graves, away from the distant funeral that has since disbanded. She turns toward the cemetery road that runs close to the burial plot she kneels at, the road that leads back towards the gates and the living. She sees Connor, decked out in his Iron Maiden t-shirt and jeans, arms crossed as the wind wildly blows his hair around, leaning against the door of his '94 Camaro. Scarlett looks past him to see Allison in the backseat, silhouetted in the morning sun, headphones on and boppin' away to some unheard music.

Scarlett wipes the welled-up tears away from her eyes and straightens out her clothes. As she walks toward them, she sets aside the conversation in her mind and starts to think about everyday things: the plans for the night, the school day ahead, and the homework she still needs to finish—anything to get her in a happier mood.

⋈⚬⚬⚬⚬⚬⚬⚬⚬⚬⚬⚬⚬⚬⚬⚬⚬⚬⚬⚬⚬⚬⚬⚬⋈

Vistrus opens the door to his house; morning light pours in from the outside. He stands for a moment, silhouetted in the doorway, breathing in the air around him. The inside is as immaculate as when he departed. Allison, perhaps, helped clean up even more than he had before he left. He rolls his carry-on luggage off to the side and lets it rest. He places his leather golfer's cap on an empty hook, sets his briefcase down on a shoe bench, slips his shoes off and into the bench cubby hole.

The inside of the Petrovsky residence is elegant yet masculine-high society without pretentiousness. It's everything a father wants for himself and everything he needs for his daughter. The framed, wall-mounted, ninety-inch flat screen LED television, while the centerpiece of the living room, is only one of the eye-catching pieces. A well-maintained, antique red velvet chair with gold rivets sits slightly off center from the television, giving way to a modern couch meant for the family. The antique chair is for Vistrus, not Allison.

An end table beside the chair holds a wooden humidor and a marble ashtray. A carved symbol adorns the top of the humidor, one Allison has inquired about once or twice in her life, but Vistrus has always less-than-convincingly dismissed as nothing.

The symbol carved into the lid of the antique humidor is a variant of a pentacle. Triangles make up the star's points. Each triangle has a line starting from each corner and meets in the middle of itself. Thus each star point is carved in a pyramid-like fashion, giving it a 3D quality. These lines join around the entire star forming an outline of a house; a base, two walls, and two slanted lines form the roof. In what is the center of both the star and house is the mathematical equals sign. A circle encases the entire design. The butt of a fully smoked Churchill rests in the ashtray. On the other side of the chair is a stand that holds a dulcimer. The decorations on the walls are mainly pictures of Vistrus and Allison throughout her years. A small section above a well-maintained, deep red, upright Steinway piano has one 8x10 photo of a young woman. Her features are similar to Allison's, a delicate jawline and prominent cheekbones. Her eyes are a bit darker than Allison's but have the same eternally sad look. A certain melancholy betrays the eternal youthfulness of her face. A blurred banner decorated with six wavy parallel lines hangs in the picture's background. No other photographs surround this one.

At this moment in the early morning, Vistrus enjoys a few moments alone after his long trip, isolated from society in the desert, and before heading into the museum for another day of acquisitions. He walks into the living room wearing a blue and black smoking jacket, holding a small glass of dark red cranberry juice cocktail, and sits in his red chair. He clicks the remote control, turning on the television to watch the morning news. He turns on his cell phone, which has been off since he landed in the Arabian

Desert. As he reaches for his dulcimer, he notices a blinking light on his outdated yet beloved answering machine. He listens to the days' old message from Tracy while the talking head on screen rattles away the story of the day. The text messages on his cell phone start flooding in, all from Tracy's desperate attempts to get a hold of him.

He reads the onslaught of text messages while also trying to catch the scrolling headlines, pop-up text at the bottom of the screen, and graphics window next to the newscaster's head on his television. He opens his humidor, grabbing a new Churchill. He lights up his cigar with the remaining match in a matchbook that rests next to the ashtray. He must contemplate how to best approach Tracy and discuss all the vague, cryptic messages she left for him. A discussion he is looking forward to having, if only out of curiosity.

As he lets out the first puff of his cigar, the graphics window on the news program changes to a picture of a brunette woman. Vistrus stops like a deer in headlights. He hangs up the phone and erases the message as his attention shifts to the woman on television. Nothing extraordinary about her looks: brown eyes, a healthy face of unremarkability, a smile showing good teeth—an utterly ordinary woman. But below the picture is the word MISSING.

He checks his Breitling watch and turns off the television. Finishing his drink in one long swig, he sets it down and heads out the door, cigar in one hand and cellphone to his ear.

>∞∞∞∞∞∞∞∞∞∞∞∞∞∞∞∞∞∞∞<

Connor takes the corner with the illusion of danger, as he does every day. Tires squeal a little, the back end drifting just enough to cause Allison to jump and Scarlett to giggle. But an illusion of danger is all it is. Pulling that off every day the same way and being in total control of his car takes practice, patience, and precision.

Scarlett enjoys her daily giggle at Allison's expense because the three-story behemoth of a late 19th-century building they call school always puts Scarlett a little out of ease. From the towering rotunda entrance—where you can stand in the middle and look up past the third floor to the ceiling—to the darkened doorway of the always-locked, urban legend of a fourth floor, the building has never sat right with Scarlett or most of the students who attend. The once half-walled stairwells leading up to the fourth floor have since been fully walled-off after a few lost souls took the dive to end it all, plummeting from the fourth floor onto the school seal in the lobby below.

If that wasn't enough, Scarlett knows of the empty swimming pool and locker rooms below, hidden and abandoned. Forgotten relics of time's past peck away at the back of her mind, making her feel they don't want to end up forgotten, always making their presence known to the next incoming class of freshmen, a silent cry for release from their exile. It's been an internal whisper crying in her ear since she was a freshman. A whimper that stayed through her sophomore year and hasn't dwindled in her junior year.

The underground rifle range used decades ago for physical education classes is now sealed off for storage. The feeling that there's been more forgotten about this place than is remembered makes Scarlett feel uneasy. She wants to know everything. Not for some insidious reason, nothing nefarious. Only a natural curiosity and need to know. A need to know what's available, what's hidden beneath. If she can make friends with the monster under the bed, so to speak, then she doesn't have to fear it.

As Connor pulls into a spot and they hop out of his car, Scarlett knows today is another day to befriend the monster that is her school. All three of them look to the overcast sky that warns of rain and indoor gym class and inhale their last bit of fresh air for the next eight hours. The wind whips by as they enjoy the moment.

"Don't you just love Fridays?" Connor rhetorically asks as they leave his blue baby in her temporary resting place and start off to the school in front of them.

"Shit!! Today's Friday!" Allison's pace quickens with a hopping start. These are her only words as she makes a full-on dash ahead.

Scarlett's arms in the air, she shouts, "Hello?! What's the rush?"

Allison turns toward them, doing a sideways run causing her to stumble a bit. "I had detention! I hate this place!"

Scarlett and Connor watch as she turns around and trips over a parking block, stumbling forward, arms flailing out sideways but catching herself in an uncharacteristically graceful way. She looks like she is about to go down; her right foot slides out from underneath and hovers just above the ground, and her left swings out and in front, taking the leading step. She stands and continues on her run. "Ha! I didn't fall!"

Connor and Scarlett chime in with a sarcastic slow clap. "Well done, Al! I give that an 8.2," Connor shouts. He turns to Scarlett, whose smile is fading. "You don't always have to go alone."

Scarlett turns her head toward the ground. Watching each step in front of her as she walks. "I know." She leaves it alone as they walk in uncomfortable silence for half the parking lot. "Today just sucks." She grimaces at herself for using such a poor descriptor.

Connor puts his arm around her shoulders. "I could be there with you. It's what family is for."

Scarlett moves into a one-armed embrace but stares away from him. A "thank you but not now" response of mixed appreciation. Connor understands the unspoken cues and tightens his hug before letting her go.

"What damage we doing tonight? Tomorrow?" Connor asks, changing the subject to something he hopes will be more exciting.

"Taking Al to The Attic. That girl needs to unwind. You should come," she says, looking at him again. His shaggy hair blows across his face.

"Of course, The Attic. What better place for the delinquent youth of West Haven to congregate and come together as one," Connor jokes. "I look forward to joining you two. Wanna come chill in the cafe with me?"

"Can't today. Meeting to talk about my tutor mentoring thing," she says with a hop to her step.

Under the old, orange paint of the steel awning, he grabs the stainless steel handle on the school door, swinging it open to a sea of students inside. Stepping inside, they disappear among the crowd of peers and blue lockers.

<hr>

Connor, Jack, and a small group of classmates laugh over a joke about breakfast condiments whose punchline is best kept among the ears of juvenile boys or crass men. They enter the biology classroom in a jovial mood that elevates upon seeing Mrs. Espinoza's low-cut top that teases the boys to at least pretend to pay attention as they daydream about her breasts. But as much as they may want to see her in her birthday suit, the stack of graded tests she holds in her hand turn the boys' mood from hot to not in one beat of their teenage hearts.

The class finishes filing in—an almost even mix of boys and girls. Linda stands at her desk, waiting, letting the anticipation build over the grades on their tests. She enjoys watching the worry and anxiety grow in their eyes—most of their eyes. Connor leans back at his desk: cool, calm, collected. He turns to Jack.

"Ninety-four," Connor says, a sly smile on his lips.

Jack turns to him, ungluing his eyes from happier places. "I'll be lucky if I pull eighty. I blew it this test."

Linda moves forward and starts passing them out. She slows her approach as she nears Connor. She holds out her arm, test in hand, but keeps the paper tucked toward her. "I overheard you a moment ago. How'd you know? Ninety-four."

Connor changes his smile to a shit-eating grin as he slides down to get even more comfortable in his desk chair. "Can't get a hundred on them all. It would be suspicious."

Linda turns the test to him, shaking her head. "One day, you'll be proud of being smart and actually accomplish something."

"Nah. Too much work," Connor says as he starts flipping through the test to see if he was right about the ones he got wrong. He was. A purposeful act of incorrectness to prove to himself that he can. A game he plays with himself. He doesn't remember where and when this juvenile act began. Nor why. But it's something he does. He thinks it will keep expectations just below where they would otherwise be. A high bar he lives by but not as high as it would be if he applied himself—a slacker with standards.

Linda continues passing out the tests with the usual assortments of pleasantly surprised compliments and unexpected disappointments. However, Connor doesn't hear any of this as he's confused by the last page of his test. Question fifty. It's there, and it's correct. He knew it was. But the bonus question, fifty-one, is no longer there. No traces on the paper of it having been erased, whited out, or otherwise removed. No pen indentations to indicate disappearing ink. Nothing. Just a blank spot after question fifty. But in true slacker fashion, he doesn't put any more thought into it, closes his test, crosses his arms, and feels self-satisfied. At least for the minute. He turns to Jack to see what score he received, but Jack still sits empty-handed.

Linda returns to her desk and looks around the top of it, under a few notepads and in a few drawers, searching. After a moment of doing so, she looks up at Jack. "Mr. Taylor, it appears I have misplaced your test. My apologies. If you'll see me privately, though, I'd like to go over it with you and give you your grade."

Jack and Connor lean toward each other at their desks. Connor, a bit surprised at her misplacement, says, "Dude, she lost your test?! What the hell?!"

Jack smiles at Connor. "Yeah, but dude, she wants to give it to me privately!" Jack scrunches his nose and nods his head with rebellious intent.

Connor joins in the devilish nod. "Let me know how that turns out."

∞∞∞∞∞∞∞∞∞∞∞∞∞∞∞∞∞∞∞

Allison sits at her usual picnic-inspired cafeteria lunch table, brown bag in front of her still folded at the top. She peers around at the other kids, laughing, joking, and enjoying their daily break from the grind of studies. The disdain for each student is evident in the sneer on Allison's face. Allison knows the growing unpleasantries in her mind toward her peers may be misguided, but she lets it wander since no one is guiding her. She spots Brianna at a table halfway across the open room of a cafeteria and makes eye contact. The piercing evil eye projecting off Allison sends Brianna back to her friends with a little less of a smile on her face. A hint of self-satisfaction allows Allison to open her brown bagged lunch.

Scarlett, lunch tray in hand, walks up to Allison and cops a squat across the table from her. The two girls dig into their respective lunches.

Allison's angst-filled mood seeps out of her mouth between bites of her homemade steak sandwich. "I don't get it."

Scarlett tries not to smile as she knows the conversation that is about to happen. A conversation that happens a few times a month and, while never exactly the same, the gist of it never changes. "Get what, Al?" Scarlett plays into Allison's leading question.

"Are we dumb?" Allison says as she eyeballs the stereotypical geek table of white collared shirts and pocket protectors.

"No," replies Scarlett, her mouth half filled with crappy pizza topped with more unflavored sauce than cheese.

"Are we ugly?" Allison continues as she stares down the preppy table trying to blow them up with her mind.

Scarlett laughs as she swallows her almost inedible pizza. "Hell no. We're sex."

With that reply, Allison looks around the empty table that surrounds them. No one within five feet on either side. "Then why do we always sit alone, Scar?"

Scarlett leans over the table as if to tell Allison the answer to life. She motions for Allison to lean forward, and as she does, she turns her head to hear her whispered answer.

"Because Connor doesn't have lunch with us this semester." Allison lets out a small laugh and sits back on the bench. "Plus, who cares? It doesn't matter. In ten years, we'll be at the class reunion and find out most of these kids are still living at home with their mommy and daddy, working some dead-end job that pays just above minimum wage because they are still fighting the system. Whatever that means. Hell, a few may have good jobs, but I'm sure a bunch will have come out of the closet by then, and they will be the only happy ones. Everyone else still clinging onto the memories of the past. It's so clichéd."

Allison softly laughs at all of Scarlett's words. But from all she just heard, a question pops into her mind.

"Then why are you doing this? Running for class president? To lead a bunch of future stay-at-home-adults?"

Scarlett thinks about the implication of Allison's question for a moment. She chews on both the words forming in her head and the bite of pizza. "Why not? Try something new. Maybe we're wrong about this fleeting phase of life."

As Allison ponders Scarlett's answer, she looks back to Brianna, who seems to be enjoying her popularity. "Maybe I should've run.

I could be president." The conviction is lacking in her words. "Eh. You'll make a good president."

Scarlett puts down the crust of what she hesitantly calls pizza. "I won't win."

Allison's eyes shoot from Brianna back to Scarlett. "What makes you say that?"

Scarlett opens and finishes her paper carton of chocolate milk in one down. "It's a popularity contest. Our lunch table is empty."

Allison smiles. "One day, we'll be something cool."

Scarlett nods in agreement. "One day. As soon as we get out of this place." She scans the cafeteria before returning to the conversation. "Oh, Connor and Jack are coming."

Allison's face drops. "I thought it was a girls' night."

Scarlett pulls out her cell phone. "It could be. I'll text him."

Allison quickly jumps in, "No, no, no. It's fine. Don't text him."

The mid-period bell rings, causing the Pavlovian response of the necessary students to rise en-masse and retreat to whatever their schedule has them doing. The stream of students surrounds the girls who continue enjoying their lunch. They sit, invisible to the rush around them.

"So, where are you going?" Allison chimes in.

Scarlett takes a moment to think about the question and its ambiguity. "After a few more classes, home to shower, eat, finish homework. Then to The Attic. We just talked about this, like, literally two minutes ago, unless you are stuck on life's master plan. In which case, just stop."

Allison grasps for the words to say that will turn Scarlett's interest on the subject but comes up empty-handed.

"I don't know where, Allison." Scarlett placates Allison's need to beat a dead horse. "I just don't want to live here when I'm old. West somewhere. East. I don't know. We still have another year before we graduate, and I haven't figured out what college I want to attend, let alone what I want to do for the rest of my life. Hell, I haven't even figured out what I want to wear tonight. What's eating you?"

Allison searches for her words again because the reality of her situation is that she doesn't know. The heavy weight of uncertainty presses down on her chest. She doesn't understand why it's there. She doesn't know how it got there. She knows that this impending feeling of the unknown holds her down, and she doesn't want it to. "I just think that … sometimes … that sometimes I'll never leave West Haven. Like I'm destined to live here forever."

Scarlett breaks out laughing at the absurdity of Allison's words. "You need to make out with someone or something."

"Lol. Or something," Allison chimes in. The thought of actually making out with someone puts a smile on Allison's face for the first time today since dealing with her morning detention.

The two girls stand up to throw away their garbage. Scarlett runs to Allison before walking off from the conversation. "You'll be fine."

Allison smiles in hopes that Scarlett is right. But as much as the thought of foreplay makes her smile, the uneasy weight on her chest makes her feel like Scarlett is wrong.

><><><><><><><><><><><><><><><><><><><><><><

The late afternoon sun casts its warmth on the outfielders passing balls back and forth and on the infielders throwing underhand passes from base to base. A batter stands at the plate, swinging at balls tossed for batting practice. Everything happening here would seem ordinary to the passerby. Even the player in the dugout taking the coach's accosting is a common sight on the athletic field.

But this player that Coach is yelling at is Connor. Finger wagging in his face, he listens to Coach use him as a punching bag for his frustrations. Connor tries to remain calm in the agitated moment but feels his blood starting to flow stronger with each passing moment. The beating of his heart echoes in his ears. Connor's anger and frustration grow with each sentence hurled at him, but he tries to remain calm. He takes a deep breath; the sound of the air filling his lungs begins to calm his nerves. All this yelling so Coach can vent and take it out on Connor that Jack ditched school and practice. The coach, who doubles as eighth-period Phys-Ed teacher for Jack, explains that he wasn't in class but had run into him in the hallway before the fifth period.

While most of the details of Coach's tirade pass through the pulsating ears of Connor, those particular devils stuck. And especially so because they have biology together third period. This means, in his mind, Jack left school sometime after biology, possibly before fifth period started and definitely before Jack's English class. Connor needs to figure out why he left school without so much as a text to Connor, through the screaming, coupled with the bulging vein in Coach's forehead.

"You and Jack might be great players, but you're slackers! Both of you! So don't cover for him!" Coach's spit-covered words hit Connor in the face.

Connor feels the sting of the saliva-soaked speech but can't hold in the swelling anger. The sound of Connor's voice drops in pitch with each passing word. "I'm not covering for him! I have no idea where he's at!"

Connor turns his back to the coach out of a realized need to calm down, a move that buys him a second to try and clear his throat of the sudden low, guttural voice. He reaches into his sports bag and grabs his cell phone. While Coach is spitting more words in his direction, Connor is more concerned about the lack of any text messages or voicemail from Jack.

Connor stands up, dials Jack's number, and without waiting for a beat in Coach's diatribe, he interjects, "You could not have flown off the handle and been such a presumptuous dick. All you had to do was ask me to call him." He shoves the phone in Coach's face. "Here."

Connor's worry grows with each passing moment Coach holds the phone. His concern is confirmed when Jack's voicemail message ends, and Coach lays into him, spouting the usual assortment of empty threats and heated words. As much as Coach is angry, a look of concern washes over his face knowing that Jack didn't pick up for his best friend. Coach's words end, and the calm after the storm sinks in. Both Coach and Connor stare at each other for a moment. No blinking. No flinching. Not even a tightened jaw muscle. Only a slight rise of the eyebrows from each of them. A silent question to the other as to who will act next.

At this moment, Connor recalls the empty threats hurtled toward them about being benched, running laps, all the usual scare tactics to get things running smoothly again. Connor doesn't seem to care right now. All he wants is to make sure his friend is all right. No word from him means he left in a hurry—no text after leaving means no access to cell phones. No missed call or voicemail tells

Connor he's not near any phones. All of those thoughts and the numerous possible answers to them pass through his mind while having the staring contest with Coach. Connor knows what he has to do, and he knows Coach will not be happy.

"I have to go. Do what you have to do."

Connor turns around and leaves a speechless Coach standing frozen, unsure how to react. Connor notices that the rest of the team has stopped practice and is watching the events unfold. He looks around at his teammates but doesn't say a word. No captain-of-the-team-motivational-words or commands to get back to training.

At this moment, he is not an athlete, not a captain of the team. Right now, he is a friend on a mission. Damn everything else.

⋘∞∞∞∞∞∞∞∞∞∞∞∞∞∞∞⋙

Heavy landscaping decorates the outside of the Waldgrave residence. Strategic plantings of Orange Butterfly Milkweed, Purple Coneflower, Goldenrod, and Blazing Star Kobolds make up most of the flora with some spotting of Spiderwort. They even keep their lawn's Fine Fescues and Kentucky Bluegrass edged and trimmed to perfection. In the lawn's center, a Kentucky Coffee tree stands nearly twenty feet tall with a modest three-foot-diameter trunk. All that landscaping surrounds a sidewalk leading to the outer, Stucco walls, an uncommon sight in the Midwest among the readily found brick-walled homes. The natural wood color of the barn-inspired front door and window work contrasts the surrounding houses. On a clear evening such as this one, one can see the Chicago skyline in the faint, far distance beyond the roof of her home.

Hidden by the shadows of night, a pair of green irised eyes otherwise camouflaged by the tree watch as Sylvia goes about her business. The pupils of the mysterious stranger have grown large to adjust to the low evening light. The sclera, though white, is paled by a touch of grey, perhaps helping with the camouflage.

The eyes watch through the open windows as Sylvia, dressed in a blue and white Bohemian-chic dress, sprays down the plants that hang outside her windowsill with a bottle of eco-friendly plant feed while her left hand holds an appletini in a stemmed glass. The green hue of the drink highlights the red cherry that has sunk to the bottom. Sylvia peers out into the quiet sky, enjoying the moment. The eyes outside squint as if to further hide among the tree.

The news story playing on the television in the background catches her attention. She turns away from the plants and shuts the window, latching it. On the couch in front of the TV is Brianna, oblivious to life around her, giving her thumbs a high-intensity workout as she texts with speeds found in Olympic sprinters. For the moment, Sylvia lets her daughter sit in a blissful state of oblivion. The newscaster's words, too crucial to miss, echo in Sylvia's ears, "…a developing story. A young man of 16, who authorities have identified as Robert Burns, has gone missing while on his way home from school. Friends say they were walking home with him but parted ways a few blocks from his house. We urge anyone with pertinent information to call the local authorities."

After the newscast cuts to a brief commercial, Sylvia sets her plant feed beside the window and makes her way into the kitchen, where she sprays down the counters with blue ammonia.

"We're having Eggplant Parmesan for dinner tonight. I know it's your favorite." Sylvia sets the blue bottle down and begins to wipe.

Brianna's attention shifts from her phone to her mother. Frustrated at what she hears, Brianna sits upright on the couch, debating her next move.

"I won't be home. I told you at least three times last week that I have book club tonight."

Sylvia opens the refrigerator, grabbing eggplant, yellow squash, and jarred marinara sauce and ignoring her daughter's words. "Well, dinner will be around nine. I'm making it just for you." Choice words to sting her daughter with the guilt-poisoned tipped dart only she can throw.

Brianna stomps into the kitchen. The frustration is visible on her face as she knows what is about to transpire again. Trying to calm her growing disappointment in her mother, Brianna grabs a bottle of sparkling water to calm her nerves. The hiss of carbonation floods her senses as she opens it, tickling her nose and filling her ears. After taking a sip, she inhales a deep breath.

"And I appreciate that, Mother, but you do this sort of shit all the time."

Sylvia, chef's knife in hand, turns unexpectedly to Brianna and points it at her. Brianna takes a step back. "Watch your mouth, young lady! And do what all the time?" She returns to further slicing the eggplant and pouring breadcrumbs into a bowl.

Brianna places the cap back on her bottle of Perrier as she sets it back on the counter. Slightly shaking her head in disbelief, she motions to the dishes on the counter. "This! You knew I had plans and then cook my favorite just so I feel like crap about having a life. It's not my fault you haven't had a life since dad left you, like, fifteen years ago."

Sylvia stops her preparations and places her hands on the counter. Her head hangs low in parental failure. "That's not fair, Brianna."

Brianna picks up the stemmed glass that holds the remains of Sylvia's appletini. "And neither is this!" She tosses the stemmed cocktail glass in the sink, causing it to shatter, shards and booze spilling down the drain.

In a sudden, indefensible moment, Sylvia turns, hand flying, and slaps Brianna square across the face. Brianna's head spins sideways, a bright pink handprint immediately visible. Brianna storms out of the kitchen, leaving her Perrier behind. She swings open the door to the outside with one hand while grabbing her car keys off the hook with her other.

Sylvia runs after her but gets to the doorway as Brianna is already starting up her lilac-colored BMW. Standing on the front doorsteps, Sylvia pleads to Brianna, "I didn't mean to! You just get me ... so angry!" Brianna backs out of the driveway, ignoring her mother's weak attempt at an apology. Sylvia watches her daughter drive away from the situation instead of stoking the fires. A coping tool she wishes she had but had never seemed to develop. After her daughter is out of sight and around a corner, Sylvia turns to go back inside, head hanging low.

From the corner of her eye, she notices a piece of rolled parchment paper placed on the edge of the stoop. Curious, she picks it up and opens it expecting to find a drawing or some inconsequential scribble. But the seemingly blank paper causes her eyes to widen in fear. An unsettling feeling overcomes her as she starts looking back every few seconds. She bolts shut the door to her house and draws the curtains closed. She turns on a lamp in the living room even though the recessed ceiling lights are on. Entering the hallway, she flicks the switch illuminating every corner. She peers into the bathroom and, in one quick swing of her arm, opens the shower curtain. She turns on the light as she leaves the bathroom. She searches under the beds and in the closets but finds both her bedroom and Brianna's bedroom to be empty, but she doesn't turn off the lights for just in case. The spare bedroom is the only unlit room in the house. She opens the door to the unused space, the window facing the coffee tree on the front lawn. Inspecting the room and deeming it empty, she turns on the light. But the bright LED light causes her not to be able to see out into the dark. If she had left the lights off, she would perhaps see the green eyes camouflaged in the coffee tree start to move.

At first, the eyes and head of a humanoid move away from the tree. A bark that matches the tree covers the entirety of this entity. Small, leafy vines circle the arms and wind down the torso. The definitively female shape of the humanoid limps away from her lawn toward the side of the house. As it does, her left-footed limping gait slowly dissipates. The bark covering her also shrinks and retreats into smooth skin.

If Sylvia had left the lights off and seen the glowing eyes, perhaps she would have an answer to why someone left parchment with words only she could read—words that reflect ultraviolet light. Words composed with the knowledge that she isn't an ordinary, everyday human—that she is something special, something more. And those words, written so eloquently, so simply, have struck fear that everything Sylvia loves and works for can be overturned in an instant.

We Know.

Back in her living room, Sylvia picks up a landline on a tiny, glass-topped end table next to her couch. She dials, impatiently waiting for an answer. She turns around and peeks out her window but sees nothing unusual. After many unanswered rings, her face relaxes a little—a voice on the other end.

The stainless steel sink and countertops reflect the light from above, shadowing the worry on Vistrus's face. The cordless landline in hand, he talks with Sylvia about the parchment. His minimal-effort attempts to placate her are in vain, perhaps from Sylvia's past overreactions or because he feels there isn't much to worry about. Vistrus likes a more Napoleonic approach of wait and see. To him, the one parchment isn't enough to warrant a frenzy. However this plays out right now, he must keep calm.

His daughter is seated just a few feet away, awaiting his return to the dinner table. Her eyes dart around in anticipation. She wants to continue the meal that waits for them on the table. The medium-well ribeye seasoned to perfection, still juicy from the marbling entwined within, calls out to her, begging to be eaten. While delicious, her side dish of balsamic sautéed Brussels sprouts always reminds her of tiny cabbage patch dolls, making her feel like she's cannibalizing small heads wrapped in lettuce. But the flavor reminds her that they are one of her favorites. She sips on her can of cola.

"I would not worry about one piece of blank parchment paper," Vistrus tell Sylvia as he tries to keep things vague in front of Allison. But Sylvia seems to be inconsolable for the moment. "I am eating dinner right now with my daughter. Let me finish, and I will meet you at the museum." Not the first time he's had to withhold the whole truth from his daughter. It pains him to do so because, from his viewpoint, honesty is paramount to a good relationship. He knows this little lie is a necessary evil until she starts to come into her own.

"Yes. I will meet you there when I am through. I shall see you in a bit," Vistrus says, hanging up the cordless phone on its wall-mounted base. He turns to Allison. "Sorry about the interruption."

"No worries. Just want to dig in. Looks delish." Allison picks up her fork and knife as he sits back down. Vistrus motions for her to start eating.

"Everything okay? Sounded like a problem at work." She shovels steak into her mouth.

"Yes. A small concern with the delivery of old parchment scrolls from a dig out in Africa. She was worried because one was blank," he says, cutting into his blue sirloin, blood dripping out and pooling underneath his brussels sprouts. He chews his steak as well as his lie. He hopes Allison drops it before she asks too many questions.

Allison swallows a bite of sprout, the remainder still on her fork. "I'm going out tonight with Scarlett and Connor to The Attic." She lets the sentence trail off as he sips a glass of deep red wine, piercing her with his eyes. "If that's okay with you?"

His eyes light up as she changes from statement to question. He sets down his glass and smiles. He looks out the window toward a waxing crescent moon that does little to calm his nerves. He knows she is due to start her changes soon—a phenomenon every parent of his genetic disposition worries about. He was around her age when he first noticed his changes. He wonders how long it will be before she starts noticing—before she finds out, before the last remaining bit of childhood innocence is lost to their … condition.

"What time?" he asks, taking a bite of his sprouts, pretending nothing is worrying him.

"We'd be there around ten. Home by midnight or so," she says with hopeful eyes.

He squints his eyes. He senses there's more to this than his daughter is letting on. "Connor is picking you up?"

Allison shrinks in her chair. "No?"

Putting on his best dad-voice, "Are you asking me?"

Allison sits back up in her chair. She knows she needs to display a confidence that has not yet found her. "No. I'd either take the bus or…" He stops mid-bite, waiting on the rest. "You can give me the Porsche."

Vistrus swallows, cutting into what's left of his steak. He withholds a response for a few moments, milking the anticipation for what he can. "How have your nightmares been? I do not want you driving if you have been up all night."

She perks up in her chair. "Good. I mean, fine. I mean, I haven't really had any lately. Well, one last night, but I always have bad dreams around this time of the month." An honest answer; she knows that will garner her points.

"Did it wake you?" His decision to loan her his car shifts toward no.

"No. Not that I remember. If it did, I fell right back asleep. I do think a therapist could help me with these. Someone to talk to," she says, sipping her Coke.

He points a fork full of bright red, blood-dripping steak at her. "No, you do not. Therapy is a crock." A lie he's said to her before, and each time it makes him feel worse and worse. But he knows what her dreams could mean. He knows that she will be able to use them one day. Harness them for good. A therapist who was not a Legend or had no knowledge of The Nation and their abilities could squash that ability, make her close her mind to it for good. But he knows she's old enough to start making her own decisions. "Why do you want to go?"

Allison sits back in her chair, searching her mind for the words to the reasons. The ineffable answer to the question asked. Scratching her ear with her index finger. "'Cause ... I don't remember much of the dream, but I do remember Ms. Waldgrave dying."

Raising an eyebrow but not wanting to sound an alarm, he takes a sip of wine as he sorts his words. He finds just one. "Sylvia?"

Allison nods. "It was sad. I remember feeling sad. Except, why her? She's just a teacher. Brianna and I haven't been friends for a few years."

Vistrus continues searching for the words to discourage her at the moment from seeking help but not altogether. He doesn't want her to start analyzing her dream now. He knows where that path can lead. But he can't keep her away from them forever. That's not their nature.

Before he can say anything in response, she pipes back up.

"Maybe talking with someone will help me understand my dreams—what they mean. Like, maybe I'll learn something. About me, or my internal thoughts..." Grasping for a word to convince her dad that she is right, her mouth utters, "Subconsciousishness." And while that might not have been a word to win his praise, she feels it drove her point home.

Her father takes a slow, deep breath to help him think and for dramatic pause. But the skyward look in his eyes has admitted defeat. At least for now. "Fine. I will make some calls and find you someone good. Here," he says, reaching into his pocket. He pulls out a set of car keys and places them on the table, keeping one hand on them. "I shall give you my keys after you try a bite of my steak. This is fantastic."

He cuts off a bite-sized chunk of overly rare meat. Juice dripping out from the muscle fibers, Allison unwillingly bites down and chews it.

"Cook it, dad," she says, forcing down the bite. "Try using fire to cook it."

He shakes his head, smiling at his daughter. "Not one scratch. On you or the car. This is my second child you are handling. I want you both back home safe."

In an ironic petulant-sounding moment of being a teen, Allison stands up and half-stomping her foot in a playful fit, says, "Daddy, I'm seventeen. I'm not a baby."

"But you are still my baby." He feigns throwing the keys. "You will be safe?"

Allison nods, excitement overtaking her neck. He tosses her the keys. She catches them left-handed while finishing off her steak with her right. She chugs the last of the soda, swallowing that and the chewed steak simultaneously.

"I thought you said ten, young lady?" Vistrus is confused by her sudden eating binge.

Allison steps to her father's side. "We have to get ready at her place," she says, planting a kiss on his cheek. She looks at the keys in her hand. "I can't have the Porsche?"

Vistrus shakes his head. "Not while you are having nightmares. You are lucky to get the Solstice."

Allison low tosses the keys and catches them with the same hand. She smiles as she skips out the front door. He watches her with worry in his eyes from the kitchen window as she starts the car and heads out.

∞∞∞∞∞∞∞∞∞∞∞∞∞∞∞∞∞∞∞∞∞∞∞

Scarlett stands in front of her mirror, tugging at the green lace trim top, half a size too large. She tilts her head side to side, judging herself and the top she once loved. Scarlett mouths the words to Linkin Park's "Numb" that plays on the radio. After a moment of silent thought filled in by the music and Allison's inordinately noisy rifling through the walk-in closet, Scarlett decides this is not the top she wants to wear tonight.

Something about the lace trim on her top seemed a little less akin to the *Pretty In Pink* movie poster hanging in the background and more in line with *Pretty Woman* when Vivian Ward was still working the street corner.

She reaches behind and grabs a bottle of water off her over-stuffed bookshelf. As she sets it back down, she yells over the music to Allison, "I don't like this. Toss me a different top."

No sooner than she finished her sentence, a red, plunging neckline of a top with black trim hits her across the face. "Here. Try this one. Show off the girls for once."

Scarlett holds out the top. She turns it over to examine it. The thought in her mind of her pushed-up bosom on display is not making her excited for the evening. But nothing is making her eager for the evening. She wants to be thrilled about the night out. Her friend needs a fun night out and tonight is the night. She needs to be a good friend, and maybe a push-up bra and a low-cut top are precisely what she needs tonight. Perhaps this night needs a thought process more in line with Allison. So Scarlett grabs the bottle of cabernet at her feet and takes a swig. Cutting loose once in a while never hurt anyone.

"I feel like I'm going to be sluttin' it up in this," she says, taking another small sip.

Allison grabs the bottle out of her hand and takes an exaggerated gulp. "It's not sluttin'-it-up. It's just a low-cut top. Man up and be proud of what you got."

Scarlett slips on the top and examines herself in the mirror. She looks over herself, unsure of what she sees reflected at her. "I don't think 'man up' is really what they mean in this instance."

Without hesitation, Allison corrects herself, "Then Betty White up. But either way, you look gorgeous."

"Betty White up?" Scarlett says with a raised brow.

"Yeah. I'm starting it. It'll catch on," Allison replies.

As much as Scarlett would like to deny it, she admits to herself that she does look gorgeous. It's not because of the liberal-leaning top either. It's the sight of her in something out of her comfort zone—a feeling of something different and new. The sensation of adventure elevates her mood a little closer to where she wants it to be.

Allison shoves the almost empty bottle of cabernet in Scarlett's face, a gesture that it needs to be polished off. Scarlett downs the last few sips of wine and holds it out from her. She stares at it for a moment, examining the label. "We're out already?"

A sheepish grin breaks across Allison's face as she plops down on the bed. "Sorry?" She holds her palms to the ceiling, indicating she has done no wrong.

"I may have some more," Scarlett says as she tosses the bottle into a small trash can hidden in the back of her closet. Allison leaves the bedroom to search for more wine.

Allison makes her way to the liquor cabinet above the oven. She finds a few bottles of wine stowed away in the back. However, the dust collecting on a bottle of cheap vodka grabs her attention. She figures if that goes missing, no one will notice. "Where is everyone tonight?" she yells to Scarlett.

Scarlett, again rummaging through clothes, can only make out a few words above the Slipknot song now blaring out the speakers. She turns it down to a more manageable level. "What?!" she yells.

Allison enters the bedroom equipped with a plastic bottle of half-drunk vodka. "Where's everyone?"

Scarlett emerges from the closet. "Out. Living. Con's at practice. Running late, I guess, but he should meet us there, and the 'rents are out."

Allison unscrews the top to take a swig, but Scarlett snatches the bottle out of her hand and caps it back up. "We'll bring it with us."

Scarlett stares down Allison, who's standing cross-armed. The look in Allison's eyes silently demands more of an explanation for the policing of her behavior.

"Al, your dad'll kill you if you scratch his baby."

"Seriously? That's your reasoning?" Allison pouts.

"Seriously. Yes. Now come on," Scarlett hesitates before putting the bottle in Al's purse and pulling out the keys to Vistrus' Pontiac.

The tires of Connor's Camaro screech to a halt outside Jack's house. He shifts his baby into park and jumps out the driver's side door, leaving his cell phone on the passenger seat. Looking at the house, he sees the interior lights are all on—an uncommon occurrence for a friend whose parents are especially eco-minded. The front door to the house is open, and the screen door softly flaps in the wind. As he approaches, he sees the interior is a mess.

He runs up the lawn, side skirting the front door. His fore-thought that there may be people inside takes control. He scurries to a tree for cover. Various thoughts run through his mind of the possibilities of what could have happened and who could be inside. Shuffled into the thoughts racing in his head is his realization he has no idea how to handle this situation. Something is wrong, and he wants to help. He wants to figure out what happened to his friend and his friend's house but has no realistic approach.

Trying to shake the doubt from his head, he lets instinct take over. He drops to the ground, recalling the great action movies he saw as a child, and army crawls toward the house under cover of late evening. He makes it through the imaginary gunfire to the safety of the outer wall, just below Jack's bedroom window.

He rises slowly to sneak a peek through the glass, but the drawn curtain blocks his attempt. The silhouette of a moving figure casts a shadow on the curtain. Connor moves about, trying to see around the curtain but to no avail.

"Dude! Jack!" he whispers in a borderline shout. "Why the hell weren't you at practice?! What's going on?! I know you said you needed to clean before your parents come back, but this raises some serious red flags!"

He looks around the yard and out to the empty street, checking for anyone who might be around. A clean sweep, and he looks back in through the curtain. The moving figure is gone. No silhouette. Nothing. Failing a response from the inside, Connor skulks along the walls to the front door. His head floats past the open doorway to survey the situation. A vintage plaid-cloth-covered couch straight from the 1970s lies overturned and broken on an arm. A coffee table is flipped upside down. The coasters and books that were once on the coffee table are strewn about the room. Pictures hang askew, and a crack runs through the mounted television. An antique bookshelf lay busted and the wall behind it broken, exposing the wooden studs. The many tell-tale signs of a long, well-fought battle are everywhere. Yet at first glance, Connor sees nothing out of the ordinary.

He exercises caution when opening the door and takes a light-footed step inside. He hears nothing. The sound of violence has calmed; even the wall-mounted clock's second hand has stopped as a timestamp for the event. The person he thought he saw silhouetted through the curtain has disappeared. He only hears the sound of his heart beating and lungs breathing.

"Jack!" No response. "What the hell is going on?!" He spins about in the clutter, trying to comprehend its entirety. "Jack?!" Connor stops spinning and reaches into his pocket for his phone. Realizing he left it out in his car, he calculates the risks of leaving the scene prematurely versus staying inside, mostly unexposed. Liking the latter of the two scenarios, he heads for the landline in the kitchen.

Broken glass and ceramic pieces crunch under his feet with every step he takes. He reaches for the phone dangling from the wall. He picks up the receiver, putting it to his ear, thinking maybe someone held the line for a just-in-case scenario. But no luck. Only the loud repetitive EIH-EIH-EIH-EIH of an off-the-hook receiver. He uses his finger to hang up the phone when he notices the small red indicator light of a missed call. The last name on the caller ID is his own: DESALVO. He frantically dials his dad's cell phone. In his haste, he misdials. "Damn it," spews forth from his mouth without his consent. He dials again but only to be greeted by a voicemail message.

"Dad! Where are you? I'm at Jack's, and something's wrong. Like they've been robbed or something. I can't find Jack, and his house is … a mess. I don't know what to do." His message is interrupted by a call waiting beep. His rapid-fire train of thought halts. He looks down at the caller ID once more to see who is calling, and once again, it's his surname. "Oh, it's you."

And with that final interjected thought, he clicks over to the other line. "Dad?! I'm at Jack's! Something's not right!" Cut off by the commanding tone of his father's words, he stands listening intently. He nods along in unreceived affirmation with every word he hears.

"Should I call the police?" His eyebrows raise as his father's uncharacteristic commands not to phone the authorities stop short of falling right out his other ear. "Um, okay. I understand. But I don't understand what you mean by anything unusual. Like, besides the fact it looks like a tornado rampaged through here?"

He falls silent again, listening once more to his father's words. After a deep breath to collect himself, he speaks once again. "I don't know. I'll keep looking. I'm freaking out, dad, but I'll let you know." With that, he hangs up the phone and backs up against the wall. His eyes scan the room as his head methodically rotates left to right, like a robot on watch. After taking a moment to calming down his built-up hysteria, he tiptoes back into the living room, further crunching the glass underfoot.

He starts picking up what he can to put back in place. Connor hefts the overturned and busted couch back upright. He sets back a small overturned rocking chair back into rocking position. He looks around, unsure of how he will make sense of any of this and manage to find anything unusual when everything about this situation is unusual.

He starts to move the bookshelf back into place when he notices a small, plain shelf behind the drywall, mounted between two studs. Two small, dust-free rings indicate someone took something. He examines further, unsure what he's looking for. Seeing nothing else, he finishes resting the bookshelf in its rightful place.

He continues cleaning up the mess by turning the coffee table back over and placing the scattered books and coasters back on top. He notices on the floor where the table had just been covering a piece of parchment, blank but old. He places it back on top of the table between two books.

Continuing his wade through the wreckage back into the kitchen, he looks around at the pristine kitchen, save two chairs pulled away from the table. On the fridge, he finds flight info under a magnet and two phone numbers. He pockets the information and heads to the bathroom just off the kitchen. Finding it untouched, he sweeps the rest of the house to see everything else is intact except for a small portion of the hallway off the main room.

He stands, trying to recreate the struggle in his head, imagining the thrown punches, grappling, and bodies tossed against the furniture—an image somewhere between professional wrestling entertainment and an MMA cage match. Satisfied with his amateur sleuthing skills and having found nothing of consequence, he heads out.

Slipping into his Camaro, he looks over the flight itinerary. As Jack had said, they should have been home by now. The possibilities of what happened are way off-base from the reality of the situation. He knows his mission to find his friend has only just begun. A reminder dawns on him that he should have already met his cousin and Allison at The Attic.

><><><><><><><><><><><><><><><><><><><

Marbled floors and pillars, vaulted ceilings with fantastic, painted murals, and historic artifact displays sparing no detail, each designed with meticulous precision, make up the marvelous wonder and beauty of the interior of the West Haven Museum of Natural History and Art—second home to Vistrus Petrovsky, Director of Cataloging and Acquisitions.

He stands alone, surrounded by the beginnings of what will be a beautiful yet eerie display of caskets and their residents from mid-16th century Europe. The setup juxtaposed the gallery showing of locally selected abstract art surrounding both sides—a mix of ancient and obscure.

Light footsteps approach him from far behind. His ears tweak backward to hear better. His arms remain crossed as he stays forward, a slight smile crossing his lips. As the footsteps grow near, he uncrosses his arms.

"Sylvia. Good to see you." He turns to her as she gets within whispering distance.

She stops, sending a playful sneer his way. "I hate that you can do that. You're like a cat, you know. They can identify a specific individual's footsteps within a few hundred feet of them."

Vistrus smiles at her, emitting a dry meow.

Sylvia shakes her head. "We can't do that, you know. That trick of the ears is reserved for vamps and werewolves."

"I hate when you call us that. We are not those things," he snaps back before collecting himself. "But, yes, well. I enjoy my gifts. My ears give me more time to enjoy what I was looking at."

"When The Nation settles on a name, I shall use that. Until then, it's just a placeholder." Her quick apology falling on deaf ears, Sylvia changes the topic.

She looks around at the display under construction. "Very nice setup you've got here."

Vistrus nods and cuts to the chase. "What do you have to show me?" He holds out a hand.

Sylvia pulls out the rolled-up parchment from an inside pocket of her custom shawl. She hands it over to Vistrus, who opens it and turns it over. He sees nothing. "I suppose this is related to what my kind lacks?" he states.

"Yes. I forget you can't see into the UV spectrum. But it's there. Someone knows, and they want me to know they know," she says, panic creeping out in her voice.

He shoves it back toward her. "Hide it. Before someone sees it."

A bright light shines around the corner as she pockets it back within her shawl. A security guard making his rounds on patrol interrupts their rendezvous. The light stops on Vistrus and Sylvia. "Just me, Javier."

"No one mentioned you'd be here so late. Is everything okay?"

"Just a little work I did not want to leave till tomorrow. We will be out soon."

With that, the light falls off them as the security guard nods and turns away.

Vistrus turns back to Sylvia, a decidedly frustrated look on his face. "How did you get this?"

Sylvia's defensiveness kicks in. "I found it on my doorstep when Bri was storming off. I didn't do anything that would expose…"

Vistrus waves a hand to cut her off, evident frustration on his face, even in the dim light of the nighttime museum. "Never thought you did. The Taylors never made their flight."

Sylvia's defensiveness fades, joining Vistrus in frustration. "That was two days ago. Why are we just finding out now?"

Vistrus gains a sternness to his tone. "That is how The Nation wanted it. I am only telling you because they are your friends." He waits for a reaction that never comes. "Did you know?"

Sylvia shakes her head. "I haven't talked with them in a few weeks." She stares at Vistrus for some reaction, but his intense stare doesn't break. He is thinking, and this moment is no time for words. Sylvia, however, is not done talking. She taps the parchment tucked away in her shawl. "Could the two be related?"

Vistrus thinks for a moment before giving an answer that may set off a degree of paranoia. "Perhaps. But let us not jump to any conclusions."

Sylvia looks to him for help. "So now what do we do? I can't just sit around being an easy target."

"No. Take that…" Vistrus indicates to the concealed parchment, "…and meet me outside the Mandarin Garden at Ballard and Potter."

><><><><><><><><><><><><><><><><><><><><><

Scarlet and Allison sit slouched on a plush, comfy couch set off to the side wall below a row of grated windows in the all-ages music venue, The Attic. Most of the teen and young adult crowd haphazardly dance to the music on stage. The pop-punk band's music is more reminiscent of Blink 182 than G. G. Allen despite them being dressed to the nines with studded leather accessories, Mohawks dyed green and blue, piercings too numerous to count, and torn jeans and home-modified shirts to round out the look.

Allison stares across the room to the far wall separating the main floor from the bar—the forbidden, liquor-filled room crowded with the 21-and-overs. Something inside Allison's mind yearns to be the jean-jacket-wearing rocker girl surrounded by swooning suitors. Her ability to pick whomever she'd like to entice for the remainder of the night. But no, she's stuck on the couch. Not that she minds. She has Scarlett at her side. Scarlett, who, soda in hand, stares into the sea of dancers and mosh pit participants, working up the courage to go out there and dance. Not to dance with a boy, but to dance with herself. For herself. To say to herself and show the world that she doesn't care if she is good or bad but is enjoying her life.

Scarlett takes a sip and immediately stops herself from spitting it out. She leers at Allison, tucking away the bottle of vodka they snuck in. Allison shrugs her shoulders. "You needed more."

Scarlett laughs. "Oh, I did, did I?" She takes another drink, proving Allison right.

Connor enters through the main door, finally out of his baseball uniform, though not dressed appropriately for a night at the club. He hurries past the line of people waiting for the bathroom, bumping into a muscular man as he does, but Connor is in rescue mode. He could have walked through a wall and would not have noticed. Luckily, the bigger man didn't seem to notice either. Connor stops in front of the girls, urgency dripping off him.

"Nice to see you made it, Con," starts Scarlett as she holds out a drink. "Have a drink. It's Allison approved. She's helping me relax."

Connor shakes his head, eyes wandering the room. Scarlett pulls the drink to her mouth and chugs a bit. Both girls glance at each other for a moment, wondering the same thing; they are trying to figure out what has Connor so distracted.

Scarlett decides to call him out. "Eyes darting around, doesn't take a drink, what's going on, Cuz'?"

Without stopping his scan of the room, he says, "I dunno. Maybe nothing. I can't get a hold of Jack."

"Maybe he's busy?" Scarlett offers up her thoughts.

Allison sits up and takes a drink, or two, or three. This catches Connor's attention. He raises an eyebrow at her zealous drinking habit tonight. "Perhaps. In class, he said he'd be at practice, but he never showed."

Allison stops her drink-a-thon for the moment with a nudging interjection, "And?"

Connor returns to scanning the room. "Something's wrong. I can feel it."

"So kick back and have a drink until you don't feel it" is Allison's not-so-wise solution to the problem at hand. But Connor finds a bit of comfort in that idea. He grabs Allison's glass from her hand and finishes the mixture of vodka and cola.

"I was at his house. It's a war zone."

Allison pours vodka into her empty cup, letting it dilute with the melting ice and remains of cola. "What are you gonna do about it?" nudges Allison once more.

"Find him," Connor replies with resolve.

The girls start to gather their belongings. "We'll come with you," Scarlett begins, checking around her immediate area.

"No, you two stay. Enjoy the show. And try not to get a dewy after polishing off that bottle."

"I won't," Allison reassures.

Connor looks at both girls. "Scar, you should probably drive, or Ally should stop drinking and wait it out. But don't let them catch you with that. You'll get kicked out … *again.*"

Both girls give a coy smile like they're invincible. "Yeah, yeah." Scarlett waves off his concern. "Go. If you need us, call."

Allison, feeling the better effects of the alcohol, adds with a sultry tone, "Yeah. If you should need us."

Connor smiles at the girls, shakes his head, and runs off.

Scarlett turns to Allison in a bit of disbelief. "If you should need us? Really? Have another drink."

Allison takes her up on that offer and sips her glass of mostly vodka. Scarlett relaxes back into the seat while watching Connor hurry to the front of the venue.

The song on stage ends, and the pounding bass drum settles down, but a vibration still runs through his right pocket. Connor reaches down and pulls out his beckoning phone to read an unknown number. "Hello?!" He tries speaking over the noise of the venue but can't hear who's on the other end. "Hold on a sec." Connor quickly pushes his way out the front door to the quiet of the parking lot. The street lamps illuminate the night.

Connor stops off to the side of the building to concentrate on the call. "Hello?" The frantic, familiar voice of Jack is on the other end. He is speaking so fast that Connor can't hear him. He is piecing together what he can. "Where?" A beat while his mind works on the puzzle of Jack's words. "Yeah, I got it. I'm on my way." Connor pockets his cell phone and runs to his car.

Connor opens the doors to a newly constructed police station. State-of-the-art security cameras stand watch over the stainless steel entryway doors. Just inside, a rounded reception desk, high off the ground, lords over any who may enter. Connor approaches, and his confidence and resolve start to fade in the presence of armed authority. He stops shy of the desk as a man whose badge reads Officer Smith turns around. A friendly smile breaks across his face as he sets down his drive-thru coffee cup. "May I help you?"

A question for the ages. Connor knows that Jack is here, but unsure as to why he's there, he feels a bit of unease inquiring. "Um. Yes." He hesitates, then corrects what he thinks was an unintentional disrespect. "Yes, sir." He pauses, gathering his thoughts. "My friend is here. I know it's late, but he just called."

Officer Smith smiles and chuckles. "No worries, son. What's his name?"

The kindness of the officer puts Connor more at ease. He smiles a bit—a way to show appreciation for the officer not playing into stereotypes common to teens.

A second officer stops directly behind Connor. He turns around to see who is looming over him but only catches the badge number 0051 before the officer moves his badge and name tag out of Connor's eye line. The two officers engage for a moment in casual talks about hitting the streets and being safe, but the demeanor in Officer 51's voice seemed anything but relaxed or kind. To Connor, it sounded more like a man with deep-seated anger issues, ready to pounce on a traffic stop for any small thing. The voice of someone who became a cop after seeing too many action movies. The kind of officer who gives the rest of the badge a bad name. After the two officer's brief conversation, Officer 51 turns to Connor. All ease that Connor just began to feel flees from him.

"You all right, kid?" Officer 51 queries.

Connor tenses up a bit but tries to feign relaxation. "Um, yeah. Just tired, sir. Long day."

Officer 51 nods to Connor and waves to Officer Smith. Connor watches as 51 exits the station. Connor turns back to Smith, who is still waiting. "What's your friend's name?"

"Jack," Connor blurts out.

"Just Jack? Or does he have a last name?"

"Sorry, sir. Taylor. Jack Taylor," Connor apologizes.

The officer turns to his computer and types away at the keyboard. The sound of tapping keys stops after a quick moment as he reads the screen. Shaking his head in disappointment, Smith turns back to Connor. "We have him. Yup. Just don't end up in here too for getting 'jacked.'" The lousy attempt at a pun is lost on Connor as he stands confused and without a response.

Officer Smith steps down from the reception desk and heads down a side hall. Connor hesitates, causing Smith to turn around and motion for Connor to follow.

"So, how do I sign him out?" asks Connor in a show of apparent naïveté.

The question causes Officer Smith to stop in his tracks. He turns to Connor. "Doesn't quite work like that. He's got a $2500.00 bail. If that can't be paid, he'll be released in the morning."

They continue walking down the relatively short hall, which seems to go on for miles. "Here you go." Officer Smith steps a few yards away to give them some privacy.

Connor sees Jack lying on a corner bench, eyes closed. He looks unharmed. "Jack!"

Jack shoots upright and hops to the cold metal bars of the cell.

"What the hell is goin' on, Jack?"

Jack, the ever-so-confident wordsmith, stands swaying like Michael Keaton, or Chandler Bing, about to deliver a short monologue.

"I was, uh, chilling in the courtyard during my free period." His pitch raises as he says "free period," an unnecessary punctuation on the words. But that's just how he speaks. "I saw a cop; this cop walks up to Mrs. Espinoza. He started talking to her, and well, she looked at me and nodded. In my direction. The next thing I know is, the cop walks toward me and tells me to come with him."

"So?"

Jack squints, unsure of what Connor is missing from his story. "He had, like, no reason to say so, so I was all, 'no.' Then, well, he went all Judge Dredd."

"Why?"

"See, well, uh, that's the thing. He said I looked like I was on PCP. And I … laughed. Who the hell does PCP anymore? No one, right? I mean, no one I know. But I was all defensive about it cause baseball." His voice again rises with the last word. "So he throws me up against his car. He drags my ass back here. Well, drove me here. But yeah, told me I had to do a pee test. It came back positive. Not for PCP, though, for steroids."

Connor's face turns to disbelief. He takes a small step back from the bars separating them. "Dude. Tell me you aren't doing steroids."

"No way in hell. You've known me fifteen years. Have I ever done anything to even … warrant that question?"

Connor hangs his head, upset with himself in his momentary doubt. But the hang of his head tells Jack that yes, he does trust him, and no, he's never done anything that should warrant the question.

Jack continues, "Exactly. So why trump up some charges for no reason?"

Connor's head lifts back up to look Jack in the eye. Both stare at each other, knowing there's got to be more. But they need to figure out what. Jack walks back to the bench and takes a seat. He bobs his head, hands to his ears, pretending he has headphones on.

"Do I look like a guy on, well, PCP? I was just sitting there, chillin'! And my biggest, um, question is," Jack pauses as he gathers his words, "How did he even find me back there? You know, that's a spot not easily visible from, like, anywhere."

Connor rubs his chin, trying to think of something that could help his friend, when an idea strikes, "So who was this cop? What about witnesses? I mean, somebody had to see?"

Jack shakes his head. "Mrs. Espinoza walked off after she pointed me out. No other students around. It was strange."

Connor seems momentarily defeated. "Did you get his name?"

Again Jack shakes his head. "Only a badge number. 0051"

Connor pauses for a moment, knowing he has to say what needs to be said, but he doesn't want to leave his friend. "Here's the thing, Jack."

"Crap."

"I don't have the money to get you out tonight."

Jack looks around the holding cell. "I have to spend the night in this place? I, uh, don't think I can, well, do that."

"It'll be okay. The cop at the desk said you'll be released tomorrow morning. So just hang tight, and I'll be here when you get out."

Jack looks to Connor again with urgency as he walks back to the front of the cell. "Find out why I can't get a hold of my parents."

"That's the other thing."

Jack's eyes get big. He grabs the bars of his cell, waiting to hear some unpleasantry.

Connor continues, "When you weren't at practice, I went to your house to see why you skipped."

The worry on Jack's face grows. "And?"

"And I'll find your parents."

"Connor, what did you find?" Jack grows visibly agitated. His hands tighten around the cell bars. His veins course with blood, pulsating more and more as his agitation grows. The skin on his hands and face darkens a couple of shades, though Connor doesn't seem to notice.

"Remember when we started playing ball?"

Jack half-smiles as he knows Connor is trying to calm him down. "Little league. We played on the A's."

Connor waves a reminiscent hand. "Before little league, when we played t-ball. All that youthful, big talk about going major."

Jack laughs at the break from reality. "Who would have thought we'd have scholarship potential? Well, me potential. You offers."

Connor nods at the way life works out. "But that's how we met—T-ball. I was horrible. But you told me to stick with it. It was your idea that I try pitching."

"Cause you couldn't hit worth a damn."

"And you couldn't catch a ball to save your life. But look at us now. College-bound, then who knows. Maybe the pros."

Jack's smile fades into angry, puckered lips. "Who knows? But see, here's the reality of it. I'm stuck in this, uh, cell for no fuckin reason! My parents are nowhere to be found, and you won't tell me what you found at my house!" His voice again raises as he speaks the last few words.

"I'll find your parents and figure all this out. It has to be some sort of mistake. Just hang tight. I'll be by in the morning to pick you up."

"Hang tight? Really?"

Connor slyly smiles. "I could've said 'stay put.'"

"Wiseass."

Connor salutes Jack while nodding as he walks off, leaving Jack alone once more.

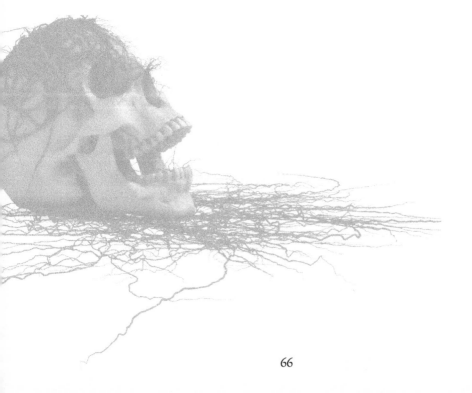

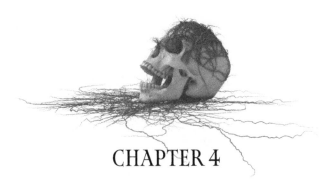

CHAPTER 4

"You're wrong."
~K. DeSalvo~

The interior of The Attic still buzzes, and so do the girls. The bottle of vodka hasn't moved much since Connor left last. Their ability to focus regains minimal ground.

The band finishes their current set on stage, says their rock n' roll graces, and steps off. The dance floor dies down a bit too, but the music on the house speakers keeps some rump shakers shaking. The girls look around the club through their unfocused vision. Scarlett rubs her stomach and her eyes.

"I think we should call Con-Uber or something to drive us home."

Allison laughs a little more than she should have at Scarlett's word mashup. Scarlett joins in on the chuckling though she is slightly unsure why. "Scarlett, you just said 'Con-Uber.'"

"I didn't say that." Scarlett denies it, realizing she had let her guard down a little too much tonight. A sobering thought for someone whose concerns about her friend are rooted in this same activity.

"Yes, you did. But we're fine. Well, I'm fine. You're not. I got this," Allison says, standing up from the couch. She almost fumbles her landing but sticks it at the end.

"No. Yes. You know what I mean. And you know why we should call someone?" Scarlett says as she too stands up, albeit with less trouble than Allison.

Allison shakes off the cobwebs of her buzz. Her focus is steady on Scarlett for the moment as they weave their way through to the exit. "Okay. Look. That happened, and it was not your fault. You were a baby. Damn."

Outside, the parking lot is half-full. The street lamps shine down, illuminating the late-night humidity on the parking lot and car windows. The girls walk with a bit more confidence than inside.

"Why you gotta kill my buzz, Scar?"

"Cause you drink more than Sinatra," she retorts.

"Who?" Allison asks, ignorant of the name.

Scarlett stops walking for a moment and fixes her dumbstruck gaze on Allison.

Allison ignores the jaw-dropped stare. "So, do I need to hail an Uber?"

Scarlett weighs the possibilities in her head, playing out every scenario she can think of, but she trusts her friend. Even when she feels it goes against her better judgment. Scarlett opens the passenger side door and takes a seat.

Allison gets behind the wheel and starts the car. Before backing out, she shuts her eyes hard to help clear away any ounce of unfocused vision. She pulls out and begins the journey home.

Scarlett changes the subject to something from a few hours ago. "So what was that 'if you should need us' bit earlier? You got a thing for my cousin?"

Allison feigns shock and surprise before the surprise that she can't honestly answer the question sinks in. "What?! No! Maybe. I don't know. He's cute. And a senior. But I've known him for, like, ever."

"Interesting."

"Interesting?! What the hell does that mean?" Allison defends.

"It means interesting. Don't read into it, Al."

"Look. I'm seventeen. I have needs. Don't you?"

Scarlett closes up, starting to regret her opening inquiry into the subject. "This conversation, sober or not, I'm not having it. Not if it involves my family."

Allison pokes at Scarlett by pointing out the excessive amount of "nots" in her response and, while doing so, stares just a bit too long at Scarlett for her comfort. Scarlett gets her phone out and pulls up Connor's number.

"Neither of us should be driving. Should I call him?"

Allison turns back to the road, still centered in her lane. "I know your rules and no. I promise I'm fine."

Scarlett again drops the subject in hopes Allison will continue driving responsibly. "You want Connor, go for it. I just don't need to hear the explicit details."

Allison's simple head nod and "heard" finishes that subject. The next few minutes of the ride are an awkward silence that, at least for Allison, becomes too much. So Allison decides to have a little fun; she takes her hands off the wheel and uses her knee to steer.

"Look! No hands!" Allison says, laughing.

Scarlett's eyes grow wide. She says, trying unsuccessfully not to laugh, "Not funny. I thought you were good?"

Allison wraps her hands around the back of her head. "Yeah, it is. That's why you're trying not to laugh. And yes, I am. Just messing with you."

"Sure, but can you put your hands back on the wheel?" Scarlett's freckled hand goes to grab the wheel but passes right through it, and she falls onto Allison's lap, causing the car to swerve. Allison grabs the wheel again to straighten themselves out.

"And you thought *I* wasn't okay to drive. You can't even grab the wheel."

Scarlett is sure she grabbed the wheel. As sure as she is that she saw her hand go clear through it like she wasn't even there. But from Allison's response, Scarlett is sure Allison didn't see the occurrence and she is fine with that. Scarlett's more logical side chimes in, putting doubts in her mind that she missed the wheel and perhaps had too much to drink.

"Crash your dad's car, and he'll kill you. No scratches, remember."

The girls continue driving, eyes straight on the road ahead. But as Allison uses her thumbs to align the car with the white and yellow lines in the street, neither girl sees the police car pull up behind them. He follows them for a few minutes, running the car's plate. As they turn, Allison checks the mirror and sees the cop.

"Is that?" Allison asks, gesturing behind them.

Scarlett tries to peek behind her but is obvious nonetheless. "Yup. Just drive normal."

"Normal?"

"Yeah. Like you're not a lush."

When the squad car lights up his cherries, Allison shoots Scarlett a frustrated stare.

"What do I do?! What do I do?!" Allison freaks out.

"Just pull over. Don't say a word. And don't blow," advises Scarlett.

"Ew. Why would you say that? That's so not how I'm going to try and get out of a ticket," Allison defends herself.

"No, you moron. Breathalyzer. Don't blow."

"Oh. Yeah. Gotcha," Allison says, pulling the car to the shoulder of the road.

Allison watches the officer in the car. Her stare focuses on the rearview mirror when the interior light of his vehicle shines on his badge, and even from this distance, she makes out the number 0051. Realizing the impossibility of seeing numbers that small, that far away, she squints to clear her eyes, but the badge number is still there, plain as day—as is the forged detail in the badge and the seams on his shirt. It is as though the mirror is acting like a magnifying glass. She looks at Scarlett, but all Allison can focus on is every pore in Scarlett's perfect complexion. Every tiny hair that covers her arms and face is in sharp focus. Whatever this is that Allison is experiencing adds to her momentary mental meltdown. She turns back to the rearview mirror and sees the officer on his CB radio. He speaks into the handheld set, and Allison sees him mouth the words, "Copy that. I'm on my way."

The cop car pulls out from behind them, cherries still flashing, and zooms away in a frantic hurry. Both girls sit there for a moment, visibly shaken. The girls' pounding hearts echo through Allison's ears like the bass drum from the band earlier tonight. Allison tilts her head, unsure what she is hearing. She looks around the car, searching for the source. Scarlett watches her, oblivious to the sound.

"You okay, Al?"

Allison realizes the sound she hears, where it originates from, and that it's not audible to Scarlett. She stops and rests her head on the headrest. "That was close. Too close."

They spend the rest of the drive home in silent concentration. Neither girl wants a repeat of what just almost transpired. The fates seem to be on their side as they pull into the driveway of an empty house. No scratches on the car, no worrying father to question them and smell their alcohol-scented breath. Just a place for both of the girls to sleep it off.

><><><><><><><><><><><><><><><><><

Vistrus stands, arms crossed, outside a small Chinese restaurant called The Mandarin Garden. The wind blows on an otherwise calm Chicago suburban night as he watches Sylvia approach from around a corner. She walks past the strip mall of closed-for-the-night shops toward Vistrus. Only a few lamp posts and the neon signs in the windows illuminate the streets.

"It's two in the morning. They're closed," Sylvia says, pointing to The Mandarin Garden.

"Not why we're here," Vistrus replies, dry as a soda cracker.

"Then why are we here?"

Vistrus doesn't answer her question but rather, he walks off and looks back to ensure she is following. He turns down a dimly lit alley off the main road. They begin walking the back alleys for a while, keeping an eye out for things. Vistrus explains to Sylvia that the trick to their activity tonight is that nothing will look out of place—at least to the casual observer. It will be small details they must spot. A task that Vistrus has been doing for more than a few centuries. Sylvia, on the other hand, not so long. She is a younger Legend. Younger than most, and with that comes much to learn.

"So, is this just something to do until the sun rises? What does Nick have to say about this?" she starts on a tangent of questions.

Vistrus shuts down her line of questioning. "No. This is what we must do to stay protected. To make sure those learning of their true self stay hidden. What Nick or the Council knows is not your business. You are not on it. When you are, you can ask." The sternness in his voice warns her not to tread in icy waters.

Sylvia ignores the caution tape, "You didn't even tell him about the note, did you?" The honest concern in her voice rings clear to

Vistrus, and while he may find her a tad annoying for his liking, he's not one to be mean for no reason.

"No, Sylvia. I did not. We know nothing about what it means, and missing members of The Nation are far more important." A teaching moment if there was one to have.

"If attention from the Council is a hard no, then at least some from you. It deserves something until we know it's nothing," Sylvia rebuts.

Vistrus looks at her with almost-apologetic eyes. "Perhaps." The thought that she may have a valid point is not something he subjectively likes, but he's proud of her from a more objective position. The doubts in his mind of her yearning to be on the Council momentarily ease. They are still there but relaxed for a moment. She may not be as intellectually stunted as he thinks. Then again, he realizes every idiot has their moments.

He's about to move on when he realizes Sylvia has no idea why they are strolling through back alleys or what they are particularly looking for tonight. He stops and turns to her. In hushed tones, he speaks, "There was a missing woman on the news—a member of The Nation. It could be a simple abduction. Possibly more. But she is local. We need to keep an eye out for anything unusual."

"But why back alleys?" Sylvia whispers back, still confused.

"One, if whoever took her had to unload her from a vehicle, they would not do it along Milwaukee Ave or any major street. They will do it in an alley, out of sight. We might be able to pick up the scent of blood, spot a light creeping out from under a doorway, or hear something. Two, remember the first time you transitioned? You hid. We all hid the first time. What better place to find a scared youth than curled up back here trying to figure out what they went through."

Vistrus continues his walk again.

"I guess that makes sense. But wouldn't they hide in their room?" Sylvia hushes to herself as she follows him.

"Perhaps. But we cannot break into random houses." Vistrus turns back to her, still speaking in hushed tones. "This night has been fruitless. One more alley, and we will call it."

As they are about to make a turn into their last stop, his ears pick up a sound—a slight shift in the rhythm of the wind and a change in ambient sounds. He knows it is something. He motions for Sylvia to halt. He pushes himself up against a shadowed wall. He feels the chill of the bricks through his clothes. Sylvia follows suit though the look on her face indicates she does not hear what Vistrus hears. He holds his index finger to his lips and listens to the sounds.

Footsteps and whispered talking from down the alley. From the sounds of the footsteps, Vistrus counts one person, and from the sound of him talking to himself, a man. The steps weigh heavy. Vistrus peaks around the corner to see a tall, muscular, blonde man with chiseled features carrying the teenage boy displayed on the news as missing, Robert Burns. Robert appears injured and hangs limp as a rag doll over the man's shoulder.

The man talks in hushed tones to the young boy. "All I needed was the correct sample, then none of this would have happened. See what they make me do. These filthy creatures—diseased and despicable. It would have been so much fun if you had been a vampire. The experiments are almost complete. Results happen, but not without breaking some eggs. And with the broken eggs, the cure is almost complete. No more vampires. No. I have seen beneath the surface. I know their secrets. But for you, kid, I am sorry. There's a war going on out here."

He pauses as he sets the young Burns down against a dumpster. He adjusts the young man's head, so it is not hanging off to the side or down in front of him but back against the metal dumpster. "And you may not know it, but it's been going on for a long time. I don't know how you and the other two back there got caught up in all this … but … we can't let it get out now."

He continues squatting in front of the kid making adjustments to his clothes. An apparent sign of respect for the mix-up. "Sometimes. Good people get caught in bad situations, you know. Have you ever heard of friendly fire? Funny phrase. Being shot is never friendly. It's just a nice way of saying someone stumbled into something they shouldn't have. It wasn't your choice or your fault."

Vistrus has heard enough but decides to play it out casually without knowing the man's abilities. He turns the corner to the alley. Sylvia takes to the shadows. He takes a nonchalant stroll down the backstreet toward the man and the unconscious teen.

Vistrus walks forward, keeping his ears focused on the surrounding environment. He listens for the possibility of others breathing as they wait in the shadows—shifting winds, doors closing, anything that might indicate the blonde man has company.

The man watches as Vistrus approaches him, though he continues whispering to the unconscious Robert, unaware that Vistrus's ears can hear every word he says. He also seems oblivious to Sylvia's skulking. "There are bad men out there. Men. Hmm. Creatures. Malicious, evil creatures. From myths and fairy tales you heard growing up. Yes, they exist. Believe you me, they exist. But we plan on changing that. You can't say anything to anyone, though. You never know who might be one of them."

He stands up as Vistrus gets closer. He looks back down at the boy once more. "Which brings me back to friendly fire."

Vistrus pretends he hasn't heard the blonde man's entire monologue. His experience has taught him that he must play this just right. Caution is never a bad thing. "Everything all right?"

The blonde man gestures to the boy. "I was walking home and found him here. I can't seem to get a response."

Vistrus decides a subtle hint is the way to go. "Found him? In this alley?"

The blonde man's eyes get shifty, darting back and forth between the boy and Vistrus. He squats back down and lifts Robert with one hand. "Yeah, help me, please."

Vistrus takes a step closer and plays into the blonde man's hand. Just as he does, the blonde man pulls out a Ruger 9MM handgun from behind his back and jams it into the teen boy.

Vistrus stops walking and takes a few steps back. His ears stay focused on his surroundings but sense nothing more out of the ordinary. His eyes scan the area for makeshift weapons, escape routes if things don't work in his favor, and other objects that may be of use.

"What makes you think I won't kill him?" A possibly rhetorical question to perchance force a move.

Vistrus chooses his words carefully, hoping they won't be the last for the Burns kid to hear. "I am thinking you have a bit more humanity than that." Vistrus starts inching closer to the blonde man.

The answer throws off the blonde man. He still holds the gun against the boy, but his thoughts are off kilter. "Perhaps. But I'd stop where you are if you don't want to test that theory."

Vistrus heeds his warning. "So how do we conclude this encounter? You have the gun."

The blonde man smiles a cocky, confident smile. "With me leaving and you not following."

Vistrus shakes his head. "I do not see that happening."

Still hiding in the shadows, Sylvia has made her way closer to the blonde man. Seeing an opportunity in the exchange between the two men, she lunges out from the shadows at the blonde man. As she topples him to the ground, his finger squeezes the trigger sending a bullet flying.

The blonde man stands up, brushing off the tackle. He waves the gun between Vistrus and Sylvia. "Should have just let me go," he says, shaking his head.

Sylvia has taken to tending to the young man's bleeding chest wound. She looks at the blond man in disbelief at what he is saying.

"Now his blood is on your hands." With that, the blonde man runs off, arm behind him, waving the gun as he runs.

Vistrus kneels to help tend to the boy. Looking him over, grief strikes Vistrus for the kid. Sylvia looks at Vistrus, and with a quick gesture of her head, and an "I got this," sends Vistrus running off to find the blonde man.

Sylvia stays behind, holding the dying boy. Trying to save him in his final moments, she applies pressure over the exit wound, but her effort proves fruitless. Robert opens his eyes and looks into hers, silently pleading for help. She begins to weep for him as blood pools from under her hands. She calms him with whatever soothing clichés come to mind. Anything to bring peace to the boy as he leaves this world.

Vistrus races down the streets; his speed dwarfs even the fastest sprinter. As he runs, his movements are smooth and graceful. His ears twitch as he runs so he can follow the distant sounds of the blonde man's frantic footsteps. The physical changes happening to his body offset the gracefulness of his run.

His hair grows longer with each step, darkening till it is jet black, yet grotesquely thinning simultaneously. Veins and capillaries on his face rise to the surface, becoming more prominent. The color of his skin pales out.

After a few turns, he catches up to the blonde man, who is still running as fast as he can. Vistrus throws him against a brick wall, smacking hard against it, knocking the wind out of him. The gun falls to the ground and under a dumpster. In a flash, Vistrus is face to face with the blonde man.

Vistrus' face is now in complete vampiric form. The veins and capillaries bulging out, pulsing with blood. The pupils of his eyes have dilated, leaving no trace of irises. Hundreds of tiny red capillaries now dominate the once white sclera. His nose is recessed and withered. He snarls, revealing elongated, pointed incisors streaked brown. No other teeth are visible, having all recessed back into his gums. Blood spills out his mouth from his transition as he speaks.

Vistrus spits out his words, "You should not have done that!"

The blonde man's eyes widen in excitement. He laughs through the pain of being thrown like a rag doll. "I knew it! Vampire! You'll die next!"

The blonde man open-palm punches Vistrus in the sternum, knocking him back. The man reaches for a knife, but Vistrus takes a deep breath, lunges forward, grabs the man's arm, and yanks him down. A visceral pop wrenches the night air. The blonde man screams in pain. His arm falls limp as the knife clinks against the ground.

Vistrus scares himself with that attack. He backs off before he does more damage, but it is already done. The blonde man holds his lifeless arm.

"This is why I kill your kind," screams the blonde man as he pops his arm back into the socket.

Vistrus watches as the cracking sound of his arm relocating pierces his ears. "You killed that boy! Not me!"

The blonde man laughs. "Not yet … if you can get back to him in time."

Vistrus makes a quick head turn toward Sylvia and the boy. The blonde man grabs the knife on the ground and side-arms it at Vistrus. The blade grazes his forearm, catching his attention. He turns back to the mysterious figure who is running off. Vistrus catches up to him in a flash, knocking the man to the ground. Before the man can turn over, Vistrus is on top of him. He grabs a handful of the blonde hair and pushes his face into the deteriorating cement.

"Whatever you think you are doing, you have no idea what you are up against. Whoever you think you are, you are *not* strong enough," Vistrus threatens.

The blonde man quietly laughs as a bloody smile crosses his face. "You and your family are already dead."

The thought of this man threatening his little Allison makes the blood pulsate harder through his visible veins.

The man continues laughing at Vistrus, taunting him with each soft laugh that spits a mix of blood and saliva onto the concrete. All Vistrus can do is imagine that his little girl is already lying in a pool of blood somehow missed by him while he exited his own home. Then the thought of unwelcomed strangers invading his private residence becomes the icing on the cake.

He lets out a roar and smashes the blonde man's face into the ground, grinding it against the rough, worn road. The loud, stomach-churning sound of the man's jaw breaking and teeth cracking echoes through the alley. The man falls unconscious as Vistrus realizes what he just did.

Vistrus stands us and looks around at the carnage of what just happened. All concentrated in a tiny area around the blonde man's bleeding face. Dizziness sets in as his veins recede, his teeth flatten out, and the rest of his appearance returns to normal. He falters backward a few steps as the dizziness overtakes him. After gathering his bearings, he searches the man's pockets for a cell phone. He finds one with a locked screen, though the 911 access is still available. He calls in the emergency with the location, but as the operator says to stay on the line, he wipes the phone clean and sets it on the man's back.

He rushes back to Sylvia and Robert. He arrives to find Sylvia surrounded by a puddle of blood and Robert's lifeless eyes staring blankly into hers. She weeps for the boy she doesn't know. Vistrus stands a few yards away, his face in his hands. The world around him spins, a feeling usually reserved for when he shifts back to his Normal self. But this time, it spins for the boy. The lost, innocent life that left behind the body of Robert Burns.

Sylvia looks up to Vistrus, tears flowing and voice broken by sadness. "What do we do?"

Vistrus stares deep into Sylvia's eyes. They say nothing as the approaching sirens break the silence of the night.

After a long stare with sirens fast approaching in the distance, Vistrus speaks, "Go. I will take care of this."

Sylvia's stare turns scared. She holds the boy closer to herself, tightening her grip around him. She was the last person he ever saw. The maternal side of her can't leave him.

"This is not a request." A sternness in his voice reinforces his words.

Sylvia buries her head in the boy. Vistrus knows he needs to temper his words and voice. He calms down for a moment, the imminent sirens drawing ever closer. "I promise he will be treated well."

Sylvia sets Robert's body down on the ground. She stands up and retreats to the shadows. A small trail of blood from her shoes fades from the body.

Vistrus is quick to cover the fact that Sylvia was ever there. As the ambulance turns the corner to the alley, Vistrus stands up, waving his arms. As the ambulance stops, he keeps his face hidden by shadows and constant movement. He points to the boy and the blood and spins a story of a late-night walk after a long day to clear his mind. The story is enough to sound believable but not enough to demand attention away from the boy.

The paramedics tend to the boy as Vistrus finishes his story. By the time the medics have a moment to turn back to Vistrus, he has disappeared. They take a quick look around before turning their attention back to revival efforts. Vistrus watches from a concealed rooftop vantage point. A squad car pulls up from the other direction. The lights from both vehicles illuminate the alley in a blinding dance.

Vistrus hops a rooftop or two back to where he left the unconscious blonde man. He looks down to an empty alley. The blood has been diluted and smeared. The broken teeth are gone. The unmistakable scent of bleach wafts into Vistrus's nose.

In a very short time, someone completely cleaned up the mess.

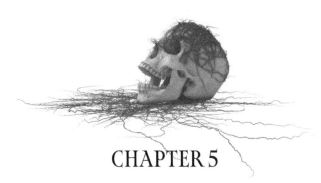

CHAPTER 5

"All the lore about your kind. Vampires.
Reading all those books, watching all those
movies trying to separate fact from fiction.
Time wasted. They tell you it's viral.
Contagious. Get bit and turn into one.
Bats and such..."
~M. Espinoza~

Vistrus enters a greasy-spoon mom-and-pop diner to see Tracy seated at a small corner table, wringing her hands and sipping coffee. A smile crosses her face as she spots him. Tracy takes a deep breath to calm herself, which stops her hand-wringing. She puts a hand to the side of her face as if to hold back tears.

He walks past the booths lining the windows; elderly patrons enjoying their Early Bird Specials fill most of these, while suited businesspeople and their business partners take up the rest. Tracy's anxiety is visible on her face as Vistrus makes his way to her. The tempting pies on display in their countertop case across from Tracy do nothing to calm her nerves right now.

Vistrus takes a seat and motions to the server for coffee. "What is going on? You would not say anything in your messages," he starts.

Tracy shakes her head. "Hi, Tracy. How are you, Tracy? I'm good, Tracy. Thanks for asking."

Vistrus nods to her. "Sorry. I assumed you were not good and wanted to get straight to it." He pauses for a moment, but Tracy is not getting any more comfortable.

He continues, "How are you, Tracy?"

She takes a quick look around and shifts closer to him. "Me?" she says, pointing a finger at herself. "Not good. Not good at all." She shakes her hand and keeps her wide-eyed gaze on the man in front of her.

"I think you do not need any more coffee," he quips, pulling her mug closer to him. "Start at the beginning," Vistrus redirects.

"I'm late," she starts.

"No. We are right on time," he says, looking at his watch.

The waitress walks up with coffee and pours a cup for Vistrus. Before continuing, Tracy and Vistrus order cornmeal pancakes, bacon, and sausage patties. Tracy waits until the waitress walks out of earshot. She quickly scans the room, making sure everything is normal; no one is listening or even looking in their direction.

"Not now. I mean, I'm late and won't be on time for another nine months," Tracy whispers.

"Have you seen a doctor?" Vistrus asks.

Tracy leans closer and lowers her whisper, "Multiple tests."

Vistrus's eyes widen, and he takes a deep breath as the realization hits him. "How?"

"Exactly. That's why I contacted you." She notices a bruised cut peeking out from his rolled-up shirt sleeve. He tries to pull the sleeve down. She looks him over more closely and notices multiple subtle bruises. "What happened?"

"Nothing important." He lowers his voice to an almost inaudible level. The outside observer—someone who is not a Legend—would see their lips flutter, quiver, or twitch, but no audible sounds would usher forth. To vampires, this is a way to communicate in public when prying ears may otherwise hear words not meant for them.

"There must be a mistake. Legends cannot get pregnant twice. There has never been a case of a second child being born. It is hard enough for females to conceive once, let alone twice."

Tracy taps her temple twice and points to him. "There's the rub." She lowers her voice to the same imperceptible level as his. "I've taken three home tests."

"What does Ken think?"

Tracy looks away. "He doesn't know. I don't know what he'd say. I thought the Council should know first."

"Wise decision. I shall inform them."

She reaches out and grabs his hand. Her fingers brush across rough, scabbing cuts. "I don't want them to take my baby."

Vistrus rests his free hand on hers. "They would not."

She looks at his hands. "A bit more than a scuff, I'd say."

"It is nothing." He pulls his hands away.

Though the patrons around the restaurant seem oblivious to their conversation, Tracy keeps an eye out for any busybodies trying to eavesdrop. Her tingling skin tells her something is amiss, but because of her anxiety, she is unsure if her senses ring true at the moment. She listens to each of the surrounding tables for tell-tale signs of intrusion, but the usual conversations about weather and daily plans tell Tracy that she is the only one being intrusive.

Tracy pulls back from him, sitting upright and staring at him. Her eyes try to read his mind. He stares back, waiting for her to speak. He knows she does not believe him, but he wants to focus on the task at hand.

"You're hiding something, Vistrus. And the fact that you won't tell me isn't helping any."

"I know the history of our people, and this is something they will want to protect. You will be safe. I promise you that."

"Promise me that what happened to you isn't something against The Nation. Tell me the scuff was random."

Vistrus looks her dead in the eye, staying calm and collected. "The encounter was random. I promise."

Tracy seems to calm down a bit. "I want to keep my family safe, V. All of them. Ken, Connor, Scarlett. I just need them to be safe."

Vistrus nods.

"Scarlett already lost one family," she adds.

The blaring ring tone of Tracy's cell phone interrupts the moment; people turn to see the sound. Tracy looks around at the crowd as she pulls out her noisy phone. She checks the caller id to see it is Ken. She mutes the ringer but does not send it to voicemail.

"Should I answer? What do I tell him?"

The waitress delivers the food to the table, sets down the plates, and asks if there is anything else she can bring, but the question goes unanswered.

"Yes, answer. Do not tell him anything you do not want to." Vistrus and Tracy have far more pressing concerns than a need for extra pancake syrup. The waitress sighs and walks away.

Her finger slides left to answer the call. "Hey, baby." She smiles, calming herself down with controlled breathing.

The smiling eyes fade as the person on the other end delivers unwanted news. Vistrus watches as tears well up in Tracy's eyes. Her fear and paranoia set back in as she begins to shake. She listens for a few more moments.

"Thank you. I'll be right there."

She stands up from her chair and starts to walk away. Vistrus turns to her. "What is happening?"

She turns to Vistrus as tears stream down her cheeks. "I have to go. I'm sorry." She turns back to leave, but Vistrus quickly catches up.

"What is going on?" he inquires.

"I'm not sure," she says, anxiously edging toward the door. "I don't know much." She continues walking.

Vistrus can tell it is something terrible, but it is not his place to force or coax it out of her. He must do what he needs to about her situation and the Council. He will leave her to her own devices.

"Go. We shall continue this later. I will take care of the bill and let the others know." He tries to leave her with some silver lining, but he knows he is only fooling himself with such comforts.

><><><><><><><><><><><><><><><><><><><><><

Connor stands in the lobby of the police station, surrounded by the early morning bustle. The officers leaving the station to attend to their assigned tasks whiz past him. He sees a few early morning offenders seated and staring him down. The bright light of the dawning day shines on the face of Officer Smith, still seated at his desk, lost in his computer screen. The blinding light in his eyes helps keep him awake. The steaming cup of coffee next to him helps, too. Connor takes squeamish steps toward him.

"Hello, sir," Connor starts. "I was here last night."

Officer Smith looks up and blinks with wide eyes. "Yes, young man. I remember."

"You said to come by this morning to pick him up or whatever."

Officer Smith laughs at his "whatever." He leans back in his chair, crosses his arms, and tilts his head back for a moment as if he's going to nap. Connor tries patiently to wait for a response that never comes.

"So, how do I sign him out?"

The officer adjusts forward in his seat. "He's not here. He got out last night."

Anxious fidgeting overthrows Connor's attempt at a calm demeanor. "But I don't understand. You said he had to spend the night and I should come back today. It's today and…"

Officer Smith interrupts, "Look, son. I don't know what to tell you. He ended up getting out last night."

Connor whips out his cell phone and dials Jack. He waits for it to connect, but as soon as it does, he fumbles the phone, tossing it between his hands as he tries to regain control. As he puts it back to his ear, all he hears is the beep indicating he should leave a message. Connor looks back to the cop who watches him with a look somewhere between concern and suspicion.

"What time was he released?" Connor asks with hopeful concern.

Officer Smith types on his keyboard. The increasing number of keystrokes and passing seconds add to Connor's anticipation. "Looks like shortly after you left."

"But you were still here when I left."

"Look, kid. I'm on desk duty. I have my computer and am nothing more than a receptionist with a badge for the next few weeks." He breathes in, squinting his eyes at Connor as he tries to determine Connor's end game.

Connor's eyes light up as an idea strikes him. "Does it say who came to get him?"

Officer Smith looks at his screen with a raised brow. "Looks like no one."

Connor stands confused and unsure what to do or how to compose himself at this moment. He looks around for some outside help from a strange passerby. Not surprisingly, no one comes to his aid. He looks back to Officer Smith. "No one? That can't be right?"

"Sitting here drinking coffee all shift leads to restroom breaks, if you know what I mean," the officer hints.

Connor tries to pick up the hint the officer drops. "I can wait if you need to go. It's no problem."

The officer laughs. His impatience fades as he sees the naiveté in Connor's youth. "No. I meant last night. I was away from the desk." He looks back to his computer screen to confirm what he is about to say. "It looks like Officer Espinoza released him."

Connor slides his finger across the phone screen and calls Jack again. Still straight to voicemail. "He couldn't have just walked out? Is that even how it's done?" he asks Officer Smith.

The officer smiles. "Nice to know you've never spent a night here." He leans forward with a smile on his face. "Yes, once released, you are free to leave."

Connor takes a slow, deep breath in and out. His face twists in thought as he tries to imagine last night's events.

"Is there a problem, young man?" Officer Smith inquires, leaning in a little closer.

Connor, unsure of the officer's tone, chooses his words carefully. He does not wish to eat them. He also doesn't want to say no to a man of power who might be able to help him in his cause, except that he is still not entirely sure what his cause is.

"No, sir. It's just that his phone goes straight to voicemail."

The officer leans toward Connor. "Look, son. You seem like a good kid. I don't know why you would associate with someone like him. Maybe you don't know the whole story."

Connor stands with an unmistakable look of confusion covering every inch of his face. He shakes his head. "What don't I understand?"

"That address, where your friend lives. It's a reported drug house." Connor stumbles back a step at the news. "Crack den." His world is spinning around him as the information hits him with the impossibility of that being an accurate statement. "Dealer."

He watches as people pass by him, unaware of his imminent mental and possible physical collapse. He sways back and forth from the sting of the officer's words. He stumbles back a step before regaining his footing. "That's not true."

"Look, son. Don't call me a liar," his tone of voice reinforces his authority.

"I mean, that can't be right. There must be a mistake," Connor pleads.

"I'm looking at reports from that address. Things happen that you don't see. I suggest finding new friends."

Connor feels his heart racing. The sound around him amplifies as he grows angrier with each word the Officer speaks.

The officer continues, "Now, if there's nothing else, have a wonderful day."

The sounds of the station drown his eardrums in white noise. Connor looks around and inhales. The sudden, overwhelming whiff of sweat and dirt from the cops at the end of their shift assaults his nose; gunpowder and steel top off the aromas. He looks around, overwhelmed by the new sensations, unsure why he smells what he smells and hears what he's hearing.

Connor swings his head all around, trying to locate the source before he realizes the world around him hasn't changed. Something in him has.

He looks at his phone but notices his fingers. Still flesh toned and human, he sees tiny, raised veins. He has a few from the workout of pitching, but this is more. Much more vasculature than he is sure he usually has. He makes his way to a bench and sits down. He put his elbows on his knees and his head in his hands. He tries to relax, hoping the world around him will stop spinning.

He takes a few deep breaths while buried in his hands. After the third breath, he raises his head. The sounds around him return to normal. The smells that besieged his nose have dissipated. Even the veins he swore he saw have receded. He's sure he didn't imagine it though.

><><><><><><><><><><><><><><><><><><><><><><><><

Allison creaks open her eyes from a deep slumber, blinking a few times as she adjusts to unfamiliar surroundings.

She rubs the sleep from her eyes and shoots upright in bed. She looks at the eggshell white sheets and cornflower blue comforter, a far cry from her usual pink and black. Intricately carved posts corner the bed. She remains calm as the realization sinks in that this is definitely not her room. She did not think she was intoxicated enough not to remember falling asleep here last night. She does not remember leaving her house again after driving home.

The color scheme hints at country living with a dash of suburbia, not her rebellious rock 'n roll youth. The dresser matches the bed with eggshell white drawers and a cornflower blue frame. The wood is well worn but otherwise sturdy—an intentional shabby-chic look. Allison picks up a small 5x7 store-bought picture frame off the dresser. The photo of Brianna and Sylvia, enshrined in some happy memory from long ago, confirms she is not at her home but at the Waldgraves'. Bri looks to be around eight or nine years old. Her mom, however, hasn't seemed to age a day since this picture was taken.

Allison looks around the bedroom, searching for some sign that this is not real, that she did not take a walk and crash at an old friend's house late last night. She thinks to herself that she couldn't have. Brianna would have been in her bed. But this doesn't feel like an ordinary dream to Allison. Everything is far more tangible. Her senses are far keener than in her dreams.

Allison grabs the knob to exit the bedroom. Thoughts swirl through her mind trying to figure out what excuses will dig her out of this situation, but nothing convincing manifests. Giving up hope of not getting grounded or worse, she opens the door.

As the door creaks open, bright red light shines from the other side, blinding her. The light floods the room, drowning her in a sea of red. Allison tries to cover her eyes to see past it into the hallway, but to little avail. The shapes she can make out aren't of another person, at least that she can tell.

"Can someone turn off that light?!" she cries out.

There is no verbal response, but the lights dim, leaving a clear, red-tinted view of her surroundings.

"Thanks," she responds. Again, no one seems to be there.

She walks down a short hallway and descends a set of carpeted stairs that end in the living room. She looks around at the picture-perfect setting—throw pillows placed and fluffed on the couch with precision, undisturbed in any way. The carpet has vacuum lines all in impossibly straight rows. The television is on but plays only white noise and static. Overcome with a sense of peace, Allison senses that maybe she won't get in trouble for sleeping at an old friend's house.

Ms. Waldgrave holds a feather duster while she cleans. Allison doesn't want to make assumptions about her peculiar, torn business attire.

"Ms. Waldgrave?" Something in her mind holds back Allison from taking a step toward Ms. Waldgrave. She continues dusting, oblivious that Allison is behind her.

Allison tries a more general greeting, "Hello?" She looks around, knowing something isn't right. Ms. Waldgrave still doesn't react.

Allison watches as she moves to a spray bottle on a shelf in graceful, dancer-like motions. She lifts the bottle with exaggerated movements and sprays it three times. A loud, irritating, grating, buzzing sounds each time she sprays. Sylvia wipes the surface with the duster and squirts the bottle three more times. Again, it makes that ungodly sound.

It all goes black.

Allison is jolted awake, her unfinished dream interrupted by the buzzing alarm clock.

She suspects the dream may have led somewhere had she not set her alarm clock so that her father wouldn't worry. Not that sleeping in is a cause for worry, but she knows her dreams are a point of contention. When she sleeps too late, he knows her night was not restful.

She falls back onto her pillow and looks around her room. Yes, it is her room. She smiles, knowing that she doesn't have a cornflower blue comforter. She stretches and shakes off the last of her sleep before heading to the kitchen.

Making her way closer to the kitchen, the smell of bacon, pancakes, and sausage stirs Allison's senses. The smell of brewing coffee accents the deliciousness of those aromas. She hears soft chatter between her father and Scarlett, who woke earlier than Allison.

Vistrus stands next to a tall stack of warm buttermilk pan-cakes stirring a skillet full of scrambled eggs. "Did you girls have fun last night?"

Allison ignores his question as she spots a subtle bruise on his chin. "Daddy, what happened to your jaw?"

He keeps stirring the eggs without hesitation. "I got hit by a door going out for breakfast with Aunt Tracy."

Allison grabs a plate and throws a couple of pancakes onto it. "Got hit by a door? Where's the syrup?"

"Here," Scarlett chimes in, waving the syrup decanter. "I grabbed it for my stack."

Vistrus pulls the eggs off the stove. "A gentleman, distracted by his cell phone, opened the door into my face while I walked in."

Allison raises an eyebrow. "And you didn't move?"

Vistrus, pan in hand, doles the eggs onto the girls' plates, "I, too, was distracted." He puts the pan back on the stove to cool. "So, how was last night?"

Scarlett finishes sipping her OJ. "Fun. We just watched the band."

Vistrus gives a stern eye to his daughter. "Rough night?"

Allison shovels pancakes and sausage into her mouth. "Damn dreams."

Vistrus clears his throat at her.

"Yeah," Scarlett mocks her friend, "darn those dreams."

"She gets nightmares," Vistrus says in a very matter-of-fact tone.

Allison eats while propping up her head in her other hand. "Vivid, crappy, strange, shitty nightmares."

"Young lady," he reprimands.

"Sorry, dad." She turns to Scarlett. "They suck, and they always make me feel like I didn't get any rest."

Vistrus turns off Dad-Reprimand-Mode and returns to being concerned. "Same as the last one?"

Allison shakes her head as she swallows a bite of egg. "I was there this time. It was more real. I could feel everything. Smell. It was all very touchable."

"Tangible," Vistrus corrects while he drinks some cranberry juice. "You are still keeping your sleep journal, yes?"

Scarlett sips her OJ while eyeing Allison. "Sleep journal?"

Allison's eyes widen as her face turns a faint blush. "Dad!"

Scarlett chuckles. "I'd love to peek in that thing."

Vistrus raises an eyebrow at his daughter. "Well?"

Allison's head drops a bit. "Yeah. It's … somewhere."

Vistrus turns back to the dishes in the sink. "Glad to hear. Eat up." He waits for Allison to get involved with her eating again; it's hard to ask questions with a full mouth. "I have some business to take care of at the museum today."

Sometimes having a full mouth doesn't stop the questions. "I thought you were off Saturdays?" Allison asks as a little bit of food falls out.

"Attractive, dear," he says, motioning to the pancake that took a dive. "No rest for the wicked, love." He starts filling the sink with soapy water.

Scarlett's attention perks up. "New showcase setup?"

Vistrus shakes his head. "Just some inventory. Nothing fun." He checks his watch and turns off the water. "In fact," he says, picking up a towel and dryings his hands, "I have to leave. Can you finish the dishes?"

"But I have to work soon, too," Allison pouts.

"Don't worry, Mr. P." Scarlett stands up. "I got it."

Vistrus heads to the door and gathers his briefcase, jacket, and hat. "Have a good day, girls."

The two watch him through the window as he pulls away.

Allison whips around to Scarlett as her father leaves her vision. "Close call last night, right?!"

"What?" Scarlett asks, honestly unsure of to what Allison's referring. "With the police?"

Allison gets up and heads down the hall. "Yeah."

The girls stop in the bathroom. "Yeah," Scarlett says, dripping with sarcasm. "Can't wait to do it again."

"Come on. It was fun." Allison nudges.

"You like close run-ins with the cops?"

Allison sees Scarlett's viewpoint and changes her tone. "No. The night, I mean. It was fun. I just wish Connor didn't ditch out like that, but I had a good time." She waits for a second for Scarlett to respond but receives stares. "Tell me you didn't have fun." She grabs her toothbrush and toothpaste.

Scarlett smiles a bit, taking a seat on the bathroom floor. "Yeah, I did. What time you gotta be to work?"

Allison talks while brushing her teeth. "In about half hour. Day shifts are always so boring. But weekends are the only time I can work mornings. Better than a Monday morning would be, I guess," she says, drooling out toothpaste. "All the real customers come in at night." She spits out her foamed toothpaste.

Scarlett laughs. "You don't like all the pop lovers coming in on lunch to grab the *Fresh Children In Town* reunion album?"

"Exactly," Allison agrees as she taps off her toothbrush. "So, what are you doing today?"

Scarlett leans against the wall next to the bathroom sink. "It's time I get a job, or so I've been told."

Allison looks down at her as she flosses her teeth. "Nice. You should come work with me."

"I think I can apply there. I was thinking maybe a restaurant or something. Maybe park district something. I don't know."

"Have fun with all that. I'm hopping in the shower," Allison says, taking off her clothes.

Scarlett stands up as Allison closes the shower curtain. Allison pulls the little silver tab to change the flow from the tub faucet to the shower head. Scarlett debates trying to carry on a conversation but decides to leave Allison to her vices. Time to get a job though it may be, now she just has to find one.

∞∞∞∞∞∞∞∞∞∞∞∞∞∞∞∞∞∞∞

Tracy tries to gain control of the thoughts infesting her mind as she rides the elevator to the third floor. She imagines her husband, bloodied, mangled, and unrecognizable, though stable—whatever that means in her mind. A new image of him fading away flashes in her mind, the grating drone of the ECG's flat-line tone buzzing in her ear as she shouts to the gods above, "Why! Oh, why!"

She doesn't know what to expect. He could be lying in a body cast but otherwise uninjured. She doesn't know and can't stop thinking about the possibilities. But as elevators inevitably will, it dings, and the door opens. Eager eyes of people needing to ride the elevator stare her down, willing her to exit before they can enter.

She takes a deep breath and steps out onto the floor. The busy-bodies rush past her into the elevator before the doors close. She guesses that since he is not on the ground floor intensive care unit, he can't be that bad. But since the doctors are not discharging him, she knows the reality lies somewhere in between.

She walks past a nurse's station and sees the nurses looking over clipboards and computer screens. One male nurse stands off to the side, trying to be inconspicuous while reading some celebrity-studded pop-culture magazine. He looks up as he flips the page and nods at Tracy. She turns her head reading the room numbers. She finds his room. 351.

She stops outside his closed door. She doesn't hear any disconcerting noises from inside. She closes her eyes and takes a deep breath, preparing for the worst of what she imagined, hoping for the best.

Upon first laying eyes on his bruised face, she rushes to his side as tears form in her eyes. A doctor in his lab coat, button-down shirt, and black slacks stands by his side, typing away on a hand-held tablet. She hugs him, careful not to further damage whatever might be injured. Ken smiles back at his wife, arms wrapped tightly around her.

"I didn't know how bad it was. All anyone would say is that you were here," Tracy says, holding back tears of relief.

Ken holds his wife's face in his hands. "I'll be fine. They just have to run some tests and give me time to recover." He looks over his wife to make sure she's doing okay. "Have you told Connor?"

She steps back and looks him over. She notes that he wears no casts, meaning no broken bones. She notices some cuts, scrapes, and many, many bruises but nothing broken.

The doctor stops typing on his tablet and looks up at Tracy. "Nice to see you again, Tracy."

She looks at him and smiles. "Thank you, Dr. Wong." She pauses for a moment and looks at her husband before returning to Dr. Wong. "Nice to see you too. How is everything?"

"No internal bleeding nor any broken bones. Obviously, no concussion. You're lucky your husband is…" Dr. Wong lowers his voice, "…who he is. His strong constitution saved him."

Tracy nods. "Otherwise?"

Dr. Wong shakes his head. "I'll leave you two alone while I check on other patients. I'll be back in a bit."

Tracy sits next to Ken on his hospital bed. The air around them settles down as Dr. Wong leaves. She inspects her husband, astonished his condition is not worse. Mrs. DeSalvo looks down at his bed and grabs the television remote, muting the sound of screaming people who grace the stage on some trashy talk show. "I can't even begin to tell you how worried I was," she says.

Ken grabs her by the waist and pulls her in. He moves his hands to hold her head and gives her a deep, passionate kiss. It only lasts for a few moments, calming Tracy down in his embrace, but it felt longer to her. A moment that she did not want to end and never wants to forget. He stops after her small nervous shaking calms, too.

"Sorry about the bloody lip," Ken jokes.

She laughs. "Bloody kisses from you don't bother me. As long as you're alive." She can't help but continually check him for something the doctors may have missed. "How did this happen?"

"I was walking from my office to grab an early lunch. I was on my cell phone," Ken says, looking around while he searches his memory.

As he begins to speak of the incident, nervousness overcomes him. He continually surveys the door and around the room. As if he is searching for someone lurking in the shadows that he missed before. Tracy sees his failed attempts to hide his newfound paranoia from her. She understands as she has troubles all her own.

"I was hit from behind. I fell to the ground, and he was on top of me," Ken continues.

"Who was?"

"I don't know. I don't think I've seen the man before. I tried beating him off, but that didn't work. He was too powerful," Ken responds, still unsure of what happened. An unsettling look crosses his usually confident face. He has a jittery look that screams something is wrong.

Tracy sees this and holds his head in her hands. She looks him in the eye. "Hey, you're alive. Anything you can remember will help."

Ken lowers his head. "I never thought this could happen. With what I am. I didn't think I'd ever have to worry."

Tracy senses all confidence he once possessed, fleeing his body with each passing word. She lifts his chin to make his eyes meet hers. "What can you remember? It's okay."

"I remember thinking that I can't protect myself. I can't protect my family. My thoughts turned to you and Connor. Scarlett," he pauses and looks down again. Tracy doesn't lift his chin. His mind wanders, lost in thought, so she waits. After a long pause, he looks up at her, eyes wide, "He was a blonde man. Blue eyes. Something was off about his face."

Tracy kisses him on the forehead. "It's a start. Can you remember what was off?"

He slouches in his spot, dejected. "I'm sorry. It's not much of anything. Did you tell Connor yet?"

Tracy shakes her head. "He left already. Mentioned something about Jack as he ran out the door."

Ken looks past Tracy and out the hospital room window. "Don't. He doesn't need to worry. Tell him … say I had to go out of town for business or something."

><><><><><><><><><><><><><><><><><><><><><><

Connor stands amid the remaining mess of Jack's house, surrounded by broken remnants of furnishings. The chaos of the unknown, recent events is still palpable in the room. He looks around in disbelief at his surroundings.

His mind is having a hard time comprehending the mess of it all. One moment his best friend is sitting with him in class, the next he is in jail—then gone. Nothing. Nowhere to be found. The only thing that adds to the story is this disaster that adds no constructive value to where he might be and what happened—only more questions that need answering.

He grabs a broom and dustpan from the mudroom and starts sweeping up what he can of the glass and splintered wood. It doesn't take long to make it look less chaotic than it was but still not usable by societal standards. But it is as straightened as he can get it.

He looks over the living room as the setting sun shines its light through the frame of the bay windows and across the old parchment resting atop the magazines still in their place from his last visit. From where Connor stands, he sees the parchment and the words *"We know"* scrawled on it.

He remembers it being blank when he first cleaned yesterday. Connor could have sworn it was blank. Did he miss the writing somehow in all the confusion? As young Mr. DeSalvo steps to the paper to pick it up, a glare off a large piece of glass he had set aside blinds him for a second. As he shakes off the sun spot, he picks up the paper. Once again, the parchment is blank. A doubting thought enters his mind that he might be overthinking this whole situation.

He starts to set down the paper, but the words stick in his mind, nudging at the furthest parts of his curiosity and wonder, so he picks it back up, and the words flash again in the sunlight before disappearing as he rolls it up and pockets it. *We know.*

CHAPTER 6

"We all want the best lives for our children.
It's why we protect them.
The hardest part as a parent is when
you can no longer do so."
~T. DeSalvo~

C onnor bursts through the front door to his house, surprising
his mother, who is cooking breakfast for a child she didn't
know wasn't home. The pounding footsteps of an excited teenager racing to the kitchen ring through the house. He stops when
he sees his mother cooking. He pants, catching his breath from the
run into the house.

"Where were you all night?!" Tracy asks as she turns to her son.
"I thought you were in bed asleep!"

"Spent the night at Jack's," he says, looking around, unable to
focus. "Where's dad?"

Tracy takes the flapjacks off the stove and sets the pan down,
turning off the flame.

"Take a seat, Connor," she says, wringing her hands.

Connor doesn't seem to hear her. He continues racing from door
to door, looking for his father. "Where's dad?"

"Connor," she says in a tone only a mother could use, "take a seat."

Connor hears the seriousness of her tone and halts his jumpy
behavior. He looks at his mom, whose eyes are screaming for him

to sit while simultaneously searching for the words to tell him about his father.

"What's going on, ma?" Connor asks, taking a seat by the kitchen table. "Where's dad? Where's Scarlett? Who are you cooking all this for?"

"I was cooking it for you. I thought you were sleeping in your room."

"No. I was at Jack's like I said."

"Well, I know that now. Here." Tracy plates up the flapjacks and sets them behind Connor on the table. "Eat."

Connor takes a bite of his pancakes while Tracy watches her child eat. While chewing his pancakes, he looks at his mom. "So? What's up? I need to talk to dad about something."

Tracy knows what she is about to tell her son goes against her husband's wishes. She has thought about it from every angle but can't understand Ken's reasons for not wanting their son to know. She also knows that she is not telling Ken that she is pregnant and yet is going against him here. She sees the hypocrisy of the situation.

"Your father's … been in an accident." She grimaces as she says those words—not wanting her son to worry.

"What, like a little fender bender?" He says, taking another bite.

"No. He was mugged. He's at the hospital." She takes a deep breath awaiting his response.

Connor stops chewing. He feels his heart start to race. The thought of his strangers attacking his father because of some misguided want to make easy money off him boils his blood coursing through him. He feels his mouth start to salivate uncontrollably. Pins and needles sting his arm and grow worse with each passing moment, though his arm didn't fall asleep. He shakes them to try and regain feeling. The pain swells with each moment, causing tears to well in his eyes.

"Connor. He'll be fine. Don't get yourself all excited over this. It's nothing to worry about," she says, hoping to calm him down. She sees the signs of his changes starting to manifest and wants to calm the beast before it takes control.

He looks at his mom. A thought enters his mind that if his dad was all right, why did she feel the need to make a grand scene to tell him. What is she trying to protect him from, or hide from him? How can he say something that won't raise any alarms?

"I want to see him. I have the day off."

"You don't work today?" Tracy asks, making sure her son is not bluffing.

"I don't work Sundays. It's the only day I don't have school, work, or practice."

"Eat first. You're a growing boy. We'll go afterward."

He turns to his food and, as a teenage boy can do, begins vacuuming the food into his mouth and down his throat.

<hr/>

Scarlett sits in a tchotchke-style restaurant across from a man in his early 30s, dressed in cheap department store business clothes—a man who might be offering her a job if she can keep herself composed. The televisions behind him provide a tempting distraction from the interview at hand, but the nervous teen tries to stay focused. She looks around at the few patrons eating while the interviewer scribbles on her application.

"I actually haven't ever had a job yet. I need one, though." Her lips tighten as she realizes the pointlessness of the last sentence.

The manager looks at her with a raised eyebrow. "I assumed so. Otherwise, you wouldn't be sitting here."

"Yeah, I guess I didn't need to say that." She hangs her head, trying to get her confidence back.

"You're fine," he says, restoring her confidence for her. "Can you work weekends and holidays?"

She smiles. "Yes! I love working weekends and holidays." She stops herself, realizing the over-excitement in her voice and the borderline desperation in feeling the need to say such obviously false words.

The manager tosses her a glance and smile before returning to his notes.

Scarlett continues, "And I know you mentioned a book or something if I ever need time off."

"Yes, the request-off book," he responds, smiling back. "I only have one more question for you."

"Sure," she says, straightening herself up in the chair.

"When can you start?"

"Whenever works for you," she says, trying to hold back an ear-to-ear grin.

"Let's say this coming Saturday at 11:00. Wear black," he finishes as he stands up, extending his hand.

She stands as well. "Thank you. Thank you so much."

She peers up at the newscast as she walks away from the interview. She stops dead in her tracks, noticing a picture of Jack and his parents displayed in the upper left corner of the screen. She reads the subtitles as they appear across the bottom of the screen.

The family was much loved by everyone. Preliminary talks with friends concluded there were no warning signs to foresee this horrific event. With the deaths of these four, there are no surviving family members.

×○○○○○○○○○○○○○○○○○○○○○○○○○○○○○○○○×

Connor stands in the back of a crowded hospital elevator riding up to see his father. He looks around at the other visitors wondering who they are visiting and if they are all right. He sees an older man with a sad look in his eye and a bouquet in his hand. Connor can't help but think that this man is on his way to say goodbye to a loved family member or friend one last time. Connor's phone screams for attention through his pants pockets. He reaches for it as the door opens to his requested floor. He slides his phone to take Scarlett's call as the door starts to close.

"Hold the door," he says as he pushes his way to the front of the elevator. A guy in scrubs puts his arm out to hold the door for him. Connor looks at his name tag. "Thanks, Scott." The guy nods as Connor exits the elevator.

Connor walks to his dad's hospital room as he finally responds to Scarlett on the other line. "Hey."

"Well, hello to you too, Cuz," she quips. "Where are you?" Connor can tell she is forcing the nonchalant sound, so even though he has bigger things on his mind at the moment, he plays along with it.

"Long story, I'll explain later. What's up?" Connor states matter-of-factly.

"Um," she starts, "I don't know how to say this."

Connor stops walking. "What now?" He backs against a wall to get out of the way and to catch himself—the shift to dead-serious in her voice enough to almost knock him down. He knows she thinks what she says is no doubt serious. He is just hoping she is wrong.

"Have you seen the news today?" She tries to be gentle.

"I'm at the hospital now. I didn't realize it made the news," Connor sounds almost relieved.

"Yeah, of course, it did. If something like this isn't newsworthy, nothing is," Scarlett responds, confused by her cousin's seeming nonchalant-ness. "Let me know what they say."

"I will. I'm about to step into the room now. Love ya, Scar."

"You too, Con."

He takes a breath to collect himself before stepping in to see his father. He knows he's alive and will be fine, but much like his mother when she was ready to step into the hospital room, he doesn't know what to expect. He puts the conversation he just had to the back of his mind and enters.

He is pleasantly surprised to see his dad watching cable news and eating gloriously bland hospital food. He smiles and hugs his father.

"What happened?"

Ken pats his son on his back. "Just some thugs. Nothing to worry about."

"Scarlett said it was all over the news."

"Probably because of my position at Town Hall. Nothing more. I didn't even know it broke the news."

"I'm just glad you're alive. The injuries don't look too bad."

Ken looks himself over before turning back to his son. "I see your mother didn't listen to me."

"You really surprised by that, dad?" Connor jokes.

"Not at all. I just didn't want you to worry," Ken starts. "What happened at Jack's?"

Before Connor answers, they both hear the newscaster start up again on the television, "More of the ongoing story. A local family slaughtered on the north side of West Haven by one of their own."

They look to the television to see a picture graphic of Jack and his parents next to the same picture the news used on Friday of Robert Burns, with the words Triple Murder/Suicide underneath.

The newscaster continues, "Sources are uncertain but speculate a young family member, possibly a nephew of one of the parents, brutally shot his aunt and uncle and his cousin before turning the gun on himself. It is uncertain if drugs were involved. More to come as the story develops."

Connor's face drops. He feels the blood rush out of his head, and for a moment, it feels like it stops flowing. A slight tinge in his chest as the smack of the news takes his breath away. He turns to find his dad staring at him. The look on his father's face shows that he is unsure what to say now.

Connor goes rapid-fire. "That's not true, dad. I was there—all night. I saw the disaster. There was no blood. I mean, a little. But not enough to be a murder, let alone a triple murder/suicide. They are lying!"

Ken grabs his son by the shoulders. "Calm down, son—just breathe and start from the beginning. Forget what you already told me and tell me again. Tell me everything."

Connor takes a few deep breaths trying to calm down. His face contorts in ways only a teenager can do as he tries to recall everything he saw and all he cleaned at Jack's. Connor stares at the floor as the images start to recollect in his mind. He takes a long, deep breath one more time before he starts.

"It was a mess." He pauses as he tries to clarify the images in his mind. "Everything was turned over, broken, or just wrecked." He knows he needs to be more precise but doesn't know where to start.

"What did you see when you first opened the door? Start there," Ken says with soft words that try to guide his son.

Connor nods while still staring downward. He closes his eyes. "The door was open. The screen door was unlatched, too, slightly moving in the wind. I could see inside. The couch was overturned. So was the coffee table. There were magazines all over the floor and blank papers. But the kitchen was untouched. As were the bedrooms." He continues recalling everything he can, including the hole in the wall exposing the hidden shelf and the dust rings. "There was blood, but not everywhere. Not like you see in movie murder scenes. Just little spots, speckles, splurts, and smears on the walls and maybe on the crap all over the ground. But I've had worse nosebleeds than the blood I saw."

He opens his eyes and looks up at his father. He sees the look of concern on his father's face. He is not able to read if his dad believes him or not. That doesn't matter to Connor because he knows what he saw.

"He's not dead," Connor says, shaking his head in short bursts. "There wasn't enough blood to be. Something's not right. The newscaster is wrong."

Ken nods in agreement and hugs his son. "We'll figure this out, Connor. Just know that I believe you."

The newscaster smiles into the camera at the return from the commercial break. "Sources confirm that James and Lucretia Taylor along with their son Jack Taylor have been killed by Lucretia's nephew Robert who had recently lost his parents in an automobile accident." The newscaster takes a breath that seems like a lifetime to the anxious Connor. "Sources have also confirmed that drugs were involved in Robert's short-lived but violent rampage. Speculation that the loss of his family contributed to his downward spiral into his drug-fueled rampage." The newscaster makes a slight nod as the story concludes. "Stay tuned for more on this. In other news, city hall deemed a local business a landmark."

Ken picks up his remote control and turns off the television. Connor sits speechless, stunned at the news, his face red with anger.

"This is not right. Jack's not dead! He's my best friend and would have told me if his aunt and uncle were damn killed in a car crash. He would have said something. The media is straight lying about this! I saw him at the police station in a cell," Connor's panic escalates.

The hysteria building up in Connor worsens. He shakes with each breath and can't focus long enough to maintain eye contact with his dad.

Ken puts his hands on his son's face. "Hey, Connor. Calm down. Breathe. When did you see him last?"

"Two days ago! He was fine. He said he was getting out in the morning," Connor says, unable to rein in his emotions.

"And?"

"And that's it. Jack was already gone when I went back to get him." And with that, a lightbulb goes off in his mind. The cop behind the desk told Connor who had released him. He has a starting point.

"Did you do what I asked on the phone? When you were there?"

Connor nods. "I put the shelf back over the hole and tried straightening up. I spent the night there straightening up as much as I could. I don't think it was enough."

"It's fine. I'm sure you did a good job. Was there nothing else out of the ordinary?"

Connor shakes his head.

"Can you take one more look around?"

"Of course. But why?"

Ken puts on his best parenting face. "Because I asked you to."

><><><><><><><><><><><><><><><><><><><><><><><

Vistrus sits in a rolling leather chair behind a burgundy-colored oak desk in his office with windows overlooking downtown West Haven. The early evening sky illuminates the earth in silver and orange tones. A few pictures of himself and his daughter decorate his desk; shipping manifests from new and old inventory clutter the rest. A single framed photo of his late wife rests on a crowded bookshelf off to his right. Across from him sits a nervous Tracy.

Her paranoia has calmed down a bit. While more collected than at the diner, she can let her guard down a little more in the solitary company of Vistrus.

"What did the council say, Vistrus?" she asks, repeatedly making fists. "I mean, do they have a reason why I was able to get pregnant?"

Vistrus remains the calm in her storm. "Yes. We had a long talk and addressed all your concerns. They were very excited to hear about this."

Tracy takes a breath, perhaps her first breath since she first read those two parallel dashes that read positive. She smiles a massive smile as tears fall from her eyes.

"Do not feel too overjoyed yet. Some of their shared worries are some of your worst." Vistrus knows what he said and how it sounded, but it needed to be said.

All the joy she felt for those three and a half seconds, the first moments of true comfort since reading the pregnancy test, ripped away in a moment broken by seventeen words. Her face straightens, and anger shines through her eyes.

"Damn you, Petrovsky. You couldn't have let me have a few more moments of relief? A few more moments of not worrying myself sick. Of not wondering what's happening to me or how it will affect my family. A moment of relief from thinking this is related to Ken's mugging." She breaks down crying again, sobbing frantically at the joy Vistrus ripped away.

"What mugging? What are you talking about?" Vistrus, a man whose calm is always on display, lets it slip for a moment to let Tracy see under the veil of quiet collectedness. "When did Ken get mugged? Why haven't I heard?"

Tracy snorts in her dripping nose and wipes her tears away. "Yesterday. It was in the news," she sniffles. "Well, some news at least."

"I caught something about a fellow Legend. Local too," he replies without defense. "Is that what the phone call was about at the diner?"

Tracy nods at him. "Yeah. He'll be fine. They got caught in the act and ran off. But who knows otherwise. How do I know that someone doesn't already know? That someone somehow isn't after my family and me. You can't tell me that the week I try getting a hold of you is the same week my husband almost gets killed doesn't look suspicious."

Vistrus thinks for a moment without response to her last statement. The recent events that had seemingly been against members of The Nation are unusual. What weighs on his mind is that if Tracy is correct, or even close to right, and these events are not happenstance and coincidental, then there is something much bigger going on that he must figure out how to stop. But as a council member, he can only discuss things like this with other council members. Tracy is not on the Council.

"I need you to listen. Be mad all you want, but listen. The Council does not want your baby. Your baby is far more special than you know. There will be people who will try to take it from you," he pauses for a breath, "if they find out. The Council will do everything in its power to keep that from happening. But you cannot tell anyone. Anyone else who knows is a risk."

Tracy's growing concern is visible on her brow, which has become so furrowed her face has almost disappeared. "Ken?"

Vistrus slowly shakes his head.

"But he's on the Council. How won't he find out?" Her concerns are well-founded.

"I approached only a few members. Ones I trust above all others. No one else will know," he assures.

"Connor?"

Again Vistrus repeats his slow head shake.

"What the hell am I to tell them when I start showing? When I can't hide the fact I am pregnant?"

"We will cross that bridge when we get there. For now, you did the right thing by not telling anyone but me, and it needs to stay that way."

Tracy takes a deep breath and nods her head. "I understand, but I don't understand why someone would want to try and take it away from me. What about my doctor's appointment? Should I cancel that?"

Vistrus pulls his chair closer to her. His knees touch hers as he leans in. "No. For now, keep it. If anything changes, I will let you know."

"So I can't tell my husband, but I can tell my doctor?" she asks, still a little confused.

Vistrus looks to his office door to make sure it is closed. He looks around his office and all over the ceiling to make sure nothing seems out of place, and nothing looks suspicious. Tracy watches him as he does all this; she feels her heart pounding harder every second he looks around. Every heartbeat is louder than the last, pounds harder than the previous.

"He has been the Council's doctor for centuries now. They trust him above anyone else to not say a word. He has not given anything up yet," Vistrus assures. He once again leans in to whisper in her ear. "I do not want anyone but you to hear this. And no one else can know. Telling anyone means you have told them you are pregnant."

Tracy nods almost imperceptibly, but Vistrus sees. He knows she senses the urgency in his voice—the gravity of the situation.

"For as far back as it has been known, Legends could only have one child. The hormonal changes pregnancy puts on the body are added to by our…" Vistrus scans their surroundings again to ensure their privacy, "…conditions." He stops and looks at her to make sure she is still listening. She is looking down at her stomach as her hand rubs it.

"There is a prophecy, a long-held secret, but secrets have a way of getting out. It claims the second child born to a legend will be the Grey Fairy. The one to combine the split that made the light and the dark fairies. To bring about change so that we, as The Nation, can live openly— without fear of persecution."

He stops and looks at Tracy again. This time tears are streaming down her face. She has heard every word he spoke, and each word he has said is as much a blessing as a curse. Both are her burden to bear until the child can't be kept secret. Thoughts of joy and worry intertwine in her mind crashing into each other to form new joys and concerns that she can't share—not yet, anyhow.

"How? How will one child do all this? How will one prophesied Legend let my body conceive again? I don't understand." She looks at him with desperate eyes.

He takes her hand in his. "The science is what you want to know?"

Tracy nods. "The science. The physiology. The "How" of one child changing people completely unrelated except by our disease." She catches her last word. "Conditions, you know what I mean."

Vistrus pulls away from her, the most precious of his words spoken. He has one more thing to say. "The Council has a plan."

⊳◈◈◈◈◈◈◈◈◈◈◈◈◈⊴

Scarlett sits in the dining room of her home, a home that took her in after her parents died when she was young. A home that is as much hers as it is her cousin Connor's. But it is his parents who live there, not hers. She wonders what her mother and father were like. What it would be like to sit with them at a dinner table, recounting the day's events. She smiles to herself because she does all these things with Tracy, Ken, and Connor, but there is something that makes her wonder how different it would be, better or worse, if they were her parents.

This evening though, it is just her and Tracy. She sees Tracy sitting at the table, staring a thousand miles away. Scarlett watches as Tracy, lost in thought, spins her fork in her mashed potatoes and brown gravy. Tracy's pork chop, too, sits untouched because her worries distract her from the food—worries that poke at Scarlett's curiosity. Scarlett finishes the chop and digs into the potatoes, the silence of the dinner making for a quick meal. Tracy sits ever-staring into oblivion as Scarlett takes a bite of her mash.

"Aunt Tracy?" Scarlett asks, swallowing her potatoes.

Tracy sits, oblivious to Scarlett's inquiry.

Scarlett stops, unsure if she should ask again, but her concern is pure.

"Auntie? Are you doing okay?" she asks after swallowing another bite of her mash.

Tracy snaps out of her daze and smiles at Scarlett. "Sorry, just some work stuff weighing on my mind. How's the pork?"

"Good. You'd know yourself if you took a bite," Scarlett urges.

Tracy lets out a quick, forced chuckle. "True." She cuts into her pork chop.

"Where's Uncle Ken? He's usually home by now."

Tracy looks at Scarlett, a sad smile on her face. "You weren't home yesterday."

"No, spent the night at Al's, then went job hunting." The excitement in her reply attempts to lighten the mood. "Got a job, too."

"Good for you. It'll put some cash in your pocket," Tracy replies as she continues eating.

"So, Uncle Ken?" Scarlett asks, trying not to bring the mood back down.

Tracy stops and gives her niece a silent stare for a moment. She takes a deep breath. Replying with her exhale, "He's in the hospital."

Scarlett drops her fork. "Is he hurt? Did he break something?" she asks, spitting out mashed potatoes.

Tracy shakes her head. Her mood lightens with the thought of her following words. "He'll be fine. In fact, should be home tomorrow."

Tracy explains the situation of his attack but insists he's okay. She doesn't feel the need to lie or hold any information from her about the occurrence. The guilt she carries about withholding her pregnancy and her family's Legendary condition is heavy enough.

"Where's your new job?" Tracy asks, changing the subject.

"Manic Mondays."

"Nice. Will you be serving?"

Scarlett shakes her head. "Not old enough. Next year though. So just a host."

Scarlett's phone buzzes, alerting her to a text message. She opens it.

[Allison: *Come. Keep me company. I'm so bored.*]

Scarlett sees Tracy watch her read the text message. "Everything okay?"

Scarlett looks up. "Yeah, Al wants me to go hang out at the store while she works."

"Go on." Tracy smiles. "Have fun."

"I can stay home with you if you'd like the company. I don't mind." The earnestness in her voice lets Tracy know Scarlett's sincere in her words, but, as an adult, knows Scarlett would rather be elsewhere.

Tracy laughs. A thought enters Scarlett's mind that hopes her last words didn't seem like pity.

"No, I'm fine. Go see your friend. Tell her hello for me," Tracy says, easing the budding guilt in Scarlett.

>○○○○○○○○○○○○○○○○○○○○○○○○○○○○<

The night's moon shines light through the hospital window onto Vistrus, who stands next to Ken's hospital bed. The constant drone of the overhead fluorescent lights and machines beeping sound beneath the conversation as the distant echoes from the nurse's station carry into the room fill any bit of silence.

Ken sits upright, revealing the fading bruises that earlier today were considerably more prominent. Even his bandages are devoid of any seeping blood. Ken's outward healing belies his emotions.

"A bloodline has been severed," warns Vistrus.

"Whose? How do you know?" asks Ken, keeping to himself the news he watched earlier with his son.

"It was in the news. No confirmation yet from the rest of the Council, but it is something we must take seriously. One less family in the nation is one less to carry on our kind."

Ken's smile fades. "If I haven't heard and you haven't heard, and the rest of the council hasn't heard, then perhaps it's not true."

"Perhaps," adds Vistrus, "but it is something worth looking into. Add that story to your attack and—" Vistrus pauses, realizing he is about to go against everything he told Tracy not to do. He continues, "Other events that have started happening. I think we need to get you out of here."

"Where? Put me in hiding?"

Vistrus shakes his head. "Home, work, any private place. Someplace less accessible."

Ken thinks for a moment, looking around the room. He stares out the window towards the waning moon in the sky. "I don't know. I always thought that I was strong—near invincible. I mean, aren't we? But now. Here, there are doctors. Home, what do I have?"

"Hey!" Vistrus chimes in, not wanting to let Ken sulk in any self-pity. "Here, you have doctors, but doctors cannot help a dead man. At home, you have comforts. You have your family. You have home court. Even in your office, you have an advantage. Here, who knows?" Vistrus finishes with a hint of hopefulness.

"I don't know. How can I protect my family? What do I tell my son?" Ken says, losing confidence in himself again.

Vistrus grunts. "There is no time for your self-pity. Something happened. Something bad. Get over it and protect those you are meant to. Protect yourself. Don't wallow about it in a hospital room."

A nurse knocks on the door. "May I come in?"

Ken forces a smile as his nurse peeks his head into the room. "Yeah. Hey Scott. Haven't gone home yet?"

Vistrus turns away from the nurse so he can eavesdrop with a bit of conspicuousness.

Scott looks at the clipboard hanging off of Ken's bed. "Not tonight. Going onto hour ten of my twenty-four." He looks at Ken. "Everything's looking good. You are healing very fast."

"Thanks. I've always been told I have a good constitution," Ken lies to the nurse.

"A phenomenal one, I'd say," Scott corrects. "I think, if you keep up at this rate, we can let you go home first thing in the morning. I'd like to run a few more tests just to make sure nothing is wrong."

Vistrus perks up, turns, and shoots Ken a look that lodges right in his mind. Ken understands.

"What tests? I thought you said I was fine? Healing very fast. I feel a hundred and ten percent better," Ken rebuts.

"Just to make sure that your healing rate isn't going to dissolve all the progress. We just want to test you for a few autoimmune diseases. To cover all our bases," defends Scott.

"Aren't you just a nurse? Isn't it up to the doctor to order these things?" Ken interrogates. "No offense."

But Scott looks at Ken with offended eyes. "Nurse practitioner. Thank you. I cover for the doctors when they are off and can order tests if I deem them necessary."

Ken looks to Vistrus, who has turned his back on the situation and is looking out the window. Ken watches Vistrus' reflection and notices him observing the conversation, not looking outside. Ken makes eye contact with Vistrus through the reflection. Vistrus tilts his head a tad while looking at Ken.

"I'd like to go home now. I feel fine and want to leave," Ken starts.

"I can't let you do that," Nurse Practitioner Scott replies.

Ken starts getting out of bed. "You can recommend that I stay, but you can't stop me. I can and will sign myself out against medical advice."

"The last thing I want to do is hold you against your will. I'll draw up the papers. It shouldn't take long." Scott leaves the room.

Vistrus turns to Ken, who is up and gathering his few belongings. "I do not like this place."

Ken finishes putting on his shoes. "Neither do I. Neither do I."

"I will call the doctor to make sure whatever tests they run did not leave leftover samples for prying eyes to play around with," Vistrus assures.

⤖◇◇◇◇◇◇◇◇◇◇◇◇◇◇◇◇◇◇◇◇◇◇◇◇⤕

Allison stands behind the counter of a vinyl record store made up of rows upon rows of vinyl records and compact discs. The employees dedicated a corner section of the back wall to cassette tapes and 8-tracks. There are two back rooms opposite the checkout counter; a curtain closes off one room reinforced with a crossing chain and hanging plaque that reads: Employees only. The other area has a custom sign above the door that reads: METAL HÄUS.

Allison shakes her head in disappointment at the young girl as she scans a Hamsin album—four prepubescent boys with long blondish hair sprawl across the cover. To Allison, this is a symbol of everything wrong with modern music, but her job is not to tell the customers what to buy, just to take their money.

As the young girl leaves the store, Scarlett enters. Allison watches Scarlett look around the otherwise empty store before approaching the register.

"Slow shift, huh?" remarks Scarlett.

"It's why I called." Allison's eyes shoot toward the leaving customer. "That girl was buying..." Allison starts.

Scarlett is quick to interrupt, "I know. I saw it through the bag. How lame."

"You hear the news?" Scarlett changes the subject.

"Yup, how bad do you think Connor is taking it?" inquires Allison.

No sooner than she finishes asking the question, Allison sees Connor rush out of his car and run through the doors.

"Good. You're both here," pants Connor as he catches his breath.

"How you holding up, Con?" asks Allison.

Connor looks around the room and does a quick run to see down each aisle, making sure they're alone before he responds. "It's not true," he says, eyes still scanning around.

Scarlett hugs her cousin. "I understand. You don't want it to be true."

Connor pulls away from Scarlett. He splits his glance between the two girls. "No, I mean it's not true. I was there. At this house. It's not true."

Allison's face clouds with confusion as she asks, "You mean he's at home? Alive?"

Connor paces back and forth. "No. Yes. I mean, I don't know. But I know that what the news has been reporting is not true."

Allison steps around the counter and slides up close to Connor. "Is there anything I can do for you?"

Connor keeps looking around, oblivious to her ill-timed advances.

"Is there a place we can talk?" he asks. "Someplace that's alone."

Allison gives an exaggerated look around the store. "Don't see anyone here, Con."

He looks at her. "But there could be. You can't trust your eyes. Is there anyone in the Metal Häus or the backroom?"

Allison shakes her head. "Just us, dude."

He locks the deadbolt on the front door and flips the "Back in 15 minutes" sign. "Let's keep it that way."

"Hey," Scarlett scorns, "you could get her in trouble. Fired or something."

"No, Scar, it's cool," Allison interjects. "I haven't taken lunch yet. There's no one else here tonight." She starts walking to the curtained-off door. "Follow me."

The backroom is nothing more than a cramped eating area meets storage closet. A small round table sits surrounded by boxes, filing cabinets, and various cleaning supplies, leaving barely enough room to pull out the chairs and sit down, but they all manage to squeeze in. They sit for a moment waiting for Connor to speak. The eerie silence pierces their ears and digs into their souls.

After a moment of the girls watching Connor do or say nothing, he speaks in a whisper. "Okay. So yeah. I don't think he's dead, at least not yet."

Both girls look at him, confused and curious to know more. "You need to explain yourself. How do you know? I mean, Scarlett saw it on the news. So did I," Allison says.

"Yeah, Connor," Scarlett confirms.

"Okay, long story short. Jack was missing from practice even though he was at school. I left practice and went to his house, but it was all a hot mess, as mom used to say. Like he got robbed. I looked around, and it was clear there was a fight of some sort, or something bad, 'cause a little bit of blood on the walls. But not a lot at all. Then, when I went to the Attic and had to rush out, he was calling from the police station. He said his parents never got home from their flight. Some vacation or something, whatever. Says he'll be released in the morning."

"Wait. Wait. Wait," interrupts Allison with a huge smile on her face. "Why was he in jail?"

Scarlett sees her smile. "This is what makes you smile? A boy in jail?"

"No," Allison says as a smile forces its way across her lips. "I'm just curious as to what he did."

"Okay, not as short a story as I was hoping. Nothing. Jack did nothing. But he lands in jail. He had no idea about his house. When I went to pick him up this morning, he was already gone," Connor continues in a hurried fashion.

"So?" says Scarlett.

"So," retorts Connor. "If you knew what I knew, the story wouldn't add up. It doesn't add up."

"Then tell us the long version," Allison forfeits.

Connor proceeds to fill them in on all the details surrounding Jack's house and arrest. The blank parchment he thought said "We Know" slips his mind, and per his dad's wishes, he doesn't mention the hidden shelving. Connor brings the girls up to speed on everything he can remember. After rambling off the story in rapid-fire succession, he falls back in his chair.

"So, what?" Allison pipes up, "You wanna go investigate?"

The girls watch as an ear-to-ear grin slowly crosses Connor's face.

"So, what's the plan?" asks Scarlett. "Do we get a green van and a talking dog?"

Allison is distracted by a rapping on the window. A couple of scraggly teens want records and don't seem to care about the "be back soon" sign.

"I gotta open up again. I'll meet you at The Attic when I'm off."

"How much planning can we get done at The Attic? We need a place we can concentrate," Connor objects.

"No one will pay attention to us. We'll be all alone in public. It's the perfect spot. Added bonus, no parents," defends Scarlett.

Connor sighs in defeat. "Fine. See you there."

><><><><><><><><><><><><><><><><><><><><

Scarlett and Connor sit alone among the sea of people on an unusually crowded Sunday night show. They sit on their usual comfy couch that the venue relegated to a corner even farther back than usual.

Connor stares past the indie rock band on stage while thoughts swim through his mind, casting doubt on his convictions. A perfect soundtrack to his profound moment of apprehension. He replays every detail he saw at his friend's house against everything played out on the nightly news. Something isn't right, and he's starting to think that maybe it is he who isn't right. Maybe what he saw could have been four murders. Not all deaths are bloody. The vagueness of the scene casts an uncertainty in his mind that perhaps they could have been suffocated or strangled. Something that didn't cause the need for pools of blood. But then, where were the bodies? Jack was in jail, which means that he couldn't have been party to such atrocities. But then again, Connor knows that such traumatic events can cause people to rationalize. He begins to think that maybe his timeline might be off.

"I don't know," sighs Connor.

Scarlett looks at him, her personification of conviction crumbling in front of her eyes. His distant look tells Scarlett he is anywhere but here.

"What's going on, Con?" She smiles at the unintended rhyme and immediately hopes it makes him laugh. But no. Nothing but a stoic stare into the abyss of thought.

"What if the news was right? What if I was wrong and everything I've been thinking is just … wrong?" His words ooze with uncertainty.

Scarlett turns to him. She needs him to know she is actively listening. "But you said they weren't right," she implores.

He turns to her as his stare comes back to this room. "Denial is the first stage of grief."

With a raised eyebrow, she says, "Where'd you get that crap from?"

He gives a half smile. "I took a class. Denial, anger, bargaining, depression, acceptance."

"So you took a class. You memorized the stages of grief. So what? When the hell has that ever mattered to you?" She says, trying to use his slacker-may-care attitude to his benefit.

"What the news says makes sense," he replies, half trying to convince himself he's wrong about being right.

Her voice strengthens as she sits up, still facing him. "Not according to your story, and I'd believe your eyewitness account over some mass media news outlet any day."

He turns to her. She has caught his attention. "Eyewitness account and mass media news outlet? You've been spending too much time on Face-Ta-Gram," he says, dismissing her encouragement.

"You took a class. Memorized the stages of grief and all probably while not paying attention. You paid attention at Jack's. You took notes ... well, mental notes, but you took them. Trust yourself and your instincts," she urges.

He turns back to the crowd for a moment, staring at the people enjoying the music. Little do they know what rages inside his head right now. They know nothing about his friend and the unfolding conspiracy against him.

Connor turns back to Scarlett. There is a look in his eye that something is brewing. "But if they were right and we all go sneaking around God-knows-where and get caught…"

Scarlett does not let him finish that thought. "We get a slap on the wrist. As long as we keep our mouths shut."

His eyes remain all business as a smile crosses his face. "Not if we follow a cop."

"The cop that harassed Jack?" Scarlett confirms.

"Yeah, that cop. If he catches us, we could get in deep trouble or worse. Maybe I should just let sleeping dogs lie."

Scarlett stands up and looks down at him. "No! I want to do this. It'll be the most fun I've had in forever, and if you're right, it'll be the most exciting thing that's ever happened in West Haven."

Connor spies Allison as she makes her way through the crowd and cops a spot next to Scarlett.

"So, what's the plan, man?" Allison starts.

"Chicken shit over here is having second thoughts," answers Scarlett.

Allison pulls out a flask from her hoodie. "Betty White up, Con," she says, extending her hand to him. "This'll bring you back around to whatever it is you need be brought back around to."

Connor grabs the flask but doesn't drink from it. He holds it in his hand, twisting the cap back and forth.

"You know if you get caught," Scarlett starts.

Allison interrupts, "I won't be allowed blah-blah-blah. Such a mom." Allison grabs the flask from Connor and takes a swig.

Scarlett stands up, back to the dance floor, and faces Connor and Allison. "I'm going. I don't know where I'm going, but I'm going. I'll do this even if you won't. I believe you even if you don't. Somebody has to." Scarlett begins her trek to the front door of The Attic.

Allison scooches up close to Connor and wraps her arm around his shoulder. Connor turns to face her, and his nose is close to touching hers. He can hear her soft breaths even through the loud music and ambient talking in the background. This is Allison, his friend, his buddy. In this moment, though, there is something new in the air. A buzz of electricity he can feel inside him. A shiver runs down his spine.

A nervous energy makes him want to run away. Excited butterflies in his stomach make him want to stay. A connection he has never felt before. The newness of this encounter makes him tingle inside for the uncharted territory that is Allison.

"You okay?" he asks with a cracking voice.

Allison cracks a sly smile. "Great. Why?"

Connor shifts, unsure of what to do or how to move. He feels he should move his hand somewhere, maybe on her hand or on her thigh. Instead, his hand hovers just off of her. Afraid of the spark that could ignite by touching her. But he freezes. "Just wondering," he replies.

"Just having a bit o'fun after work. That's all," Allison says as she grazes his knee.

"Oh? Um, okay. What did you have in mind?" he asks, trying to assess the situation.

She looks him square in the eye with a devilish grin. "I don't know. Whatever pops up?" She gives him a mischievous wink.

Connor's face turns a bright shade of red, even under the dim lights of the venue. He scoots out from the intimacy of the moment.

Allison's face drops. Her sinful smile disappears, turning into a frown. "What's wrong?"

"Just a bit unexpected. Not wholly unwelcome but unexpected. Let's just relax for a bit."

Connor sees Scarlett as she finishes her swim through the sea of people to the exit of The Attic when he sees a police officer enter the building. The officer looks Scarlett up and down as if suspecting her of some uncommitted crime before moving on. Connor squints as he tries to read the badge and name tag. As his eyes close, his vision periscopes. Everything not in the laser line of sight gets pushed aside in a blur as the name tag is magnified into focus for him to see. He reads with crystal clarity the name Espinoza. Thoughts are ringing back to the morning when he listened to Officer Smith tell him that this was the officer who released his friend—his now missing and presumably dead friend. Connor figures he could approach the officer; after all, they are tax-dollar-paid to serve and protect. Perhaps officer Espinoza could tell them what happened to Jack after his release.

Connor stands up and grabs Allison's hand. "Come on. That's the cop who released Jack from jail. Maybe he'll help."

"Or maybe he'll kill us. You even said something's rotten. He could be the one doing the rotting," Allison thinks out loud.

Connor pulls her through the crowd making their approach for the cop. As the crowd clears away and he has an unobstructed view of the officer, he reads the badge—Badge 0051. The same badge number that Jack said harassed him. The same four numbers that arrested Jack for "looking like he was on PCP." If there was a cop who would help find his friend, everything in Connor's gut was screaming to him that this was not the cop. His gut cries out that Officer Espinoza, badge number 0051, is not a friendly face in the events of their lives. He continues walking past the officer, dragging Allison along.

Allison points as they pass the officer. "Here's the cop," she says to Connor.

Connor tries to play it off, "Yes, dear. Leave the fine gentleman to do his work. It's late and time to get you home."

Officer Espinoza stops the two youths as they try to move past. "Is there something I can help you with?" The authoritative tone in his voice comes across as lacking any ounce of compassion.

"She was just wondering what time curfew was?" Connor lies.

A smug laugh from the officer alerts them of his amusement by their transparent effort not to get in trouble. "Time now for her to get home."

Connor nods in agreement. "Thanks, sir. That's what I said, too."

Allison scrunches her face as Connor pulls her through the remaining crowd. They make it outside The Attic and stand in the parking lot. Connor conspicuously glances back inside to confirm that 0051 is not heading back out. Connor and Allison start walking toward Scarlett, who is already past the lot.

They hasten their pace to a full-on run, quickly catching up to Scarlett as she passes a hedge of bushes. She turns to them as they stop next to her to catch their breath.

"Oh, so now you want to do this," Scarlett scorns.

Connor's hands are on his knees, far more out of breath than he should be. He waves a hand in the air while shaking his head no.

"The cop," he starts. "The one that arrested Jack," he says, panting. "That was him in there."

"So, what do we do?" Scarlett asks.

Connor takes a moment to recover. He stands up and looks at both of them. "We wait."

"For how long?" Allison inquires.

At that moment, officer Espinoza exits The Attic. He doesn't even glance in their direction, but the guilty teenage conscience takes over, causing Connor to jump over the bushes. "Come on!" His whisper borders on shouting.

The girls follow suit. "Not long, I guess," he answers.

"So we're going to follow a police officer? That's a smart idea," says Allison.

"He may lead us to Jack," Connor answers.

"Or chain us up next to him like Sloth. A bunch of Goonies all chained to a wall," Allison objects.

"If he's even involved. We don't actually know anything," Scarlett reasons.

Connor watches as the squad car strolls past their bush cover. They remain hidden. "I know Jack," Connor replies. "Jack said there was something off about him. I believe him."

"All right," concedes Scarlett. "Let's follow the law. The cop. Let's break the law and follow the law."

Connor puts his finger up. "Stop. We get it," he says, shaking his head.

Allison takes a swig from her flask. Scarlett glares disapprovingly.

"Hey, Al. Let me get a drink," Scarlett says, extending her arm.

Alison hands it over. "See. I am a good influence."

Scarlett nods in agreement as she turns the flask over and begins emptying the contents. Allison sees this and jumps at Scarlett's hand as she moves it away.

"We are tracking the movements of a cop. A cop who may possibly be holding Jack in some sort of hostage crisis," Scarlett begins.

"And I thought being a little relaxed may help me stay calm," Allison defends.

"Yeah," Scarlett mocks. "We all know how relaxed you can get." She finishes pouring out the flask and hands it back to Allison.

Allison caps it back up and puts it back in her hoodie. "Fine. Fine. I was just having a little fun. Like anything that exciting ever happens in West Haven," Allison quips.

The squad car takes a slow turn right as he patrols. Connor watches with wary eyes making sure he doesn't lose sight of the cop. After the policeman finishes making his turn, Connor jumps up and runs off after it.

Scarlett and Allison are still crouched behind the bushes watching Connor, unsure if they should follow. Connor makes it to the corner and hides behind a large oak tree. With his eye still on Espinoza's squad car, he looks back to the girls for a quick second and waves them over. He looks again for the squad car as the girls head over to him, but it is gone—no lights shining out from anywhere and no sign of it.

"What the hell?!" Connor's frustration takes control for a second.

Scarlett moves next to him. "What?"

"What?! Where did he go? He was just there?" he says, gesturing around the empty streets.

"Calm down," Allison reasons. "It's not like he just disappeared."

"She's right. Let's hurry and try to catch up. He probably just turned a corner," Scarlett says, starting in the lead this time.

Connor and Allison keep pace behind Scarlett as she runs down the suburban street toward the next corner. Allison's lack of cardio quickly catches up, and a little over halfway down, she stops to catch her breath. While panting, she turns to look up the driveway next to her.

"Con…" she pants but loses the rest of her words in the distance between them. "Scar!" she yells a little louder but also doesn't want to draw attention to them.

Scarlett hears her and turns around. She waves her arm inward, urging Allison to catch up. Allison returns the gesture with a dramatic finger point-and-wave in her direction. Scarlett isn't sure what Allison wants, so she pulls out her phone.

[Scarlett: *Now what?*]

[Allison: *Cop car in driveway. Come here*]

Scarlett and Connor both catch up to Allison. They all speak in whispers.

"I think this might be it," Allison starts.

"How do we know?" Scarlett asks, playing devil's advocate.

"Touch the hood," Connor answers her riddle. "If it's warm, it's gotta be his. And it explains why it disappeared on me."

"Or it's another cop, and we break into the wrong guy's house. I can't believe I just said that," Scarlett reasons.

"I got this. You two stay here and be nonchalant," Connor says, walking toward the cop car.

Scarlett leans against a tree, taking to the shadows, while Allison sits cross-legged in the middle of the sidewalk.

"What are you doing?" Scarlett whispers to Allison.

"I don't know what nonchalant means," Allison admits.

"It doesn't mean that! Get over here!" Scarlett demands.

Allison hops up and skips to the tree.

Connor squats next to the squad car. He looks around to make sure no one unsuspected is outside. After he feels more secure in his surroundings, he feels the warmth of the hood, confirming Allison's suspicion.

He waves the girls over. As the girls walk up the driveway, they all hear the handle on the side door unlock and turn. Connor jumps behind a tree on the opposite side of the car as the door opens. The two girls dive behind a row of bushes lining the driveway as officer Espinoza exits his house. Their anxious eyes watch as Max locks the door and enters his car, oblivious to the amateur criminals hiding about. They wait while he backs out of the driveway, fading into the darkness of the night after turning a corner.

The three teens gather by the tree on the side of the driveway.

"This is it!" says an excited Connor. "He's gotta be in there!"

Allison whispers with excitement, "This is so cool! Hiding in shadows and skulking about! We're like ninjas!"

"Oh my God! We are not ninjas. We're juvenile delinquents. Ninjas are quiet," Scarlett whispers back as she rolls her eyes.

"I am quiet!" Allison defends.

"No, you're not," confirms Connor, still whispering. He looks around at the windows of the house, trying to observe movement from within the darkened rooms. "We need to find a way in."

Allison pulls out her flask again, forgetting it has been emptied, "The door, duh." She bends her wrist outward as if making an obvious revelation.

"We need to be sneaky," says Scarlett.

"Something that is hard to do with a wine-o," replies Connor. "It's empty, remember."

"I'm not a wine-o," she pouts, replacing her flask in her hood.

A light shines through a ground-level window next door. The three teens back against the brick wall, wishing to stay hidden from eyes within the neighboring house. They hope the fence separating the properties will keep them concealed from any eyes that happen to be outside as well.

Connor looks at the cop's house and points to the basement window. He motions to each of them, then walks his fingers to indicate that's their way inside.

Scarlett's eyes widen as she mouths, *"But what if someone's in there?"* to Connor.

He wags his finger and mouths, "I don't think anyone is home."

Scarlett scrunches her nose and shakes her head. "What?"

Connor whispers, "I don't think anyone's home."

"Then why are we whispering?" whispers Scarlett.

"Cause other people are still alive on this block," he retorts.

The girls look to Connor for the next move. He puts up his hand to wait. They hear the front door of a neighbor's house open and shut. The keys turn the lock, and the screen door shuts behind the unseen neighbor. A few footsteps later and a car door opens and closes. After the car drives out of sight, Connor squats down and pushes on the window. The fates align for the amateur sleuth as the window is unlatched and opens for him. Tilting inward, he sees more than enough space for Allison to slide in first and maybe enough room for Scarlett to slip through.

Connor looks at the petite Allison and whispers, "You first."

Allison is taken aback. "Why me?"

"Cause you're the smallest. I won't fit, and you'll need to unlock the back door," Connor says, tilting his head and giving her his best puppy dog eyes.

Allison purses her lips and gives him mean eyes as she squats to slide in the window. Allison falls to the floor, having barely squeezed through, as she commits her first actual crime of breaking and entering. Connor and Scarlett press themselves against the wall in case anyone outside heard anything. Without making any noise, the flask falls from her hood as she stands, slipping onto the carpeted floor behind her. She pulls out her cell phone and starts the flashlight app. She shines it on the floor in front of her to see her path and minimize what shines outside. Connor knows the back door is the only option for Scarlett and him.

The two try to be quiet as they wait for Allison. Connor continually surveys his surroundings, partly out of paranoia and somewhat out of his love for cheesy action flicks.

"What's up with Al tonight? She seems a little off. More so than usual," Scarlett starts.

"I think she likes me. Something happened at The Attic. Well, almost happened. Maybe. I'm not really sure."

"Maybe? A smooth operator you are not." Scarlett looks to her cousin. "I think you might be right, though, about her liking you." The door begins to unlock. "The question is, how do you feel?"

They make their way to the back door as they hear Allison make her way through the house. The one thing Connor, Scarlett, and Allison missed while making sure nobody saw them was the small security cameras around the house's exterior.

Allison opens the back door, officially cementing the three teenagers' criminal status as they enter a stranger's house. They go back down to the basement and fumble for the light. Connor's heart drops as he doesn't find his friend anywhere, both a relief and frustration. Relief that he may still be alive somewhere and frustration that this isn't the evil lair of some comic book supervillain he was hoping for. After he can put his personal feelings aside, he knows he has to search, and search quickly. He doesn't know how long this cop will be gone, and the last thing he wants for any of them is to get caught here of all places.

First things first, they shut the window, and Connor, having watched too many Crime Scene Investigation style shows, wipes the window down for prints with the sleeve of Scarlett's hoodie. As he finishes, he sees moonlight shine off the flask on the floor. He picks it up and, with a fatherly look in his eye, hands it back to Allison.

"This could have cost us everything," he scorns.

"Sorry, Con. Won't happen again." Her apology seethes with shame.

Connor looks around the otherwise ordinary room. "Shit! Shit! Shit!" Connor lets rip out in a fit of frustration.

The girls both turn to him. "What did you expect? To find Jack?" Scarlett asks.

"Well … yeah. Kinda," Connor replies.

Allison starts walking around the room toward a desk along the side wall. She picks up a notebook lying open on it. "I mean, we're here; we could snoop around a bit." She invites the notion into their minds.

"Or it means the news is right." Connor sounds resigned.

"No. I just committed a felony, I think. I'm not leaving without trying to find something. C'mon, Cuz."

He nods his head. "But make it quick."

Allison has already begun rifling through the notebook as he decides to rejoin the search. "Hey, guys, I think Connor was right."

Scarlett and Connor turn to Allison.

"Why? What did you find?" Connor inquires.

"Yeah, I'm not seeing anything, Al," Scarlett objects.

"I'll explain," Allison starts, "but we need to get out of here. Like now."

Without question, Scarlett and Connor start upstairs. Allison is in tow with the notebook in hand as they exit out the back door. Connor locks the doorknob, wiping it all down with his sleeve. As he shuts the door, the moonlight reflects off the door window illuminating a picture on the wall of Max and a woman. In the dark, the faces in the photograph are hidden in shadows. However, Connor can see that the lady in the photo is wearing a silver and opal pendant in the shape of an infinity symbol frosted with tiny diamonds.

They all walk back down the street toward The Attic, hearts racing at the excitement, terror, and stupidity of what they just pulled off. Allison hides the notebook under her hoodie, tucking it into the waistband of her jeans. After a few blocks of silent contemplation of the night's events, going over every square inch to guarantee they left nothing behind, wiped down what they touched, and covered all their tracks, they stop outside Connor's car, still parked at The Attic—hiding in plain sight among the other vehicles. Perhaps this was the moment they all needed to help put their friend to rest—or to find him.

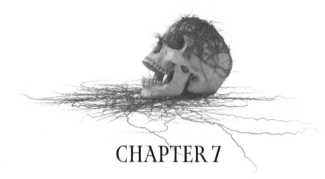

CHAPTER 7

*"A failure is just another success in
how not to do something.
It is not an indicator that one
should stop trying."*
~E. DeSalvo~

S carlett sits in her art class, molding clay into a well-shaped vase as it spins on the wheel.

She'd know this if she focused her mind on the task at hand. Instead, the anxiety of waiting for the voting results of the student council election weighs on her mind. It's been over a week since the voting began, and she gave her hunger-induced speech, but she still holds onto a thread to hope. A part of her is still uncertain as to whether she even wants to win.

There is another part of her—perhaps a larger part—that knows Allison is correct; there must be more to life than what she is living and what she sees. She must make herself get there, get out of West Haven, but how? The plan has never been to stay here, but that plan contains no direction on how to leave. The plan to leave West Haven is half-baked at best—more like mixed ingredients waiting on the oven to preheat. All she knows is that if she wins, it will be something more—a chance to do something of impact, perhaps.

The loudspeaker crackles to life, and the class stops their work. The little, whispered conversations start up. Scarlett takes her foot off the pedal and watches the potter's wheel slows to a stop. The principal clears her throat over the intercom, "Good afternoon, students."

The art teacher, Ms. Waldgrave, hushes the students so she can listen to the results without interruption. She feels nervous for all students involved, especially her child, Brianna.

Good, the afternoon was anything but. Scarlett can't vouch for the other candidates, but she can feel the ulcer that formed in her nerve-wracked stomach, perhaps added to from last night's excursion. She can't ignore the burning and tightening sensation in her lower abdomen as she awaits the election results. It is screaming for attention.

"The votes are in, and we have our new student council leaders!" Her voice booms over the loudspeaker.

Scarlett's heart starts to race. The excitement in her stomach rises to her chest. A nervousness takes her over—anxiety that she has not felt before. A feeling that she may involuntarily projectile vomit at any moment. But she can't because she needs to hear the results. Right now, at this moment, she knows she wants this.

The principal begins rattling off students' names and elected servant duties for the council. She starts with the Representatives, the sure winners of the many open positions. Next, she announces the winner, and the only candidate for Activities Social Chair, some quiet, keeps-to-himself kid that everyone knows by face but couldn't tell you a thing about him. After that, she announces Secretary, Treasurer, and Vice-President. All names that no one is surprised to hear. The excitement and nervousness start to dwindle in her chest. The butterflies begin to die down. None of the underdogs have won so far. The principal calls out the name of the president. It wasn't Brianna, but it wasn't Scarlett. The butterflies that were starting to die in her stomach drop dead. Their weight adds to her nausea, not so much in that she lost but that she knows, as sure as her name is a shade of red, that she wants something more. She needs something more.

She puts her foot back on the pedal and slowly starts spinning her pottery wheel. Ms. Waldgrave opts for a cautious approach toward Scarlett, who doesn't look up at the teacher but dives into the task at hand. The teacher stops short of Scarlett.

"Sorry for your loss, Scarlett," Ms. Waldgrave starts. "Keep working on your tutoring idea. Seeing that launched would be a legacy of its own. I know you are destined for bigger things. The universe has a plan for you, I'm sure."

Scarlett smiles at the thought of doing something more significant, be it her brainchild tutoring program in the works or something else. She can't help but think that if she can't even do what she wants to now, how will she ever accomplish the more exceptional things she wants to do?

><><><><><><><><><><><><><><><><><><><

The time has come, Sept 19. The appointment Tracy hopes will answer all of her so far unanswerable questions. She finds her anxiety in the waiting room of Dr. Wong's OBGYN office higher than perhaps she thought it would be or should be.

She looks around at the other waiting moms, moms-to-be, and young women looking after their health. The waiting room television plays the daytime soap opera where a pregnant lady with twins just found out one twin is from one husband and the other is from her secret lover. Tracy would have found such a nonsensical medical dilemma laughable only a few weeks ago. Now, though, she feels such a situation may be possible. The thought of such things seeming strange and unusual to her is a bit unnerving given her already legendary and mythical genetics.

She turns inward to go over a list of questions she has for her doctor, a list that she has gone over numerous times every day since the positive tests came back two weeks earlier. There has been no word from Vistrus about not seeing this doctor and, therefore, no reason not to see him. The knots in her stomach tighten as the receptionist calls her name for the doctor to see her.

After the nurse goes through the motions of the regular vital and statistic routine, Tracy treks over to the exam room. An excruciating twenty-minute wait for the doctor, who with each passing minute she feels will never come, to walk through the door. But he enters with a smile on his face and her file in his hand. She holds the paper exam garb she stripped down to against her chest as she sits upright on the examination table. Clutched in her other hand is the test.

Dr. Wong begins as he closes the door, "How are you doing today?"

She waits to say anything until he latches shut the door behind him. She hands him the test.

He looks at the two lines reading positive—the two lines forever ingrained on the plastic stick.

Dr. Wong turns around and double-checks the door to secure it all the way shut. After turning back to Tracy, he puts on exam gloves.

"Are you sure?" Dr. Wong asks, shocked at the implications.

"Yes," Tracy replies. "I've taken multiple tests."

"Lay back and let's start the exam," he says, pulling out the ultrasound equipment.

She watches him apply the lube to the ultrasound wand. As she scoots down the table, putting her feet in the stirrups, she asks, "I don't understand how this could happen? Is something wrong with me?"

He leans down to perform the procedure. "Let's first make sure everything is correct and healthy here."

He inserts the wand, and the monitor springs to life. An image of varying grades of gray and green on the monitor indicates her uterus is healthy. Just off center is what looks like a black hole, inside of which is another small fuzzy spot.

He points to the black hole. "There it is." He hits the save button on the test and pulls out the wand. "Congratulations, Tracy." He wipes the wand and puts the machine away. "Everything looks healthy."

He then continues with the standard barrage of questions about painful urination or menstruation. Burning, itching, and every other uncomfortable situation he must think of. After Dr. Wong clears Tracy of anything unordinary, he leaves for a moment, taking her file with him, allowing the impossibly pregnant woman a moment to get dressed.

He returns after knocking to make sure she got dressed. He no longer has her file with him. He takes a seat and takes a moment to think. Running his fingers through his hair, he searches for words on the current situation.

"I didn't mark anything in your file," Dr. Wong says.

"Thank you," Tracy replies.

"I don't know how to explain this," he begins. "You are around 220 years now, yes?" he continues in a quieter voice.

Tracy nods in relative agreement with his question.

"I have never seen this in anyone your age. I know, physically, your body looks much younger. It will even perform at the relative age you look. But this, pregnancy…" he trails off, unsure where to go.

"What does this mean?" Tracy asks with desperation creeping out of her voice.

The doctor shakes his head. "I don't know. I know the council will want to know. But I don't see any reason for concern at the moment. From a medical standpoint, you are a hundred percent healthy."

"But I'm … pregnant," she reconfirms with a pause.

"Yes, you are. And as long as anyone who isn't in The Nation doesn't know your status, you will be fine. You can play it off as any normal person would. Any other human would be overjoyed, and you should be too," he assures her.

"But what about people in The Nation? There are those who wouldn't understand—those who might not see this as a good thing. Like a bad omen," Tracy rebuts as paranoia surfaces again.

"One step at a time. First, I must tell the council I have found someone who is twice pregnant," the doctor says.

She snaps back with an annoyed tone, "They already know. Vistrus told them, and he said to see you. To find out if you can answer any of my questions."

Those words knock Dr. Wong back in his seat. Tracy waits for him to speak, but he remains silent, perhaps waiting on more harsh words from her. But she is done talking for the moment.

"What other questions do you have? It's why I am here for you." He tries to calm her down.

"You said the baby looks healthy now. But will it stay that way?" she starts.

"Honestly, I don't know. The hormonal changes from your first pregnancy mixed with your," Dr. Wong pauses, searching for the right words, "genetic disposition are two wild variables that, even by us, are not fully understood. While I see no reason for things to go wrong, only time will tell. But I can tell you that the added stress of worrying does not help." A blunt but honest reply.

"What about my other, more myth-like condition? Could it affect that? Is there a chance it won't be acute anymore? Can the hormones of this pregnancy make it become chronic all of a sudden? Or worsen the acute symptoms?" she says, working herself into a worse frenzy.

"Acute symptoms over time can lead to chronic conditions, like an asthmatic who constantly wheezes and needs to carry an inhaler. But our kind is different. Legends are built on chronic conditions that have mutated into acute conditions. I don't see that being an issue," Dr. Wong says, further trying to calm her down.

"Okay," she says, resigned, "I guess that's better than nothing. But will you continue doing what you can to see why this happened and assure everything will be all right?" Tracy stays planted in her seat.

"I will," Dr. Wong says, rising from his chair. "Stay here as long as you need. I will begin looking into all the possibilities as soon as I'm out of the office tonight."

"Thank you, Doctor," Tracy says as he exits the room, closing the door behind him.

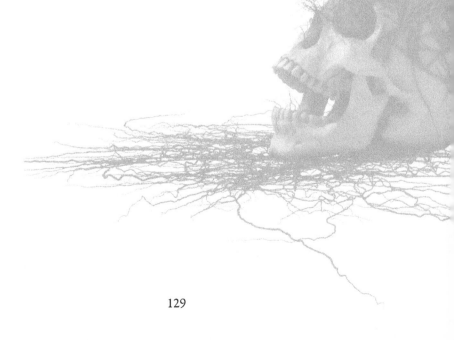

CHAPTER 8

"Life may stop for the dead,
but it doesn't stop for the living."
~K. DeSalvo~

K en raises the blinds causing the sun to shine through
Connor's bedroom windows. Hitting his eyes as he sleeps,
the ray's heat immediately wakes him up. This morning of October
2nd marks two weeks of school absences while he has attempted
to deal with the apparent loss of his friend.

"Come on, Connor. Time to get up," his dad barks.

Connor rubs the sleep from his eyes, "But…"

Before he can even get another word out or thought formed in
his head, his father interrupts, "But nothing. It's been two weeks,
and I feel for you. I do. We knew them too, but you can't keep wal-
lowing. It's not healthy. You've had time to grieve in solitude. Now
you have to get back to school. Surround yourself with people who
can and will support you."

Ken starts piling the books and notebooks on Connor's desk
into a neat stack. He straightens loose papers and puts them into
the first folder he grabs. He even hangs Connor's backpack on the
back of the desk chair.

"Breakfast in three minutes. Be out there. You have to leave in
one hour." Ken turns to leave.

As he grabs the handle to shut the door, he notices a notebook on the floor under the chair, seemingly knocked off the desk. It is the stolen notebook from Officer Espinoza's house. Ken picks it up, looking at the amount of writing in the book. He doesn't read the words but stares in awe at the volume of notes.

"It's nice to see you studying. Even if it's with someone else's notes," Connor's dad says, flipping the pages.

Connor's eyes shoot open, fully alert to what his father holds. "Yeah, yeah. It was Jack's. He took a ton of notes. Just something I figured I could use to help me."

Ken closes the notebook and places it atop the pile. "Just glad to see you are dealing with the loss. Now, come on. Chop, chop." He says those last two words with simultaneous claps.

He shuts the door leaving Connor in his last three moments of mournful solitude before rejoining the world. Connor gathers his books and papers, putting them into his backpack. He holds the notebook and contemplates leaving it at home. Connor considers hiding it in his desk, away from parental, prying eyes but decides to bring it with him —something to study in his free periods while he is away from the adults who carve out his future for him.

Connor spent an overwhelming amount of time these past fourteen days of mourning scouring the notebook he obtained from the cop's house. He has read the whole thing, cover to cover, at least a dozen times, but nothing stood out. There seems to be no direct evidence of where these people might be holding Jack and his family, or why anyone would even have done such a horrific thing as to abduct, or worse, slaughter a whole family. The notebook is laden with code, though, which is a start; if only he could have cracked it in the past two weeks—half a month in which he has refused to see either Scarlett or Allison. A boy locked himself away in his bedroom, hidden from the world. While his parents may have worried, the girls knew what he was doing and knew that space and time were what he wanted. The time for isolation has ended, even if it was at his father's behest.

Connor meets his first day back with an underwhelming welcome from no one. His classmates act as if no time has passed between now and when they last saw him, an incredible ability of both the closest friends and the most apathetic strangers. He makes his way through the first half of the day with little fanfare from teachers as he buries his face in his newly obtained notebook, searching tirelessly for a way to break the code.

He focuses on parts of a few sentences he has read a thousand times.

> *...at the base ... prescribed the medicine. VP-HFE1 ... VP-PPOX ... HCP ... CPOX ... Broken chains. Missing links.*

What Connor can't seem to put his finger on is where the base might be. A word as generic as that could be located anywhere. His instinct leads him to believe that it must be near. A locally fixed base only makes sense if grabbing Jack was a random act. If it wasn't random, then the headquarters, or whatever it is, could be anywhere. And a post of operations not near to him means all is lost. So he has to hold onto the hope that it was random so the base would be nearby. The medicine mentioned in the notes has him confused, as do the chains that "broken chains" and "missing links," but the initials vex him the most. Connor may only be seventeen, but he's heard of insurance PPOs before. Even HMOs and with the push to single-payer, even that. But his mind can't wrap around HFEs, HCPs, and the CPOXs. He figures that insurance isn't going to lead him to his friend, so he tries to push it aside to focus his efforts on the rest. Something just isn't resting as it should in his mind. Maybe his father was right. An end to the mourning process, at least for the day, to get back into the swing of life.

He stops at his locker between classes to put the notebook away, at least for the moment, and grab his advanced placement biology books. Off to see the teacher all the kids are hot for.

As he steps into class, he stares at Jack's empty desk. He hesitates at the door while other kids push past him. He doesn't respond as a few students pat him on the back and give him a half-hearted welcome back. His mind focuses on the friend who isn't there.

The board is set up for today's lecture. An overhead projector waits to light up to life with the flip of a switch, a transparency on it readily waiting to show the class its contents. He looks toward the desk at the teacher, oblivious to his return, her nose buried in her teacher's log.

Connor takes a deep breath and steps into the room, taking a seat at his desk. The teacher looks up, surprised to see Connor unwillingly ready to get his life back together. A few stragglers shuffle in as the bell rings.

"All right, class, take out your books and turn to page 451. Start looking over that chapter. I'll be back in a few to begin the lesson." She twirls her necklace as she makes eye contact with Connor. "May I see you in the hall for a moment?"

Connor sighs but, not feeling up to an anti-authoritarian fight, nods his head as he stands. The class stares at him as he makes his way through the few seats, like a moviegoer taking a break in the middle of the climax.

The empty halls hold an eerie feeling of melancholy as Connor and Mrs. Espinoza stand outside the room. The only other visitor to these halls is the silent janitor Raymond mopping the floor a few doors down. He divides his time between the concrete floor and watching the student-teacher conversation. Mrs. Espinoza stops twirling her necklace as she begins.

"How are you holding up?" she says with a softness to her voice. A sense of concern that teachers reserve for the few occasions something life-altering happens to a student.

Connor avoids eye contact in true teen fashion by watching Raymond clean the floor—as if that is more interesting. "Fine. Just trying to get an education."

"Hey," she says, twirling her necklace again, "you've had a rough few weeks. Do you want to talk about it?"

Connor looks at her, a bit confused. Why would a science teacher want to talk about his loss? What does she care? Why wouldn't she suggest a counselor or shrink? He watches as she twirls the necklace; some type of pendant snakes through her fingers.

He looks her in the eye. "I'm fine. Excited to learn about the human body." He nudges his head toward the door. "So, whaddya say we go learn the good stuff?"

She drops the necklace out of her hand. "You need to talk to someone. Talking is a good thing. I'm here for you, Connor."

She could have been talking about anything from the task at hand to feudal Japan at this moment because all he heard was the slide trombone of the Peanuts characters when the adults spoke. All the audio in his world shot to background noise as he noticed the pendant that fell from her hand as she stopped twirling it. He would bet his life that it is the same silver and opal infinity pendant outlined with tiny, 1/15 carat diamonds that he saw while ending his first official B&E. How did he not notice it before? How did something so obvious not cross his mind? Officer Max Espinoza and Connor's advanced placement biology teacher, Linda Espinoza, are married. How was he so stupid not to have seen this before? Perhaps because Espinoza isn't a terribly uncommon last name. Maybe because he never would think that this friendly, seemingly caring teacher is somehow involved with teenage abduction and possibly murder.

He looks at her and nods his head. "Thanks. If I need to talk, I'll let you know."

He looks to the janitor, whose complete attention seems to be on them. Raymond nods at Connor as he disappears back into class. As he enters the classroom, a thought comes to his mind. An idea in a voice as clear as day yet unfamiliar to him. A man's voice is telling Connor that he is right, that he needs to continue. That nothing is what he thinks. But what has Connor feeling most peculiar is that his instinct is telling him this voice, a voice he's never heard before, belongs to Raymond.

><><><><><><><><><><><><><><><><><><><><><><

The rest of Connor's first day back went by without any fanfare or noteworthiness, not even an encounter with Scarlett or Allison. No other faux-sentimental speeches from teachers. Nothing. Just a day at school. He was there. He saw the students wandering the hallways, their lives unaffected by the past few weeks' events, utterly oblivious to the pain others face daily—how Connor wishes for that ignorance to once again run through his veins. But it can't. It's been torn away from him, never again to return. It's a grave new world he must now live in and face.

His friend, his best friend for as long as his memory goes back, is gone. He knows that he may live to see the end of college, the start of a career, and retirement, but Jack won't even attend high school graduation. Won't live to see the end of baseball season his senior year. None of it more evident than at this moment, standing on the pitcher's mound staring at some new catcher. Connor focuses on a new replacement for Jack. Jack 2.0 hides his face behind the catcher's mask. Connor looks around the field to see who's not in their position, to see if he can identify who's squatting 90 feet from him. The truth is, he doesn't care. It's not Jack. It's not his other half. It's just some other student who didn't care enough to ask how he's holding up.

He winds up and throws a heater straight over the plate. The replacement catches it, shaking the pain from his mitted hand before he throws the ball back to Connor. "Nice to have you back, captain."

Connor catches the ball and nods. As he winds up to throw again, the coach calls out his name, stopping him at the tail of his wind-up. Connor turns to his coach as he approaches.

"Hey, sport. Let's take a walk." The coach turns around, expecting Connor to follow suit. Connor watches the coach for a few moments as he walks away. A bit confused by the initial greet-and-depart, he takes a few long strides to catch up.

The coach turns his head to Connor as he slows his pace to match. "How you been?" Coach asks, already knowing the answer.

"Been better, but making progress," Connor says. "What's up?"

"First of all, I want to apologize for the yell-fest last time you were here." An honest apology from a strict, win-at-almost-any-cost coach. Connor doesn't respond for fear Coach may retract his words. "Secondly, you've met with colleges. With scouts for various schools, all interested in you."

"Yes, I know."

Coach stops. Their walk has led them away from the team enough to have a clear view of the whole athletic field, not just the practice diamond. "No. You don't. Look out there." He points to the field before them. "You've been stuck on the tiny strip of dirt we practice on. But there's so much more out there. So much more than what you see. So much more than what you focus on standing on the mound." He looks back at Connor. "Those schools that want to fund your education, they pay attention. They've noticed your absences. Excessive absences."

"But my friend died." Connor's arms cross, and his back is stiffer than the words in his response.

"But you didn't. Your life didn't. I've held them at bay as long as I can. But I don't know if I convinced them for your better."

"So what are you saying, coach?"

"I'm saying that life goes on. Your life goes on. The school year, the athletic teams go on. They want you. But you're stuck. Yes, it's still new. Yes, it's hard. But if you can't put one foot in front of the other and at least attempt to make some forward motion, then they have no use for you. And that's your future. Those schools are your future, Mr. DeSalvo. They want to help fund the beginning of your future, but they won't do it if you're not in it one hundred percent."

Connor hangs his head as he nods in understanding. The coach takes a finger and lifts Connor's chin, so their eyes meet.

"I'm tough on you. You know it. I know it. I'm not just tough on you because you're the captain of this team. You're the captain of this team because you are who you are. The others look up to you. They aspire to be as good a player as you are. They aspire to be the person you are off the field, too. But if you can't lead them … if you can't show them that you can stay that person after everything that's happened … then not only do you fail me, you fail them, you fail the schools who want you, and most importantly—more important than any of the other things I just said—you fail yourself. And the harsh truth of the matter is, you fail your friend who can't be here anymore. Season is months away from starting, and you've already checked out."

Connor's stare turns to the players in the distance. He looks to them for some form of mystical guidance as to what to do next. He watches the players go about their practice, unaware of this private conversation's content.

"The question is, son, are you going to fail yourself? Are you going to fail all those who count on you when the going gets tough, perhaps tougher than it should? Or are you going to rise and find a way to overcome? Are you going to check back in?"

A smile crosses Connor's face as the coach speaks his last few words. "Rise and find a way to overcome." Those words ring in his mind. Those words are what he needs to hear. He repeats them in his mind over and over. Now he needs to surround himself with those that can help him overcome.

Connor looks at his coach. "I know, Coach. And I'll be all in."

"When?"

"Now. Starting now. I'll try to get there starting now."

Connor looks back to his team as they practice the sport they love. Connor sees the mound and imagines himself back up there, enjoying the same feelings he felt before. It may never feel the same, but he will try.

He walks back to the pitcher's mound, coach by his side. Both continue strolling in stoic silence. Connor's mind repeats his new mantra over and over again; rise and overcome-rise and over-come-rise and overcome.

CHAPTER 9

"The truth can be a scary thing, can't it."
~J. McAllister~

Connor and Scarlett sit in his bedroom. The television drones on in the background as the nightly news begins, their favorite primetime show just ending. Connor cops a squat on the floor at the foot of his bed while Scarlett lays on the well-worn mattress, her head next to his shoulder. They both scan the stolen notebook.

He shows her the initials and gives her his thoughts on insurance programs and lack of any idea as to what kidnappers may want with insurance information. But no sooner than he says that do conspiracy theories of insurance fraud and murder start to form in their heads. Theories of some last-minute name change on the beneficiaries and some strangers collect the life insurance policies of their victims. A crime that, they realize, would take a lot of false names to not raise flags, bank fraud if no false names were used, and a lot of time and paperwork for it to be worth it.

Connor tries to stop the wild conjecture. His friend's entire family is missing. Scarlett, too, can't see past insurance scams and trying to find the base's location or whatever it is. In her mind, she imagines secret government facilities with cryogenically frozen aliens behind the modern-day rendition of the medieval torture device, the rack, that Jack and his family are tied to as they beg for their lives over some mistaken identity or other misunderstandings.

This ordeal can only be a misunderstanding. Jack is a good kid, straight-laced, and as narrow a shooter as they come. But the notebook reads like a Richard Castle novel, too grandiose for reality yet simultaneously wholly realistic and frighteningly scary in the grand realism.

They stop and look at each other for a moment. Scarlett's head turned sideways to look at him. Connor stares at her owl-cocked head. They both stare, knowing they are staring for a reason, but neither is sure why they decided now was the moment to turn their heads.

"We're missing something," Scarlett states.

"No shit, Sherlock," Connor retorts. "But what?"

"The offspring of a rhino and an elephant," she replies.

"The what?" asks a confused Connor.

"Eleph-ino."

Connor shakes his head at the horrid pun. "No. Never say that again." He lets out a slight chuckle. Perhaps the first chuckle since his sabbatical from school.

Scarlett gives his shoulder a playful tap. "Hey, Homecoming is, well, coming. You still going?"

"It's not coming up. We still have, like, three weeks."

"That was, like," Scarlett mocks him, "two weeks ago. It's in nine days."

"I'm still going. I just need to find some clothes."

"Good," Scarlett says. "Al and I have a limo planned for the three of us."

Connor smiles at the thought of being a typical teen once again, but the nightly news seems to have something against him. On the screen sits the talking head and a scrambled video clip playing next to her.

The news anchor speaks, "Police are reaching out to the public after weeks of a stalled investigation. This closed circuit surveillance video shows what appears to be three individuals breaking and entering into a house off Osceola Street. The police are stumped as the scrambled video obscures any identifying factors. Authorities have no motive behind the breaking and entering as nothing was stolen. They do believe that the individuals involved are highly skilled at computer technology since they were able to scramble the video while on screen. We urge anyone with information to call the West Haven police."

Connor and Scarlett stare slack-jawed at each other as the nightly news moves past their debut criminal activity.

"We lucked out, Con. What if the footage wasn't blurred?" Scarlett offers up.

Connor nods. "We can never say anything."

Scarlett nods back. "Never. Did anything in the video give away that it may have been us?"

"Not that I saw," says Connor as he uses his hand to brush back his hair. "I don't know what to do. The police are looking for us now."

Scarlett moves her body and flings her legs over the end of his bed. "Um, no. They're not. They are looking for three unknown individuals, highly skilled at computer stuff, who they can't identify."

"Whom," Connor blurts out.

"What?" Scarlett asks, shocked by the timing of the correction.

"Nothing. Never mind," Connor says, wondering why he felt the need to correct her. "Okay, well, that's a start," getting back to the task at hand, he looks at his cousin. "How did we not see cameras outside his house?"

Scarlett shrugs. "I didn't see any, but then again, I wasn't exactly looking. It's not like any of us are pros at being cons."

"Why didn't we show up clearly on the video? That's my question? Is something wrong with the video camera, or is something wrong with us?" Connor ponders out loud.

"Or are the Espinozas toying with us?" Scarlett offers up a second helping. "I mean, what if they know and they sent the footage to the news stations just to screw with us? Like, a huge 'we know you know.'"

"But they might not know. Either way, we need to see if Al has seen this," Connor says, pulling out his phone.

CHAPTER 10

Homecoming

*"Life doesn't ask permission
to throw a curveball your way.
It just throws them."*
~J. Taylor~

Connor finishes the last loop of his tie when he hears the front door open. He looks at himself in the mirror as he tightens and straightens it. Black, button-down shirt, a crimson tie with black paisleys, a red blazer coat that matches his necktie, and black suit pants that give him a look that is both royal and gothic. An air is lent to him that says, "tonight, at least, he is a man to be reckoned with." His dress boots accent that notion. Boots that were a surprise gift for him from his two closest girls, straight off the Sinister Soles website.

The high-pitched background noises of happy females put a smile on his face and a bit of confidence in his heart. He steps out of the bathroom toward the kitchen, where Allison, Scarlett, and Tracy are all giddy over the dresses. As he crosses the threshold to the kitchen, all talking ceases. The commotion stops as the three women all stare at him, smiles on their faces. But it is his dropped jaw that has the floor. He sees his cousin, Scarlett, in a deep red, spaghetti-strap dress, accented by silver panels on each side from which silver vining creeps along the bottom. A gorgeous dress for such an occasion. Her hair is pulled up into loose curls from a high twist, all of which is held together by silver flora decorated silver clips, accents to the vining on her dress. Her sultry, evening look makeup of mid-tone red eyeshadows blends into blacks. Black eyeliner and bright red lipstick to contrast the rest of the ensemble further accent her look. Her lips aren't too red; she doesn't look like a street walker. No. Her lips are bright red enough to call attention to them but not bright enough to make anyone think she may have questionable morals.

Connor's eyes turn back to Allison, the reason his jaw is still on the floor. She stands, jaw equally dropped at the sight of Connor. The little black dress she wears leaves little doubt that though her face may look a few years her junior, her figure is anything but. Thin but curved and shaped in all the places her mind doubts and lacks confidence. Black, pointelle tights clear up any confusion anyone may have about her femininity, accented by heels that add four inches to her diminutive height.

Every teenager takes Homecoming seriously. Perhaps more seriously than is called for. An occurrence that the three of them never understood—at least until this moment. Scarlett sees how Allison looks at Connor, and she smiles. In Scarlett's mind, if Connor were ever to take a girl seriously, she would want it to be Allison, and of course, vice versa. This moment seems to be that moment. The moment where, possibly, Connor sees Allison the way Allison has been seeing Connor—as someone more than just a friend, as a possibility for that primordial thing for which people hope. A proper content feeling, calming happiness, and to not roam this desolate world alone, but with the company of someone as strange and unusual as themselves. If only Connor could say something. Allison takes a quick breath, shaking off her nervousness and replacing it with confidence. She struts over to him and, with her index finger, closes his mouth.

"Come on, tiger. We've got a limo waiting," Allison says.

Tracy, ever the mother, steps forward with her camera ready to snap away on her phone. Waving her arms, she says, "Come on. Come on. I need a picture of all of you. You three look so grown up. I need to remember this."

She rounds the three up against the door and poses them with Scarlett on the picture's left, Connor in the middle, and Allison on the right. She says "smile" as Connor grabs his tie knot in one hand and pulls down the tie with his other, all with a wink in his eye. Allison smiles and pulls the Gerber-baby-finger-to-her-lips pose. Scarlett acts like the only normal one in the group.

Tracy snaps the photo as a tear forms in her eye. The kids may not understand the need to memorialize each moment before a big occasion in photographs, but Tracy understands. Tracy knows that decades from now, they will look back, not at the youthfulness of their physical beings in the pictures, for those may very well look the same. She knows they will look back and smile at the naiveté of teen years with a fondness for when the world was simple.

The teens head out the door and trek down the driveway, all linked arm in arm—Scarlett, Connor, Allison.

Allison smiles at Scarlett before they enter the limousine. "I envy the boy you pick tonight."

Scarlett grins back, ducking into the limo. "Thanks, Al. You ain't so bad yourself."

Scarlett's response doesn't feel the same as they ring in Allison's ears. There was something in her words to Scarlett, a truthfulness she has never touched. To Allison, Scarlett's words felt like she was merely returning the compliment. Allison isn't sure what to do with these strange feelings creeping inside her head.

She smiles at Connor, pushing her newfound feelings aside. "I can't wait to dance with you."

The kids leave the limo divider up for the ride. Allison pulls out a flask from her dress, concealed in a place only God could find. She offers it up to Scarlett first. Scarlett grabs the flask and, taking a sip, playfully condemns Allison for her juvenile delinquency. Scarlett passes it to Connor, who takes a swig while never taking his eyes off Allison. Allison chugs a small swig and tucks it back into its secret hiding place.

"This is going to be a good night," Scarlett announces with a huge smile plastered on her face.

"Hell yeah, it is," confirms Allison.

"I just wish Jack could be here," Connor says, his gaze finally leaving Allison.

Allison scooches a tad closer to Connor. "No. Not tonight. We all miss him, but he's not here. He wouldn't want you to waste the night on wishing he were. So don't."

"You're right. I guess. It's just ... this is the first dance we didn't double date."

"You never even asked a girl to go tonight. Even if he was here, you don't have a date," Scarlett points out.

"True. But there was still a ton of time before ... everything happened," Connor says, wishing things were different.

Allison pulls the flask out again, opens it, and shoves it in Connor's face. "Each time you get all mopey about Jack, you drink. That's the rule for the night."

Connor takes a reluctant drink. "Fine. I'll follow that rule if you answer me two questions," he proposes.

"Ask away?" Allison asks.

"First, how are you not in some parental, or court, mandated alcoholics anonymous? You are always sipping at that thing," he begins.

"Seriously? You think I'd get caught? Dad would kill me if he found out his little daughter liked the devil's syrup," she quips.

"Okay. Two," he says, putting up two fingers, "don't ever use the phrase 'devil's syrup' again. That's just weird."

"That wasn't a question," she says, landing a playful slug on his arm.

"Third, don't you think it's an issue, drinking all the time? Once in a while, sure, we're young, we're supposed to do stupid stuff. I just think..." he continues before being cut off.

"Dude, Con. Not in school right now. Don't want a lecture. I'm not abusing it, just having a little fun. We're going to a dance and want to loosen up," Allison shuts him down.

Allison puts it back to Connor's lips. "I answered. Now drink. This night, right here, it's about how far we've come in the past years. We celebrate tonight what we've accomplished."

The Homecoming dance welcomes all the students with festive decorations and loud music provided by a decent DJ. The school's main gym holds the dance itself. During the day, this gym is empty, lined with bleachers waiting for people to sit in them. The floor yearns for the bounce of a basketball and the teams that compete.

But tonight, the gym bleachers sit empty. The basketball court and more are transformed into an assembled dance floor. A craft services table off to the side with snack food and punch is lined with students filling empty stomachs. Surrounding the dance floor and the over one hundred students groovin' out are round tables set for twelve people each. A few are bare, most of which have a wallflower or two making new friends. The streamers lining the gymnasium ceiling and balloons tied around the chairs and basketball hoops scream of the festiveness of the night.

The three friends enter the gym feeling like they could rule the world. A few heads turn to see who made their entrance, and one of the boys even does a double take on Scarlett, but tonight isn't about boys for her; it's about her and spending time with her friends.

The three of them bee-line to the crafts table for food and beverage. Allison squashes a fleeting thought about spiking the punch with the remainder of her flask when she sees Ms. Waldgrave standing guard over the craft services table.

"Nice to see you all tonight," Ms. Waldgrave begins. "You ladies look fabulous tonight. And Connor, quite handsome yourself."

"Thank you, Ms. Waldgrave," he says, thanking her on everyone's behalf. "Having fun playing chaperone tonight?"

"So many things I could be doing, but it's always nice to see the students out of a classroom setting," Ms. Waldgrave replies. "Go, enjoy your night. You don't need to talk to me the whole time."

With those words, Connor nods his head to her, and the three turn to the dance floor. On the floor, Scarlett moves about in a flowy manner—not quite Woodstock-hippie but nothing too disjointed. She's having fun and doesn't care what anyone else thinks. Allison inches close to Connor but keeps it friendly. Connor plays the oblivious teen boy dancing the gentle boxer dance of awkward boys everywhere, hands held in a loose fist mid-chest, swaying about in something that resembles rhythm to the music.

For a few moments, they forget the recent events. They let go of any school work on their mind, all the dreams plaguing Allison, Scarlett's lost bid at student council president, Connor's loss, and overwhelming obsession. They forget all their worries in a moment of joy—a moment where the kids can be kids and not worry about the ever-approaching adulthood and never-ending onslaught that is life.

A boy Scarlett's seen around school, but couldn't tell anyone his name if asked, dances his way up to her. She dances with him for a moment as they try to say hello over the loud music blaring through the tripod-mounted speakers ten feet away.

Allison sees the interaction between the boy and Scarlett and uses this moment, along with the slowed-down music, to slide in closer to Connor. Connor does a quick, momentary head tilt of confusion but doesn't shy away. Allison takes his hands and places them on her hips. She takes control of the dance, leading him in the sway of the song.

Connor looks at Allison and notices how grey her eyes are. He always thought they were a pale blue. He's amazed at how many times he's seen her but never noticed her grey, almond-shaped eyes. He could swear they were pale blue. He studies her pronounced cheekbones that will keep her looking young for far longer than she'd like. He finds himself drawn to her pinkish-toned lips that beautifully contrast her skin tone. He finds himself drawn to her and, at the same time, unable to decide if he should kiss her or continue staring at her, wondering. So the unsure teenager that lurks inside the otherwise confident young man wins this round, and he stares. He waits for something to happen, not knowing what it is that will happen or if it will kill the moment, but he waits.

Allison looks at him. She sees the budding man she's seen a thousand times a day before tonight. She's just never seen him clean up so nicely before. She sees not the high-school boy with shaggy hair in a baseball uniform but someone she wants to intertwine with. She knows she doesn't have long until the song ends and the DJ will speed up the music again. If she ever wants to kiss him, to see if they spark the way she feels they will, she'll have to make the first move. Now is the time.

She moves in closer to him and presses her lips to his. His hands leave her waist and cradle the back of her head. The butterflies in her stomach are almost too much to handle. An excitement that sends shiver after shiver down her spine. Her whole body quivers, which plants an image in her mind of her looking like a shaking Chihuahua, but she pulls herself back to the moment.

She went for it, and the young Mr. DeSalvo didn't back away. No. Instead, he moved into the kiss, joining her in the moment. A moment that both wanted to experience, but neither knew they wanted. The thoughts flying through her head of everything he might be thinking and everything she feels in her heart and stomach at this moment feels all-enveloping.

Their tongues begin to intertwine for just a brief second. A momentary exploration of new lands, but the song comes to an end, and a Pavlovian cue to stop kissing halts their brief moment of newfound intimacy. They pull away from each other and stare into each other's eyes, smiling.

"No biggie. Just something I wanted to do," Allison says, trying to play it cool while smiling ear to ear.

"Yeah, uh, no. Me too, yeah," Connor tries to form words while Allison giggles at him. "Thank you."

"You're welcome," she says with a wink.

The two of them part ways as Connor walks to a table to collect his thoughts. Allison heads to the ladies' room as Scarlett continues dancing away on the floor, blissfully ignorant of the more extraordinary things yet to happen to her and her friends.

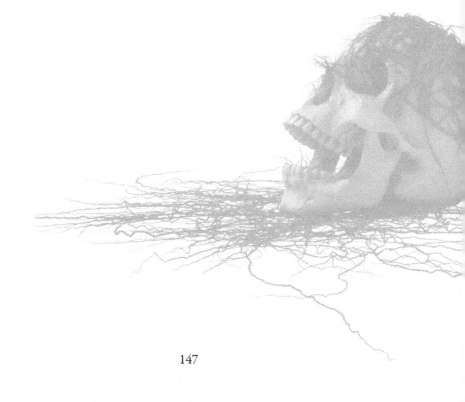

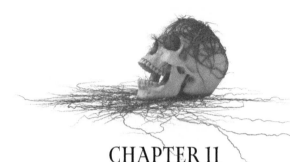

CHAPTER 11
Halloween

"Do not judge people,
for you do not see
the inner demons they live with."
~V. Petrovsky~

H alloween in West Haven is something of an oxymoron. It's a celebrated holiday in the modern sense of costumes and candy and a spiritual celebration in the old, pagan tradition, even among monotheistic households. And at the same time, it isn't made a big enough deal within the city limits to attract outsiders. As if the town wants this holiday to themselves and no one else. Any annual parties are for townsfolk only and a few select family members who may live outside city limits. It would look like any other town to the passerby, but to those who Are In, they know.

The funny thing about such a peculiar holiday in this town is that most teens and even some young adults that are Legends are still not In. Those that are not In stroll the streets trick-or-treating as they pass by the streetlights decorated with fall wreaths. The occasional house whose backyard is decorated for the commercial aspect speckles the otherwise downplayed streets. Nothing too different from any other town.

Each year the student-athletes throw a Halloween party for all their friends. It's a way for the parents to enjoy the spiritual side of their day while the kids enjoy the blissful ignorance of not knowing their true selves or what the rest of the Legend in this town know. This year, Connor and the rest of the varsity team throw their annual holiday party at The Attic. The bash of the year, the party to attend for anyone who's anyone at Maine West Haven High School.

The costumes are always a mix of homemade humor like "cool guy in leather" or "nerd in glasses" fully equipped with a white button-down shirt and pocket protector. Others are more elaborate with full gothic Victorian era vampire costumes or full makeup like Michael J. Fox from Teen Wolf. Connor has decided that his last year at Maine West Haven will be his best costume. A black karate Gi complete with a yellow logo of a black fist in front and Cobra on the back, headband to match. And because teams do what they do, the entire varsity team is dressed to match the Cobra Kai.

All of the elaborate costume coordination and party decorations take a backseat to the memorial set up in Jack's honor. The All-Valley karate tournament board with Jack's name as the grand champion. His picture hangs next to his name with #FindMyFriend in large lettering under it. Below the Halloween memorial is another one; a table set up with his catcher's mitt, mask, and uniform all laid out, surrounded by a few candles. Connor and the rest of the team stand guard over the open flames.

Brianna dresses to the occasion as Little Bo Peep while all her surrounding friends dress up as her flock of sheep. The direct insult of the costume is seemingly lost on them as they stand by the soda bar. When her ears pick up it is appropriate to do so, Brianna laughs at her friend's statement, but her mind is elsewhere. She stares at Connor as he stands center circle of his teammates. Brianna listens to her friends' trivialities on home life as long as her patience allows. She knows her friend only complains about cars and how little money her parents allot to her weekly. She knows the problems are superficial and insignificant, so she holds up a hand to stop the baa-baa of the sheep, cutting off their words into immediate silence. The sheep all stand bewildered, awaiting their shepherd's next command.

Brianna excuses herself from the group, leaving them to fend for themselves. Something that the group isn't used to doing. They all stand there, unsure where to go, what to say, or do.

She makes her way through the crowd to Connor. He tosses a look to his teammates that communicates a need for privacy in this public place. So they do what guys do, disperse into the crowd to find a girl to talk with.

She stands in front of him, not speaking, letting the uncomfortable silence suffocate them for a moment. He wonders if perhaps the words she wants to say are not coming to mind. She fidgets with her hands. She goes to twirl her hair but realizes that he might take that the wrong way. So she looks back down at her fumbling hands.

"What's up, Bri? Enjoying the party?" He realizes that if he doesn't start this encounter, they may stand there all night in silence.

"Yeah," she says, finally looking at him. "It's ... fun." She looks him in the eye, searching for permission to ask a question but unsure if she's finding it. "How you been?"

He lets out an amusing huff. "Like, recently or since you got too cool for us?"

"Hey, I'm talking to you now, aren't I?" Self-righteous indignation spews forth.

"Yeah, things have been what they've been, but thanks for asking," he says. "You okay? I mean, you have a bunch of lost disciples waiting for your command over there."

Brianna sighs, defeated by his ambivalence. "Them. Yeah. They want to be me but have no idea what my life is actually like."

"Well, what is your life actually like? Have you tried telling them?" Connor retorts.

She shakes her head. "They don't care unless I'm talking about the latest Sephora eyeshadow, Coach purses, or some stupid clothing trend."

"Then why be friends with them?" Connor asks with a hint of sincerity not lost on her.

"I don't know. Because I don't have to be myself around them," Brianna says, again staring at the ground. She waits a moment, hoping he'll say something. He remains silent. She looks back at him to make sure he's still there. He is still in front of her, full attention directed her way. "I'm sorry about Jack. Love the memorial, though. Well done. I can't imagine what you must be going through."

He looks off to the door for a momentary escape from the here and now. The universe answers his plea with the entrance of Allison and Scarlett, dressed in full costume. Scarlett wears an all-out Little Red Riding Hood costume—a red hooded cape, white dress with red trim underneath. Even a wicker picnic basket. Allison in tow as the big bad wolf. Well, Legs Avenue-sexy werewolf version of the big bad wolf. However, she has made a few modest revisions to keep some things hidden from the prying eyes of teenage hormones. Connor smiles, turning back to Brianna.

"It's been what it's been. Thanks for your condolences," he dismisses.

Scarlett and Allison gather on either side of Connor. A protective shield against whatever scheme is on Brianna's mind.

"Hi, Bri. Long time," offers up Scarlett.

Brianna cracks a tiny smile. "Yeah. Sorry about that. Life's been a little crazy."

Allison chimes in, "Yeah, popularity is such a drag. No time there for the little people you used to call friends."

Brianna's friends flock to her, further voiding the solo boy/girl conversation.

Brianna scans her following. "Yeah, Allison. It's such a drag," she says with a conniving smile. "Must be hard finding your way to the bottom of a bottle all the time." Her friends all laugh to egg on the mockery.

"Go douse your face in gasoline and light a match, Bri. Might improve your look," Allison fires back.

"Al, stop," interjects Scarlett. "She was just trying to talk to Connor."

Brianna's facade fades for a moment as she looks at Scarlett. Brianna nods at Scarlett as her head turns back to the false friends with which she surrounds herself.

Allison watches with contempt as Brianna Bo Peep and her flock of sheep walk back to their corner of the festivities.

Allison looks at Scarlett. "She thinks because I finally made a move on Connor that she can just move in."

"You kissed. Once. And you were the one who said it was no big thing," Scarlett reminds Al. "Hey Con," she says, turning to him. "Nice party."

Connor nods in agreement. "A little bit of planning on my part. It was mostly the rest of the guys."

"It's just nice to see you are relaxing from the notebook and getting back to your life," Allison chimes in.

"At this point, I don't like admitting it, but I know he's gone. Now, the book has become a puzzle for me. Something I'd like to solve just so I know why or where. Something more than simply he is gone." Connor looks around the room, trying to get his mind to where it was before all the chaos took control.

Allison moves in closer. "If that's what you're wanting, maybe I can help. It's been a while since I glanced at it. Fresh eyes may help."

"I'd like that. We can look it over tomorrow. Right now, I have to be a gracious host to all these people," he says, putting the thought on the back burner for the evening.

"So, does that mean you are leaving Scarlett and me to our own devices?" Allison asks.

"No, I figure I'd lord over the party some more while I chill with you. Let them come to me if they want," he offers. "I'm keeping you two by my side all night."

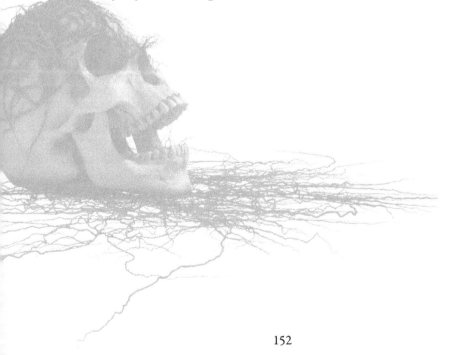

CHAPTER 12

*"The voices you hear in your head...
sometimes they are not your own."*
~D. Childers~

T he blue and white halls of Maine West Haven weigh quieter than usual. It could be the fact that not many students
have arrived yet. It could be that the sunny, 41° F weather in late
November hits the skin with a warmer tone than expected. It could
be the time of the morning. Whatever the reason, Scarlett and
Allison seem to be the only ones in the entire building at this hour.

The two girls sit on the hallway floor outside their lockers, a
little less than a hundred feet from an intersecting hall. Backpacks
at their sides, they sit and watch the empty corridors.

"It's nice of you to help Connor through this time. He's still
taking it pretty rough," Scarlett says, breaking the silence.

Allison turns to Scarlett. "I try. I thought helping him with that
notebook would lift his spirits a bit, but we're not making any progress. Honestly, I think it's just dragging him back down."

Scarlett goes into her backpack and grabs a plastic bottle of
cran-raspberry juice. "Any progress with your efforts towards
seducing him?"

Allison shakes her head. She pulls out her flask from her backpack. Scarlett's eyes widen in horrid surprise.

"You'll get expelled if they catch you! You are way beyond acceptable right now!" Scarlett scorns.

As she finishes her parental lecture, the silent janitor, Raymond, turns the corner, mop and bucket in tow. He seems oblivious to their happenings as Allison dumps some into Scarlett's juice and starts drinking.

Allison takes a swig and holds onto the bottle. The janitor turns his attention their way for a moment and sees the flask that Allison holds so dear.

Scarlett looks around the hallways as a deep voice, oddly familiar to her, sounds in her head. "Sylvia is coming. Put that away." The only person she sees besides Allison is Raymond, but he's never spoken, or at least, she's never heard him talk—not that she can recall.

She looks around, unsure why that thought, spoken in a voice she can only imagine she created, told her paranoid ramblings of getting caught.

"Come on, Al. We could both get in trouble," Scarlett urges.

"I just need one more sip. It's not like it matters. Connor still thinks of me as just a friend," Allison relents.

The voice again sounds in Scarlett's head. "Hurry. She's about to turn the corner." Raymond watches the girls with an urging look in his eyes.

Scarlett makes eye contact with Raymond, whose head nods to the close, adjoining hallway. "Hurry," Scarlett hears in that same deep voice. She grabs the flask from Allison and takes a hypo-critical swig just before Ms. Waldgrave turns the corner to the hallway. Scarlett is not quick enough as she fumbles to put the container away.

Ms. Waldgrave sees the stainless steel's shine and the flask's unmistakable shape. She quickens her pace as her hand rises in the air. Wagging her finger at the two young women, she commands, "Ladies! Stop right there!"

Scarlett grabs the flask and holds it behind her. She tries to shove it in her waistband, tucked under her shirt.

"Stand up, young ladies," Ms. Waldgrave demands.

Allison stands up.

The motion of Scarlett starting to rise gives her the distinct feeling that the flask is slipping out. She falls back to the ground. "Leg's asleep, Mrs. W," Scarlett feigns.

"You'll live. Please stand up," Ms. Waldgrave urges.

Scarlett takes a deep breath, standing up slowly, but the flask has already shifted too much and slips out of her waistband, falling to the ground.

Ms. Waldgrave raises a suspicious eyebrow at Scarlett. She picks up the flask and opens it. She takes a whiff of what she can only assume is cheap, spiced rum. "Is this yours, Scarlett?"

The voice once again sounds in her head. "No. Say you found it."

Raymond slaps the mop into the bucket and heads to them.

Scarlett decides to listen to the voice in her head. "We found it. Thought we'd turn it in," young Ms. McAllister lies.

"You found it? Then why do I smell alcohol on your breath? And why try to hide it?" Sylvia keeps up her interrogation.

"Teenage curiosity. The temptations of hormones and naiveté are too much sometimes," Scarlett continues her deception.

Raymond reaches them and taps Ms. Waldgrave on the shoulder.

"Yes, Ray?" She looks at him for a moment, neither of them talking. He points to the flask and then to himself. He makes a fist and rubs it in a circular motion on his chest while giving her sad eyes.

Though reluctant, Ms. Waldgrave hands him the flask.

Scarlett's internal dialogue sends a thank you out to that voice. What shocks her, making her look around once more, is the same deep voice in her head responding, "You're welcome."

"This isn't over," Mr. Waldgrave continues her lecture. "Yours or not, you drank alcohol at school, and worse yet, you don't know if that was poisoned or fatal. We're going to see your dean. Come on, Scarlett."

Ms. Waldgrave begins to walk off. Scarlett follows, not wanting to make matters worse. She turns her head back to Allison, pointing her finger, mouthing, "*you owe me*" and finishes with a mountainous hand motion, "*huuuge.*"

Allison hangs her head and nods to Scarlett. She turns to Raymond, who is still within arm's reach. He pockets the flask while nodding at Allison.

"*You need to talk with her.*"

Those words echo through Allison's head in a deep voice. What she doesn't know is that the same deep voice echoed in Scarlett's head.

Allison looks at Raymond as she hears those words. He nods again and walks away. Allison says to him in a hushed tone, "Thank you."

Again the voice rings in Allison's mind. "You're welcome."

She freezes in place. Shocked, a little scared, and still unsure of what just happened.

><><><><><><><><><><><><><><><><><><><><><><

Connor sits in his first-period Fine Arts Appreciation class, twirling his pen between his fingers and listening to the teacher's lectures on the differences between classical, baroque, and gothic period music. A course Connor signed up for to receive an easy A but has found an interest in learning the difference between having a subjective and an objective appreciation for things. This course has been the perfect course to get back into the swing of things after his bereavement absence.

Though, it doesn't make the class interruption of the messengered note delivered for him any more inviting. A letter that he must once again excuse himself from class, this time to see the school social worker.

After reading it over, he hands it to the teacher. "Do I have to? Can't I just stay here?" he pleads.

The teacher shakes his head, "I think it's a good idea you do this. At least once." He hands the note back to Connor.

Connor huffs as he gathers his belongings and heads out the door, note in hand, to the other end of the school where the offices are. He does not want to go through this again.

As soon as his behind hits the chair cushion to wait for the social worker, she calls him into her office.

"Take a seat." She motions from behind her desk.

Connor parks himself in a horribly outdated yet comfortable chair.

"My name is Mrs. Hsu. I've been keeping an eye on you ever since the loss of your friend," she starts.

"Thanks?" he says, unsure of where this is going.

"I would like to talk. If that's okay with you?" Mrs. Hsu says, opening a Manilla folder.

"I guess," Connor says, ambivalence frosting his tone.

She places a pad of legal paper on the folder and holds a pen to take notes as she listens. "How are you doing?"

"Okay, I guess," he replies, unsure why he's here.

"That's the second time you said, "I guess," Mrs. Hsu points out. "Let me ask you this: how are you feeling?"

She scribbles something on the legal pad before Connor even starts answering the second question.

"I feel like I lost my best friend. I'm not sure how to verbalize that. Have you ever lost your best friend?" he asks, crossing his arms.

"This isn't about me," the counselor reminds him. "I'm just here to make sure you are in a good place. Grief is hard. It takes time," she offers in a textbook-style reply.

"Yeah. I know. Why did it take you so long to make me do this if you knew about it this whole time?" Connor asks, still crossing his arms.

"I wanted to see if you would ask for help on your own. But you didn't. That and your absences in the beginning," the social worker says, still scribbling on her pad.

Connor stands up. "I'm not going to hurt myself or anyone in the school. You're safe and not liable for my behavior. I'm dealing with this the best way I know how and just because it may not make sense to you or anyone else, it's helping me. I'm coping."

"Coping is good," she says as she dots the end of a sentence on her pad. She looks at Connor with full attention. "People are worried about you. About your future. We want what's best for you."

"What about Jack? What about his future? What about…" He wants to finish by saying "the truth," but he doesn't know if he can trust her. He thought he could trust his bio teacher. Now he doesn't know who he can trust.

"I'm fine. I'll be fine. I'll be more fine when I walk out of the door. I know you are here. A resource to use at my disposal. But right now, I want to get back to class," he says, opening the door to leave.

Mrs. Hsu stands up from her desk. "Connor, you need to talk about this," she says in a desperate attempt to get him to stay.

He turns back around and slams the door. Throwing his arms into the air, he relents, "Fine. You wanna talk about this? Tell me why. Tell me how talking about this does anything. It doesn't bring him back. It doesn't tell me who took him, why they took him. If they meant to take him, or it was some mistaken identity. It doesn't say where he is and possibly rotting away."

The social worker motions to the chair for him to once again take a seat. He stands at the door, still unsure whether he is staying or going. He makes a step toward the chair.

"What good does making me talk about this do? It doesn't help me. All it does is placate some need inside of you to force me to talk in hopes that I make some revelation about my feelings. I know how I feel about this. The fact that you don't isn't my problem.

"He was my friend. Mine. You knew nothing about him besides what others could have told you. You don't know why he stuttered and dragged out his sentences the way he did. I know. You don't know why he stuck with baseball all these years when his real passion was poetry. I know why. He was my friend. My friend. And my friend is gone. Talking doesn't bring him back. Talking doesn't turn back time. All it does is make others feel better about my misery."

He smiles at Mrs. Hsu as he opens the door once again. "I'm sorry if my thoughts are insulting to you or your profession. I'm sorry if justifying my grief to you or anyone else is not at the top of my priority list. I have to get my life back in order, and it's hard. A good chunk has been torn away. Sorry if you are not important to me."

She holds up an outstretched arm urging him to wait. "One last question, Mr. DeSalvo."

He huffs and turns around one more time, frustrated at her blocking his big dramatic exit again. "What?" he grits out.

She looks the young man square in the eyes, making sure she has his attention. She takes a deep breath with squinted eyes. She exhales and raises an eyebrow, unsure if she should ask her question or not.

"What?! What more do you have to say?" Connor says, his patience worn out.

"Are you in?" she says as the look on her face reaches for a hopeful answer to a vague question.

"In what? What are you talking about? Orchestra? Band? Sports? Chess club? Illuminati?" He shrugs, again turning to the door.

He exits, leaving Mrs. Hsu behind, standing up and unsure what to say or do next. He walks back to class with tears welling in his eyes. He's trying to comprehend why she summoned him after all this time. She may have a legitimate caring concern for the student body and be a bad social worker. She may have other intentions in mind. Right now, Connor can't think clearly enough to sort out his thoughts on her or the timing of this meeting.

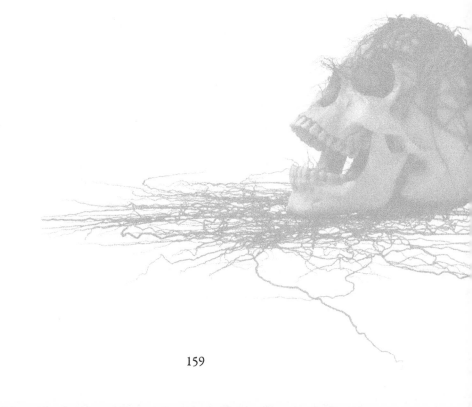

CHAPTER 13

*"Don't be frightened by that
which you do not understand.
Remain open-minded.
You may be surprised."*
~E. DeSalvo~

The motionless, late November air fills the classroom. The closed windows block out the sound of the increasing fall wind. The unseasonably warm weather sticks in everyone's mind like sweaty skin to hot leather.

Silence fills the science class while the students all bury their noses in a test, one that Connor didn't study for. His mind is still elsewhere, caught between a nagging need for closure on Jack's death and disappearance and newfound feelings flowing through his mind for Allison. But right here, right now, he splits his time tossing looks between his test and the empty desk next to him. He still imagines Jack sitting there, trying to say something funny.

Connor looks at the test and pictures his grade slipping away from him. The past conversation between Coach and him further clouds his mind. He knows he needs to get his head back in the game, back into life, and back into being himself. The self-induced stress he feels right now furthers a simmering anxiety within him. The sounds of the other students breathing, clicking their pens as they concentrate, tapping away at their desks all ring in deadening volumes through his ears. The grating sound of pens writing on paper causes the hair on his arms to stand on end. Every little noise amplifies a thousand times, and he can't turn the sounds off.

He feels his heart pounding in his chest. Each thump-ump of his heart moves his shirt in rhythm. His skin starts to itch and hurt like something is trying to tear its way out, but no one else seems to notice. No one else seems to be in pain. No one feels his pain. He looks up at Linda Espinoza seated at her desk, flipping through papers and jotting down errors while occasionally glancing up to watch her students. She mindlessly twirls her pendant necklace with her left hand. She doesn't notice his pain, but maybe it's because as he looks at his pained arms, there is nothing to see. He can feel the pounding heart in his chest; no one else can. He feels a tear fall down his face from the pain he feels. A loud, guttural, pained cry escapes his lungs.

The entire class stops taking their tests to stare at him. He realizes that in the minds of the rest of his classmates, he just yelled for no apparent reason. Linda looks up from her papers and sees the tears running down his face.

"Mr. DeSalvo, is there a problem?" she says, tapping her pen.

The pain disappears. The tearing sensation of a million little men pushing their way out of his skin subsides. His heart no longer pounds in his chest. His hearing no longer taunts him with every slight sound. He realizes that he screamed in the middle of a quiet test. He knows he needs to say something and get back to normalcy.

"Just a really tough test, Ms. E," he lies, causing the rest of the class to chuckle. "Perhaps I should've studied a little longer for this one."

"Well, perhaps next time. But keep your frustration on my test writing to yourself," Ms. Espinoza commands, turning her attention back to her work.

He shakes his head a few times, clearing away the rest of his mental distractions. Taking a deep breath and looking back at his test, he breezes through the rest of the first page questions concerning the differences between dominant and recessive genes before making his way to the second page, where Punnett squares greet him. As he fills out the squares correctly predicting the outcomes of the presented possible genetic results, his mind starts wandering back to the notebook.

He tries to push aside the distracting thoughts, but as he forges ahead on the test, answering questions about RNA, DNA mRNA, rRNA, and tRNA, his mind keeps returning to the notebook for some reason. No longer able to concentrate, he begins randomly filling in the answer bubbles, knowing he will probably fail. His mind keeps going back to the codes in the notebook they stole; a small letter followed by capitals. Something keeps stirring in his mind. He tries linking the words on the test to the stolen notebook and why the lettering looks so familiar.

He remembers what he told his coach, that he's going to put himself back in the game, not forfeit his future over Jack's death. He knows that right now, the test is what's important, so he shoves the nagging thought aside and puts his mind and effort back into the exam.

><><><><><><><><><><><><><><><><><><><><><

Scarlett sits on her bed, schoolbooks opened and sprawled out. The radio plays on low volume in the background, droning away another set of commercials. She doesn't pay attention to them, though; she buries her nose deep in a notebook. The notebook she is studying right now is not school related. She holds a pencil between her teeth as she flips through the pages, occasionally circling a word here and there that she thinks might be code.

Tracy opens the door to her room and peeks her head inside. She looks around at the books decorating Scarlett's bed and smiles. "Nice to see one little suspension hasn't lessened your academic acuity at all."

Scarlett looks up, smiling at her aunt and lying through her teeth to the only mother she can remember, "Nope. Walking the straight and narrow. Making sure I'm square for tomorrow." She gestures to the material around her.

"Any exams or tests tomorrow?" Tracy inquires.

Scarlett shakes her head. "Not that I know of, but even if there is, I'm kosh."

"Kosh?" Tracy asks, realizing she is not as hip as she once was.

"Yeah, it's an abbreviation. It's short for kosher. As in, all good," Scarlett clarifies. By the end of the sentence, her mind was back in the notebook. It hit her. The key to the code. Abbreviations.

Tracy keeps the smile on her face as she nods and closes the door behind her.

Scarlett returns to her notebook, pencil in hand, frantically circling each appearance of the words "base," "vam," "heme," and the initials "JT," "LT," "jT," & "RB." She notices other paragraphs that, while at this moment she may not understand, have initials, and she senses their importance. So she circles what she catches. Some sections—and the ones she feels will give the most answers—are short and almost entirely coded. A few of them read:

Vams canes point b/c HED. Few. Many missing. Differ fr myth. EDA. Xq13.1 EDAR. 2q13 EDARADD. 1q42.3-q43

EPP X-linkd & AIP known. FECH 18q21.31 ALAS2 xp11.21

MSRMHT MSTN 2q32.2 power source

Missing link. No cause for change. Need to find catalyst.

Paragraphs like those are scribbled between longer scrawlings of abbreviated notes. For the moment, Scarlett is not sure what to make of them, but she figures anything could help. She pays attention to a few paragraphs and lines throughout the notebook.

Unsub at base. Not jT. Must ID. PK mistake. Will rectify.

Unsub n/r to stim. Normal?

JT & LT acquired. Stim to commence.

JT & LT n/c w/ stim to JT

Subq DS JT, subq DS LT no changes. IM DS JT & LT. No changes.

Burns identified. Wrong sub. Acquire needed. PK respns

The notes seem to go on and on. Some are illegible, and some appear to be variations on the above. But the excited Scarlett starts making a list of all the initials and coded words she can find, leaving space for the decoded meaning. Scarlett figures it all out. She has heard the term unsub before. After many seasons of *Criminal Minds* and the countless times Dr. Reed has said it, she is sure that unsub means unknown subject. So she takes an educated guess and jots it down next to that code.

She continues circling code and recording her writings for most of the remaining notebook. She makes only minimal further headway on decoding but does not lose any of the excitement she feels. She can't wait for Connor to come home to share the progress. She has finally found a way to help her cousin deal with the loss. Perhaps she has found a way to help him move on and cope with it. If she's lucky, she might even be able to answer some of the questions surrounding the mysterious circumstances of Jack Taylor's disappearance.

But first things first. A knock on Scarlett's bedroom door signals the arrival of Allison, the reason she's been homebound for a week. That little stunt at school won her a week's suspension. But Scarlett values her friendship, and as a given bonus, the time off let her make headway on the notes.

Allison creaks open the door, taking guilt-filled steps like the apologetic child she is. Scarlett motions her to come in.

"Thanks, Scar," Allison begins. She holds some schoolbooks tight against her chest. "What you did…"

"I said you owe me," Scarlett interrupts. "It wasn't a get out of jail free card," Scarlett finishes in a very maternal voice.

"So what do I owe you? Like fifty bucks?" Allison asks, confused.

Scarlett chuckles. "No. You don't owe me money. You owe me a talk. A real talk with honest answers. Because the next time that happens, it's your ass on the line."

Allison lowers the books from her chest and sways about searching for words. "It's nothing. Just having some fun. I mean, don't you find the grind of it all just a tad boring sometimes?"

Scarlett shoots an evil eye at Allison. "That answer is just a tad too long for honesty, Allison. Wanna try again?"

Allison's face scrunches up. She stops her swaying to take a seat. She knows Scarlett called her out on a lie. Biting the inside of her cheek, she searches for an honest answer, but nothing comes to her.

Allison starts to realize that maybe she doesn't quite know why she does what she does. Thoughts float around in her mind that she can't tell Scarlett, not because she doesn't want to, but because they have yet to fully form. Allison doesn't know how to verbalize those thoughts. Like random pieces of a puzzle without a box to see the picture, she has an idea of parts but not the whole. A few thoughts start to form in her mind, but she shoves them aside, not yet ready to face her truth.

The moments of Allison's silent contemplation go on a little too long for Scarlett's liking. "I've got all night, and I'm not afraid to have this conversation in front of Connor," Scarlett says, breaking the silence.

"Okay. Okay. I'm not stalling. I'm just thinking about how to say it," Allison says, but still without an honest answer to give. She takes one more nibble on the inner cheek. "Have you ever felt like everything you thought you wanted was wrong?"

"I don't understand," Scarlett replies. While she may not understand what Allison is implying, at least she is talking. Scarlett knows this is a beginning of a much-needed conversation, if nothing more.

"There are parts of me I don't understand. Parts of my life that I feel are wrong. I can't explain it. It's a feeling, ya know." Allison looks Scarlett in the eye, trying to let Scarlett into Allison's weird, little world.

"How come you haven't said anything about this before? The way you feel?" Scarlett asks. It stings Scar that her friend doesn't feel she could say whatever it is that is on her mind without being judged, laughed at, or whatever it is holding her back. Scarlett has always thought of herself as someone who is there for Allison.

"I dunno," replies Allison. "I just… when you can't explain something to yourself, it's even harder to try and explain it to others."

"Understandable. Is everything all right at home?" Scarlett asks, grasping for a possible root of Allison's confusion.

Allison laughs. "Yeah, there, that's one place everything is fine. Though I do think something is going on with dad. But we'll talk about that later."

"Then what is it? What can't you explain?" Scarlett asks, realizing the pointlessness of the question.

"It's this town, this life, me. Something isn't right. Something is not right with me."

"Don't be silly. Of course, everything is right with you. You are wonderful and fun and my best friend. I wouldn't have it any other way."

Allison stops thinking for a moment and smiles. She is unsure of the thoughts running through her mind, like random words jumbled over one another in a loose pile. All meaningful as a single word but as a bunch, it's gibberish. She doesn't know what she is thinking and doesn't know how to rearrange the stack into sentence structure. She's stuck, perhaps only a step or so ahead of where she was before. But she smiles and hugs Scarlett. She'll take any forward motion she can.

"I'm sorry I haven't been there as much as I could have," Scarlett starts. "Please know that I will never make fun of you for the way you feel, and I'll always be here for you."

Allison continues to hold the hug for a moment. A tear wells up in her eye from finally opening up.

"It's these dreams, too. I have these dreams, and I don't know what to make of them."

"I remember, at your house that morning," Scarlett adds.

"They seem so real, so cryptic. I just want to talk to someone about them," Allison begins.

The door to the house slams shut as Connor drops his book bag by the door.

"Scar!" he calls out as he rushes to her room.

The girls look at each other.

"Continue this later?" asks Scarlett.

"Later, yeah," Allison replies.

Connor bursts into the room with a smile on his face. "Genes."

"Jeans?" retorts Allison.

"Are we going shopping right now?" asks Scarlett.

"Shopping could be fun." Allison smiles.

"No. That's what they are. I think," Connor says, grabbing the notebook and flipping through pages like a madman till he finds what he's looking for. He jabs his finger onto the pages. "There." He points to the code ALAS2. "Genes."

The girls' eyes light up. "Genes," they both say in unison.

"Google it," he says. "A-L-A-S-2"

Scarlett whips out her phone, tapping away with lightning speed, entering the letters and number into the search bar. She looks a little puzzled when the first results that pop up are genetic reference pages.

"Connor, you're a gene-ius," she puns as she clicks a link to a genetic reference page.

Connor and Allison make eye contact and shake their heads at Scarlett's pun. "So what's it saying?"

"It's loading. Hold on," and no sooner does Scarlett say that does the page loads. "It's just information. The ALAS2 gene helps make an enzyme for red blood cell production."

Allison's eyes go big, anime big. She starts shaking her hand at Scarlett in uncontained excitement. "Wait! Wait! Wait!"

Both Scarlett and Connor freeze in their respective poses. Out of the corner of his mouth, Connor squeaks, "What's going on?"

"The notes kept saying vam and vams. Add a 'P' to the short code, and you have vamp as in vampire," Allison starts.

Connor and Scarlett unfreeze. "There's a link to related health conditions," Scarlett says, clicking the link. She scans the page. "Just some stuff about porphyria and some anemia I can't pronounce. Nothing about vampires."

Connor decides to pipe up, "Work with me for a minute. A while back, in biology, Mrs. Espinoza taught us about the light spectrum and sound spectrum of what humans can see and hear."

Allison twirls a finger in the air. "Bring it around, Con."

"I said that those were the only spectrums we knew of, our perceptions not being able to see past those, even with mechanical help."

Allison's finger is still twirling for him to bring home the point. "Come on."

"What if the internet only tells us what they want us to know? I mean, it's not a holy high place. It's pretty much Thunderdome," he continues.

"So where do I go from here?" chimes in Scarlett.

"Oh," pipes up Allison with renewed excitement. "Try Googling 'vampire disease.'"

Scarlett shrugs and types it in. The results make her drop her phone. Connor reaches down and checks out the results; a wiki entry of erythropoietic porphyria and a picture of a severely scarred individual. "Effin'-A, Allison. You may have cracked the case."

"HA! You gotta be shittin' me!" Allison snatches the phone from Connor and stares at the screen. "Do you know what this means?!"

"That a crazy guy thinks vampires exist?" Scarlett says, bringing her back down to earth.

Allison is already in her own world, flipping pages in the notebook. Connor is looking over her shoulder as she does. His breath on her neck is almost enough to break her concentration. He spots something and stops her from turning the page. He flips back a page and points out the letter EPP.

"Here. E-P-P. The E-rhythmic poetic porphyria or whatever. It's a scientific abbreviation. I guarantee it," he states.

Though reluctant, Scarlett types it into the search bar, and five results down is EPP, Erythropoietic Porphyria. Scarlett looks up at them. "So … vampires, porphyria, and Jack and his parents go missing."

They all look at each other in stunned silence.

Scarlett continues, "What's going on?

CHAPTER 14

*"Don't choose to believe easy fictions
because difficult facts
can be hard to understand."*
~K. DeSalvo~

A knock on Connor's bedroom door goes unanswered as he sits on his bed, still in the same clothes he was in on Monday. Six days and the beginning of December have passed while he wiles away his time, nose buried in the notebook. The excitement of their previous discovery consumes him and any forward progress he has made in dealing with the loss.

The stolen notebook lays open in front of him with a new one by his side. His pen digs into the new pages as he scribbles notes while googling away, trying to break the code within the book. He no longer notices the wall-mounted clock loudly ticking away the seconds because his mind focuses on the task at hand. The dark circles under his eyes deepen with each passing hour, unable to remember if sleep eludes him for the second or third night in a row. His messy hair has transformed from playfully unkempt into greasy, scattered, and wiry like a mad scientist.

A slow twist of the knob and a cautious open follows a second unanswered knock as Ken peeks into Connor's bedroom. After seeing his son still awake and thoroughly distracted, he lets himself into his son's room.

"Came home early from work, Connor," he pauses, but Connor doesn't say a word. "You know why?"

Connor does not seem to even acknowledge his father's presence. Ken closes the door behind him.

"I got a call from your coach today. It's Saturday, Connor, and your coach called me," he says. Connor is still oblivious to his father's presence, too preoccupied with the notebook.

Ken realizes that talking will not break Connor's focus. So, he steps forward and slowly closes the notebook in front of his son. Connor looks up at his father with tired eyes and a paled face. "How've you been, son?"

Connor realizes for the first time this week exactly how long he's been working on this project. He rubs his eyes and yawns. "Tired. But I'm working on some stuff … for school."

Ken takes a seat next to him. "For school? The call I got said you hadn't been in school since Monday. That's one day this week you went. You missed the rest of the week. Is there something going on, son?"

Connor looks around his room before returning to his dad with a 1000-yard-stare. A passing thought of telling his dad what he found enters his mind, but then the following inevitable conversation pops into his head about myths and how these things are not real; about how Connor needs to accept the fact that Jack is dead. He doesn't want to have that conversation again. "Just been busy, dad."

"What are you working on there?" Ken asks, pointing to the notebooks

Connor scratches his head, unsure how to explain it if he were to explain it. He well knows the lunacy of telling your father that someone possibly killed your friend because somebody thought he was a vampire. "Just a project for school. Biology."

"Well, another string of unexcused absences and the colleges who've been eyeing you have noticed. You still want to play college ball, right?"

Connor nods his head. "Yeah. Of course, dad. Why? What's up?"

"That call I received from your coach was about that. Two colleges have taken their scholarship offers off the table in light of your behavior this year," Ken warns.

"Sorry," Connor apologizes.

"Don't apologize to me. It's your future. Once one or two colleges pull their offers, it won't be long before others start taking them off the table, too," Ken says. He puts his arm around his son. "I'm not mad. We are just concerned. Your mother and I... we worry about you. Not just us either, you know. Ever since Jack's death."

"You knew the Taylors too. But it's not just about them. You were mugged, and nothing's changed."

Ken stops to think. There is a look in his son's eyes. A quiet desperation tries to scream for help but doesn't know how. Ken knows his son will retreat from this conversation unless he plays his cards just right. If he does, then maybe Connor will finally talk with someone about what's been plaguing him.

"It's been a trying time for all of us. Between the Taylors and what happened to me. It's been hard," Ken says in an attempt to comfort his son.

"But you're on the city council. Can't you do something?" Connor pleads.

"What would you like me to do?" he says, adjusting to better face his son.

Connor stops because there's the rub. The implied question of every politician on every level. And Connor knows that for every answer someone inevitably offers, there are five reasons the proposed idea won't be a viable solution. So how can Connor answer that? What can he say that hasn't been said before? "I don't know, dad, but we have to do something to make it a better world."

"That's why I do what I do for the city. But what makes it safer for one person may not make it safer for another. Remember, in the 1940s, what one man disguised as supposedly making the world safer for some was nothing more than the slaughter of millions of others. So how do we make it safer for all? That's the question I struggle to answer every day. And the sad fact of the matter is, as you become an adult, it only gets harder."

Connor stares at the ground, exhausted and without response.

"In an ideal world, ideals would be all we need. But it's never that easy or simple." He stops to look at his son. A silent moment to try and empathize with the pain he is feeling.

"Son, I'm here for you. Whatever it is you are going through, believe me, I've heard it and been through it before. You can tell me."

But Connor can only think that his dad hasn't been through this before. His dad hasn't had friends stalked and killed by people who thought they were vampires. So how can he tell him what's really going on?

"I guess it's the realizations I am coming to that are hard. The things I'm learning that are real are hard to swallow," Connor admits most vaguely.

"I'm here for you. Just know that the strangest truths are still more real than the most believable fiction. Don't confuse the two over convenience."

"Thanks, dad. I promise come Monday, I'll be back in school. Head in the game and my future."

Ken scruffs his son's head, messing up his hair, as he stands up.

"I love you, Connor. Just remember what I said. I won't think you're lying just because it sounds strange."

Connor forces a tired smile. "Thanks, dad."

><><><><><><><><><><><><><><><><><><><><><

Vistrus and Tracy sit at the same corner table they did for their last meeting in this diner. The crowd here is unusually thin, which is okay with them. To help cover the signs of her mid-late second-tri-mester pregnancy belly, Tracy wears a loose, lightweight top and long, flowing scarves. Vistrus sits, dressed in his usual attire of jeans and a button-down dress shirt. The plates of egg, ham and cheese sandwiches in front of them sit half-eaten.

"What has your doctor said?" asks Vistrus as he chews on a French fry.

Tracy throws out her hands, palms up to him. "Nothing."

Vistrus' head falls in his left hand. His thumb presses against the outside of his left eye while his middle finger presses against the outside of the other eye. His pointer finger presses on his third eye chakra, trying to center himself. He knows he said something. She knows he said something. But Tracy telling Vistrus the doctor said nothing isn't going to move this conversation along any faster. He has a hard time believing that a doctor who's been practicing medicine for over a century said nothing. "Dr. Wong said nothing. He was silent the whole time you were in the room," Vistrus asks, looking back up to her. "He said nothing about development or health risks? Nothing at all?"

Tracy looks at Vistrus straight through his eyes. "Of course, he spoke. He's not one of the Sentinels."

Vistrus thinks for a moment. The slow pace at which Tracy relays information pecks away at his patience.

"And? What were his words?" he urges as he nibbles on his food.

"Acute symptoms in other diseases have been known to become chronic, but it's unlikely," she finally offers up.

"Good. What else?" Vistrus continues prying.

"That the undue stress on my body because of our … condition may cause some problems if complications develop, but otherwise, he said I should be good to go." She finishes with a bite of her food.

Vistrus feels that is little consolation for the current situation. "Have you told Ken yet?"

"No. He hasn't noticed anything yet," Tracy says.

He looks her over. "Are you sure? There are noticeable changes."

"I've been dressing more full coverage and avoiding intimacy, which works because he is still not feeling very secure in himself since the attack," she says, taking another bite.

"Okay. When visiting him at the hospital, I noticed changes in his demeanor. Very unsure of himself," Vistrus adds.

"Yup. And still like that a bit. He second-guesses himself at everything he does. And he's begun coddling Connor, who's got his own problems as of late," she says, cutting a would-be rant short.

"It is far enough along you can tell him when comfortable. When you do, though, keep it between you and him until you're too far along to hide," Vistrus advises.

He looks around the diner at the few patrons who are seated, enjoying their meals, oblivious to what is happening in a hidden world they don't know exists around them. He raises his hand to catch the waitress's attention and makes the motion of a check mark.

He looks back to Tracy. Her body language clearly states she is still not ready to wrap up this meeting. "What else is on your mind, Tracy?"

She looks around the restaurant watching the other patrons eat. She sees a few others who are people-watching as well. One of them happens to make eye contact with her causing her to look away, bringing her back to Vistrus.

"So much I still don't understand. The science. The why behind this. The fact that Ken's attackers still haven't been caught, let alone identified. My son, who's an A student and star athlete without trying, has sunk lower than not trying to not giving a crap. He's missed so much school ever since Jack died. I feel like my family is falling apart, and the timing of it all ... I think it's my fault, Vistrus. Like the fates are out to destroy my life."

He grabs her hand and brings it down to the table in comfort but lets go after a moment.

"It is not your fault. Do not confuse poorly timed coincidence for cause and effect. The rest of those things, bad as they may appear to you, are not related to your pregnancy," Vistrus assures.

Assure her he may try, but he knows that her worries, while misconnected, are not unfounded, and he doesn't have any good answers to give her. Partly because he shares her fears and partly because he knows neither of them fully understands the prophecy in all its vague ambiguity.

<hr />

Ken stands in front of his master bathroom sink while Tracy slips into her nightgown in the other room. A carefully timed act to avoid her husband seeing her forming a baby belly.

"He keeps saying he'll improve. He keeps saying that his head is back in the game, but I'm not seeing it," Tracy says as she slips a robe over her nightgown.

Ken spits out a mouthful of toothpaste foam. "I think he's finding out."

Tracy ties her robe as she steps into the bathroom. "How? Why would you think that?" She grabs her toothbrush and toothpaste and begins brushing.

"It's not like it's a bad thing. Not that I would think it," Ken defends.

She stops brushing and spits. "No. I just meant, what would cause you to think that our son's finding out?" She continues brushing.

Ken spits one last time and rinses his brush. Tapping it off and putting it away, he says, "I'm not sure, but ever since the Taylors were pronounced dead, he's been acting rather strange. Reclusive and always reading his schoolbooks."

"He's smart; he's studying," Tracy says, playing devil's advocate.

"Studying? When has he ever done that for more than twenty minutes at a time?" Ken retorts.

Tracy nods her head and spits again. "I need more. Otherwise, he's just getting senioritis."

"Senioritis?" Ken asks.

"The laziness that comes with knowing college is around the corner," Tracy explains. "If he is finding out, then we need to be there for him."

"I'm trying. But he's not talking. I can't make him talk, and asking him if he thinks he's a vampire or werewolf or whatever would sound completely crazy if he's not there yet," Ken says while flossing his teeth. "I'm not getting through, I don't think."

"Do you want me to try and say something to him?" she offers.

"No. I remember when my mom tried to talk to me about it. It was awkward. The whole thing sounded like she was talking about finally hitting puberty, but I was already nineteen."

Tracy laughs. "I can picture Eleanor having that talk with you. I would've loved to see that."

"That's what I mean. It was weird. Connor doesn't need that," Ken says but then pauses for a moment. "At least, I don't think he does. Maybe I'm wrong."

"So, what did you say?" Tracy asks as she slips into bed.

Ken walks into the bedroom from the master bath. "I told him that we're here for him and not to be afraid to come to us, even if it sounds unbelievable."

"Sounds perfect to me," Tracy assures.

"Now we just have to hope he has the courage to tell us," Ken says, slipping into bed and turning off the tableside lamp.

He lays down in bed facing his wife. She stares into his eyes, searching for the confident man she knew only a few months ago. She sees her husband. She sees the face of the man she loves, but the person inside is slowly slipping away. She doesn't know what to say that won't push him further. She doesn't know what she can do to restore the confidence the mugging beat out of him. Lying there, they stare into each other's eyes.

Neither one says anything; she smiles, leans into him, presses her lips to his, and closes her eyes. She kisses the man she knows is still inside, hiding in some safe corner needing a nudge to bring him out. After a moment, she lays back down, still staring into his eyes. The man she married is in there. He's just afraid. So she lays facing him in the darkened room—eyes connected as they fall asleep.

CHAPTER 15

"Troubling times are well met
by individuals of strong character.
Sometimes, though, those characters still fail."
~K. DeSalvo~

T he athletic conference room drowns in silence, despite the three different college representatives, coaches, Connor, Ken & Tracy seated at the table. The chill of the mid-December air creeps into the ordinarily nondescript conference room. An unnerving air of tension permeates the atmosphere, choking out all sound. The twelve eyes that stare at Connor pierce through him, trying to force out some response, some bodily action instead of his crossed arm, slouched-in-his-chair position that he currently holds stone-willed.

Connor looks at them all, stopping at each set of eyes, peering into them, trying to decipher the thoughts they hold within. His mother's eyes plead and beg that he return to who he was, the son who, as much as the teen boy said he didn't care and played the role, actually gave a crap because he knew the right thing to do. But what Connor wonders at this moment is why she has those eyes. Why do her eyes shine with such desperation for him? In his father's eyes, Connor finds a much more welcoming appeal. Within them, Connor sees a father who wants what's best for his son. A father who wants his son to do what makes him happy and will provide the best life for him. Connor nods at his dad before moving on. Like they always do, Coach's eyes read of an impending lecture with a finger pointed at his face, spitting about heart, love of the game, and life metaphors. All stuff Connor has heard a hundred times before.

The smile Connor shoots at his coach only causes the red on his face to deepen. It wasn't a condescending smile or one of rebellion. Just a smile to thank him for the almost four years of heart he put into coaching Connor and the rest of the team. Then Connor moves on to the three different college reps, one each from Ole Miss, Michigan, and a Wisconsin Badger. All three possess calm, collected confidence polished with annoying overtones of varying types of arrogance. All three know they will prevail over the other, not knowing for sure who will eventually win. He smiles at all three reps. His smile radiates something less than thanks.

Coach takes the floor. He pulls his chair into the table and hesitates, uncertain of his following words. He then slides his chair out, a dramatic move for the moment but decides, perhaps, a tad over the top for the occasion and pulls back in. He puts up his finger, pointing it at Connor as predicted, "We've had this talk before, and I hate that I have to repeat it, but your talent gives you a future. You're sitting on a winning lottery ticket, and none of us like seeing you throw it away."

Tracy interrupts, "He's right, baby. Ever since Jack died, you've stopped caring about school, grades, sports, and your future. Everything. All because no one ever found his body. We all knew the Taylors, son. You weren't the only one that lost someone when the news played the clip that day. You were the only one who hasn't realized life goes on."

Connor sits up in his chair. He knows his chance at a rebuttal is coming soon, so he prepares himself but doesn't say anything as the room quiets down. He watches the reactions of the three college scouts. They play their cards cool and wait for someone else to speak.

"Son," Ken starts, "we've tried letting you run with what you did to cope with the loss. We let you let your grades slip. We let you ignore your sports. We let you watch your future slip away as long as we could, but we can't let it slip away completely. That's why we are all here today."

The Wisconsin Badgers' representative throws his cards on the table. "We liked what we saw of you, and if you come with us, we can provide you with the future you want for yourself. But young Mr. DeSalvo, you have to work with us. Show us you want this. Give us something for our return. You have to get yourself in order, get your grades back up, get your performance on point for the season, and get your head in the game."

Connor nods his head in agreement, but something is unnerving in the half-smile on his face that worries his mother. It's a twinkle in his eye, accompanied by the half smile she recognizes. Ken stops Tracy before she says anything.

"I understand, sir. I've been a little lax lately. I can bring it around," Connor replies.

"Good," the Badger scout speaks up again. "I wouldn't want to see you throw away a bright future because of bad coping techniques."

Connor breaks out into laughter. Rage replaces the twinkle in his eye. His hands hit the table as he stands up. "Have you ever lost a friend, not just a friend but his whole family too? Have you ever walked into their house to find it tossed about with spurts of blood on the walls?" His voice slowly gets louder as his speech quickens. "No answers. No bodies. Nothing that actually points to death."

Connor looks the rep dead in the eye, waiting for a response. "Well, have you?"

The Wisconsin Badger rep looks away, shaking his head.

"No. You haven't. Not many people have," Connor continues as his voice starts to tremble, his head shaking. "No one able to tell you anything but then over the news, you have to hear that they've been declared dead. Do you know what that means? It means that within that given time frame, no one, nowhere, has found the bodies, but a coroner has signed their death certificate in presumption. That means my friend's body is rotting away somewhere, and I can't see him again, not once to say goodbye to my best friend. Who, by the way, was also on track for a scholarship, but now is God-knows-where not to get a proper burial. I can't see him. I can't get answers from anyone as to what happened. So sorry if my coping isn't good enough for you. Next time you accuse someone of having bad coping techniques, try putting yourself in their shoes first.

"You want bad coping techniques? I'll give you bad coping techniques." Connor flips off all three reps. "Here's your bad coping techniques." He waves his middle fingers in their faces, flipping about like an orchestral director ending an epic symphony while they all sit, jaws agape. "And for the record, suck *this* bad coping technique," he says, grabbing his crotch before walking out of the half-meeting, half-intervention.

His parents give the representatives an embarrassed courtesy smile and wave as they chase their son down the hallway.

"Connor! Hold it right there!" his father commands.

Connor stops in his tracks but doesn't turn around. He taps his foot, waiting for his parents to catch up.

"You can't do things like that and expect to have them offer you anything. That is not how one conducts themselves in those sorts of situations," his mother scolds.

"Okay, and how does one conduct themself?" Connor turns to his father. "Do you honestly think I care about baseball after what happened to you, dad? After what happened to Jack? There are bigger things in the world than hitting a ball with a stick," Connor fires off at them.

"Connor," his dad pleads, "what happens in the world is important and, yes, in the big scheme of things, more important than baseball. But baseball is what will allow you to concentrate on the things that are of more importance to you."

"No, dad. It's not that simple."

"I never said it was, son. But if you want to learn how to better the world so that things like what happened to me don't happen to others, then you have to learn to play ball with the right people. Shooting down those trying to help you get there is not how it's done."

Connor hugs his father. "It's just been such a shitty year, dad."

Ken pats Connor's back while hugging him. "I know. I know"

><><><><><><><><><><><><><><><><><><><

Tracy sits at the kitchen table, peering out the window at the orange night sky as the clouds pass over the moon. She holds one hand to her stomach, feeling the life growing inside her. A life she still hasn't told her husband about. At this moment, though, they discuss the other life they created. The defiant, almost-to-manhood life they named Connor.

Ken stands, his back to the counter, watching his wife peer out the window. Right now, he is trying to do that thing all husbands do—try to read her mind. He could ask, but that would interrupt the mile-long stare she has going on, and to him, her gaze is beautiful. He doesn't want to disturb it.

After a moment, she turns back in for the conversation. "Connor has to suspect something. This acting out, rebellion, disobedience, whatever you call it, isn't for nothing. Isn't just from coping with the loss of his friend."

Ken steps forward and starts pacing a few steps back and forth. "No, I'm afraid not." He stops pacing and takes a seat. "When Jack first disappeared, Connor went to his house."

"Why am I just finding out about this?" Tracy asks, mildly offended that Ken never said anything before.

"I didn't think it would get this far," Ken defends. "But what the news said, what we've all been told about the circumstances surrounding ... not what Connor saw."

"So what's going on, Ken?" she starts. "Could it be related to your attack? Is something going on in West Haven that threatens us, our way of life, my family?"

Ken shrugs. "I don't know. I would love to say, 'no, everything's wine and roses,' but the truth is, I don't know."

"Then what do we know about all this?" she asks with a hint of desperation.

"That our son's coping techniques may have stumbled onto something bad happening around here and hiding who he truly is from him as a means of protecting him may very well be the thing that gets him hurt?" Ken summarizes in brutal truth. "We may be overthinking this whole thing, and he's just going downhill from it all."

"So, we either tell him about his Legendary state and hope it doesn't get to his head, putting himself at risk—or chance endangering our son by keeping our mouths shut. These don't seem like good options."

"Welcome to the wonderful world of a city councilman," Ken quips.

"So, what do we do?" Tracy begs.

"If I knew, I would have done it already," Ken answers.

"Self-defeatist jokes won't help, honey. Seriously. We need to keep us safe if something is going on, and even if there isn't, we need to figure out what's happening with our son," Tracy says, a little bit of anger creeping into her voice.

"I don't know what to do." Ken's frustration grows. "I can't tell him what he is. He's young, and young kids tell everyone when they think something is cool. Everyone wants to be a damned super-hero nowadays, thanks to the movies. And telling people would put our world at risk," Ken says more rapid-fire, once again pacing the kitchen floor. "The scene he described at the Taylor's sounded like whoever it was broke through the wall and stole their 21-gram vials. I get confronted by people I couldn't take down. They were strong, strong people who knew what I was." He stops and looks at his wife. "I'm scared, Tracy. I've never been so scared, and I don't know what to do."

"Does the council know all this?" she asks.

He nods his head. "Yeah, but they are at a loss. Until something more happens and we can get definitive proof of what's happening, there's nothing they can do."

"Why not?" she implores.

"Because we can't just go out there and search for something that might not exist."

CHAPTER 16

"In life and love,
nothing is ever so simple in nature,
yet so complex in emotion as
a quiet moment between two people."
~E. DeSalvo~

K en opens the door to his home after a long day at work. He kicks the late December snow off his shoes and wipes the rest on the doormat inside the house. Taking off his coat with a little shiver as the cold leaves his body, he hangs it and his hat in the closet and sets down his briefcase next to his shoe bench. Before he calls out for Tracy, his ears have already picked up the distinct sound of a running shower. He heads toward the master bath and starts unknotting his tie. Thoughts of a romantic ending to his long day put a smile on his face and warmth in his heart. But as he unbuttons his shirt and enters the bathroom, Tracy turns the water off and opens the shower curtain. Surprised to see anyone there, she lets out a little shriek. Ken laughs at the expense of his wife's scare. She, too, laughs when she realizes who is there.

"I didn't hear you," she says, grabbing a towel.

Ken stares at his naked wife, both in admiration of the aesthetics but also at the pregnancy belly he estimates to be about five months along that she's been hiding for reasons yet unknown to him. "I was … going to make a romantic … gesture and … join you."

Tracy sees him looking at her stomach. "Words can be hard sometimes," she says as she finishes wrapping the towel around her.

"I guess," he responds.

"That's why I haven't told you," she starts.

"But how?" he inquires, still standing there with his shirt unbuttoned.

Tracy dries herself off and heads into the bedroom, Ken in tow, quietly waiting. She starts getting dressed in soft, cotton pajamas for the night.

"I was scared. I knew it shouldn't be, so I didn't know what to do. I went to Vistrus because he's on the council," she begins with meek words.

"So am I, my love. You could have come to me," he says, half-irritated, half-worried.

"So many things ran through my mind. Was I going to be in danger? Was I going to put you and Connor and Scarlett in danger if I told you? And of course, the big question of how was I pregnant again," she says, finishing buttoning up her sky blue pajama top with white clouds.

"I understand, I guess. You did what you thought was right. I just wish that you thought coming to me was right."

She sits down on the bed next to Ken. She wraps her arms around him. "I wanted to. I wanted to come to you so badly. I was just so unsure about a lot of things. And after Vistrus and I talked, some of those things were not completely unfounded. But now you know."

Ken nods his head as he stares at her stomach. Unsure thoughts are passing through his mind of everything she fills him in on, from the prophecy to all their concerns.

"I'm just so glad you finally found out," she sighs in relief.

"I don't know how I've been so blind," he relents.

"You've been distant. We haven't held each other in, well," she looks down at her belly, "about five months."

"How do we tell the kids?" Ken asks in earnest.

Tracy shakes her head. "We don't. Not until we must. I'll wear baggy clothes, keep covered as I can. Do whatever I must in order to keep it hidden. Not that I want to, but with the state of things."

Ken nods his head in agreement. "I understand." He holds his wife as a silence falls over them.

A calmness fills the room. The past months of tension, chaos, uncertainty, and coming changing times all stand still right at this moment. They hold each other, not wanting to let go. Neither of them wants to let this moment slip away. This moment they haven't felt with each other since it all began.

The serenity of the right here and now carries away the doubt in Ken's mind about not being the father he needs to be. Tracy's worries about her pregnancy, everything she felt she had to hide from her husband because of his position in the city and the council, drift away in this momentary sea of tranquility.

They hold each other, feeling the years they've spent together, the joy and fear of it all, the uncertainty of some moments, and the happiness and clarity of others. In the other person is the hopes and dream of the collective two. The life they longed for since they started dating in high school many, many, many years ago, far more than looks would tell.

The immeasurably long future they have together all comes to this moment and how they feel while in each other's arms. And they don't want to let go because outside the bedroom doors, tonight, tomorrow, and the next day is the reality that she is pregnant with a Legend.

And more so than just a miracle child, a prophesied Legend to not only rejoin the fractured DNA of two closely related Legends but to also give The Nation a chance, after countless centuries of hiding and creating campfire stories to help stay out of sight, a reason to come forward. A reason to not fear what the rest of the world will say because what they will have to offer as a whole will be far greater than any negative spin, prejudice, or unfounded fear can bring forth.

So for now, for just a few moments more, they hold each other in their arms, her head resting on his shoulder. He cups his hand around her neck, and they breathe slowly, enjoying the moment of pure happiness that eludes so many in life.

CHAPTER 17

Christmas

"Holidays are a time for family.
Blood relative or not,
they are a time for those close to us."
~V. Petrovsky~

K en, Tracy, and Vistrus sit in the family room. A fake tree decorated with blue and silver lights helps brighten the dimmed room. A warm, half-eaten apple pie sits on the table, begging for someone to finish it. Each adult sips a glass of wassail, discussing the events of the past year and the presents they've received. They pick at the remaining pie crumbs on their plates. A soft orange glow fills the air from the fireplace as the crackle of wood fills the background with quiet noise.

Connor sits against the foot of Scarlett's bed as Allison drapes herself over the edge of the bed next to him. Scarlett sits upright against the headboard.

Connor flips through pictures on his phone of him and Jack goofing off and being silly. He comes across one of the four of them from last year's Homecoming. All four dressed to the nines for a dance they thought they would repeat this year. Allison slowly reaches down and takes his phone, setting it on the bed next to her.

"I have a gift for you, Con," Allison says with an unsteady voice.

Scarlett moves forward to the edge of the bed. "Um, should I be leaving my room for this present?"

Allison laughs. "No. I've been looking over the notebook, trying to figure out the where of it all."

Connor turns to her, hoping to hear some good news.

Allison continues, "Now, you already said you've accepted the fact that he is dead." She pauses, waiting for a reaction from him.

He nods his head a few times in short bursts. "Yeah, I know."

"Okay, so I've been waiting for tonight since all our parents are together and busy, and generally, a holiday like today, people are preoccupied with other things," Allison rambles.

Scarlett has shifted to the other side of Connor. "Tell us what, Al?"

"I think I found it," she says matter-of-factly.

Connor's eyes widen as he shoots up from his seated position. "You better not be messing with me, Allison."

She shakes her head and her open-palmed hands. "No messin'. I swear." She gets up and heads out the bedroom door. "One sec."

Connor and Scarlett just stare at each other.

"Did you know about this?" Connor inquires.

Scarlett shrugs. "No idea. She did this of her own accord."

A moment later, Allison enters the room, notebook in hand, her finger holding a page ready to be shown. She plops back down and opens the book.

"I kept seeing North over and over again. I thought it was just a reference to the direction. It made no sense," Allison starts.

"Me neither. Either. Whatever. It kept referencing North, but it sounds like nonsense," Scarlett adds.

"Exactly," says Allison, "but here's what I figured out."

Connor sits with eager eyes, waiting for the mystery to reveal itself.

"The answer was in the adjectives. It made a reference to 'The Old North' once, earlier in the notes. At first, I thought it was some Southern vs. Yankee thing we kept missing. But then I was watching an old movie at work and saw a preview for *The Breakfast Club*, and I remembered Maine North," Allison explains.

Connor raises his hand. "What am I missing here?"

"Maine North is where *The Breakfast Club* was filmed," Allison says, moving her story along.

"The one in Niles," Connor interjects. "That closed down years ago and turned into a state police station."

"Exactly!" she excitedly shouts.

"I hate to be the voice of reason, but we're not driving what'll take an hour or more in the unplowed snow to break into a state trooper station," Scarlett clarifies.

Allison shakes her head vigorously. "No. No. No. North Haven."

A look of disappointment draws across Connor's face.

"Wait, Al. They tore that down before we were born."

"I know. But you're not all correct. They tore almost all of it down. Keywords, *mon frère*. Keywords. Ever wonder why they never built a mall or some crap over the old site?"

Scarlett and Connor look at each other, unsure of what to think.

"Look," Allison says, pointing again to the notebook. "The word Base is used in a few contexts. Sometimes in relation to the DNA codes we've found. Other times to refer to the North. If 'The Old North' references the same place as the rest of the Norths..."

A smile breaks out across Connor's face. "That's gotta be it," he gasps. "So, what's our next move?" he says, still smiling.

"You guys are nuts if you think you are going to go to an old, torn down, dilapidated building to try and find where Jack died," Scarlett starts, then pauses mid-thought.

Connor and Allison both give her puppy dog eyes and whimper.

Scarlett continues her thought. "...without me."

With a reactionary fist pump, Connor shouts, "Yes!"

Allison stops them. "Wait. What the hell do we tell our parents?"

"Heading out to a movie. Movies are always open on Christmas," Connor offers up.

Scarlett plays the devil's advocate, "What if they want to join us?"

"Psychopaths," Connor says with a bit too much excitement.

"They may be a little strange, but I wouldn't call Aunt and Uncle psychopaths," Scarlett jokes.

"It's a movie and one they're guaranteed not to want to see with us," Connor says, defending his choice.

"Sounds good," Allison finishes. "Let's go!"

As they open the door to head on out, Ken takes notice. "Where are you three headed?"

"Movie, dad," Connor says, keeping his answers short.

"Please be careful driving in this cold. It can be bad for the car," Ken's fatherly tone takes control.

"Enjoy! Do you need some money for snacks?" Tracy offers up, reaching into her husband's wallet.

Scarlett hops over to her aunt and takes the $20 bill. "Thanks!"

The three close the door behind them as they head to Connor's car.

"Why did you take the money? We're not actually going to the movies," Allison states.

"Maybe not, but who are we to turn down a twenty? Plus, snacks!" Scarlett exclaims.

><><><><><><><><><><><><><><><><><><><><><><><><

The wet winter roads, damp with snowfall, glisten from the moonlight above. The empty streets sit in an eerie, silent aura that adds to the mixed excitement and fear that each of the three teenagers feels during the drive. The roads are salted, making for an easy journey. Though strangely enough, no one spots any salt trucks in either direction. The few cars they pass have headlights that seem to shine a blinding light, a silent pleading for the teens to turn around. The teens do not complain that this Christmas night is quieter than others. They don't say much. The excitement of the possibility they felt in the warmth of the bedroom has turned to a silent, cold realization that they might stumble upon nothing, or worse, find a family rotting away in a basement.

If they are right about the location, Connor might get some closure as to how his friend died, Allison will have played the hero in cracking the code, and Scarlett will get to bear witness to the event. But right now, away from the outdoor cold in the car's heat, it doesn't seem like much consolation. They all stare ahead into the night.

They pull into a parking lot about a half block away from the old remains of North Haven High. The crumbling structures of what little remains after the demolition offers a foreboding presence in the night. But the trees that sprinkle the property grow dense toward the old auditorium entrance once used for the fine arts department.

They exit the car's semi-warmth into the cold night. As the lights from their vehicle fade, leaving them in darkness. The sounds of leaves falling and small animals rummaging for food and a warm place to sleep all around them fill their ears. But all these sounds amplify in their minds. They hear the footsteps of a man instead of the pitter-patter of scavenging squirrels, bricks hitting concrete instead of falling leaves. They all look at each other and take a deep breath. Now it is real, and they can't turn back.

After a careful dash to not slip and fall on the slippery, icy ground, they make it safely to the fence surrounding the property. Scarlett spots a cut in the chain-link fence they easily slip through. As they tread further through the thicket of trees onto the old high school grounds, they notice that the entrance to the auditorium still stands a short distance ahead. The roof may have caved in a bit, but it makes them wonder what's inside.

They approach the exterior entrance and stop before moving any further. "There's not much left of this place," observes Scarlett.

"No, there's not," agrees Allison. "But this has to be the place. It's the only thing that makes sense from the notes."

"Agreed, but even if it's not, we're here now," chimes in Connor.

"No turning back now." Scarlett heeds her warning.

"But where in there?" ponders Connor. "It's a mess and in ruins."

Allison pulls out her phone and starts typing away.

"Not really a great time to be checking Facebook, Al," Scarlett says.

Allison shakes her head while making a twisted face at Scarlett. "Not checking, Scar. Looking for blueprints, pictures, something that will help." She taps her phone a few times, sticking her tongue out and to the side. "And here."

"What?" Connor urges.

"Surprise, surprise. The old auditorium had a basement for the theater: dressing rooms, storage, workshops. That has to be it. Through the doors," Allison says, barely able to contain her excitement.

She puts her phone back in her pocket and tugs on the door of the auditorium entrance. To their surprise, they find it unlocked.

Allison holds the door open, waving Connor in first. "After you, good sir."

Connor tips an invisible hat in her direction and enters. Scarlett follows, and Allison last. She takes one final look outside before letting the door shut.

The mold that lines the damp corners of this place fills their nose with a musty smell. But, even in the darkness, they can see a well-traveled path that leads to a side door.

"That has to be it!" Allison whispers.

Connor stops walking and grabs onto the girls. "I don't think this is a good idea anymore."

Scarlett looks him in the eyes. "What's going on, Cuz?"

"It's just… I mean, what if we find more than we bargained for?" he says, doubting all the work put into this.

"This is what you wanted. This is what you said you needed to help you with his loss, your grief, everything," Scarlett reminds him in a gentle whisper.

"I know, but what if there's nothing there? What if, like I said a minute ago, that the notes, the codes… what if we're wrong?" Connor says, sinking further into self-doubt.

"If you don't want to do this, then we won't," Allison assures him.

Scarlett turns to both of them. "Fine, there may be nothing there. But we knew that going into this whole thing that nothing may come of it. So the question is, what if there is something? Are you ready for real closure? Because you've all but thrown away your future for this, Connor. To turn back now would make everything you did pointless. Is that what you want?"

Connor starts visibly shivering. "No, it's not what I want!" he says, trying not to yell. "What I want is my friend back! What I want is not to have gone through what I've gone through for the past few months. To not have seen the things I saw at his house, been told the things I was told."

Allison chimes in, "But you can't take all of that back. You can't change what happened to you."

"So the question is, how do you deal with it now? Are you ready to move forward?" Scarlett asks her cousin. "It's not exactly warm in here, so make a decision."

Connor takes a deep breath and stares at the side door looming before him. He knows what he must do but as with anything, taking the first step is hardest. The girls wait, also starting to shiver in the cold. But they wait for him; they cannot force him to make a move he isn't ready for. So they stand behind him, waiting. He takes another deep breath and, as he exhales, steps toward the side door.

The door is locked. The path to and from it has been trodden many times recently. He feels his heart race as the handle refuses to turn, the cold steel against his hand. Steel that is a bit too clean and dust-free to be in these shambled surroundings. He looks for hinges, but they are on the other side of the door. He pulls on the knob, trying to break through the old wood but is unsuccessful.

Tears of frustration start falling from his eyes. His face turns redder with each shoulder ram and yank against the handle in feeble attempts to break open the lock. He lets out a scream of anger because nothing will budge. Someone has taken great pains to make this door more durable than it would appear to need to be. He kicks the door a few times in vain. He stops his efforts and gives into frantic frustration.

"This isn't how this is going to end! There's something in there! Something that we're right about! Something! I need to get in!" Connor shouts in frustration at his friends.

The girls sit there, knowing he isn't yelling at them but venting about what is possibly the last roadblock toward healing. He turns his back to the door and slides down in defeat. Allison moves in and puts her arm around him, sitting on the cold ground next to him. His head is between his knees as he tries to gather himself, but Allison's attention is on Scarlett, who looks around the room. Scarlett walks over to a shadowed corner and picks up a chunk of wall or ceiling; she's not sure which. But it's small enough to hold in two hands and weighty enough to be a struggle for her.

She takes it back to Connor, still buried in himself. "If there's no knob, the door can't be locked."

Connor slowly lifts his head to look at Scarlett, unsure what she just meant. Upon seeing her holding a chunk of concrete, a slow smile crosses his face. Making his way back to his feet, Connor brushes off the dirt from his jeans and takes the rock. Heavy in one hand but manageable, he starts smashing it into the doorknob, over and over.

Each connecting strike is a blow against everyone who told him he was wrong. Each time the chunk clings against the knob is another time he feels vindicated for his past behaviors. The few strikes turn into many as the metal slowly gives way under the repeated bashing. The jagged concrete cutting into his hand causes warm blood to trickle down, cooling in the winter air. Each strike enrages Connor more and more. As he strikes with greater force, the girls see veins in his face start to bulge. Veins that previously had not been noticeable. His grunts with each strike turn into growls. Veins begin protruding from his arms, coursing and pulsating with blood. The shadows in the low light make him look more feral and wild with each passing second. The girls look at each other, unsure and scared of what they see happen to him.

He continues bashing away at the failing knob, each strike making him a little less human in the shadowy moonlight.

Allison taps him on the shoulder. "Hey, Con. You all right?"

He turns to her, his face cloaked by moving shadows and nighttime cloud cover, but she shudders at the sight. Fangs. Fangs that shouldn't be there glint at her. Shadows couldn't make that sort of thing. Varicose veins make him look more like a steroid-abusing bodybuilder about to have an aneurysm than the cute guy she knows. He lets out a growling grunt and snaps back to the door, giving the knob one last hard blow and knocking the metal to the ground.

He takes a deep breath as the knob rolls away. He turns back to the girls, sans all signs of the angry, vein-covered hulk they thought they saw with fangs to spare. He is Connor. Calm and happy that he gets to move forward.

He tosses the rock aside and enters the dark corridor beyond the door. The girls are apprehensive about the events taking place. But it is dark, and the darkness makes things look stranger than they are. To help them curb that from happening again, Allison pulls out her cell phone and turns on her flashlight—a little illumination in the otherwise dark place. As Connor moves forward, the two girls look at each other, a silent agreement between them on the unsure weirdness they just witnessed happen to their Connor.

At the end of the short, dark hall is one door, closed but not locked, from underneath which a dim light shines through. Connor puts his ear to the door to listen. As he concentrates and focuses more and more, he hears breathing.

"Anything?" asks Scarlett.

He shakes his head. "All I hear is our breathing and some sort of beeping."

Allison steps forward. "Let's do this then."

Connor nods in agreement and twists the knob, opening the door to a room lit by an old, hanging shop light with a flickering neon bulb. A table sits in the middle under the flickering light. A few notebooks closed on the table have the same front covers: black with white speckles. Medical devices line the walls: heart monitors, intravenous monitors, hoses, and breathing masks, all beeping and making subtle noise. One lone, metal cabinet is close to the door, next to which are three hospital gurneys. The three youths stopped in the doorway at the sight of the room, not from everything they just saw but what they now see against the walls, chained, gagged, and listless—Jack and his parents. All three shackled to the wall by their arms, hanging, heads limp. The monitors give the only clue that any of them are still alive, a notion that clicks in Connor's mind.

"They're not dead!" he says, rushing to his best friend's side.

Scarlett and Allison follow in. Connor holds Jack, trying to stir him. "These chains! There's gotta be a way to open them!" Connor says to the girls who are already looking around. Connor gently pats Jack's face trying to wake him up. "Come on, Jack! Come on! I know you're still in there."

The girls return to Connor with a set of keys in hand. "They were in that cabinet," Scarlett says, trying key after key to unlock the chains.

Connor continues holding his friend. "Al, see if you can find some liquid."

She looks around but doesn't see a supply of water or anything wet anywhere. She turns to the IVs hooked up to Jack. She takes it down and, possessing no medical knowledge, slides the needle out of his arm. The liquid from the bag starts flowing out the hose as she throws the hypodermic onto the floor. Allison squeezes it over Jack in an attempt to wake him up.

Scarlett tries another key on the keychain and turns it. A click in the lock and the chains open. His arm falls limp, open sores and bruises from the chains around his wrists. She unlocks the other chain, freeing him from his bonds. Allison continues to spray his face trying to wake him up.

"Get his parents. I got this, Al."

She nods and helps Scarlett unchain his parents. A short minute or two later, and all three of them now lay on the gurneys, resting comfortably for perhaps the first time in months.

The three look at each other in amazement at their accomplishment, searching for a clue what to do next. Connor looks at his friend lying on the table and starts crying in relief.

"What now?" Asks Allison.

Connor gets out his cell phone and calls his dad. "Hey, dad," he pauses for a moment, tears running down his face. "No, we didn't make it to the movies." Again he pauses. "Yes, we're fine. But dad, don't be mad. Please, I need your help." He takes a deep breath, trying to collect himself.

Scarlett and Allison can hear Ken through the phone receiver asking a slew of questions. Each is an eternity for the teen who wants nothing more than to interrupt, but Connor patiently waits for a break in his father's barrage.

"We found Jack."

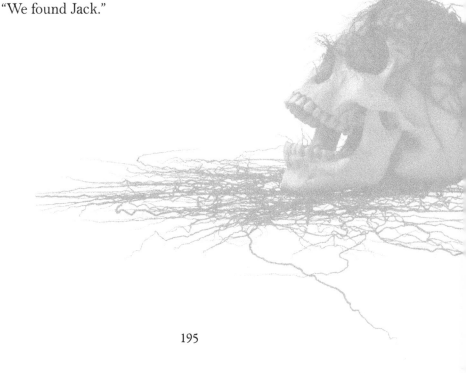

CHAPTER 18

"Coming home is the hardest thing.
No matter what has stayed the same,
everything is different."
~S. Waldgrave~

Connor sits by Jack's side as he lays in a hospital bed. Jack sleeps peacefully, still recovering from the months of unknown traumas. Armed security stands outside the hospital room doors. The festive mood of the approaching New Year outside the room provides a stark contrast to the sobering reminder of what humanity's worst are capable of inside the room.

"What a nightmare it must have been for you, bud," Connor says to his sleeping friend. "I wish I had been able to find you sooner. But you're here now." He pauses to look around the hospital room decorated with balloons, flowers, and get-well-soon cards. "Something big is going on here. If our work spent on the code is right, someone thought you were a vampire."

As Connor says, "vampire," Jack uncomfortably shifts. He stays asleep, but Connor knows he heard him.

"Whatever is going on in West Haven is big, my man. And somehow, you got caught in the center of it. But we'll figure it all out," he says as mixed tears of joy and sorrow cascade down his cheeks.

Connor watches Jack sleep, amazed that they were able to save him. He's unsure of what else to say to him. He hopes Jack hears him. He feels more sure after Jack stirs a bit, but still, he hopes. He wonders what he's been through the past few months, what he's endured. He wants Jack back and for it to be the way it was.

"So, you missed homecoming. That was something. Allison and I kissed. Scarlett was with us, but she just danced a lot." His heart rate monitor shows an increased heart rate at the mention of Scarlett's name.

"She said it was nothing, but I think it was something. So there's that." He watches the monitor as Jack's heart rate returns to normal.

"We found you. I may have lost my scholarship offers, but I don't care. We found you. I hope it hasn't been as bad as it looked. But then again, it wouldn't have looked so bad if it wasn't."

The nurse on duty pokes her head in the doorway and knocks gently. "How's he looking?"

Connor turns to the nurse. "Good. Stirred a bit but still sleeping."

The nurse smiles and looks at the clock. "Visiting hours' almost up. You can come back tomorrow."

"I know. One more minute."

The nurse nods. "Of course."

Connor puts his hand on Jack's shoulder. "I don't want you to think I did some big noble thing by mentioning my lost scholarships. I don't care about those. I was trying to make conversation." He pauses, taking a long look at Jack's bruised and battered body. "I'll see you soon. Happy new year, bro … Happy new year."

><><><><><><><><><><><><><><><><><><><><><

Connor exits the hospital lobby, leaving the festive New Year decorations that brighten the otherwise sterile decor behind him as he enters the parking garage. Making his way to his car, he hears footsteps behind him. He turns around to steal a glance at the person heading in the same direction.

"Hey! I remember you!" Nurse Practitioner Scott says in an overly friendly voice.

"Um, hi," Connor says, unsure how to respond.

"Is your father healing okay? I know it's been a while, but he seemed to be recovering faster than normal," Scott says, a tad too intrusive for Connor.

"Oh, well, you know. Just taking it a day at a time." Connor forces out a smile.

"If he still doesn't feel a hundred percent, tell him to come see me. He was such an interesting guy," he says with a side-to-side head bob.

"Yeah. Thanks," Connor says, turning back and continuing to his car. But all he can think about are the countless patients this Scott guy has had since. He pontificates that this guy has way too much interest in his father. Connor thinks, *What kinda medical professional calls another person interesting like that? Especially in front of someone who cares about them?*

All those thoughts cause Connor to quicken his step to get away from the nurse. He turns a corner and looks back, but Scott is nowhere. He enters his car and heads home for the New Year countdown.

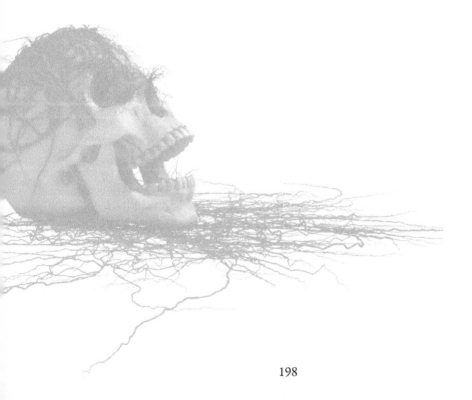

CHAPTER 19

"Birthdays.
Celebrate them
because you never know
if you'll see your next one."
~T. DeSalvo~

Connor, Allison, and Scarlett all sit in Jack's hospital room, laughing at the joyous occasion that is January 3rd—Connor's 18th birthday. Guards still stand a vigilant watch outside the door. Jack sits upright in his bed. He is awake and alive with open eyes, but he stares off, lost in some vague thought, looking for something that is not there. The laughter around him alerts him to something someone said, something he should possibly be laughing along with, but he can't. A thick fog coats the world around him, surreal after all the time away.

"We're just glad to have you back, man," Connor says, catching Jack's attention. His mind's fog blurs everything from moments before. Jack forces out a smile, knowing that whatever Connor said, he said with good intentions.

"Thank you." Jack's reply is as dry as stale toast. His thoughts drown in the pain of the previous months.

"There's still a few days left of Winter break, and I don't know when you plan on going back to school, but I'll help you catch up when you're ready," Scarlett says, trying to make Jack feel a little normal again. She notices he is staring off. "Is that okay?" she asks, waving to him.

Jack looks through her and nods. "Yeah, uh... sounds good."

Scarlett sees Jack's eyes. She sees him looking at everything but seeing nothing as if he's looking for stuff that's not there.

"Hey, guys. Can you wait outside for a second? I need to talk to Jack," Scarlett says, much to the confusion of her cousin.

Allison sees the absence in Jack's stare that Scarlett sees and taps Connor on the shoulder. "Come on, let's give her a minute," she says while her head motions to the door.

Scarlett sits on the bed next to Jack. Unsure if he is in the moment with her or lost in thought, she exercises caution when resting her hand on his. His eyes shoot to her. He sees her, not looking past her but at her through his mental fog. For a moment, he is here, with her.

She whispers to him, "I don't know what you went through. And honestly, unless you want to talk about it, you don't have to tell anyone. You don't owe anyone anything."

He looks at her and his eyes start to well up with tears. She squeezes his hand.

"You are safe now. Whatever happened, it's over, and we will help you deal ... when you are ready," Scarlett assures.

She pauses for a moment to look into his eyes. She sees despair within him that wasn't there before. She slips her other hand under his, holding his hand between both of hers.

"Connor wanted to be with his best friend since it's his birthday. But we never thought to ask you. We just figured..." She trails off. "What can I do for you?"

Jack stares at her for a moment. His heart monitor picks up a slightly quickened heart rate. He breathes in and out, trying to slow himself down. A tear falls from his eye as he tries to hold back the rest.

"Thank you for, you know, what you guys did," he says.

Scarlett responds with a few, subtle nods, not wanting to speak for fear of interrupting him. She does dry his tear with her finger.

"I, uh, I need my parents. I need to talk to my parents."

"Let me talk to a nurse, and we'll get you to them. Can you walk?"

He nods.

×°°°°°°°°°°°°°°°°°°°°°°°°°°°×

Jack hugs his parents for the first time since being rescued. He moves between both parents' beds, hugging them over and over.

He doesn't say anything but holds onto them like a small child clinging to a parent.

"He said he needed you," Scarlett says to Mr. and Mrs. Taylor.

Lucretia looks up at Scarlett. "Thank you. It's been hard for him."

Scarlett looks to the ground, knowing she can't even imagine what he went through. "For you too, I'm sure," she adds.

Lucretia realizes how she said her last words and quickly makes amends. "Of course. Yes. Us too."

Scarlett hears her but senses something is not right with Mrs. Taylor's correction; like when a friend doesn't hide a lie to cover something up, it is unspoken not to delve deeper. For a quick moment, Scarlett thinks there may be something more to this than a random kidnapping of an entire family.

"Come here, son," James says, patting his bed. "Sit."

Jack lets go of his mother and walks his saline IV bag on its metal stand over to his father's bed.

James looks at Scarlett and the others standing outside the door. "We need some time to talk with our son, please."

Scarlett looks up from the floor. "Of course, whatever you need, Mr. Taylor. We'll be outside."

"Thank you all for visiting him. Please feel free to come back tomorrow," James asks.

Jack turns to Scarlett, who forces out a smile as she leaves. She nods at all three of the Taylors. "Of course. My apologies." She exits, and the other two follow.

James turns to his son. "We have to explain some things to you, don't we?"

Jack stares at his father; the thoughts and images from the past months replay in his head, haunting and tormenting him. "What did they, well, make you? What did they make me? What did they do to me?"

James smiles in a vain attempt to comfort his son. He rubs his hands together while he thinks.

"Son," he starts before stopping again for a few moments. The thoughts in his head do not form as clear as he'd like. "They tortured us, yes. They did things to us that I will not speak of again until you are ready to talk. But..." he stops. His thoughts once again become unclear in his mind. "They didn't make us anything."

Jack looks down from staring at the ceiling, turning his blank stare to his father, unsure what he should think. "But the pain, the teeth, the veins," Jack says in short bursts.

Lucretia chimes in, "Jack, my love. This isn't how we wanted you to find out. It's supposed to be a natural occurrence. A surprising one, but natural. When your body was ready. They forced it out of you, took something from you that you will never get to experience again for the first time."

Jack shakes his head slowly. "Well, I don't understand."

James holds his son's hand. "It's not a virus like they say in all the books and movies. We hold no more capacity for evil than any other human. We also hold the same compassion and kindness as any other human because we are human."

Jack keeps shaking his head, lost in the words he hears.

"The legends that define us, our kind. They are based on fear and misunderstanding. But like all legends, their roots hold some truth," Lucretia says.

Jack raises an eyebrow as an internal light bulb slowly flickers to life in his head. "Mom?"

She smiles at her son. "Your father and I have reflections, we can eat garlic, go out in the sun, kind of, and while a stake to the heart will kill us, a piece of wood through anything's heart will kill it." She pauses, letting the words sink into her son's mind. "A silver bullet will kill you. But so will most other bullets."

James takes the floor. "We don't need permission to enter a house any more than is common courtesy and respect for not entering someone's home who doesn't want you there." He watches as Jack's slow head shaking gradually turns into a slow head nod. "The truth in the legends is that the tidal pull of the full moon will affect you more than other nights."

"There are those in the world," Lucretia says, "that think we are of legendary gods. Some immortal beings. But we can die. We can feel pain. But we are stronger. We are faster. And what makes us hide who we are from the rest of the world is that we are different, Jack."

Jack takes a deep breath. A lot of the past few months start to make a little more sense. He rises from his father's hospital bed and stands between his parents.

James takes the handoff in the speech, "We are different because of our diseases…"

Lucretia cuts him off, "Conditions, James. I don't like that word."

James looks at his wife. "An asthmatic may have a lung condition," he says with air quotes, "but the CDC and WHO still quantify asthma as a disease."

"We can't infect others with it," Lucretia says, getting back on track. "It's not a virus. It's not in the blood. It's in the genes. The genetics."

Jack sits there, shaking his head in disbelief. "No. I'm not some monster. Not me. Some monster, freak of nature, vampire. I'm a kid. A, um, normal, about-to-be 18-year-old kid who just wants to put all this, well, behind him."

James lets out a small chuckle. "This is exactly how I felt when I first transitioned all those years ago. It's okay to feel this way, Jack. It's a lot to take in."

Lucretia chimes in, trying to add a moment of levity, "You are not a vampire, Jack."

He lets out a sigh of relief. "Oh, thank God."

"You're a werewolf," his mom finishes.

"Lucretia," James reprimands, "we know better."

Lucretia shares a well-needed chuckle with her husband.

Jack paces back and forth in a small circle, scratching his head. "But it hurt so bad. So bad." Just the thought of it brings a tear to his eye.

"It gets easier, love," Lucretia says, trying to calm him. "Less painful over time, but it does stay uncomfortable."

Jack takes several long moments to let all of this information sink in. He continues pacing the floor, looking down at the tiles while organizing his puzzle-pieced thoughts. After a few mind-hurting moments, he takes his left hand and rubs his eyes.

"So, I'm … immortal?" Jack throws the thought out there.

"No," James says, shaking his head. "A Legend."

Jack now rubs his head with both hands, trying to wrap his mind around these thoughts.

"Why don't you sit back down, Jack?" James says. Without thinking about it, he does. He sits at the foot of his mom's hospital bed.

They all sit in silence for a bit while Jack attempts to comprehend the reality of the situation.

"How? How the hell did we become … these things?" Jack asks.

James looks at his son with a furrowed brow. "We were born this way. We didn't become anything; we always were."

"Then, what is it? What is this disease or CONDITION, or whatever?" His voice back to his usual fluctuation in volume.

Lucretia smiles, knowing that her son is starting to grasp the gravity of who he is, which means that he may begin to understand and, she hopes, accept.

"Vampires, the Legends with a capital L, get their roots from a blood disorder called Porphyria, specifically Erythropoietic Porphyria. But that's just the beginning. Genetics are a funny thing. There was a man named Joseph Merrick, an intelligent, kind man who just happened to be born with numerous genetic mutations. Not just one or two but numerous," Lucretia begins, with Jack listening intently. "Sometimes you hit a genetic lottery, and it doesn't work in your favor as he died young. Sometimes you play the lottery and win. But just like the real lottery, if you want to survive after the winnings, you don't flaunt it. You stay who you were before you won."

She watches as Jack nods along, finally grasping the situation.

"Vampires, werewolves, others, all genetic mutations that happen to work in our favor," she continues. "We don't call ourselves those names, though."

Jack throws out his arms like an umpire signaling someone safe in a close call. "Wait! Wait! Wait! Hold on a minute," Jack begins to laugh at the ludicrousness of the moment. "First, you tell me you and dad are vampires. Then you tell me I'm a werewolf. Now you are telling me we don't say those names and that other kinds exist?! I uh, suppose next are, well, fairies and zombies."

James and Lucretia both look at each other and smile but say nothing. Jack sees them and knows they are holding back.

"You guys need, like, help. Like serious medication and therapy. Life isn't *True Blood* and *Buffy* and *Blade*. Is this some joke, some scheme to make me feel better about what happened?" Jack starts up.

James shuts the privacy curtain around them. "Jack, listen to me. Look at me."

Jack watches as the veins in his father's forehead start bulging out and pulsating. He watches as his father's hairline starts to stretch and thin, and his nose starts to shrink, turning purplish-black. His teeth begin to recede into his gum line.

"Stop, dad! Just stop!" Jack pleads as he looks away.

"That's enough, honey," Lucretia demands.

James starts his slow transition to his normal state. "That's genetics. That's what we are, son. With that also comes some bonuses."

"Bonuses?" Jack reiterates.

"We have great hearing and increased strength, increased speed," James continues.

Jack interrupts, "Tell me I'm not going to start sparkling. I don't want to sparkle."

Lucretia laughs. "We don't sparkle, love."

"But how? What, um, lottery winnings do we have that make us these … things?" Jack asks, still not satisfied with the answers so far. "How, if it's genetics, are you and dad vampires, and I'm a werewolf?"

"Well, besides EPP, or Erythropoietic Porphyria, which is the basis of the legend of vampires, we also have what is called Myostatin-related muscle hypertrophy," Lucretia continues.

James interjects, "Which gives us all our strength. That condition, as well as others involved in more than one Legend, allows us to be vampires and you, not."

Lucretia nods. "Yes. And our lovely teeth form fangs because of Hypohidrotic Ectodermal Dysplasia."

"Wait a second," Jack chimes in. "I saw a special on the Discovery channel about that disease. And because of baseball and anti-drug videos, I know about myostatin and muscles. None of those are diseases that just pop up, like, well, as dad mentioned earlier, asthma."

"Excellent, Jack. You're right," James confirms. "The conditions are asymptomatic in Legends until the AIP and FNAH act up."

"What is AIP and FN whatever?" Jack asks.

"Acute intermittent Porphyria and Familial Non-Autoimmune Hyperthyroidism," Lucretia offers up.

"This sounds like a lot of cheap bedtime stories to keep kids from looking under their beds a million times, checking for Howie Mandel," Jack argues.

"The AIP and NFAH are like asthma. They act up and when they act up is when the other diseases," James catches his word choice before Lucretia can say anything, "conditions manifest. That's what allows us to transition into vampires and you into a werewolf."

"This is a lot to take in," Jack admits.

"Take your time, son. Take your time," James consoles.

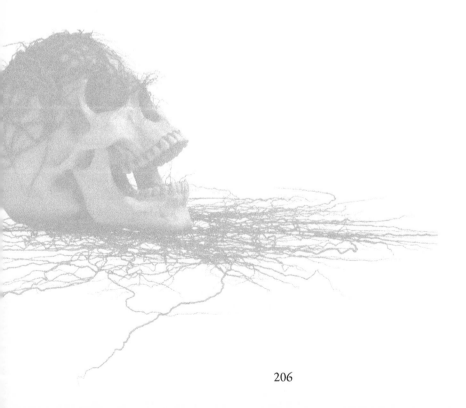

CHAPTER 20

"Telling someone is easy.
Telling the right person
is the challenging part."
~V. Petrovsky~

S till weary from their stay in the hospital but needing to do something about their recent experiences, all three of the Taylors walk into a quiet police station.

"Are you sure you want to do this?" Lucretia whispers to her husband. "We just got out yesterday. A little time to rest isn't going to hurt any."

"Yes. The sooner we do, the sooner we can start putting this behind us," James whispers back.

The front desk officer sits, eating donuts and watching something on his smartphone. A few officers roam about the station performing various duties but otherwise seems like a mundane day at the station.

Jack finds a seat on a nearby bench while James and Lucretia walk up to the reception desk.

Officer Smith looks up from his cell phone, greeting them with a smile. "How may I help you?"

James looks at the officer while keeping an eye on the other cops in the station. "Hello," James starts but pauses when he sees an officer pass by close to the reception desk.

Officer Smith's smile fades. "Is everything okay?"

James looks back to Officer Smith. "We are looking for someone. We were supposed to file a report."

"Missing persons? Just a second while I pull that up," Smith says as he types away at his computer.

James shakes his head. "No. We are looking for…"

James is interrupted as Officer Espinoza approaches Officer Smith. "Lunchtime, Smith. I'll help these nice folks out."

Officer Smith walks away, leaving the Taylors with Officer Espinoza.

James and Lucretia's eyes go wide. They stand, unable to move, frozen like a deer in headlights. From the bench, Jack sees Espinoza and rushes to his parents' side. Months of unspeakable torture and experiments all flood the front of their minds.

Max Espinoza leans over the counter, invading the personal space of the Taylors. He says straightforwardly, "I heard you say you were looking for someone. Who is it that you are looking for?"

The Taylors stand, still unable to move as Officer Espinoza waits for a response. James hesitates, unsure of what is safe around them.

Max takes his voice to a whisper, "I hope you didn't come here looking for help."

James looks to his frightened son, who holds steady. Lucretia, too, is maintaining her stance, keeping her eyes square on Espinoza.

James hesitantly says, "You don't know who you are dealing with."

Max laughs in their faces. "You are all a dying race, and you don't even know it yet. Vampires and werewolves are nothing but soulless monsters trying to hide among us."

James takes a deep breath. "We are not without souls. We are no different than you, except we can see past our differences."

James turns around. Lucretia and Jack follow suit.

As they reach the exit, Officer Espinoza calls out, "If you remember who you were looking for, please come back. And Jack, I'll see you at school."

Jack freezes in his tracks. He starts shaking, unable to move. James puts his arm around Jack for support so he can continue walking.

James whispers, "Don't worry, son. Everything will be just fine."

Jack sits in the living room of his house fiddling on his iPhone, the television streaming the latest episode of *Stranger Things* off Netflix. The evening light shines through the windows illuminating the room and casting Jack in strange, dancing shadows that would play into his newfound worries of being a monster if he noticed them.

He holds his phone in his hand. He whiles away the night with texts to Connor and Scarlett, who fill him in on any gossip from school to try and get him back to some sense of normalcy. A feeling that has still not returned to him.

He turns down the volume on the television, still high enough for him to hear but low enough to listen in on the conversation his parents and Vistrus are having in the den.

"I don't understand why he never came to the hospital to get our report," James tells Vistrus in a concerned voice.

"The council deemed it too risky with what had happened to you," Vistrus replies.

"That's not a great reason. A family is held hostage and tortured, yet they don't want a report on it," Lucretia argues.

Vistrus grimaces as he searches for words to calm her growing anger. "It is not that the council did not want you to file a report. They did not want anything going public. How would you look to a Normal officer telling him someone tortured you because you are a vampire or someone thought you were a vampire?"

"That's why you send in the contact for The Nation. Someone who knows, someone who would have believed," James rebuts.

Jack hears bits and pieces, though a few words fade from his ears. He holds his phone in his hands but stops texting. As he shifts focus to the conversation, like a volume button on a remote control, his parents' words become louder to his ears, more focused.

"We, The Council, put armed guards at your door. No one was allowed in unless you personally knew them. There was a list and a short one at that." Vistrus's voice grows sterner with each passing word. "You do not know him, and so he was not allowed in," Vistrus finishes defending.

"So when do we get to give our report?" Lucretia asks as she calms herself.

"To the police, you do not. Not after what happened at the station. To The Council, you will. A Council member will be there and take it back to the police with what information can be public," Vistrus commands.

James points his finger at Vistrus. "I respect you. Always have. But right now, I don't like you. I don't like what The Council is doing and don't like that you are a part of it. It's crappy politics. We should have come forward long ago."

Vistrus nods at his statement. "I understand your anger, but things are in motion that will bring The Nation into the public eye. Sooner than you might expect."

James sits, shaking his head.

Vistrus continues, "While you were underground, is there anything you remember? Anything at all that might help The Council?"

Lucretia and James look at each other, searching for memories in the other's eyes. James turns to Vistrus. "They injected us with something. They put it into our IV bags."

Lucretia nods in remembrance. "Yes. And when they did, it burned for a while, then got cold for a long time. When they did that, they said they were testing potential cures."

Vistrus raises a curious eyebrow. "A cure?"

The memories start to flood James' mind. "Yes. And when we were cold, they would Taser us, burn us, inflict pain in some way to try and elicit a physical response. Get us to transition."

"Please tell me none of the cures worked," Vistrus says with an uncharacteristically worried voice.

Lucretia shakes her head. "No. But one or two of them did manage to slow down the transition. Far longer time to change and much more painful. Whatever they are working on, they are onto something, and it doesn't bode well for us."

Jack gets up off the couch and strolls into the den. "I hate to, uh, interrupt, but I remember something. It may be nothing, but I remember."

"You were eavesdropping, young man?" James asks with a stern tone.

"Yeah, dad. Like, two days ago, you were telling me I'm, well, a werewolf, and you're mad at me for listening?" Jack retorts. "Couldn't really help it. Once I started hearing you guys, it just got louder and more, I don't know, uh, in front of me."

"He is gaining his abilities fast," Vistrus notes.

"I think the drugs they forced on him sped things along," Lucretia defends as if his words were an attack.

Vistrus turns to Jack. "Only if you feel ready to talk."

Jack nods a few times. "It may be nothing. Um, but they only ever said vampires and werewolves. When you sat me down and told me, well, of the monster I am."

"You're not a monster; you're human. You're a boy," Lucretia implores him.

"Whatever," Jack continues. "We're all freaks, and that's why we've hidden since, like, whenever we all began. But they only mentioned those two. Vampires and werewolves."

Lucretia continues her politically correct maternal bargaining, "Jack, no one here is a freak. We are normal, everyday people..."

"With frickin' superpowers," Jack interrupts. "Yeah, we're normal. But you're, well, missing the point. You, umm, alluded that there are fairies too," Jack continues.

Vistrus chimes in, "As well as others."

"Sure, yeah," Jack says. "But they only mentioned two. In all the talking the cop and the blonde guy did, they only mentioned those two Legends or whatever we're called."

Vistrus hears him and turns to James. "That is why I did not send a police officer in to take your report. If one cop is involved, then who knows how many more might be."

They all confirm their agreement with their silence.

"And did you mention a blonde man, Jack?" Vistrus points his question to him.

"Yeah, some blonde guy. Real ripped and scary as hell," he says as he starts to get paranoid thinking about him. "His face was scary. All tore up."

"Thank you," Vistrus interrupts, trying to calm Jack down. "That could mean that they do not know the full extent of The Nation,"

"It's a start, I guess," James says. "Not a comforting one, but a start."

Jack raises his hand. The others look at him, a bit puzzled. "Yes, son," James says, calling on him.

"I know you tried explaining it a bit before but, um, what makes me a werewolf? Am I just, well, a hairy vampire?" Jack asks.

Vistrus chuckles. The first chuckle of the night for him. "No. I trust they explained the mutations that make us vampires?" Vistrus motions to the adults.

Jack nods his head. "What I can remember, yeah."

"Well," Vistrus continues, "like vampires, you have the Myostatin-Related Muscle Hypertrophy but Strongman syndrome as well, which increases your natural strength over vampires."

Jack listens intently. Something in his mind has clicked, telling him this is a reality he will have to adjust to, and the sooner, the better.

"And of course, the hair comes from Hypertrichosis," Vistrus adds.

"What, uh, causes my, ya know, change?" Jack asks, trying not to sound offensive.

"Oddly enough, genetic Rickets," Vistrus starts. "That acts as the catalyst for the transition. Comparatively more painful than ours."

Jack's face twists in a portrait of pain, sympathy, and disbelief.

"But all of that is stuff that they, whoever they are, presumably are still trying to figure out. If you are correct, young man," Vistrus concludes in a voice that hints at admiration for the teen.

"So," Jack inquires, "what do we do now?"

CHAPTER 21

"Everything looks different
without the naiveté of innocence"
~N. DeSalvo~

On the first day back in school after the end of Winter break, the school's general population, oblivious to the events that unfolded over the past few weeks, walk around in ignorant bliss. The winter sun shines through the windows a little brighter than usual, a seeming calm after the storm.

Connor, Jack, Scarlett, and Allison hang out at Jack's locker. A kid slams his locker shut a few doors down from them, causing Jack to flinch, covering his head. Scarlett looks at the unknowing kid and gives him the stink eye. The kid shrugs and walks off.

"Jack, if you're not ready, I'll get you out of here. We'll talk to a teacher and get you home," Scarlett says in a tone that almost sounds like a concerned mother figure.

Jack shakes off the feeling and looks around the school halls for a moment, scanning every student and teacher he sees. His hearing focuses from one conversation to the next trying to pick up on some conspiracy against him, even knowing it is his paranoia in him. After an extended moment of doing so, he looks back at Scarlett and forces out a weak smile.

"Thanks. I can do this. I think," Jack finally replies.

"I'll walk you to your next class," Scarlett says as she wraps her arm around him.

Allison and Scarlett connect eyes. Allison nods Scarlett off as she stays behind with Connor.

"I don't even know what class it is anymore," Jack says. "I'm not really sure about anything right now. Thank you, Scarlett."

Scarlett helps him think while they continue walking. "We'll figure it out, Jack. We got this."

><><><><><><><><><><><><><><><><><><><

Scarlett is standing in line, paying for her lunch. The ever-silent lunch lady, December, is joyfully doling out food to the kids. As Scarlett enters the cafeteria, she sees Allison sitting at their usual table, but Mrs. Hsu, the school social worker, stands next to her. The two seem to be engaged in some conversation.

As Scarlett approaches the table, Allison nods in her direction. The social worker turns around and smiles at Scarlett.

"Do you have a moment, Ms. McAllister?" the counselor asks in a way that has only one correct response.

Scarlett lifts her tray. "I just got my lunch. I'd like to eat it." She begins to swing her legs over the bench-style seats.

"We could talk here if that's okay with you?" the social worker insists.

"Fine. I'm not sure what all this is about, though," Scarlett says.

The woman takes a seat across from the girls. "Jack is back. He's alive after being presumed…" The counselor stops so she can choose her words more sensitively. "…not."

The girls each raise a suspicious eyebrow at that phrasing.

"We, the school, just want to check in on you and see how you are doing with all of this," she continues.

"Look, Mrs.…" Allison starts on an irritated note.

"Mrs. Hsu," she says, formally introducing herself to the girls. "Sorry about the lack of proper introduction. I've been watching you for a while to ensure you are okay."

"Well, Mrs. Hsu," Allison continues in rapid-fire succession, "we're fine. Things are fine. Everything is fine. Why don't you try talking to Jack, who actually went through something? Or Connor, who is BFF's with Jack and busted his ass to find out what actually happened when no one else would? Which is the only reason Jack is back, as you put it."

Scarlett finishes her bite of fried chicken patty sandwich. "I think what Allison is trying to say is that things are all kosher over here."

Mrs. Hsu smiles at the girls. "Just because you were not the ones directly involved in what transpired with the Taylors doesn't mean you did not go through something."

Allison stops eating her lunch and turns toward Mrs. Hsu, her irritation growing with each spoken word.

"You had to go through the stages of grief," Mrs. Hsu continues. "You had to go through them all only to have your personal healing … interrupted when he was found."

Allison's tone takes a downward shift. "I just told you: go ask the guys. Go find the people who did this. Go worry about the things that actually matter." She turns back to her lunch.

The counselor sees Allison leave the conversation and turns to Scarlett.

"This is what matters to me. You, her," she nods toward Allison, "everyone involved. How you deal with things matters. How people around you deal with things matters. We care. I know it's not 'cool,'" she says with air quotes, "but if you decide you want to talk, I'm here."

Mrs. Hsu stands up from the table. "Have a wonderful day, ladies."

Mrs. Hsu takes a few steps from the table, smiling, but Allison isn't done. She throws down her chicken sandwich onto the tray.

"You don't actually care!" Allison says in a loud voice that causes more than just Mrs. Hsu to turn around.

"Excuse me?" Mrs. Hsu says, getting quickly offended.

"You have to care. You don't actually care. If you did, you would have tried sooner. If you did, you would be doing something more than a half-assed attempt to get us to talk to you." Allison walks toward the stunned social worker.

"I do care about things. My lot in life isn't to fight. It's to tend to those in need," she defends.

"Then you suck at it," Allison attacks. "There was no note given to me about meeting you and doing some preliminary talk to set up

215

a time to actually meet and talk. No. You waltz in here like we're all buddy-buddy and sit at our table."

Mrs. Hsu interrupts Allison's diatribe, "You're in pain. I know. That's why you are lashing out at me. What you are doing is not acceptable. I'm going to be okay with it this time. When you are ready, you come to me."

Mrs. Hsu again turns around and walks away. Allison stands, unsure of how to react to the social worker's non-reaction, so she watches as Mrs. Hsu leaves the cafeteria.

As she walks away, Scarlett turns to Allison. "She was just trying to help."

"Yeah, where was she or anyone who wanted to help when Jack was missing? Where was anyone who wanted to help while Con was obsessed with finding out what happened?" Allison argues back.

Scarlett wants to say something. She wants Allison to understand, but pushing buttons isn't something she wants to do right here, right now.

CHAPTER 22

"They don't enjoy hiding who they are,
nor do they enjoy the ridicule.
But what choice do they have?"
~R. Chandler~

J ack and Connor sit at a lunch table amongst a few friends from the team. While the others sit and laugh at the passing events from the day, Jack sits spaced out in his own little world. The happenings in front of him pass by like a hazy dream. Connor sits, caught mentally between the teammates' laughter and Jack's internal universe.

Connor scarfs down the rest of his processed mystery meat before excusing himself from the table. As he stands up, he taps Jack on the shoulder, finally grabbing his attention.

"Come on, bro," says Connor.

Jack shakes his head and motions with a finger for Connor to sit back down.

"What's up, Jack?" asks Connor.

Jack looks to the guys whose conversations trail off as they give their attention to Jack.

"So, as you all know by now, I'm, well, not dead," starts off Jack. He waits for the few nervous chuckles to die down before continuing. "But things are, um, different. Ya know?"

Everyone nods in agreement, whether or not they understand where he's going with this.

"I'm… uh… glad to be back. Don't get me wrong. Having all my friends around is, is wonderful," Jack continues. Then he stops talking, looking at everyone around him. "Things happened while I was … away. Life-changing things. The noises around me are a bit much sometimes." The volume rises in his voice as he finishes the last sentence.

The guys are all looking at him, unsure what to say, half wondering if he is serious, but no one betrays the team's camaraderie.

"It's like, well, uh, things happened to me. Things that made me find out, well, certain things about my family. I, uh, I don't know how to say it exactly," Jack continues.

Connor puts a hand out to control the floor for a moment.

"Bro, you don't need to say anything. I understand. And I think the rest of the guys understand enough to know that things are now different. You don't need to say anything you are uncomfortable with. I know things happened that changed the game of life for you," Connor says, trying to calm him.

"Um, you do?" asks Jack.

"Yeah, Jack. I do. Anything that you don't want to talk about, anything that you are still working out in your head … take your time, my man. If you feel like others may not understand, or if it's too uncomfortable, wait. Wait till it isn't. Wait till later. We got you."

Jack sits there half nodding his head, a little confused about the interruption.

"Well, okay, I guess," Jack finishes prematurely. "We'll talk later then, Con."

The guys sit in uncomfortable silence for a few moments until one of them releases a raucous burp, causing them all to laugh. The moment of levity allows normal activities to resume for the rest of the team. Connor and Jack, however, continue to sit in quiet contemplation. They look around and watch the other guys. Connor wonders if the rest of the team would stand in solidarity if they thoroughly knew what Jack has been through.

Scarlett can't quite place her finger on it, but something has changed. She has always thought Jack was cute in a second-hand sort of way. His lanky features but clean-cut looks, his peculiar way of speaking that seethes with lack of confidence but still drips with talent. Every aspect of him stands in conflict against everything else. This unique awkwardness-meets-cool-guy has always made Scarlett smile and made his presence welcome. She never thought of him as anything more than a friend, or at least the thought never crossed her conscious mind until recently.

She's heard of Stockholm syndrome, where the captives empathize with their captors, and Nightingale Syndrome, where a caretaker falls for the patient, but she is neither captive nor nurse. She sees Jack, and while he still looks and talks the same, his actions are different. Sometimes jumpier but other times more confident. She thinks it is this newfound confidence fighting its way to the surface that she fancies. Scarlett is conflicted about having such feelings since this change in him she finds so pleasing was brought about by such cruel means.

But here she sits with Jack, Connor, and Allison, watching some independent creature-feature that is as fun as it is campy. But the few jump-scares the movie has makes Scarlett scoot closer to Jack, grabbing for his arm. Moves which have not gone unnoticed by Jack. He wraps his arm around her so she can cuddle into him. He will protect her from the things that go bump in the night.

Connor and Allison also cuddle up on the opposite corner of the couch. The sense of youthful naiveté slips away as thoughts typically reserved for adults flow through their minds. But for now, things are left innocent. They sit, holding hands that occasionally wander up the other's arm with gentle fingertip touches.

The moments of idyllic escapism are gone as the credits begin to roll, and as they roll, youthful awkwardness and uncertainty creep back in, causing the couples to separate like settling oil and water.

"Wanna watch another movie?" Scarlett says, breaking the silence.

They all look at each other for a moment, yearning to rejoin hands and see where it may lead, but everyone is slightly too nervous to say anything.

Jack speaks up, "Actually, well, I wanted to talk about lunch, yesterday."

"Those milk containers keep tasting better and better each day closer to expiration," quips Connor.

"I meant what happened," Jack says through a half-forced chuckle.

"I know what you meant, Jack," Connor follows up.

"What did you mean when you said that you know? Do the other guys know?" asks Jack.

"No. I haven't said anything to them. I figure it's not my place to tell," Connor says.

"But, well, uh, how do you know? I didn't even know till, till I was chained up," Jack continues, his voice rising in pitch with each word of that sentence.

"To make a long story short, we became criminals and found a notebook with ramblings. It took us some time to break the code, but we did," Connor fills him in.

Scarlett quickly adds, "Actually, it was Allison. She broke the code."

"With everyone's input," Allison interjects.

"So yeah, that's when we found out they thought you were a vampire," Connor finishes summarizing.

Jack scratches his head, unsure how to correct his last sentence and still sound sane.

"So," Jack starts, "things, for me, are, um, different. That theory you discovered ... well, it wasn't so much a theory."

Scarlett gives Jack a raised eyebrow. "You aren't telling us you're a vampire."

Jack scrunches his face realizing how absurd this must sound.

"It's just a theory, right?" Connor asks. "You aren't actually a vampire?"

"Well..." starts Jack, "they injected me with so many things, IVs, drugs, that uh, I saw things: things that happened to my parents, to me."

"Like pointy teeth and bulging veins?" asks Scarlett.

"How did you know?!" Jack asks, surprised at her detailed description.

"Lucky guess," she responds.

Connor goes to his desk and retrieves the parchment he found at Jack's house. The parchment that shined words in the sunlight once again reads the words "*We know*" to Connor.

"I didn't think of it till now, but I saw this at your place when I went to look for you," Connor says, handing it to Jack. "Do you have any idea what it is?"

Allison perks up and peers over Jack's shoulder as he unrolls it and flips the paper over a few times. "Looks blank to me."

"'We know'?" Jack reads out loud from the paper. "What does that mean?"

"What are you talking about? There's nothing there!" Allison pipes up.

Connor's eyes light up. "You can see that?! It was there. Then it wasn't. Now it's back."

"What are you two talking about?!" Allison interjects.

Jack, ignoring Allison, points to the words, confused by Connor's question. "Yeah. They're, uh, written right there."

Connor's excitement grows. "At least they are now. But it wasn't when I first saw it."

"Bro, right here, plain as day on the paper," Jack starts.

"Parchment," Allison corrects him.

Jack looks at Allison. "What?"

"It's parchment," she starts. "My dad works at the museum. I know the difference..." She trails off. "Holy crap! He lied to me!" exclaims Allison as she shoots up from the jolting realization. Waving her hands around in uncontained enthusiasm, she says, "Things are starting to make sense."

"Who lied to you?" Scarlett inquires.

"My dad." She turns away to leave, then turns back to Connor and gives him a big smooch. "I gotta run. I'll call you all later."

∞∞∞∞∞∞∞∞∞∞∞∞∞∞∞∞∞∞∞∞∞∞∞

Vistrus sits in a reclining chair, sipping a glass of Bordeaux. James and Lucretia partake in the wine as well while seated on an antique day sofa. Neoclassical music playing on vinyl sets the mood.

"We know they know about vampires and werewolves, but they only mentioned those two. I don't think they know about any of the other Legends," James tells Vistrus.

"My memory is a little foggy on most of it, but I think the boys are right," Lucretia contributes.

"Knowing what they know is important, but we still need to know who they are. Do you know anything that can help with that?" Vistrus urges.

"No. Only that Jack knows the police or at least a policeman is involved," Lucretia says, sipping her wine.

"All the more reason not to have our contact take your statement at the hospital. But that is one man. We must not condemn a whole department for one rogue," Vistrus reminds them. "Last time Legends had one rogue within our ranks; we had to hide from the world for hundreds of years."

"But they did have medical supplies," James adds. "And not old, run-down supplies but fresh, packaged supplies."

"Could be someone at the hospital," Lucretia surmises.

"Yes," agrees Vistrus. "But if it is not West Haven General, then it could be any hospital within driving distance."

"In Chicagoland, that's a lot of hospitals," James says, stating the obvious.

"There is the rub," Vistrus finishes. "So we need to figure out who or what is running this operation."

"If my drugged and groggy memory serves me correct, I don't even think they know who's at the top of it," James admits.

"Why would you say that?" Vistrus asks.

"The blonde guy and the one Jack figured was a cop kept asking about who was in charge," James continues.

Dizziness sweeps over Lucretia as a burst of memories floods back into her mind. "That's right! I remember now. The blonde guy kept saying who'll find out. Like he was telling us really bad riddles or questions."

Allison bursts through the door of her house, gasping for air from the sprint to the door. "Dad! We … need … to … talk!" she gets out between breaths.

"In the den, Allison!" he calls out to her. "We have company over, too! Please mind yourself."

As she makes her way to the den, she mocks his last sentence under her breath. But as she finishes her mockery, turning the corner to the room, she is greeted by Vistrus and the Taylors.

"We know," she says plainly.

Vistrus takes a deep breath as he gathers his thoughts.

"We know what?" he responds, trying to play it cool.

"Don't patronize me, dad. 'We know.' It's what was written on the blank parchment a few months ago. You said it was a shipment, but I know you were talking to Mr. or Mrs. Taylor," Allison deduces.

He smiles, both proud that his daughter has figured it out and out of amusement that she is still partially wrong. He looks at James and Lucretia, who stare at him, waiting to make eye contact with him. Lucretia is about to speak when Vistrus subtly and slowly shakes his head "no." He then turns back to his daughter.

"That is quite the detective work you have done. But how do you know what it said?" he asks, rising from his seat. "More wine?" he says to the Taylors, who both shake their head no. He, however, momentarily walks out of the room and returns with the bottle to top off his glass.

Allison cops a squat on a reclining loveseat. "Jack saw the paper and read it. But I couldn't see it," she says.

"And how did Jack see it?" Vistrus follows up.

"Connor grabbed it from your house," she says, gesturing to Lucretia. "He thought it was out of place being blank and all." She turns her attention back to her father. "So what does it mean?"

"That is what we are still trying to figure out," he responds matter-of-factly.

"And why could he see it and no one else?" Allison asks.

The three adults turn to each other, drawing proverbial straws to see who needs to come up with a lie. James draws the shortest straw.

"While we were held captive, they injected us with a lot of drugs," he starts with a truth. "His ability to see what he saw must be a side effect from one of the drugs."

Allison hops up off the loveseat. "Interesting," she says as she skips away. She knows they are lying since Connor could also see it, but she has no other cards to play, so she remains quiet.

Vistrus calls her, "Come back here, young lady."

Allison stops and slinks back. "Yes, father?"

"Interesting?" he parrots. "You think you are going to say 'interesting' and nothing more?"

"What?" She shrugs. "I think it's interesting that things can have such lasting effects. That's all."

"And you're not hiding anything from the Taylors or me?" he urges.

"Nope," she says, skipping away once more. The thoughts in her mind of her friend being a vampire seem to add a sense of excitement.

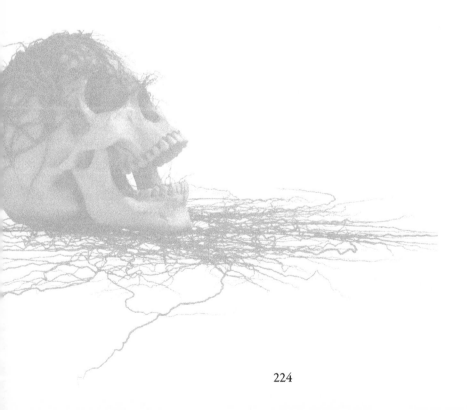

CHAPTER 23

"Enjoy the simple things too.
If not, then nothing can truly be enjoyed."
~E. DeSalvo~

The events of the past few weeks and months have overshadowed a most important event in one's life, and in this case, that event falls on February 5, 2018—Allison's 18th birthday. She and Connor sit, looking over the Cheesecake Factory's ridiculously enormous menu, trying to decide between the Avocado Eggrolls or the Tex-Mex Eggrolls and an entree to go with each. A couple of sodas and a basket of rye bread sit in front of them.

"I don't know, Con. What do you want?" asks Allison.

He surfaces from the depths of the menu to steal a glance at the young woman in front of him, shifting uncomfortably in her spaghetti strap, little black dress, looking far more feminine than he usually sees her. He, too, is dressed more masculinely than he usually does in a button-down, dress top, blazer, and slacks. Even his shoes are of the dress variety.

A smile crosses his face as a thought enters his mind. An idea that has him questioning what he did right in life to be here at this moment, with her.

"It's your birthday, Allison. Whatever you want is perfectly fine," he replies in a soft tone.

The server approaches the table, notepad in hand. "Thoughts on appetizers? Perhaps the calamari?" the server says, lifting his pen to the pad.

Connor looks up at the server, smiling while he tosses a glance at Allison, who is still lost in the menu. "Actually, we'll take the Avocado and Tex-Mex Eggrolls."

Allison shoots up from her menu with a massive smile on her face.

"And for the entrees…" the server continues but sees Allison's lost facial expression, "…another minute perhaps."

Connor gives a half smile to the server while nodding in agreement. After the server leaves, Connor returns to the entrees. A minute or two of comfortable silence pass. Connor finally pipes up, "I'm eyeing the four cheese pasta. That looks cheese-i-rific."

Allison laughs and looks up at him. "Thank you … for all this."

"No worries. I just want you to be happy," Connor offers up sincerely.

She smiles, blushing a bit. "I am. I was also thinking about the four cheese pasta or the chicken fingers."

"I know I said it when I picked you up, but you look stunning tonight," Connor says as he closes his menu, setting it on the edge of the table.

Allison looks down at her dress, turning a deeper shade of red. "You don't think I look like a ten-year-old boy dressing up in mommy's finest evening wear?"

"Wow. That was … descriptive." Connor laughs. "I think you know some unusual ten-year-old boys. Not that there's anything wrong with wearing what makes you comfortable. But no. I think you look amazingly beautiful and very much not like a ten-year-old boy. I don't date ten-year-old boys."

"Thank God for that." Allison laughs.

The server approaches once more, appetizers in hand. "Tex-Mex and Avocado Eggrolls," he says, placing them on the table. "Ready to order or still need more time?" He grabs his pen in hopes they know what they want.

"Thank you," Connor starts. "We'll take the chicken fingers and the four cheese pasta."

"Any sides or anything?" the server continues with the order.

"No, thank you. Just an extra plate to share," Connor finishes and hands the menus to the server.

Allison looks over the amount of food in front of them, her eyes wide and ravenous.

"You can always take some home if you can't finish it all," Connor says, almost sounding like a father.

"Challenge accepted," she says with a sly smile. Allison puts down her fork after taking a bite of her avocado eggroll. "Do you think he can die?"

"Come again?" Connor says as he swallows a bite of the Tex-Mex roll.

"I mean, being a werewolf," she whispers. "Do you think Jack can die?"

"Okay. One … Jack's not a real werewolf. He was just kidnapped or whatever by some psychos who thought he was," Connor begins.

Allison interrupts, "And his family."

"Yeah, sure. And two, real vampires and werewolves don't exist. They can't. They are just legend, myths. He's just dealing with the situation in a way that makes sense of everything that happened to him."

"So you don't believe in vampires or ghosts or anything?" Allison's curiosity is piqued.

"I'm not saying I don't believe, but logically, it makes sense that they don't," he answers.

"But you just said 'real vampires don't exist,'" she replies with a wink.

"I don't know. Someone somewhere close by sure thinks vampires and things are real. Real enough to capture, torture, and possibly kill for. So maybe I'm wrong," Connor says, backpedaling a little on his previous statements.

"Well, real or not, what do you think it would be like?" she nudges.

Scratching his head, he says, "Cool, I think. Super strength and fangs and all. Being different like that. I think it'd be pretty neat."

"Being different can be neat but also lonely. Think about it. Who could he tell? His best friend doesn't believe him, so who would? Who would actually listen, take him seriously? Then if someone did, who would not treat him as diseased, outcast, or as some dangerous influence on the precious youth of today?" she says, bringing the fun down a notch or twelve to very serious.

Connor sits back in his chair, shocked at the weight of her statement. "Never thought of it that way."

"And then there'd be the people trying to cure them or suppress their transformations. Some weird conversion therapy to make them believe they aren't what they naturally are. Or they'd all be locked up and killed off cause it'd be easier just to get rid of something they don't understand instead of learning about what's different cause people always fear what doesn't act or look like them," she finishes and takes a deep breath.

Connor sits there smiling at the gravity of her words. He has never realized that someone who hides from the world and herself as much as she does could have such profound thoughts circling her mind.

"You have never looked more beautiful than when you speak with fire," he compliments.

Her passion fades into self-consciousness as she slinks back into her chair. "Just saying. But thank you. I think people are too quick to judge. I, myself, would never want to be a vampire or anything like that. It would be harder than life already is."

The server returns with the entrees giving them a needed distraction from the conversation.

"Oh, I got you something," Connor says, reaching into the inside pocket of his sports coat.

"You didn't have to, Con. This night out is more than enough," she says.

"It's just something I saw and thought of you," he says, handing her a small black velvet box.

"Thank you," she says with a smile.

"You have to open first. Then you can thank me." He gestures for her to open the box.

Allison looks down as she opens the box. A pair of onyx-crusted pentacle earrings shines darkly in the restaurant light. A huge smile crosses her face.

"These are perfect! Thank you so much!" She takes out her current studded earrings and wears her new gift. "These are my favorite ones now."

"Happy birthday, Allison."

CHAPTER 24

*"There's a fine line between being
sarcastic and just plain mean."*
~T. DeSalvo~

Girls' choice dance, Turnabout, Sadie Hawkins, whatever name it's called, can be a very trying time for young girls, especially those who aren't overly confident in themselves to begin with. But the dance is part of high school culture and a valued experience each year. It's a time when even the less outgoing girls muster up the courage to ask the boys to a school dance, and if fate favors them, things will go their way.

There was no doubt in Allison's mind who she was going with and no doubt as to if he was going to say yes. So the nervous, butterflies-in-stomach moment of standing in front of him, hesitantly asking the question, hoping he'll say yes, was much more anti-climactic than, perhaps, for other girls. Meaning that the most challenging, most painful part of Girls' Choice preparations was finding that perfect, not-too-over-the-top-not-too-understated dress that would make her feel the way she wanted both inside and out. She and Scarlett had spent hours trying to find the ideal dress for Allison, something that would let anyone doubting her know she is a young woman on the rise and, at the same time, have an edge that screams come too close, and she will cut you.

They found that dress from some store out at Gurnee Mills. A black dress with red lace overlay on the torso, black, sheer sleeves that flare at the red, lace cuffs, and a skirt with red panel sides that gave way to silver vining over the rest that disappears into the red lace on the torso: busy, edgy, badass, and feminine. A perfect dress for her. She loves every inch of it and how it makes her feel empowered, indestructible, and sexy. But a nagging feeling in the back of her mind hopes Connor likes it too. She will soon find out.

Scarlett's dress was an easy find. Red dresses aren't terribly rare. She found a form-fitting deep red that goes down just below her knees. Red lace top center starting at her neckline and fading down about five inches. She is slightly more confident that Jack will like this dress than Allison is about Connor loving hers.

Standing in Allison's bathroom, the girls finish the final touches on their lipstick application as the doorbell rings.

"I got it, dad!" yells Allison from the upstairs bathroom giving her lips one last smack to ensure color dispersion.

She runs down the stairs, followed by Scarlett. They both stop at the door, looking one another over and straightening themselves up. They both give each other an indicative nod of perfection before Allison opens the door.

Connor and Jack stand there, corsages in hand and slack-jawed at the beauty before them.

Jack extends his corsage outward, "You look ... wonderfully beautiful, Scarlett." He places the flowers on her wrist.

"Thank you, Jack," she says, smiling. "You look very handsome, yourself."

Connor hasn't moved since the door opened. Allison and Connor stare at each other, eyes connected.

"You look perfect," he says, breaking the silence.

A mile-wide smile crosses her face as she turns a light shade of red. "You don't look half-bad yourself, big guy."

He places the corsage on her wrist and takes her hand, planting a kiss carefully on her cheek so as not to ruin her makeup.

Vistrus turns the corner, camera ready, and snaps a couple of candid shots of the teens. "You all look very well groomed. It is good to see you boys clean up nicely."

"Thank you, sir," Connor says with a tenseness reserved for teenagers around the parent of the girl they are currently consensually defiling.

Vistrus poses them for a few photos to later frame before releasing them to their waiting limo ride to the dance.

The event itself is a bit lackluster to their liking. Not that the DJ isn't talented or that the decorations aren't up to par, but it is a general feeling that somehow Homecoming is supposed to be paramount, and this is only its neglected stepchild. The irony is that Homecoming is the lesser loved sibling of Senior Prom.

Through dancing with the boys, the girls couldn't help but notice Brianna surrounded by her usual entourage of characterless followers. What catches their attention isn't the usual crowd she surrounds herself with, or even the boys added into the mix on this night. It isn't even that their dresses are over-the-top enough to stand out at Girls' Choice—dresses that belong more in a prom setting.

No. What catches Allison's and Scarlett's attention is that under the right light, a dancing spotlight covered by a yellow gel, they notice a bruised, black eye that Brianna attempted to cover with concealer and foundation and the accompanied pained smile that goes with a nasty shiner like that.

After a while of dancing and enjoying the night, the slew of ballads begins. Jack and Scarlett share a dance that puts them close. His unsure hands sit on her waist; hers rest easy on his shoulders. She moves in close to him, resting her head on his chest, forcing him to move his hands around to the small of her back. She leans an ear against his chest, smiling as she listens to his racing heart.

Allison and Connor sway in rhythm to the song as they gaze into each other's eyes. A shared private moment in a public place. No one else in the auditorium exists at this moment, just the two of them. A longing peek into the possibilities of their futures.

As the second slow song in a row comes to an end, the young adults separate and grab a seat at a table, a momentary break from the evening's motion as well as a mental break from the thoughts floating around their heads. Brianna separates from her social circle and makes her way to the table.

"The girls would like some punch," Brianna commands Connor and Jack with a forced smile.

The two take her not-so-subtle hint and get up to get a few glasses and perhaps will make another stop to stay away from her.

"Enjoying the dance, I see," she begins with obvious intent as she stands over the girls.

"It's been fun," Scarlett says, keeping it light. "What brings you this way?"

"Just seeing how you've been. How's Connor been holding up since the whole thing with Jack?" Brianna says, getting to her point.

"You sent him away to ask me about him?" Allison responds.

"Fine. Whatever. Maybe I wanted to talk to you and didn't exactly know how to start," Brianna admits. "Jesus, Allison. You can be very off-putting, ya know."

"You can just leave friends behind for popularity, ya know," Allison retorts with a seething smile.

"Fine, whatever. Don't say I didn't try," Brianna says, turning around.

Scarlett hops out of her chair. "Hey, Bri. Hold up."

Brianna stops and turns around again. "I'm not going to sit here and be insulted by you too."

"No, nothing like that," Scarlett starts. "Actually, I was just wondering," she says, lowering the volume of her voice, "what's up with the black eye? Everything okay?"

As Scarlett finishes asking her question, a few girls from Brianna's social circle walk up and surround her on both sides.

"Peachy keen. Just an accidental fall," she says, pulling out a compact mirror to check her makeup.

Her friend makes a forced laugh and quips, "Fell into a doorknob. Can you believe it?!"

"Unbelievable. Really," Scarlett's reply is saltine.

The girls pull Brianna away from Scarlett and Allison as Connor and Jack return with five glasses of punch.

"Where'd Bri go off to?" Jack asks the girls. "We have her punch." He hands the girls a glass each.

"Whisked away by her fans," Scarlett jokes.

"Well, if she comes back, it'll be here," Connor says, setting it down.

Allison responds, "Don't see that happening anytime soon."

CHAPTER 25

"Say what you will,
but to be a good and effective parent
is the hardest job in the world."
~T. DeSalvo~

[Ken: *Where are your college admissions?*] Connor reads the text sent in hopes it helps him give more thought to college. Also, so that Connor knows that his dad will have to search his room for the papers. The text is met with a relatively fast response, barely enough time for Ken to take a quick bathroom break.

[Connor: *IDK. Desk somewhere, dresser drawer. My room.*] Ken is glad he didn't waste too much time waiting for the response, as Connor had it narrowed down to the same area of the house that he did. Ken enters Connor's room and begins rummaging through the mess of Connor's desktop, a bit overwhelmed by the clutter. "So glad he inherited my organizational skills," Ken muses.

The desk drawer is even more cluttered and sticky with something that once was a Jolly Rancher, Popsicle stick, or some other sugary sweet. The sticky mystery substance made almost everything else in the drawer sticky too, but he finishes going through when he sees the notebook from Espinoza's basement. It is suspiciously out of place among the loose papers, crumpled facial tissue, and leaked dried-up pens. So he pulls it out to see what it is.

At first glance, Ken knows this is not an ordinary school note-book. He knows he's seen it before, too, hiding in plain sight among the schoolbooks that his son pretended to bury himself in as a way to cope with the seeming loss of Jack. No, this book that Ken wishes he had found sooner is not school related.

Ken wishes he had seen it while Connor was grieving so he could have explained it to him or at least come up with a good fairy tale about it till Connor himself transitioned. But he didn't; a healthy respect for his son's privacy would have been violated, and this was something Connor did not feel comfortable approaching his dad with. Why would he? Connor has no idea about his true self or that his mother and father are Legends. His son holds no other secrets from him that he knows of. But then again, they would not be secrets if he knew. So maybe.

But he can't think about that now. Now he has to figure out a way to explain this to Connor and make him know he wasn't trying to violate his trust. But first, he must find those papers he came in for, set up a meeting, and get the ball rolling on his son's future.

Ken sets a meeting with one short, painless phone call. Ken knows there are perks to his government job, even if the city he represents isn't where the college is located. But that easy task checked off his to-do list; he now has to show his findings to Vistrus, show him the notebook.

It doesn't take long for Vistrus to respond to Ken and make his way over to the DeSalvo's. The two sit in silent concentration, examining the notebook in Ken's home office. Vistrus is quick to confirm this parent's fear: that his child is finding out on his own what his true nature is. But it also raises a new concern, something more rooted in them: a fear that after centuries of hiding in plain sight and living peacefully among Normals, a well-organized insti-tution has begun hunting and torturing them.

"Why would not he have come to us?" Vistrus ponders out loud.

"Because we spent more time trying to get him to believe his friend was dead instead of trusting him and his instincts and the fact that he was there at their house," Ken says, pacing back and forth.

"Point taken," Vistrus says, thumbing through the notebook. "A bunch of this is DNA code, but there is more code. This is not good."

"What do we do?" Ken asks, finally taking a seat at his desk.

Vistrus looks up from the notebook. "You do nothing. We already know where the Taylors were held captive. I will go back there and take Sylvia along." Her name rolls off his tongue with a distasteful pucker.

"Council prep?" Ken asks.

"Yes," Vistrus dryly replies. "The things we do. Plus, it will be nice to have someone who can see in the dark."

Ken nods in agreement. "What should I do with the notebook?"

"Scan it. Make a copy."

Ken nods in agreement. "I'll email you the files. That way, we both have them."

Vistrus turns to leave. "Thank you. I have to go but make sure I get those files.

Vistrus and Sylvia open the door in the ruins of old West Haven North—the door that led to torture, drugging, and horrible human experiments, all for some unknown reason. Vistrus hopes this room will reveal the method behind the madness.

"See Sylvia," he says while rummaging through the abandoned room. "The Council is not about some new world order. They are waiting for a time to step forward."

"I just don't understand," she says as she searches the room, not knowing exactly what she is looking for. "There's been no time in history that would have been okay?"

"Not enough for The Council's liking. Witch hunts, religious fanatics that would brand us, politicians that would distort and use us to further their agenda. The list goes on."

Sylvia examines one of the hospital beds. "But is waiting until after our entire culture is systematically killed off or made out to be villains the right time?"

Vistrus takes his usual deep breath before answering a question he doesn't have a complete answer to, but before he can, Sylvia speaks up again.

"These beds are all stamped WHG. They came from West Haven General," she deduces.

"I shall inform the council. Any members of The Nation will need to know to go elsewhere."

"But what will they do besides send out some metaphorical memo?" she asks while pilfering the cabinet of anything useful.

"Search for a safe hospital, safe doctors, find places we can call sanctuaries," he starts. "Protect The Nation as they have since the beginning," he pauses and looks in her direction. The low light makes it harder for him to see. "Anything useful?"

"No. Just more stuff to implicate West Haven General," she responds as she fumbles with IV tubing.

He searches the medical and miscellaneous debris of the center table area. A small, torn, but not crumpled notebook page catches his attention. He reads it:

> WH founded as a sanctuary for their kind. A little on the nose with the word Haven but they are monsters, after all. Damn vampires. The entire Organization (illegible writing) kill ... all.

Some scribblings are smudged or smeared with spilt liquid, but more notes at the bottom of the page are legible.

> Must find the beginning of it all.

A few words are no longer clear, but it ends with one word; a word that hits close to home for Vistrus and a word that also instills a sense of wonder and adventure for him.

... *museum.*

CHAPTER 26

"We will find our voice.
We will be heard."
~R. Chandler~

Sometimes the screaming voice inside our head wants to be heard. The voice inside our head begs for someone to listen and understand, for anyone to listen without forming uninformed judgment or prejudice. The voice inside our head screams at us that what is happening, the way an entire people have been treated, isn't right, isn't just, and isn't humane. Not because of some choice, some outside option that a whole community of people has made, or some iota of control they may have to change such things about them that have caused such bad images, stories, fables, and myths. No.

An entire people, known to themselves as Legends, must find each other without being able to reach out to like individuals. An entire people must live in secrecy for as far back as written history can recall, hiding half of who they are, not because of some flawed ideology or hate-filled religion. They must hide for fear of being rounded up and killed, experimented on, and treated like scapegoats for no other reason than genetics. Something that cannot change. Something they cannot opt out of. Now, in light of a small piece of thrown-away notebook paper, Vistrus informs The Nation that a far greater threat looms.

The recent events do not stem from a madman and his friends. They are not incidents isolated to some half-off-his-rocker guy who has seen *The Lost Boys* one too many times and thinks this threat is, as the image of the word is ingrained in his mind, an "Organization." An organization that seemingly knows more about the town's history than most townsfolk. An organization that knows there are more things hidden about the town than anyone outside The Nation should know.

So he tells them. He informs The Council of the recent findings. Connor, Jack, Allison, and Scarlett will know the meaning of "Are you In?" sooner than expected. Whatever it is this town hides won't be hidden for long unless they do something instead of sitting and waiting. This safe haven of West Haven is no longer safe. Vistrus tells the Council that some outside entity knows of the existence of vampires, and the organization is not an ally. The Council must do something before they don't have a choice anymore; they must make a decision and forge an option that works for them.

So Vistrus tells The Council all these things and lays out what is known by him, what he knows that Scarlett, Connor, Allison, and Jack know. He tells them all of this because they need to protect themselves. Vistrus informs them of this because the boy who lost his life in the back alley was innocent. He tells them this because he needs to tell Tracy everything he can to keep her baby safe and the prophecy intact.

><><><><><><><><><><><><><><><><><><><><

He sits with Tracy at the same small diner, each having what they try to pass off as a tuna melt and fries. A delicious sandwich if you can get past the plated presentation that looks more like yesterday's upchuck than freshly made tuna salad.

"You wanted to know the science," he starts in the same almost imperceptible volume they spoke in last time they shared a meal here.

She nods while taking a bite.

"The science behind it is only hypothesized now," he starts while studying her reaction.

The look on her face is far from satisfactory. "There has to be more," she insists in the same almost indiscernible volume.

"There is, and you won't like it," he prefaces. "What they do know about the science is deadly."

She stops eating and looks at him. "But I thought you said the child was somehow the savior of our people."

He stares at her, not saying anything. He hopes that the gravity of his words will sink in and make sense to her before he has to be the messenger of horrible news.

"You're wrong," she starts. "They are wrong. They can't ask me to give up my own life, leave my family behind, all in hopes that this child is who they say she is. This isn't fair, it isn't right, and I won't let it happen like that."

The two eat the rest of their meal in silence. Each contemplates the recent news bestowed upon them. Neither says anything more to the other but silently acknowledges the other person's struggles.

⬦⬦⬦⬦⬦⬦⬦⬦⬦⬦⬦⬦⬦⬦⬦⬦⬦⬦⬦⬦⬦⬦⬦⬦

Seated behind his desk at the museum, Vistrus studies a map of the building. One of the charts on the front kiosk for any visitor to take. He is searching for something that will give him a clue as to what the scrapped notebook page was referencing. He knows where all the "employee only" rooms are located, the doors that lead to back halls, the doors that lead to other offices.

Nothing on this map seems out of place, nothing but museum artifacts and displays that have rotated countless times since the museum opened. But he knows the restoration room, storage vaults, and more rooms kept off the general visitor's map, rooms that will be on blueprints, not public-use maps. Blueprints he has never seen but now must locate. He knows that if this torn, mostly illegible paper is correct, this place where he spends 40-plus hours a week holds more secrets, questions, and answers than he ever imagined.

CHAPTER 27

"Whether you want it to or not,
life goes on and so must you."
~J. Taylor~

T he time has come again, and for the final time.
A moment in Connor's high school career that nearly
eluded him because of his past truancy, grieving process, and insub-
ordinate behavior. The moments in life he handled the way he did,
and at the end of it all, shouts deafeningly into his ears that life
does not care. He must care about himself and be the one to make
sure he deals with things in a way that won't hold him back. He
is here, in a moment that should have passed him by: a meeting
that should be with some other kid, in some other school. But the
gods of fate have chosen mercy on him. Here he sits, next to his
father and across from his coach and the scout from the Wisconsin
Badgers, the only talent scout who still wants to recruit him to
their college to stand on a pile of dirt and throw a baseball past a
guy holding a large stick.

"I'm here because last time we met, it did not end well," the
Badger's rep begins. "I may have had a hand in that, which is why
I kept an eye on your activities, grades, whatever I could." A smile
breaks across his face.

Ken interjects, "Thank you for your reconsideration."

"It is my pleasure," the recruiter continues. "I know that Jack and his family have been found and are alive, due in no small part to this young man before me. Last time, we didn't get a chance to ask you about your post-collegiate plans. We like to know what we can about those we may invest in."

Connor nods at the given recognition. He shifts upward in his chair, straightening himself. He doesn't speak immediately to make it seem like he's searching for the right words. "The truth is, sir, after everything that has happened, I stopped putting too much thought that far ahead into the future."

The college rep tilts his head—a far cry from the typical answer he expected.

"Now, it's not that I don't want a future, or that I don't have ideas. But I think that given recent happenings, I would like to keep my options open for the future," Connor continues unconvincingly.

The rep's twisted face motions for Connor to explain himself more clearly.

"Okay, it's like a road trip with no specific destination. You know the general area and the road to get there, the road being Wisconsin. But the exits you take are up for grabs. I don't want to pigeonhole myself to do only one thing to find out later it's not what I was meant to do. I need to explore a little more before I commit to an endgame that far out." Connor finishes up with more certainty than he started.

The agent gives the DeSalvos a friendly, honest smile as he straightens his head. "I can understand and appreciate your thoughts on finding your future. We know your talents on the field, and this," he pauses to choose his words carefully, "extracurricular activity of finding your friend, shows us the true depths of your dedication and loyalty," he says. The scout takes a moment to look at and take in the emotions of the entire DeSalvo family. "We would like to help narrow down the future possibilities as you see fit. That brand of dedication and loyalty are traits that will go a long way with us and give you a bright future. So, the Wisconsin Badgers would like to offer you a full ride for the next four years."

As the parents and coach break out into a joyful chorus of congratulatory relief, the representative finishes his thoughts, "Of course, that comes with behavioral and academic stipulations that are standard on this sort of offer."

Ken nods in acknowledgment of the representative's words while hugging his son. Ken looks his son in the eye, "Do you have anything you would like to say to the nice man?"

Connor turns to the college recruiter. "Thank you for continuing to believe in me and keep me in mind for the team and the school. I look forward to pitching for the Wisconsin Badgers starting in the Fall of 2018."

The rep extends his hand out as he stands up. Connor stands to meet him. "Then this wraps up a long overdue meeting, and we are glad to see you come our way. We are positive you will be glad you chose us," the recruiter says, shaking Connor's hand. He retrieves a stapled pile of papers from his briefcase. "Give these a look and call me with any questions. This is just a sample but covers most everything that will be in his contract. We will be in touch," he says as he leaves.

The coach shakes Connor's hand. "Mr. DeSalvo, you've done it. Somehow, against all odds, as you've stacked them against yourself, you did it. Not that I'm surprised. You've been pulling stunts all four years and always remained on top. Now that you landed this, finals should be a breeze."

Coach pauses and drops his smile. "Practice is over. The real game has begun. These past four years have been just that, practice for the next big thing. And that big thing has arrived, so, ready or not, here you come," he finishes with a slight chuckle.

"You're ready, though. You've always been ready; whether you want to admit it or not, you're future is here. The real world waits for no-one and holds no favorites. It will be cruel and unforgiving because to the world no one is special." He extends out his hand for a shake, and Connor reciprocates.

"Now, go prove the world wrong."

CHAPTER 28

"The enemy of my enemy
is not always a friend.
Sometimes they are a worse enemy."
~D. Childers~

The piercing sound of the second hand clicking away each moment in a constant reminder of the timed test that will decide if they can take one less class during their college tenure breaks the room's hushed tones. Connor finishes the last question of his Advanced Placement Biology test but, per instructions, doesn't get up from his desk. Instead, he stares at Mrs. Espinoza, a face he has come to associate with all that is wrong with the world but has no proof or voice to say anything about it.

So, Connor sits and thinks about the past year at school. The academic, athletic, and personal tests have helped shape who he is. The future that lies ahead of him in college, playing baseball in exchange for an education. More importantly, he watches Jack finish his test while he thinks about what Coach said behind closed doors after Connor accepted the offer presented to him by the Wisconsin Badgers. He thinks about the fact that practice is over, and that the real world awaits him.

As Connor sits there, he can't help but wonder what the real world holds for not only him but his friends as well. Connor knows he aced this exam, will graduate high school, and move on to college.

He wonders what will be different. If they will have the opportunity to hang out as often as they did these past four years, or if they will grow apart and not see each other as often, then eventually, not at all. Maybe they will only see each other on Facebook, Twitter, and Instagram in political posts and holiday greetings. He knows this, though; Scarlett will always be his cousin, and right now, Jack is his best friend, and whatever is blossoming between himself and Allison feels nice.

So yes, the future is unclear and possibly uncertain, but he knows he is looking forward to whatever it may throw at him. If practice is indeed over, then he is as prepared as he is going to be and feels ready to face it all.

Jack finishes filling out the last question on his test and turns it over, setting his pencil on top. He glances at Connor with a sneering lip nod that says he feels good. He is ready to move on; perhaps that is what these four years have prepared them for. To be able to move on when the time comes. To be able to deal with memories, joyous and painful, to forge new friendships and relationships and bring them into the future with them. These four years have prepared them, most of all, to be able to know when they are forced to move on from the places that have brought much joy and memories into their life, that they can leave them where they are. So they will always have a lifetime of memories that, when needed, can help carry them through tough times. Memories that no doubt will one day be replaced by more important and, hopefully, more joyous memories.

The uncertainty of everything still unanswered is the bittersweet icing on the cake that was these last four years.

><><><><><><><><><><><><><><><><><><><><><><

A patrol car skulks through the parking lot close to Connor and Jack as they walk past a few strip mall stores toward a Men's Warehouse. They pay little mind to the usual activity of the chilled evening. As they enter the store, the only visible employee sets down his cell phone and comes out from around the counter.

With an upturned nose, he looks down at the boys, "May I help you?"

Connor steps forward. "Yes. We are here for our tuxes."

"For senior prom," Jack adds.

The salesman huffs as he walks to a rack of pre-ordered tuxedos. "Names?" he says as if he has better things to do.

"DeSalvo and Taylor," Connor replies. He gives Jack a funny look about the salesman's attitude. Jack chuckles in reply.

A moment later, the salesman comes out holding the two matching tuxedos. After handing them to the boys, he points to the dressing rooms. "Try them on in there. Make sure they fit properly."

The boys enter the rooms and begin undressing. They hear the bell to the front door chime as they finish zipping their tux pants. As they emerge, they look at each other, nod, and do a half smile at how cool they look. They turn to the salesman, now engaged in a quiet conversation with a cop.

Jack and Connor both stop in their tracks as their smiles wash away. They are stuck at the far end of this tiny tux store. Standing between them and the exit is Officer Max Espinoza. Jack locks eyes with the officer and begins to shake. Tears well up in his eyes. He tries to hold them back but can't. The fear of the past months overtakes him. He runs back into the changing room and cowers in a corner.

Connor looks at the salesman

"They fit great. We'll take them."

The salesman's snooty attitude turns soft as he witnesses Jack's breakdown. "Is everything okay with your friend?"

"Yes," Connor begins but shifts his stare to the officer, "he's recently had some issues with corrupt authority." He turns back to the salesman. "He'll be okay."

Officer Espinoza stands unfazed by Connor's dig at him. "Looks like you boys are gettin' ready for prom. Big night."

Connor stares down the officer.

"Let's see, that wouldn't be Maine West Haven's prom? Would it?" Max continues.

Connor keeps staring him down.

"It's not polite to not answer a question when asked, young man," Max preaches.

"Yes. It is Maine West Haven," Connor says through gritted teeth.

"Well, isn't that something? I might have to chaperone that night. It sure would be nice to see all the youngins getting together for one last party," he says, looking in Jack's direction. He turns back to Connor "That is until college starts. Well, I must be goin'. Maybe I'll see you boys at the prom." He winks at Connor and turns to exit.

The salesman looks at Connor. "What was that all about?"

"The officer is convinced my lanky friend is either on mass amounts of PCP or some type of vampire. It's a little game we play," Connor says, walking into the dressing room and lifting Jack to a standing position. "It's okay, bud. You got this."

"I can't go. If I go and he's there, it'll be, well, the past few months all over again," Jack says, still trembling.

"It's our one and only prom, but if you can't do this then I won't either," Connor promises.

Jack shakes his head. "No, no, no. It's one night. We'll figure something out." He peeks out of the dressing room. "Is he gone?"

Connor nods yes and starts walking him out of the dressing room to the counter.

The salesman looks at Jack, "I think I heard about you. You're that kid who," he pauses, searching for words, "just returned not too long ago."

Connor nods at the salesman. "That's him."

"So the rumors are true," the salesman confirms.

"What rumors?" Connor asks.

"In a small circle of my friends, there is a rumor that he and his family were suspected of being … more human than human," the clerk answers.

"Well, if that's the rumor…" Connor lets the sentence trail off.

"So? Are you in?" the salesman asks.

"In what? School?" Connor asks, completely confused by the question.

The guy nods and turns to his computer. "Your rentals are due back by closing time the day after prom."

The dress racks of Okora sit half empty, having been pilfered by high school girls searching for the perfect prom dress. The lucky ones can still find one worthy of purchase, but most of the remains sit hanging half off the hangers like leftovers from a second-hand store. The smart ones, like Scarlett and Allison, shopped early, tried on the dress, and had alterations made.

The vast amount of women, young and older, roaming the racks the night before prom fills the air with a sense of panic and wonder. Some girls emerge from dressing rooms after trying on the dresses post alteration with smiles on their faces, glowing at how beautiful they look and feel. Others appear with tears falling down their cheeks, not feeling confident even though the dress fits wonderfully.

Allison and Scarlett knock on a door to check its availability. A familiar voice within quivers back a response, "One moment, please."

Allison and Scarlett turn to each other as the less than confident response sounds like their old friend.

"Bri?" Scarlett says back.

"Yeah?" Bri meekly responds.

"Everything okay?" Scarlett asks with sincerity in her voice.

Bri unlatches the door to the dressing room and emerges in a gold sequin, form-fitting dress that flares into a flowing skirt. "The other dress didn't fit, and this was the closest they had, and now I'm going to prom dressed like the golden ticket from Willy Wonka," she cries.

Allison freezes in awe of the beauty before her. She sees Bri as the down-on-her-luck young woman who stands before her, not as the self-righteous betrayer she formed her to be in her mind. A sense of guilt and remorse fills her, making her wonder if the past four years of pointed anger and resentment could have been better spent rebuilding a friendship.

"You look…" Allison stops while searching for the perfect word.

Bri looks at Allison, awaiting some snarky quip. "Like what? The wrapping to a Ferrero Rocher?" Bri adds.

Allison shakes her head, still in awe of the sight before her. "No. I was going to say perfect."

Scarlett and Brianna stare, speechless at the nice and utterly real comment that just came from Allison's mouth. Allison, however, stares slack-jawed at Brianna as thoughts run through her head she has never experienced before. Feelings that can turn into realizations and such emotions about someone who has been an enemy for the past four years make Allison want to run screaming. But she stays. And she stays to face her inner demons and beat them back into their hiding place.

Brianna sniffles away a few tears and smiles a bit. "Thank you, Ally. That means a lot coming from you." Bri turns to Scarlett. "I just want prom to be perfect, and the other dress was perfect."

"Prom's not all about the dress, Bri. It's about the company you keep that night," Scarlett says before adding with a smirk, "and the dress."

Brianna takes a quick look around the store to make sure no one of value is within earshot. "Thank you," she finishes with a smile. "I have to change back. The room next to me is open." Brianna enters and latches the door shut.

The girls each enter a room and try on their perfectly altered dresses. As Scarlett tries on her dress, she imagines what it will be like next year at prom with all her friends and classmates, one final time together before embarking on a journey that is the rest of their lives.

Allison slips on her dress and looks at herself in the mirror. Mixed thoughts enter her mind. She sees a female who looks years too young to be in such an exquisite dress. The baby-faced teen and coltish body trying to burst into full womanly form in the guise of a prom dress.

On the other hand, she sees someone who has been through a lot these past three years. Someone who someone else thought was worthy of spending their one prom night with, which means she will get two prom nights. She tries to see the woman that Connor sees, the woman that her father sees. She tries to see the woman that everyone else around her sees, except for her.

Scarlett stands staring at herself, tugging her dress down to get out every and any wrinkle that may have scrunched up. She feels elegant and classy as she does mock poses in the mirror. Scarlett knows that she, too, has one more year before her prom, but she is glad she gets to go with her friends, even though Jack isn't ready for such a grand social situation. She stands there thinking about the year ahead, what it might be like, what the last year at West Haven holds, and how it will all end.

The girls both step out of the dressing rooms, already changed back into their street clothes. A smile on both their faces as they sling the dresses over their shoulders and carry them home in plastic protective covers.

><><><><><><><><><><><><><><><><><><><

The still air of the evening brings a strange silence to the familiar surroundings as Brianna stands in front of her bathroom mirror wearing her prom dress, still uncertain about her final choice. She snaps a few selfies that tease the top of her dress, as she doesn't want to give away her complete look before prom, then posts it to Instagram.

From the other room, Sylvia excitedly calls out to her daughter, "So!? Let's see it!"

Brianna cat walks into the living room where Sylvia is drinking an appletini. Brianna finishes her walk with a twirl to show off the sequin under the living room lights.

"It's gold," Sylvia says, sipping her martini.

The little bit of confidence Brianna had in her dress has been washed away by those two alcohol-soaked words. She looks down at her dress, once again questioning her choice. "But I was told I look perfect in it."

"Probably by some boy just wanting to defile my daughter," Sylvia says as her voice becomes more confrontational.

Brianna looks back up. "No, actually, it was Allison. My ... friend. She saw it and gave me a compliment for once."

"Well, that's nice," Sylvia says, polishing off her appletini. She walks into the kitchen to pour another. "When we first went shopping, I thought we settled on that blue and white princess-style dress? Didn't they take your measurements for alterations?"

Brianna walks into the kitchen. "Yeah, and they messed it up. So, I was left to pick something out on my own. The day before prom doesn't exactly leave a ton on the racks."

Sylvia pours the next martini and downs it in one swift gulp. She begins to concoct another. "The dress is gold. It makes you look like a streetwalker."

"Damn it, mom! Prom is *my* night! Why are you trying to ruin it for me?!" she says, stomping her feet in raging frustration.

She pours and chugs down the next martini. "You have no idea," she starts with a pointed finger circling at her daughter. "You think life is all about high school and boys and looking cute. You have no idea what the rest of the world holds." She sips whatever leftover alcohol pooled back at the bottom of her empty glass.

"Yes! Yes, it is all about high school and boys and looking cute! It's not like you're ever sober enough to teach me about what the rest of life will be like! I just know I don't want it to be like you!" Defiance grows with each word.

Sylvia meets Bri's words by throwing a martini glass that busts across her face. Little shards of glass pierce her skin, sticking in and stinging from the alcohol coating them. Before Bri can react, Sylvia shoves her daughter against the table. Bri tries to keep her balance but falls back onto it. Her mother stands over her, keeping an iron grip on Bri's arms.

"You're hurting me!" pleads Bri.

"You ungrateful little brat! Everything I've done for you! You can't be thankful for any of it." Sylvia emphasizes her words with a light cheek smack across Brianna's bloodied face. "Wait until you find out what life is really like! Who you really are! You won't be able to look at yourself in the mirror!" She throws her daughter against the table, Brianna's head slamming against it as blood trickles down her face.

Bri shoves her mom off of her and runs into the bathroom. She locks the door behind her. She pauses for a moment and takes a deep breath to try and calm down, but her hysteria only intensifies. She twists the handles to turn on the water and looks into the mirror. The cuts over Brianna's body look worse than they feel. She grabs a tweezer from the medicine cabinet and starts pulling out the shards of glass. Each tiny piece stings horribly as she tugs them out. Each sting sends a shock through her face and more blood dripping into the sink in an increasing flow. She sobs through her pain. Her entire body heaves with each uncontrollable breath. She continues pulling out the shards of glass and tries cleaning the wounds, but the blood continues to drip.

Through her tear-clouded eyes, she sees her face in the mirror. Her teenage skin, which she moisturizes daily, begins to wrinkle and sag. In a frenzy, she makes fruitless attempts to push it back into place. The skin keeps returning to its new drooping state. Her eyes develop puffy, dark bags under them as her lips start chapping and peeling apart to raw flesh beneath as blood drips from each cracked line. Her crying grows ever more hysterical with each passing second. Her sobs are uncontrollable.

Sylvia pounds on the bathroom door, trying to get in, but Brianna can't stop crying. She can't understand why she feels like she is dying at this moment. Her mother continues to pound on the door demanding Bri let her in, but Brianna continues standing over the sink, trying to wash away the blood and tug on her loose skin.

She notices her neck skin sags and sways like a turkey wattle. She starts pulling on it, stretching it too far to be healthy. She wipes away the tears from her eyes to try and get a clear view of herself. She looks in the mirror and sees all the youthful beauty she possesses now replaced with grotesque aging. She tries opening her eyes wide and giving a closed-lipped smile, but both are in vain. She has become old and decrepit in a matter of minutes. A monster of her former self, looking like a newly zombified victim from some movie or television show. All external beauty has been ripped away and replaced with a horrid sight.

The pounding continues on the bathroom door. Sylvia's words sound distant beneath the running water and Brianna's hysterics.

Brianna opens her mouth to have a look inside. As she does, some of her teeth fall out into the sink, which only adds to the confused hysterics Brianna feels at herself right now.

"This can't be happening," she says to herself as blood pours from her mouth. "I'm seventeen years old. I'm going to prom with Troy, star football player. I can't be … this. I'm not a monster. I'm beautiful."

The loose skin of someone many, many decades beyond her years wrinkles her hands.

She falls to the floor, blood dripping from her face onto her prom dress. She holds her old hands to her aged face and cries into them. The sound of running water and pounding floods her ears. She sobs, "This isn't me."

The pounding stops. Brianna looks to the bottom of the bathroom door and sees the shadow from Sylvia's feet disappear. Now, only the sound of running water drones above her.

"What have I done to deserve this?" she asks herself as she stands back up to look in the mirror.

Her reflection stares back at her—old and liver-spotted. Her once thick and silky blonde hair has become grey and wispy.

The pain that courses through her has subsided a little. Her face still hurts from the glass and her entire body throbs. The piercing pains that run deep inside her, penetrating all her muscles and bones, are still present.

"Is this what I get?" she asks herself through a mostly toothless grin. "Why?" she asks as she slinks back onto the bathroom floor. "I can't go to prom like this," she sobs. "I can't go anywhere looking like this!"

CHAPTER 29

*"Prom is just an excuse
for teens to drink, have sex,
and make bad decisions.
But then again,
it's where I met your grandfather."*
~E. DeSalvo~

Scarlett and Allison put the final touches on their makeup; a couple of lip smacks ensure even distributions of their lipstick, mascara to make their eyes pop, and a dab of sparkle to their cheeks for an added element of magic to this once-in-a-lifetime night—juniors at Senior Prom.

They turn to each other to see how the other girl looks. Scarlett wears a form-fitting deep red dress that flares out, starting right below the knees into a wide mermaid tail. Her hair, styled in an up-do that falls into a few loose curls and a makeup palette matching her dress, finishes her look, making her feel like the beautiful, young woman she is.

Allison wears a black, evening-style dress with shoulder caps of a woven, floral design that holds a sheer black cape that flows behind her. Her tightly styled hair and makeup finished in a darker, evening look give her a hint of an evil movie queen.

The girls smile at each other and giggle at the potential of the night ahead.

"You ready?" Scarlett asks, grabbing both girls' clutch purses.

Allison turns to give herself one more look in the mirror. Her face turns to uncertainty as she tosses glances between herself and Scarlett. Glimpses that are not unnoticed by Scarlett.

"You look beautiful, love. If I were Connor, I'd be falling in love right about now," Scarlett offers up. The compliment itself further adds to Allison's confusion ever since her thoughts muddled her mind in front of Brianna.

"Thanks," Allison says, turning away from the mirror. "I think I just heard Connor come in."

"That's some super hearing you've got if you're right," Scarlett says.

Vistrus shouts from the main level up to the girls, "Girls! Connor and your limo are here!"

Allison nods to Scarlett as they head downstairs. On the main level, Connor, fully decked out in a tail-coated tuxedo, and Vistrus, camera in hand and a light deflector set up as well, greet them.

"Goin' all out, dad?" Allison quips at the lighting gear.

Vistrus rounds them into a setup spot for pictures. "Hey, this is your first prom. Think I would let this slide? Now, come on. Your limo and prom await," he says, gesturing for them to scooch closer. He snaps a good twenty to thirty pictures in various poses ranging from serious to comical, something to remember this night by.

On their way out the door, the three teens giggle and laugh as they make their way to the limo that will drive them to the dance.

"I know that you were feeling a bit down about Jack not going, but he got you in, and I didn't want you to feel like you were going without him," Connor says in as many words as possible. "So I got you something," he finishes sliding into the limo. He hands Scarlett a corsage.

She looks at the wrist corsage and sees Jack's face flawlessly painted on the flower. "He and I thought you might like that, maybe." Connor sees her face scrunching up as she tries not to cry. "Or not..."

"Shut up," Scarlett interrupts. "This is beautiful. Perfect," she says, sliding the corsage onto her hand.

"Good," Connor says. "One more stop before prom." He turns his attention to the driver. "To our first stop, good sir."

The driver nods and pushes the button to raise the divider. A few blocks later, the limo stops at Jack's house. Outside the door, Jack waits in a full tuxedo that matches Connor's. Scarlett gives Connor a confused look.

"He wanted you and him to have some pictures together. To remember the night by. They'll be his only pictures of the prom, and wanted you in them," Connor tells Scarlett.

Jack walks down to the car as the driver cues up Eric Clapton's "Wonderful Tonight" on the stereo.

"May I have this dance?" Jack says, extending out his hand.

Scarlett takes his hand and looks back at Allison with a smile while Jack pulls her into him.

"Thank you for the dance," Jack says.

Scarlett whispers into his ear, "The pleasure is all mine."

The two enjoy the few minutes of closeness as the song plays out. Leaning against the limo, Connor and Allison watch their friends.

"I could stay here with you tonight. If you'd like," Scarlett offers up.

Jack looks her in the eye and gives her a deep, passionate kiss. "No. You go have fun. The school knows I won't be there but, uh, you will, and they've made an exception to let you in. Special circumstances and all."

Scarlett returns the kiss. The two of them are oblivious to the cameras snapping away from the porch as James and Lucretia watch the moments that let them know their boy is growing up.

As the song ends, Jack pulls away. They both stop and look into each other's eyes for a few moments. Jack struggles hard not to let his eyes wander too much.

"You look amazing and beautiful, and there's no one in the world who has helped me more since everything. Thank you so much," Jack says in a concise tone that generally eludes him.

"I know it might be too soon for this, but…" She pauses, searching for her words. "I think I'm falling in love with you."

He smiles big. "I'll take an 'I think' since I'm right there with you, my love."

"Are you sure you don't want me to stay?" she offers up one more time.

"No, but yes." He steps back and lets go of her hand. "Go, have fun. Stop by after prom, well, uh, if you want. My parents said it's all good."

Scarlett smiles and beams with excitement. "Then I'll see you later then."

Connor enters the limo first. Before Allison gets in, she turns to Scarlett, "I had no idea you felt that way."

The driver shuts the door after Allison and Scarlett enter. Jack watches as they drive off to prom.

Scarlett says to Allison, "Seriously, what is up with your hearing? But yeah, some things creep up on you."

⸻⸻⸻⸻⸻⸻⸻

With his daughter off to prom and all quiet at work, Vistrus finds himself back in his office at the museum, searching various blueprints from the city's files. Sprawled out on his desk, somewhere within the papers that show the floor and structural plans of the entire museum, are the answers to the questions he now asks.

Starting with the newest plans and working backward, he searches for discrepancies or anything that stands out from his knowledge of the building. His backward search hits on something that raises his eyebrow. An old, cracked and partly faded blueprint from the first renovation of the museum shows a sub-basement that renovations have long since sealed off.

The prints show venting that leads in, a fire code no-no of a dead-ended hallway being the only way to or from this room. Perhaps that is why some past museum directors decided to seal it off. The layout of the room itself is a simple square design, but blueprints do not show how the room was decorated or finished.

He journeys to the back end of the vault that hides the hallway to this mysterious room. Vault access is severely restricted, but his position in acquisitions allows him entry to places within the museum where few are allowed to go. Any access to the vault must be registered, so he signs in under the guise of checking old inventory for a project in the planning stages.

The far side of the vault holds little to be concerned with, mainly filled with cobwebs building upon replicas and unimportant set decorations, which leaves Vistrus to his own devices. He takes his time rearranging what he needs to access the back wall better.

Years of minimal foot traffic in this back area have left it surprisingly close to what Vistrus imagines it looking like when renovations first hid away the hallway. A wall bordering cyclopean architecture stands between him and his hidden treasure. The question added to his growing list about the town and its history is, why hide away something so seemingly mundane? Why put forth the effort to cover up a room that could have been repurposed?

After around half an hour of inspecting the wall for seams and weak spots, he happens upon a soft piece of mortar that immediately begins to crumble away as he rubs it. He pulls at this spot, rubbing over and over again until the mortar stops falling apart. After it finishes falling away, a small, hollowed hole, a few inches tall and barely wide enough to fit his little finger and ring finger inside, remains. After all these decades, this spot is the only weak point in the masonry. He carefully slides his fingers into the missing mortar, feeling the smooth, stone surface. As he nears the end of his reach, he feels something out of place—a slick bump in the otherwise flat stone. The stone itself was even but still finished with the gritty feel of rock. This is different, polished like porcelain or metal. He pushes on the polished piece and finds it sinks into the stone. A noise clicks from behind the wall causing Vistrus to pull his fingers out of the hole quickly.

He watches as the stone wall separates perfectly from its mortar seams and opens on hinged ends to reveal the hallway behind it. The dark, damp hall fills his nostrils with mildew and dust. The dim light in the far reaches of the vault fades quickly in this hall. There is no end to the hallway in sight. He enters the corridor, pulls out his cell phone, and turns on the flashlight application.

A quick inspection of the doorway mechanism finds him a way to close himself into the hallway and get back out, safeguarding his newfound secret.

The light illuminates the hallway of the same cyclopean architecture and cobblestone walkway leading downwardly sloped to what, at first glance, is a dead end in the corridor where the architecture changes to large, solid blocks of what appears to be marbled Lime and Obsidian. From his limited knowledge of geology, he assumes this is some form of Serpentine Subgroup stonework. The choice of which has him wondering.

After the initial shock and awe of the sudden stop in the hallway, he notices a small inset of a cosmetically hidden handle. He pulls on the handle, and the door opens with a poof of dust from between the cracks.

As the dust settles, he spots a small light switch a few feet from the door. As he steps toward the switch, the door leading into the room shuts behind him. He jerks his head for a quick look back, shining the flashlight at the door, but no one is there. He flips the switch causing dozens of tiny overhead lights to illuminate the room in a brilliant yet eerie glow. The interior is the same marbled serpentine stone. The height of the room stands just over ten feet. The two long walls tilt backward about fifteen degrees giving the ceiling more surface area than the floor. The extended length of the room is about twenty feet, and the width is about ten. There are no windows or any other outlets to the world outside. No storage containers or anything else indicating what this room was once used for.

He looks around at the seemingly barren room, taking in the beauty that has evaded him for all these decades in West Haven. The smell of stone and stale air replace the scent of mildew from the hallway. There are no tables, no shelves, or boxes of any kind. The only thing that accompanies Vistrus in this room is a piece of parchment that lays face down in the center of the room, on top of which sits a white glove.

He instinctively looks around the room before stepping toward the items. A defensive measure to make sure no one else is around. Finding no one waiting to ambush him, a notion he feels yet knows is unfounded, he steps to the two things.

He first lifts the white glove; not the most pristine of items but still reasonably white. Nothing a proper washing couldn't fix. Though he knows from his time in the museum that old relics, still yet to be examined, do not get washed. So this glove will be as it has been for some time more. The glove is made of soft cloth, feeling like some sort of silk blend. Finding no tags, he presumes this predates mass manufacturing of any kind.

Second, he carefully lifts the parchment, maintaining a cautious hand as he doesn't want to possibly tear or cause the paper to crumble. After taking a moment to flip it to the other side, he almost drops the parchment when he sees the charcoal drawing on the front. He stares, unsure of what to make of the portrait. He wonders why this portrait is here. How long has it been here? And how could it be so accurate in depiction? The shock of the discovery holds him motionless. His stare locked in on the parchment, unable to tear his eyes away from what he holds before him.

><><><><><><><><><><><><><><><><><><><><

A masked and hooded man dressed in all black, carrying a black backpack, skulks around the outside of the Taylors' home, hugging the exterior walls and staying in the shadows. Only the occasional small reflection off his bolt cutters betrays his location. He creeps up to a set of landline phone wires and cuts through them with ease. He quickly makes his way to the main power box and clips the lock guarding the switch inside. He sneaks a peek inside the house through a window and sees the three of them in the family room watching TV. Jack is still in his prom tuxedo.

He readies the bolt cutters around the main power line to the house but doesn't cut. He holds the position with his left hand. With his right hand, he switches off the central power, then quickly uses both hands to slice through the main power line, metal conduit, and all. He slinks back into the shadows.

He listens to the conversation inside the house as James tells his wife and son, "Jack, go check the basement. I'll look outside."

Jack, following the command of his father, heads downstairs. James heads out back, the darkness concealing the things that go bump in the night. He approaches the power switch and flips it back on. The lack of power in his house alarms him. He looks down and notices the main power line severed. As he turns around to rush inside, sensing something is wrong, a blow to the face from the bolt cutters stops his progress. The stun from the hit gives the masked man enough time to shock him with a Taser gun.

The masked man pulls a length of rope out of his bag and makes quick work of tying James's hands and feet together in a fisherman's slipknot, preventing James from coming loose should he awaken. He then drags James's limp body to the back door, where James exited the house. He opens it and lugs the unconscious body inside.

"Is everything okay, dear?" Lucretia calls from the living room.

The man drops James and rushes Lucretia in a surprise attack. She sees him and knows she needs to make time to fully transition before he reaches her. Her mind races, unsuccessfully calculating how to counter this intruder. He lunges at her, bolt cutter pulled back, ready to strike. As he swings down, she jumps over the couch, starting her transition. The bolt cutter grazes her calf. Her muscle cushions most of the blow. She turns around in almost complete vampiric form. Her beautiful, smooth skin has stretched and scarred. Her nose recedes fully into her face, leaving nothing but holes where her nose should be. Her lips have scarred over and disappeared from her face. Her teeth, too, have retreated into her gums, save her elongated and stained incisors. Her thin hair whips around from the commotion. The masked man dives over the couch, landing on top of her. His Taser fires up and sparks. He jabs it into her neck, not worrying whether that is a fatal spot to shock someone.

She quickly falls unconscious, and her vampiric form retreats from sight. The man ties her up in a similar fashion. He sits her on the couch and drags James to prop him up next to her.

"I know you heard the commotion, boy," the masked man calls out to Jack. He removes his hood and mask to reveal himself as the blonde man. His face healed but scarred and disfigured from Vistrus's attack in the alley. "Come out, come out. Wherever you are," he taunts.

Jack watches from the darkened hallway as the blonde man starts tiptoeing around the living room, searching for Jack while keeping the parents in his line of sight. "I know you're here," the blonde man continues.

Jack waits, trying to use his anger to transition himself. He knows he's done it. Jack remembers being chained to the wall and the force-fed drugs that transitioned him before. He concentrates but can't get the change he needs. He knows he must react and soon. The blonde man will find him eventually.

Jack sneaks into the kitchen, blindly reaches for the knife block, and slowly pulls out a bread knife. Jack watches as the blonde man takes off his backpack and pulls out a belt. The blonde man unrolls it to reveal stainless steel dental instruments that glisten in the moonlight—pointed, sharp, and menacing.

The blonde man takes a pointed tool out of the belt and turns to Lucretia. "Time's running out, Jack. Don't you want to save your mommy?"

Jack creeps into the living room, bread knife ready to strike down all its serrated fury on the blonde man. As he gets within striking distance, the blonde man suddenly turns around and pokes Jack in the chest with the tool. The sharp, sudden pain causes Jack to drop the knife and grab his chest.

"Them's the smarts, huh?" the blonde man says, using the instrument to point at Jack's chest.

Jack stands, clutching his chest. He looks up at the blonde man's scarred and disfigured face. "What do you want from us?" Jack pleads.

"Sit next to your father," the blonde man gestures.

Jack defiantly looks at the blonde man and remains resolute in his stance.

The blonde man shakes his head at Jack's stubbornness. He takes a scalpel from his rolled-out tools and slices James' bicep.

"Stop!" screams Jack.

James wakes up from the pain of the injury. He looks around, trying to figure out what has happened to him.

"Sit down, boy!" the blonde man reiterates, once again jabbing Jack in the chest with the pointed tool.

James holds back the tears from his arm being sliced open. "What do you want from us? Why are you doing this to us?" he asks the intruder.

The blonde man ties up Jack but is distracted by James' questions. The blonde man yanks the knots on Jack's ropes while looking at James. "Why am I doing this? Research. We must find a cure for your kind. A way to eradicate everyone like you. A way to make you one of us."

"We're no different than you! Just people…"

The blonde man jumps at James with a tool in each hand. He holds the scalpel to James's neck. "No! You are very different. I've seen your kind for decades try and hide among the normal people. Your kind made fables and legends of what you are, all while walking among us. We don't know what you are planning or what you want from us. But we will stop you. We will cure you. Then there will be no difference. Nothing to separate us. Nothing to make you superior to us."

"No one is superior. Please. Let us go!" James implores.

The blonde man stands up and walks back to his tools. He pulls out an empty syringe and walks back to Jack. Without saying a word, he jabs the needle into his arm and draws a vial of blood. He then proceeds to do the same to James and Lucretia, who, upon being stuck, finally regains consciousness.

The blonde man walks over to James and Lucretia. "Change for me! I need more samples! Show us who you really are!"

"If we change, will you let us live?" Lucretia asks.

The blonde man laughs. "No. I will still kill you."

"Then why would we transition?" James inquires.

The blonde man slashes James' neck, causing blood to spray everywhere. The gurgling sounds of life leaving James' body are too much for Lucretia as she transitions back into full vampire form.

"Mom!" Jack yells. "Mom!"

Lucretia looks to her son. "It's okay, Jack. We love you and always will."

The blonde man collects blood from James as it spurts out of his neck.

Lucretia keeps eye contact with her son. "Be strong, Jack. You've always been stronger than you know."

The blonde man pulls out a plastic bag and places it over Lucretia's head. He ties it tight around her neck, cutting off all oxygen.

Jack struggles against his ropes as he sees his mother gasping for air. "You're dead meat!" Jack screams to the blonde man in a panic.

Jack feels his blood coursing through his veins. An unimaginable pain starts in his head and quickly spreads through his whole body. He feels the agony of his teeth shifting around, growing. He can taste the blood pooling in his mouth. His clothes start to tear as his muscles expand drastically in size. His hair grows long and thick and starts covering every inch of flesh. Even his nails grow long and dense, like a canine.

"Look what we have here. A change without drugs," the blonde man starts. "You are now a real, living myth and shall die like one."

Jack ignores the taunts of the blonde man, keeping his eye on his mother, whose life is diminishing with each passing moment he stays tied up. Jack watches as the blonde man turns around, searching through his tools. The pain is almost unbearable as Jack's vision starts to go white for a moment, but he stays focused on his mother. Jack continues struggling against the ropes when the pain suddenly washes away. His senses heightened; he hears his mother's shallow breathing from inside her plastic coffin, the breaths of the blonde man, the blood trickling down his father's neck, and the birds outside chirping away. Jack hears everything and sees in greater detail than moments ago. His nose has picked up a scent, too. An aroma he has never smelled before this moment. Something that wreaks of faint urine and sweat coming from the blonde man; Jack can smell the blonde man's fear.

Jack takes a deep breath and, with all his might, pulls against the ropes. They do not break, but his hand slips out from one of the knots, freeing him from his bindings. With a vicious roar, he lunges at the blonde man, who turns around, scalpel in hand but the ropes still around Jack's hand knock the blade free. Jack tackles the blonde man onto the floor, landing on top. The blonde man scrambles for anything nearby that he can use to defend himself. He stops, eye-locked with Jack. The blonde man sees the anger and the pain, the rage and the sadness, the confusion, and the humanity all within one boy's eyes. The blonde man also sees Jack move in. Jack sinks his teeth into the blonde man's neck, ripping out his throat in one great and terrible motion.

Jack rushes to his mother and tears a hole in the bag, but there is no response. He shakes his mother, trying to wake her from her endless sleep. Tears fall freely from his eyes as the young Jack Taylor sits among the carnage. He continues shaking his mom.

"Mom! Wake up! Mom!" he cries out over and over but still no response.

After a while, he gives up his efforts and falls onto the couch in between his deceased parents. The blonde man lies dead on the floor at his feet. Jack sits, unsure of the unreal events of the evening, his prom tux covered in everyone's blood. His home is now a sight of a massacre.

He sits on his couch in full werewolf form. Drying blood covers his face and mats his newly grown hair. He sits in shock at the events and is uncertain of what to do next. He can't call the police. But he realizes he can dial his friends if he can return to his Normal state.

He reaches into his coat for his cell phone but can't find it. He looks around and sees his phone on the floor, drowned in a pool of blood, lifeless as everything else around him.

⋙⋘⋙⋘⋙⋘⋙⋘⋙⋘⋙⋘⋙⋘⋙⋘⋙⋘⋙⋘

"I could just die tonight," Scarlett says, taking a seat at their table. She looks around, taking in all the prom after an exhausting night of dancing.

The event is everything a senior student could ask for; glorious food and drink, a DJ that was well worth the money, all decorated to the nines, nothing overlooked.

Allison and Connor join her. "Me too," Allison agrees. "This has been so much fun." She reaches into Connor's tux jacket, slung over a seat back, and pulls out a flask. She holds it low and pours some into a glass from the table. She caps it off and slips it back into the jacket.

"I'm surprised there's still some left," Scarlett says. "We've been hitting that all night."

Allison takes a big gulp of her drink. "Last of it." She turns to Connor and whispers in his ear. "Speaking of things to hit tonight, how about we head back to your place."

Connor hops up out of his chair. "I'm ready to go. You ready to go, Al?"

She nods her head yes.

"Scar?"

She shrugs. "It's been fun, and the night is almost over. No after-prom party for the varsity players?"

Connor shakes his head. "Decided to break tradition this year since everything that happened to Jack. Didn't want him feeling left out."

"Have the limo drop me off at his house. I'd like another dance," Scarlett tells them.

As they leave prom, Scarlett pulls out her cell phone and sends Jack a text.

[Scarlett: Coming over. Hope you still have your tux on. I want another dance.]

They enter the limo and begin to drive back home. Allison and Connor use the excuse of having been drinking to be a bit more handsy in front of Scarlett than she'd like, but she finds shelter in her Facebook app.

Scarlett checks her texts, but Jack has not responded. She hopes he is still awake. Scarlett wants this to be a night he'll never forget. She sets the phone down for a moment and closes her eyes to avoid the sight of Allison fumbling around with Connor.

The limo stops, and the driver opens the door. Scarlett steps out and turns back before the door closes. "Have fun," she says, but Connor and Allison are busy burying their tongues in each other's mouths.

Scarlett walks up to the darkened house as the limo drives off. She sees the lack of lights or any electronics turned on. She knocks on the front door and waits. No response. She hears rustling inside the house and checks the knob. Locked. She knocks one more time. Someone turns the knob from the inside.

><><><><><><><><><><><><><><><><

The two lovebirds exit the limo, walk up the driveway, and stop outside the front door of the darkened house. They listen for a moment but hear nothing inside.

"Looks like your parents aren't home," Allison says with a wink.

They enjoy the moment outside, kissing and their hands wandering. Connor holds Allison's head in his hands and looks her in the eyes.

"You sure you want to do this?" he asks. "No pressure."

She shakes her head enthusiastically. "So ready," she says, jumping up and wrapping her legs around him as she dives back in for another kiss.

He carries her into the house, both lip-locked and ready to feel what's next. He carries her past the entryway and living room. Neither of them saw the shining, dark-colored pool of liquid on the living room floor. Connor stumbles over something but never looks down to see what it is. Her legs fall back to the ground as he regains his footing. His eyes stay locked on Allison. She leans against the wall to help Connor unbutton his tuxedo shirt. A devilish smile on her face as they both hurry to unbutton him. She runs her hands across his chest, and he again lifts her off the ground. She wraps her legs around him once more as he pulls her away from the wall to carry her to his bedroom. Connor unzips the back of her dress as he opens the door to his room.

They shut his bedroom door, and Connor takes a deep breath to prepare himself for this moment. As his lungs fill, he catches the scent of something unfamiliar but metallic.

"Do you smell that?" he asks, taking himself out of the moment.

Allison looks around and takes a deep breath in. She shakes her head. "I don't smell anything." She grabs his shirt and pulls him toward her. They both tumble onto the bed. The moonlight shadows shine through his curtains into the darkened room, adding to the beauty of the evening.

Allison and Connor explore each other's bodies in ways they had only fantasized about. All those daydreams and flights of fancy have led to this moment. An act that they both feel is meant to be on this night. What else is an occasion such as prom for if not this?

Allison takes in all the emotions of the moment. She is with the boy she has always wanted. That this is far more physically painful than she thought it would be. That the pleasure she feels far out-weighs the pain. That, at this moment, the two of them connect in a way they can never connect with anyone else. First times never happen twice.

Connor's smile says it all, that he is with the girl he has always admired. A girl whose spitfire personality is only outdone by her loyalty to those she considers family. And he gets to share that with her.

Connor and Allison wish this moment could last forever, but like all great moments in life, when they are over, they're over. As momentous as the moment was and disconnected from the rest of the world as it was, things must get back to normal. The night must march onward. That life goes on. They both smile because they know that this ending is only temporary—that it can happen again.

Allison hastily redresses herself so they can leave his room. He zips his tuxedo pants and turns on the light. Connor notices a small amount of blood on his sheets where Allison was lying down. While he has heard stories about this moment, the placement seems to be where her back laid.

"Turn around, love," Connor asks.

Allison, oblivious to the spots of blood, says, "Don't worry about zipping me up. I'll be fine."

"That's not it," he replies.

Allison shrugs and turns around. He sees a smear of blood across the back of her dress.

In an instant, he flicks off the light again, leaving them in the dark room. He puts his finger to his lips.

"What's going on?" Allison whispers.

He shakes his head while slowly opening the door. "I don't know. Follow me."

They sneak out of his bedroom and make their way to the living room. Again the unfamiliar scent overtakes his sense of smell. He stops and sees a streak of mostly dried blood on the shadowed wall where Allison was leaning. Connor now realizes what he was smelling so strongly before.

Allison stumbles back toward the bedroom a few feet before regaining balance. As Connor continues, he sees a broken lamp that should be sitting on the living room end table instead lying in the hallway.

As they turn the corner to the living room, a sight greets them that burns itself into their minds and forever eclipses the moment they just shared.

Etching into their minds to haunt their psyche is a glistening pool of dark crimson blood and a pile of mangled, ripped-apart bodies.

BOOK CLUB QUESTIONS

1. What is the significance of the title? Did you find any meaning in it?

2. What did you think of the writing style and content structure of the book?

3. Were there any quotes (or passages) that stood out to you? Why?

4. Who was your favorite character? Why?

5. What motivates the actions of each of the characters in the book?

6. Which character would you most like to meet in real life?

7. What scene resonated with you most on a personal level? (Why? How did it make you feel?)

8. What was your favorite chapter and why?

9. How have the characters changed by the end of the book?

10. How did you feel about the ending? How might you change it?

ABOUT THE AUTHOR

Nick Savage is an award winning and Amazon best-selling author.

Nick lives in the greater Orlando, FL, area with his wife and two cats.

He is an avid video game nerd, artist, and musician.

Other books by Nick Savage

The *Fairlane* Series:
The Fairlane Incidents
The Fortunate Finn Fairlane
The Fragile Finn Fairlane

Other books in *The West Haven Undead* Series
So We Stay Hidden
The West Haven Undead

Coming Soon:
World Whore, D

MORE BOOKS FROM
4 HORSEMEN PUBLICATIONS

PARANORMAL & URBAN FANTASY

AMANDA FASCIANO
Waking Up Dead
Dead Vessel

BEAU LAKE
The Beast Beside Me
The Beast Within Me
Taming the Beast: Novella
The Beast After Me
Charming the Beast: Novella
The Beast Like Me
An Eye for Emeralds
Swimming in Sapphires
Pining for Pearls

CHELSEA BURTON DUNN
By Moonlight

J.M. PAQUETTE
Call Me Forth
Invite Me In
Keep Me Close

JESSICA SALINA
Not My Time

KAIT DISNEY-LEUGERS
Antique Magic

LYRA R. SAENZ
Prelude
Falsetto in the Woods: Novella
Ragtime Swing
Sonata
Song of the Sea
The Devil's Trill
Bercuese
To Heal a Songbird
Ghost March
Nocturne

MEGAN MACKIE
The Saint Liars
The Devil's Day
The Finder of the Lucky Devil

PAIGE LAVOIE
I'm in Love with Mothman

ROBERT J. LEWIS
Shadow Guardian and the Three Bears

VALERIE WILLIS
Cedric: The Demonic Knight
Romasanta: Father of Werewolves
The Oracle: Keeper of the Gaea's Gate
Artemis: Eye of Gaea
King Incubus: A New Reign

SciFi

BRANDON HILL & TERENCE PEGASUS
Between the Devil and the Dark
Wrath & Redemption

C.K. WESTBROOK
The Shooting
The Collision

KYLE SORRELL
Munderworld

NICK SAVAGE
Us of Legendary Gods

PC NOTTINGHAM
Mummified Moon

T.S. SIMONS

Antipodes
The Liminal Space
Ouroboros
Caim
Sessrúmnir
The 45th Parallel

TY CARLSON
The Bench
The Favorite
The Shadowless

**DISCOVER MORE AT
4HORSEMENPUBLICATIONS.COM**

Lightning Source UK Ltd.
Milton Keynes UK
UKHW012047310123
416284UK00025B/152/J